Alan Fisher grew up in the Notting Hill area of London and worked in Kensington libraries when he was sixteen. With time on his hands whilst doing his National Service, he began writing short stories. Back in civilian life, he worked as a clerk in an underwriting syndicate at Lloyds, as a porter at London University, and as a clerk in Paddington General Hospital. He attended night school and entered teacher training. Teaching history in secondary schools in Sussex and Kent, he later gained a degree from the Open University and a postgraduate diploma from Sussex – but feels he learned more from reading Arthur Koestler.

Alan Fisher is married and has two sons. *Yangtze* is his fifth published novel. His fourth, *The Terioki Crossing* (also published by Corgi Books), was set in Russia in 1917 and won the Georgette Heyer Prize for an outstanding historical novel.

Also by Alan Fisher

THE TERIOKI CROSSING

and published by Corgi Books

YANGTZE

Alan Fisher

Heaven's net is wide;
Coarse are the meshes, yet nothing slips through.

Tao Tê Ching: *The Way and its Power*

CORGI BOOKS

YANGTZE

A CORGI BOOK 0 552 13298 5

Originally published in Great Britain by The Bodley Head Ltd.

PRINTING HISTORY
Bodley Head edition published 1988
Corgi edition published 1989

This book is set in 10/11pt Ehrhardt by Goodfellow & Egan Ltd,
Cambridge

Corgi Books are published by Transworld Publishers Ltd.,
61–63 Uxbridge Road, Ealing, London W5 5SA,
in Australia by Transworld Publishers (Australia) Pty. Ltd.,
15–23 Helles Avenue, Moorebank, NSW 2170,
and in New Zealand by Transworld Publishers (N.Z.) Ltd., Cnr. Moselle
and Waipareira Avenues, Henderson, Auckland.

Printed and bound in Great Britain by
Cox & Wyman Ltd, Reading

To my Literary Agent
John McLaughlin

I wish to thank Allen & Unwin (Publishers) Ltd. for allowing me to use extracts from the Arthur Waley translation of the Tao Tê Ching, *The Way and its Power*

CHAPTER ONE

The *Star of Asia* was old, creaking, only a few voyages from
the scrapyard. Forward movement sluggish, it wallowed
gently in the warm swell, bow wave stained brown by silt
streaming out from the Yangtze delta.

In the hot season the monsoon picks up moisture from the
East China Sea and carries it landwards. The air is leaden
and there is a faint haze where sea and sky meet.

Reed had left his cabin door open. He stirred on his bunk
and rubbed sweat from his eyes, wondering at the change in
the thumping tempo of the engines. The humidity was like a
blanket. He sat up, scratching irritably at the damp patches
on his drill shirt. A fool returneth to his folly. He groped his
feet into his boots but remained seated for a moment longer.
I should have stayed in the States, or gone to Spain to fight
Franco, he thought. Or some damned thing.

The small effort of standing made him sweat again.
Voices in the next cabin were indistinct. Peggy Rittenhouse
said something then laughed harshly. Reed frowned to
himself as he heard Linda Bishop reply. Seventeen days of
avoiding that girl. A little of Linda Bishop went a long way.
Still scratching he peered at himself in the mirror. There
was grey in his hair. And he needed a shave.

A Chinese steward knocked on the open door. 'Two
hours, Mister Reed.' His mouth curved up in a professional
smile, and he waited.

Reed pulled a few dollar bills from his crumpled roll and
stuck them in the boy's white coat. 'Buy your cousin's chow
shop.' He paused as he reached the door. 'And pack for me.'

The boy grinned. 'Will do, Mister Reed.'

He went on deck, leaning on the rail and staring at the low flat line of the China coast, hazy, yellow tinged. Still far off, the pilot boat was buzzing across the silt-laden water.

The *Star of Asia* was approaching a bay of immense width and there were more ships, all drawn on invisible threads towards the Yangtze and Shanghai. Reed took a cigarette from the damp packet in his shirt and watched a square-headed junk as it passed slowly astern. It was moving slackly, lug sail balanced to catch the slight stir of air. He recognized the deck cargo – a wood oil trader from round the coast, on its way up river to Hankow. In 1934 the boat yards in Kiangwan would build you a junk like that in three weeks for four thousand dollars Mex. Three years on and the price has almost doubled. He dragged on the cigarette. And he was no richer.

The grey-bearded archaeologist came to the rail. He was returning to Honan after a sabbatical at a Midwest university. He'd seen Reed and carefully distanced himself, but Reed didn't give a damn.

Further along the estuary lay warships of the 3rd Japanese Fleet – they'd come to settle the Shanghai matter peaceably. He shielded his eyes, counting. Eleven – twelve of them, and more at Woosung. He'd picked a bad time to come back here.

Seabirds gathered from nowhere as stewards emptied buckets over the stern. The dull thump of the engines ceased and the *Star of Asia* slowed in the swell as the pilot boat bobbed alongside. A Chinese river pilot caught the rope ladder and swung himself up. White shoes, white trousers, white shirt. His gold-rimmed spectacles gleamed under his peaked cap. The pilot boat's propeller churned, and it pulled away. And the engines started to thump again.

Reed flicked the cigarette over the side and pondered the enigma of free choice. Rubbish from ships floated, half submerged in the dull water. There was a sort of inevitability about coming back. Here, along the lower reaches of the great river the need to compete diminished and his transgressions seemed smaller.

8

A newly-married couple walked hand in hand past him. Twenty-one, twenty-two perhaps, they seldom emerged from their cabin. And they looked exhausted. Reed wondered how they managed in the oppressive heat.

He could see the shoreline distinctly now. Thousands of sea birds squawked, picking at the mud flats. They looked unnatural, ill-adapted, until they lifted off. He watched a gull, wings spread, riding on the warm air. Over a million years of natural selection to achieve that completeness. The perfect act. So birds had tiny brains. What had brains got to do with perfection? He scowled as the *Star of Asia* passed a Japanese cruiser; grey, efficient, guns pointed at the China mainland.

The cruiser was lowering a seaplane over the side. It bobbed gently, crew strapping themselves down, then it took off, flying in a wide arc. Reed caught a glint of reflected light as the observer peered down through binoculars at the *Star of Asia*. Did that Jap know they were carrying aero engines for Chiang Kai-shek? It seemed likely. The Japanese knew just about everything – they'd spent years building up an intelligence network in Asia – traders subsidised by Tokyo, prostitutes with sharp ears. Polite, white-suited young men – he'd encountered two of them in a bar on Butterfly Row just before he'd left for the States. They'd stood him drinks – a high-class whore hovering in the background as bait – and they asked him questions about CPC's new installations at Wuhu. There was money there for him but he hadn't gone along with it.

Wild fowl flapped over the shifting delta of silt. The Chinese pilot followed the deep channel where the river ran faster. Other passengers dressed for the end of the journey had come on deck. White, linen suits – thin cotton dresses and wide-brimmed hats.

Reed groaned softly as he heard Linda Bishop's voice. Middle class, New England. She had a direct, imperative way of speaking that left little room for argument. Now she and the youngest of the ship's officers had paused, leaning at the rail and watching a Japanese destroyer. 'Surely it's

9

against international law to assemble warships in China's territorial waters?'

The young officer was still new to the sea, his first voyage to the Orient, and he mumbled something about Japanese concessionary rights. He was more interested in Linda Bishop. She adjusted the lens of her expensive camera and pointed it at a laden junk. 'It smells quite awful even from here – I'd prefer you didn't tell me why.' Click. She turned her head briefly, qualifying her abruptness with a quick smile. 'Why the huge eye painted on the bow? To see its way?'

Reed stifled his irritation. Seventeen days. There had been no way of avoiding the presence of Linda Bishop and her questions. He'd hear her low-pitched voice on the deck above, or as she passed his cabin. And at meal times from the end of a table. Or maybe I'm just listening for her, he thought. She was a puzzle. A brittle, hands-off manner if you got within two feet of her, and a persistent Puritan sense of justice. That combination in a woman made him contentious. Twice, however, he had become suddenly aware of her cool attraction. Seeing her alone, peering down at the bow wave, a frown on her face and her thoughts a long way off. And that other time four days out from San Francisco – a momentary scene that hung in his mind, waiting for an answer. Now she was moving along the rail to take more pictures of the junk. Click. She wound on film, and as she raised her camera again he noticed the perspiration stain under her arm. So Linda Bishop was human and felt the heat like everybody else.

Reed's attention was focused on her and he missed what was happening. She called out, pointing to the junk, and in the same moment the Chinese pilot shouted and span the wheel. Reed saw the top of the lug sail veering across the bows of the *Star of Asia*, and he tensed, waiting for impact. There was an ugly sound of timber grinding along the metal side, then the junk was astern, wash cascading over the deck cargo.

'We nearly ran it down!' Linda Bishop was staring

10

anxiously back but the young ship's officer had remembered his duties and was running towards the bows. She called angrily to the pilot. 'We could have drowned those people!'

He looked down at her through his gold-rimmed glasses and shrugged, spinning the wheel again to bring the ship back into the deep channel.

'He doesn't even care!'

'It was the goddam junkman's fault,' Reed growled wearily. 'He crossed the path of the ship.'

'But it was so small!' And now she directed her anger at him. 'Don't small sailing ships have the right of way?'

'This isn't some snob yacht club, Miss Bishop. This is the Yangtze. The Chinaman broke the rules. See there, where the current is slow?'

She looked but didn't see and he reflected briefly on the impossibility of explaining to her. 'The river is too shallow there for a ship this size. Y'have to have rules. The Chinaman probably wants his lousy junk run down so he can claim the insurance.'

Her mouth tightened. 'You can't just assume that.'

'Why not?' He wondered at his perverse pleasure in angering her. 'Asiatics are the same as the rest of us, but a bit more crooked.'

An unattended child ran into Linda Bishop's thigh. She turned her briskly and pointed her in the opposite direction. 'Go and find your mother, little girl – she's that way.' And to Reed she said, 'I had the strongest impression that it is *we* who exploit the Chinese.'

'Sure, we take from them. They need our know-how and they've got to pay for it – that's the way of the world. China is a hundred years behind the West.'

'Are you really so cynical or are you trying to be irritating?' And she looked at him in that way she had of making him defensive. 'The Chinese had a written language four thousand years before Christ. They had a code of laws before Europe discovered America.'

'So did the Red Indians – it didn't save them. Y'have to pay for your weaknesses.' In the end you had to pay for every

11

damned thing. 'China is squalid, brutal and backward. Go a few miles outside the towns and you'll find yourself back in feudal times.' What was she doing here, anyway? 'You on some sort of grand tour, Miss Bishop?'

She pursed her lips and stared at the shoreline, trying to make up her mind whether or not to be civil. 'I'm here to write a series of articles on the mid-China Methodist missions.'

'Yeah?' He tried to sound interested. 'Are you a missionary, or a journalist?'

She continued to frown at the shoreline. 'Both – neither.'

Ninety years of mission money and effort poured into China, but the great mass of people had never responded – to them Christianity was an alien faith. Reed leaned on the rail and noticed again that Linda Bishop edged slightly away from him. 'Peggy Rittenhouse says your father is a missionary. That right?'

'He *was*. For twenty years. And he never became cynical about the Chinese,' she added.

'Well now, I'll bet they appreciated that.'

He wished he hadn't said it.

She seemed about to make a sharp reply, but paused, listening to a sound like the tearing of silk over their heads, then a rumble like distant thunder. 'What was that?'

Guns. He peered back at the mouth of the estuary. That damned Jap cruiser. 'Your cultured Asiatics are killing each other, Miss Bishop – just north of the International Settlement.'

She didn't look at him. 'I suppose men are fools the world over.' And she turned away, a long girl with a swinging decisive walk so you knew exactly where she was going.

He stared at her legs until she was lost to sight among other passengers. With women he'd always worked on a simple principle. You probe at their values until you find the point at which they are prepared to oppose you – not always easy because they are usually playing some game of their own. But once they take up a position, you've got them figured out. It didn't seem to work with Linda Bishop. Her values showed through all the time, but she was still a puzzle. He remembered her four days out from San Francisco, and the question. He'd found her quite by accident alone on the boat deck. She'd thought she was unobserved, lying in the sun, eyes closed, long limbs browning. Then she glanced at her wristwatch, as if waiting for a specific time, and took pills from her bag, swallowing them with practised ease. She lay back in the sun again. Like a convalescent – the thought had surprised him.

He ought to go and shave. But he delayed, fingering the last cigarette from the crumpled packet in his shirt pocket.

The *Star of Asia* entered the Whangpoo River on the incoming tide. A few casual villagers dotted the flat shore. He looked for the oil companies' silver tanks. Socony Wharf. A tanker was discharging its load. A Japanese carrier with a gunboat escort was moving slowly upstream ahead of the *Star of Asia*. There were other warships moored up at Yantzepo and Japanese marines in olive green uniforms were unloading supplies. But Reed searched with his eye for the high crane at the China Petroleum Company wharf – he'd worked for CPC for four years. Offices in Shanghai and Nanking; installations at Woosung, Chen-chiang, Wuhu, and Hankow. He'd repaired their trucks with the help of two Chinese mechanics, but mostly he serviced the ageing Stinson seaplane used as a ferry by CPC. And I grudged it, he thought. But I don't know what else to do with my life. I guess that's why I've come back.

Linda Bishop groped down the steep companionway and found the cabin she had shared with Peggy Rittenhouse. 'Dear God, it's even hotter in here. Did you hear the guns?'

'Was that really guns?' Peggy was leaning over her trunk, large breasts sagging inside her faded kimono. 'You're *kidding*.' She had a marked London accent and used it unashamedly, Linda thought, to amuse or get round people. 'Don't worry, love. They wouldn't dare fire into Shanghai.'

'That drifter, Reed, says there's fighting just to the north.' Linda lowered herself onto her bunk, suddenly weary. She

13

winced as Peggy threw slippers on top of dresses. 'It took him precisely one and a half minutes to get under my skin.' And she eased down until she was flat on her back. 'I timed him.' The limp, spent feeling would pass in a while.

Peggy paused, holding up a skirt and frowning to herself. 'Reed is all right.' She glanced at Linda. 'You feeling off colour?'

'Just hot, and a bit tired.' She could hear the soft hiss of the river beyond the porthole.

'You don't look too good.'

The cotton dress was sticking to her thighs and her arms shone wetly. 'I'll be fine in a minute.'

'And you're all packed.' Peggy pushed a strand of moist hair from her forehead. 'Americans make me feel sloppy and ineffectual.'

Linda closed her eyes and listened to the water. She wouldn't have chosen to share with Peggy – thirty-five or thereabouts; sensual, gaudy, untidy. 'You're probably good at other things.'

'Arch says I have no will power.' Peggy giggled. 'He should know. What do you think of my shoes?'

'They're beautiful, they really are.' Linda could say it honestly. 'They suit you.'

'When I was young I used to dream about having shoes like this.' Soft red leather. Teetering high heels. Peggy looked wistful. 'I'm blowed if I know where I'm going to put them. Perhaps I'll have to wear them.'

The trunk was over-filled with her tasteless wardrobe.

'You can pack them in my case – just until we reach the hotel,' Linda added quickly, already hoping she wouldn't have to share with Peggy again. But at worst it could only be for three more nights, then she could be alone. 'I don't know why Reed insists that he must travel with us.' The sudden heavy feeling of fatigue had passed and she leaned up on her elbow. 'I swear he hasn't shaved for three days.'

'We're travelling on the same route.' Peggy took off her kimono. 'Reed has to go to Chen-chiang.' She adjusted small straps on her bra with no noticeable effect then stuffed

14

the kimono into a corner of her trunk. 'It's safer, love, having Reed with us. I know he's irritating sometimes, but he's been good to me. We probably won't see much of him while we're in Shanghai, if that's any consolation to you. He kips with a typist from China Petroleum. Her name's Sao. Arch and I have done the town with them a couple of times.'

'Sao? A Chinese girl!'

'Don't look so *shocked*.' Peggy stepped into her skirt and zipped it up. 'We all need somebody. She's good for him.'

The simple assessment of Reed left Linda feeling prudish and mean-spirited. 'How long have you known him?'

'He and Arch used to fly together out of Cuba.' Peggy held up an orange cotton blouse. 'Will this do?'

'Great. You mean they were with an airline?'

'Lord, no!' Peggy laughed, white teeth perfect. 'They were running liquor into Florida. I used to do their washing, and cook for them sometimes. Then Prohibition ended, so they went off to a war in South America – but don't bring it up in conversation because Reed doesn't like talking about it. When they came back I married Arch.' Her mood switched and a slight frown crossed her face. 'I've been living in hotel rooms ever since. We came out here with CNAC but now Arch flies for the Chinese Air Force. He says we can rent a small house when I get to Nanking. I'll believe it when it happens.' Peggy continued to frown. 'Bloody trunk won't close.' She leaned on it. 'His mother lives in Oakland. She got sick and he couldn't go home so he sent me. Outlive us all, she will.'

Linda noticed the tightness about Peggy's mouth whenever she talked about Arch. 'I'll give you a hand.' They both pressed down on the trunk lid. What made people marry, then stick together when love was absent? She was sure now that Peggy Rittenhouse didn't love her husband. The trunk locks clicked. But then what did she know about love? – she'd only observed it from a safe distance.

Peggy fell back exhausted on her bunk. 'God Almighty! This heat! You'd think they'd do something about the electric fan. Nothing on this ship works properly. Have you tried flushing the toilet along the passage today? – it left me feeling limp.' She wiped her moist forehead with the back of her hand. 'You're a glutton for punishment, you are – actually *choosing* to come out here at this time of the year. Whenever women do anything apart from eating and sleeping I assume it's because of a man.' And she glanced sideways at Linda.

Linda looked round the cabin to see if they'd left anything. Peggy's toothpaste.'Don't you want this?'

'It's nearly empty.' Peggy smiled. 'You're very good at avoiding questions about yourself.'

'Am I?' A subconscious defence. 'I'm sorry. I'll try not to.' She paused momentarily then dropped the toothpaste tube in the wastebin. 'It isn't because of a man.'

'Sorry, love. It's none of my business.' Peggy changed the subject. 'Arch was in Shanghai until the twelfth of August. *If* the ship hadn't had engine trouble, and *if* we hadn't been delayed in Honolulu, I could have met him here. By now he'll be at the Chuying air base near Nanking.'

'I don't think there was anything wrong with the ship's engines.'

'Why would they say it then?'

Linda sat and cupped her chin in her hands. 'I think it was an excuse – so the ship couldn't make the call at Yokohama.' She frowned. 'And I think it's because of the cargo. We're carrying aeroplane engines for Chiang Kai-shek – I saw them being loaded at San Francisco, at night, just before we left. Big wooden cases.'

Peggy looked at her blankly.

'The embargo,' Linda added. 'Aren't you just a bit curious? Aero engines are war materials – it's a breach of the embargo to carry them. If we'd gone to Yokohama the Japanese would have prevented them reaching Shanghai. I tried questioning that young deck officer, but he went all stiff-jawed and British – wouldn't tell me a thing.' She shrugged. 'Don't you think it's all a bit – a bit secretive?'

But Peggy wasn't curious. She buttoned her blouse, thought about it then undid the top two buttons. 'Why don't you talk to Reed. He'd know if there's anything going on.'

Her faith in Reed was boundless. Linda sighed. 'Reed and I don't have conversations, we snipe at each other. I think he actually enjoys being obnoxious.' She stopped herself. 'I'm sorry. I know he's a friend of yours.' Reed wore his sweat-stained shirt and three-day stubble like a calculated insult. 'I guess I'm not used to men like him.'

'What sort of men are you used to?'

'Oh, I don't know.' Linda felt the need to evade again but she didn't know why. She picked up a pair of Peggy's discarded stockings and threw them in the bin. 'Safe. Presentable . . .'

'Clean-shaven?' Peggy smiled lazily.

'Definitely clean-shaven.' Linda smiled back. 'Ambitious.' There had been several back home, but in the end she hadn't wanted any of them.

'Well, you won't find many like that where you're going, love. Sure you don't mind me putting the shoes in your bag?'

'No. Go ahead.' Linda took a comb and peered at her reflected image. My face is thin, she thought. And something's gone.

'All these pills of yours.' Peggy was snooping in the open bag. 'You been ill?'

'I had an operation a while ago.'

Peggy turned to her, curious and concerned. 'You have to look after yourself out here.'

'Yes. I guess so.'

Boys arrived to take the heavy luggage. The two girls followed, groping upstairs to join other passengers at the rail. More Japanese warships were tied up at the wharves of Hongkew on the west side. Seen up close they were awesome: grey, long guns and towering superstructures. But the life of the river seemed unaffected. Yellow-bronze figures stooped, working on the junks – they didn't even glance at the ship as it passed. Rubbish floated in the slack current – a great dead fish, white belly upturned.

The *Star of Asia* moved slowly behind a large American freighter, sampans and launches rocking in its wash. The ship had been part of that other world that Linda had left

17

behind and now everything seemed alien. Even the sounds were unfamiliar and she felt anxious. Why had she come so far from home?

Peggy chattered and pointed. 'That's Pootung Point on the far side, and over there is the Japanese Concession.' But Linda barely heard her. She watched as a police boat buzzed alongside a junk and bobbed to a stop, and a Chinese in a blue cotton shirt and dirty shorts spat over the junk's high stern. They'd been building junks like that for two thousand years. And men and women had lived out their lives along this river for far longer. She peered down at the water. If she died tomorrow it would all go on just as it always has. The thought was unexpectedly comforting.

A small seaplane of the river service roared over and alighted, trailing white furrows. Peggy dabbed at the per-spiration in the vee of her blouse. 'Look, love. Shanghai.'

The *Star of Asia* was turning a bend in the river, and above masts, sails, and funnels loomed the ugly but impressive skyline of Shanghai International Settlement. High, West-ern, squared off piles of ferro-concrete upjutted into the yellow-tinged haze. Linda stared. 'My God, it's vast!' The city sprawled west, south, north.

Reed joined them. 'Broadway Mansions – over there,' and he jerked his head in the direction of a slab-sided skyscraper.

He'd shaved after all, Linda noticed. And he'd had a drink.

'That's the highest building in Asia,' Reed was saying. 'Nothing's done in moderation here.'

Tramcars, automobiles and rickshaws were crowding along the Bund, Shanghai's main artery facing the river. And behind were the smart white towers – Glen Line Building, Jardine Matheson, Yokohama Specie Bank, Bank of China.

'I'd expected something more Oriental.' Linda peered at the tramcars.

'It's a modern Babylon.' Reed shrugged. 'An unreal world of money, and the awful fear of losing it.'

18

But Peggy was looking beyond the Settlement to a huge column of black smoke rising six hundred feet out of the Chapei district to the north. 'Is that where the fighting is?'

'Yes.' Reed grinned sourly. 'That's reality.'

Linda felt a small presentiment.

And on the Bund a man in a white suit was seated reading a newspaper while a boy cleaned his shoes. Mother of God, what a strange world I've come to, she thought. She glanced sideways at Reed. He's just a little uneasy too.

CHAPTER TWO

The cold shower ran tepid despite all her adjustments.
Linda turned her face up, letting the water cascade through
her hair. The city had smelled of smoke when she'd woken.
It drifted in from the war zone beyond Soochow Creek. And
the hotel was crowded with nervous Westerners from
outside the Settlement, so she and Peggy had been forced to
share again.

It wasn't that she disliked her – Linda rubbed soap over
her shoulders. And Peggy, singing like a bird, was kindhear-
ted. But the thought was there if she was honest about it, her
room mate was embarrassing.

> Love is the greatest thing,
> The oldest and the latest thing.

Linda turned her face up to the shower again. They'd
'done' the Cathedral and St John's University, like a couple
of tourists, which of course was what they were – Peggy
clicking away with her box Brownie and talking too loudly.
And yesterday, the evening meal in a Foochow Road
restaurant that turned out to be a nightclub, with the men
eyeing them as though they were whores because Peggy
dressed like one.

Water drummed on the shower curtain, and Peggy called
something.

'I can't hear you.'

'We'll go shopping. I'll show you Nanking Road.'

She couldn't think of an excuse. 'Fine.'

'I'll show you where ladies have fits.'

'Fits!'

'Honest. Fits!' Peggy came in and poked her head round the curtain. 'Cross my heart and hope to die.'

Linda quickly turned her back to her and Peggy withdrew. 'Sorry, love.'

She's assumed I'm unduly modest. Linda stared at the water streaming between her breasts and down, rippling over the scar. I don't like people seeing it – I don't even like looking at it. Sudden drastic surgery. Another few hours and they would have gutted me. The scar, purple and obscene, curved round the soft flesh of her belly. She touched its unevenness. It will always be there. And I'll never be able to have children.

'We've got a visitor,' Peggy called. 'Mister . . .' Linda couldn't hear the rest.

'Who?'

'He's from the American consulate.'

Linda cursed softly. Her clothes were in the adjoining room. 'I'll be right out.' And she put on her bathrobe and wound a towel round her hair.

The visitor was young, expensively dressed in a white linen suit. 'I have to apologize, Miss Bishop, I've surely come at the wrong time.' And he shrugged hopelessly. 'We had a cable from the Methodist Foreign Mission Committee in Chicago. Sorry I didn't get to meet you off the boat.'

'Don't worry about it. Mrs Rittenhouse and I managed fine.'

'I hear there was a little trouble.'

'Trouble?'

'The *Star of Asia* was carrying war materials in breach of the embargo.'

'Really?'

'Aero engines for Chiang Kai-shek. They were off-loaded and delivered to the Chinese agent's warehouse.' He shrugged. 'We would have turned a blind eye, but the Japanese consulate lodged a protest, so the Port Authority has had to impound them. It's created a lot of paperwork for our office.' He glanced at Linda's figure and allowed his appreciation to show.

Linda pulled the lapels of her bathrobe together. 'I can imagine.'

'Well, we'd like to greet you officially – the mission service does a splendid job.' His smile tightened as he turned to Peggy. 'And of course we're glad to see you again, Mrs Rittenhouse.'

He isn't glad to see her at all, Linda thought, and wondered why.

Faint sounds of gunfire trembled the window.

'We offer what help we can to American citizens.' He took out a pocket notebook and a silver pencil, frowning slightly as he adjusted the lead. 'Now you would have been going inland, to Dr Foster's mission at Hsia-kang, but as that's no longer possible . . .'

'No longer possible?'

'I assumed you knew – you've heard the news, surely? Our government has ordered wives and dependents of American residents home, and it follows . . .'

'I'm not a wife or a dependent. I've just crossed the Pacific. I don't intend turning round and going back again,' Linda said.

'You're not familiar with the situation here, Miss Bishop. There has been bombing. The British Ambassador was wounded on his way from Nanking. And Madam Chiang Kai-shek's car was strafed – I believe she's quite badly hurt. The consulate staff are here to see that nothing unfortunate happens to you.' He smiled, white teeth showing. 'Now, I *could* get you passage home on the *Hoover* . . .' He didn't even glance at Peggy.

'I'll tell you exactly what I'm going to do.' Linda kept the edge out of her voice. 'I'm catching the Nanking Express from Shanghai West station tomorrow night. It will take me as far as Ch'ang-chou, and I'll travel the rest of the way by bus, car, ox cart, whatever.'

He tapped his teeth with the silver pencil. 'Well, of course, nobody can force you to go home.'

'Absolutely right.'

'But the consulate can take no responsibility for you if you make that journey. You could stay here for a week or two, that might be wiser. Shanghai is a fascinating city.' He smiled. 'Come to think of it, I could probably find some time to show you around – and you too, of course, Mrs Rittenhouse.'

He'd barely included Peggy in his concern. Linda decided she didn't like him. 'I'm expected in Hsia-kang, and that's where I'm going, Mr . . .'

'Call me Frank.'

'Oh, that's a really nice name, so – so frank.' Peggy stared at him. 'I'm going as well. Arch is expecting me in Nanking.'

'I hope your husband knows what he's doing, Mrs Rittenhouse.'

'Arch always knows what he's doing.'

'Well, I'm sure nobody would doubt Captain Rittenhouse's integrity . . .' He tailed off. 'Okay. I'll report to the consul. He may lean on you a little, but I wish you both good luck.' He paused at the door. 'By the way, as an accredited journalist, Miss Bishop, you may care to attend a press conference in the Japanese Concession tonight. I could take you there. Might be interesting for you. General Matsui, the Japanese Commander in Chief will be answering questions. He's expected to confirm the stop line limiting the advance of his troops.'

Linda hesitated. She was pretty sure that the young man had had this proposition saved up against the possibility that she was passably attractive.

'The General speaks pidgin English and incomprehensible French. Actually he's become quite a popular figure with the business community here in the Settlement.'

'Yes. Yes, I'll go,' and she added reluctantly, 'thank you.'

'Then I'll pick you up around seven thirty.'

It wasn't until they went out shopping that Linda learned why he had shown so little concern for Peggy.

'It isn't really his fault, love, he just does as he's told. America doesn't want to get involved in the war, any more than do the British or French.'

'But all that stuff about showing us Shanghai.' The

23

temperature was up in the eighties and Linda tried not to look at the rickshaw boy's sweating, painfully thin body as he grunted, swinging them round into Nanking Road. 'I think young Mr what's-his-name is a real pain.'

'He's ambitious,' Peggy smiled maliciously, 'clean-shaven – and he fancies you.'

'Oh, c'mon, Peggy! Be serious. He was washing his hands of you and Arch.'

'American pilots who stay on here are in the dog house – they've even dug up some law against flying for a foreign government. And Arch is a big embarrassment to them because he was famous in the Great War.'

Linda had never heard of Arch Rittenhouse until she'd come to China. She could feel her spine wet against the back of the seat.

'You can see their problem,' Peggy was saying. 'The more pressure they put on Arch, the more they draw attention to what he's saying. They won't get him to go back to America, and I'm going to Nanking no matter what.'

Linda pondered. What strange lives people lead. Would I do that – live out of a suitcase, drag across this country for a man I don't even love? No, I wouldn't. No man I've ever met is worth that.

The rickshaw passed smart Western shops; Kelly and Walsh, The Chocolate Box, Whiting and Laidlaw. Then it seemed to Linda that they had crossed abruptly into a confused cultural mix. Smells and combinations of colours were strange, and she stared, trying to adjust to signs painted vertically in garish hieroglyphics. Drug store – she could figure that one out by the merchandise. There were open-fronted shops selling alarm clocks, bottle openers and American shoes. And cheap restaurants – some had framed pictures of General Chiang Kai-shek in their windows.

'You feel sort of separate.' Peggy took out a handkerchief and dabbed at the vee of her blouse. 'It's like nowhere else you've ever known.'

It had an ugly vitality, Linda thought.

A bearded Sikh policeman regulated the traffic from a

platform at the intersection of Tibet Road, and large American motor cars edged among the rickshaws, tramcars and bicycles. Chinese in blue cotton gowns and black trousers crowded the paving of Nanking Road; and girls in pairs, with stiff little collars and ankle length dresses slit up one side to the knee, Shanghai style. There were Europeans. Linda watched a nun lifting her long gown to scuttle across the path of the traffic. What peaceful, cloistered community had she left far behind? The nun put a coin into a shrivelled out-stretched hand and muttered a blessing.

'So many beggars!' Linda looked quickly away from the twisted figure – she assumed it was a man – intricately maimed and disfigured for his calling.

'You get used to them.'

'I hope I don't. I hope I don't get accustomed to this kind of poverty.' But the bent, sweating back of the rickshaw boy made her feel accomplice to a hundred and fifty years of exploitation. 'You know, we have to carry our share of the blame for all of this.'

'In Shanghai the Chinese exploit each other. Even the begging is organized.'

'That sounds to me like the excuses Westerners make.' Linda fanned herself limply. 'All right, who organizes the begging then?'

'The Greens, love. It's a secret society but everybody knows it's run by Mr Dou.' Peggy said it as if it was quite ordinary and acceptable. 'Reed says Mr Dou lives in a great villa in the French district. The Greens organize the protection. And whores and dope. And smuggling up river as far as Nanking – just about everything. You can't peddle shoe laces in Shanghai without Mr Dou's say-so.'

'Don't the French and British try to stop him?' They were passing a temple and Linda looked, puzzled, as a yellow-robed figure emerged and climbed into a large Buick automobile. 'I mean, if everybody knows this man, Dou, is running it all.'

'Oh no, they couldn't do that. Mr Dou keeps everything

25

running smoothly. He's a director of the Commercial Bank of China, and he backs Chiang Kai-shek.'

Maybe it wasn't so different from some of the city politics back home – just a bit more blatant, Linda thought.

When the rickshaw boy let them off she gave him an extravagant tip. He grinned uncertainly, bad teeth showing as he backed away.

'The fare is really forty cents. He thinks you're crazy,' Peggy said. 'He's already overcharged us.'

'I don't care what he thinks.' She'd answered too sharply.

'It's no good feeling guilty about things you can't alter, love.'

'I'm not sure about that.' But Linda smiled at Peggy to make up. 'Okay. Now show me where ladies have fits.'

Extending southwards towards the French Concession, Yates Road was squalid but almost European. They passed a reeking alley leading off and the stench caught at Linda's throat. 'Dear God! Imagine living there. My nose could never accommodate itself to that.'

'I could show you Soochow Creek. The smell is absolutely *indescribable*. Reed says it has to do with the tides.'

She quoted Reed all the time, Linda had noticed. Maybe she'd once had an affair with him? And there was that slightly irrational distaste as she remembered that Reed slept regularly with a Chinese girl.

'"Pants Alley",' Peggy said. They'd reached a narrow turning of small tailoring shops. It was claustrophobic, high buildings on either side and crowded along its fifty yards. 'You can get almost any kind of cheap clothes – they'll even run them up overnight.'

Linda felt uneasy. This was Shanghai sweated labour. 'I only want to buy a flashlight.'

'We'll get that at Wing On's on the way back.'

A Chinese in a long blue cotton gown touted from his shop doorway. He spat loudly then showed his uneven teeth. Linda permitted her disgust to show. How many tired children sewing in his back room?

'See! What did I tell you?' Peggy pointed to a neatly

painted notice in English over a shop doorway. LADIES HAVE FITS UPSTAIRS. 'I'll bet they haven't got a bra to fit me.' And she laughed loudly.

Linda forced a quick smile. Two more days of Peggy's company. 'Remember we're just browsing.'

But they left "Pants Alley" with additions to Peggy's gaudy wardrobe.

'You're crazy, Peggy. You didn't *need* them,' Linda said accusingly. 'And how are you going to pack them? There isn't a cubic inch of space in your trunk.'

'I'll throw something out, honest.'

They found a battered motor cab plying Yates Road. It smelled musty. The driver was Russian. He offered to show them where the Chinese Air Force had accidentally dropped a bomb near the racecourse. 'They left the bodies wrapped in matting, hundreds of them – pouffe – in this heat.' He grinned. 'It took two days to move them all. I will show you.'

'Just take us to Wing On's,' Peggy insisted.

He shrugged and told them his cousin was an accountant at the store, and to buy cotton goods but not shoes because they were overcharging. The cab moved slowly with the traffic along Bubbling Well Road. 'We came out of Russia along the Trans Siberian, the Reds just behind us. My cousin had frost bite, I had to cut off three of his toes.' He turned to the two girls, his beard jutting proudly. 'We are related to the Stroganovs. You have heard of the Stroganovs?'

Linda wondered why an old man was pointing up at the sky. And others were looking up.

In that moment she felt a sudden pressure on her eardrums. An explosion rocked the cab. Linda gasped, her whole body rigid, and the cab slammed to a stop. For a moment there was near silence – just glass tinkling from high windows – then people began shouting. Small bits of debris clattered on the cab roof, and five hundred yards further up the road a cloud of smoke and dust gouted upwards into the hazy blue sky.

She could breathe again. Peggy kept swallowing, hands pressed to her ears.

27

'Another bomb!' The driver began cursing in Russian, peering round and trying to reverse the cab. But they were caught up with rickshaws and cars, and there was a tram directly behind them. '*Nelzya*!' He banged his forehead with the flat of his hand and turned his anger on Peggy and Linda. 'I am *stuck* here because you would not go via the racecourse!' And he thumped his forehead again. 'You must get out.'

People were milling between the close-packed vehicles and somewhere an alarm was ringing insistently.

'Can't we wait a moment and . . .'

'*Nyet! Nyet*! Get out please.'

'Is this a licensed cab or isn't it?'

But they climbed out, aware of the heat, and the pressure of the crowd peering up Nanking Road to where the bomb had dropped. Glass was still tinkling down intermittently.

'We won't get any further.' Linda watched the smoke fanning out over the high tower blocks of Shanghai. Safely distanced, she'd seen it all in war newsreels of Ethiopia and Spain. But war had still seemed separate from her when she'd woken that morning. 'We could try going by the backstreets.'

'I need a drink.' Peggy's hands were shaking. 'Do you need a drink?'

'Oh, I don't think we should go into a bar on our own.' Linda had seldom done that even at home.

White dust was settling on the motor cars. The clanging bell of a fire engine sounded at the rear of the traffic jam now extending several hundred yards, and Sikh policemen were clearing a side street to allow through ambulances of the US 4th Marines.

Peggy peered over heads in the crowd. 'I think the bomb hit Wing On's. God! This heat!'

They edged through the press of people. Linda's dress was sticking to her thighs and her arms shone wetly. Even this far from the bombed store the paving was littered with broken glass. British soldiers had roped off a section and were only letting ambulances through. Already a sort of normality had emerged, with ordinary traffic diverted round the racecourse.

'It's no good being prim.' Peggy pushed her way past a curio shop and an arcade. 'We've got to get out of this crowd or I'll have a stroke.' She stopped outside Boyd's bar and restaurant. 'It's nice in here, you'll like it. One drink.'

If Peggy likes it, it's probably awful, Linda thought. 'No whores, I hope?'

'Not so you'd notice, love.'

It was almost cool inside. Three large fans revolved slowly and silently. Patrons ate at the rear. A long, curved bar with high leather stools dominated the front area and already there were shocked, white-dust-covered Europeans seated at one end. They all seemed to be talking at once – nobody listening to anybody else.

Linda sat on one of the stools and glanced at herself in the long mirror behind the bar. There were smudges of dust on her face and she wiped them off. The mirror was cracked almost corner to corner.

'Bomb did it.' The proprietor had a cummerbund round his waist. 'Funny though, none of my windows are broken.' He had an Australian accent.

The bearded Russian cab driver was talking loudly at the far end of the bar. 'We didn't pay him,' Linda said.

'He can buy his own.' Peggy sagged on her stool. 'What's good for the feeling you should never have got off the boat?'

'I'm like that every morning, Mrs Rittenhouse.' The Australian mixed cointreau, brandy and lemon and shook the mixture vigorously. 'Try this.'

'Have one yourself.'

'Bit early for me, this stuff – it rots yer brain. I'll just have a Clover beer. Here's to a short war and back to business.'

The bar was filling with gin-drinking traders. Somebody passed round a jagged fragment of metal, supposedly from the bomb.

'You certainly came back at the wrong time, Mrs

Rittenhouse.' The Australian watched his clients but his eyes kept returning to Peggy's large breasts. 'By the by, I saw your husband – the captain – what? – three days ago.'

'You couldn't have. Arch left for Nanking on the twelfth.'

'No, it was Captain Rittenhouse all right – going into the America Club.' But he paused, eyes narrowed, aware that he'd perhaps said something he shouldn't have. 'Well, I could have been mistaken. You know – these old eyes.'

Linda quickly changed the subject. 'Does anybody know who dropped the bomb on Wing On's store?'

'Bloody Chinese pilots – excuse my French, ladies. They're trying to sink the *Idzuma*. Couldn't hit their rice bowls with their chopsticks.' The Australian moved off again.

Peggy had gone silent, staring down at her drink. She suddenly looked her thirty-five years.

'The crowd is clearing out there,' Linda said. 'We could go back to the hotel – if you want?'

The Australian came back. 'Sorry about the gaffe I made, Mrs Rittenhouse. The man I saw probably wasn't the captain.'

'Forget it.'

'I've got to get myself some glasses. Can't even read the race results. You having the same again?'

'Why not?' Peggy looked up at herself in the cracked mirror. 'You're only young once.'

CHAPTER THREE

Reed rose late that morning.

The bombing of Wing On's department store had shaken the windows of the apartment block, stirring him into consciousness, but he drifted back into near sleep. He'd adjusted to sounds of explosions and gunfire to the north and it was the persistent clanging of fire engines that aroused him the second time. He groped sleepily for the girl then remembered that she'd gone to work. The redolence of her was in the sheets and pillows.

Oddments of Sao's underclothes were draped over a chair next to the bed. Reed hauled up on his elbow and felt for a cigarette. What was it she'd asked him to do? Something about the refrigerator. He frowned, flicking the lighter and dragging in smoke. She'd chattered at him, hurrying naked and still wet from the shower, sorting through the wardrobe to begin her day. The refrigerator door. He remembered. She'd said it wouldn't click, and would he get out of bed and do something about it. With Sao it was a bit like being married.

The net curtains moved gently as a slight stir of air carried the stench from acres of sprawling slums adjoining the apartment block – Sao never noticed. It mingled now with the faint pungence of funeral pyres north of Soochow Creek. The Japanese were burning their dead. Reed rose and padded to the window to close it. Further down Nanking Road the dust cloud over Wing On's was settling. Another bombing error. The Chinese pilots must have been trying to hit the *Idzuma*. The apartment block was just high enough for him to see the ageing Japanese battleship moored a hundred yards off Broadway Mansions. It wasn't as easy as it looked hitting a great slab-sided thing. Not like unloading your bombs into smoke, sure that something was down there and it didn't much matter about aiming. He and Arch knew about that – he suppressed the thought. You had an image of yourself, barely noticing as it tarnished – until one day . . . For a moment he watched the slow, deliberate flight of the gulls over the river, then he went out to the small kitchen.

There was coffee in the percolator. While it heated he looked at the curling snapshot fastened to the wall with an open safety pin; he and Arch, taken by Peggy just before they'd sailed for South America and the Chaco war. They'd got their arms round each other's shoulders. And we were a bit younger then, he thought. Arch looked sure of himself, jaw stuck out, sweat-stained shirt. He peered more closely at the face. How old is Arch now? Forty-one – maybe forty-two.

There was a little shrine in the corner of the kitchen, shaped like a tiny house and lit with a red electric bulb. Sao had put a bowl of rice in front of it. Her religion was quite practical, to keep the spirits happy. She was just afraid of what they might do.

The coffee simmered. From somewhere across the acres of slums a gramophone played constantly. Reed whistled softly to himself as he poured coffee into a mug. Twenty dollars left under a plate for him – Sao knew he was broke. She'd tidied up but left the makings of breakfast. And there'd been no word of reproach about him not writing while he'd been in the States. He had in fact sent two picture postcards – one of Michigan Avenue, Chicago, and the other from San Francisco with the bare message – 'Getting a boat Friday. Reed'.

He cracked two eggs into the frying pan and stuck bread under the grill. It was a relief the way she'd appeared to adjust to his return. But he frowned slightly, remembering that flat feeling last night in the Del Monte, when she'd chattered over dinner. An awareness that her words were

32

not relating to what she was really thinking. Maybe he ought to marry her and settle down. She'd seemed to want that before he'd gone away; not exactly saying it but implying the advantages and letting him savour the delights. But he'd put it off, unsure what he wanted.

The shelf over the handbasin in the bathroom was crowded with Sao's cosmetics, and bottles and jars the purposes of which he never thought of. He showered, then rubbed the mirror and began to shave.

Maybe it really was time to start thinking about marrying Sao. She was attractive, breathtakingly practical, and good in bed. Even Arch had been envious – 'I'll bet she's a lay and a half, that one.' And in all honesty where would he find anybody better?

Drill trousers washed and pressed for him, draped over a hanger on the wardrobe door. He hauled them on and rummaged in the drawer for a shirt. The more he thought about it the better the idea of matrimony seemed. He could squeeze a raise in pay out of Claud, and they could get a small house in Chen-chiang's suburbs, beyond the smells of the city. So she was Chinese – what did he care?

He found the shirts and paused, looking down. One of them wasn't his.

He picked it up, feeling its texture. Khaki drill, slightly better than anything he wore, but Sao probably wouldn't have noticed the difference. Pin holes for insignia on the shoulder straps – an officer's shirt. Frowning, he held it a moment, then folded and carefully replaced it. Well, we had no deal – no binding arrangement, he reflected. I didn't even say I'd be back for sure. But there was that flat feeling again.

A girl chatters too much at dinner. You mention your friend's name, she turns the conversation, and you know at some subconscious level that something has changed. That shirt belonged to Arch.

He fetched the twenty dollars and stuck them in the breast pocket, then he put the shirt back in the drawer.

It was gone mid-day, and he left the apartment with just

33

his one scuffed bag and his toolbox. Rickshaw drivers pestered but he shook his head, he was down to his last few coins. Smells of cheap restaurants hung in the air – there was one every few yards, smudgy counters crowded with Chinese. The paving was shaded intermittently by gaudy banners hanging over shop fronts – they were all familiar. Sao bought vegetables there – he'd seen her bargaining, shaking her head and pointing, voice pitched high. I guess I was too comfortable, he thought, with the smells and the crowds and the bars.

A midget, head too big for his body, was squatting on an old blanket. He looked up at Reed. 'Something bad waits, not far off. I tell your future?'

He shook his head. He didn't want to know his future.

'May you receive what you deserve.' The midget looked innocent but a Chinese girl laughed as she stepped round the blanket and walked on. '*Yan kwei Tzu ta-ren.*'

His Excellency the Foreign Devil. Reed scowled. A drifter in a city of expatriates, that was what he was.

A general passed in his limousine. A few years ago they were all poor; each with a few thousand troops and a field gun or two. Now they had villas in Frenchtown, and concubines, and bank accounts in Macao or Hong-kong. Reed's train of thought triggered a jagged reminder of Chinese soldiers and a man kneeling in the dust – a thief maybe, or a Communist. It had seemed ordinary enough. Then the ugly chopping sound, and the shock of watching the officer light a cigarette as one of his men held up the severed head. Reed deposited the bag and tool box at the left luggage office in the municipal bus depot; relieved, he walked in the direction of the Bund. Distanced decently a few yards from the non-conformist chapel, a Russian whore with good legs was examining her reflection in a shop window. She turned and smiled. He couldn't have afforded her even if he'd wanted. Chinese prostitutes were cheaper – beautiful, but dull and greedy; they used perfume instead of soap. Reed hadn't paid for a woman since he was seventeen and in fact the thought disgusted him a little, a totally wrong

34

basis for a cash transaction – I've become a prude, he thought. Or maybe I'm a romantic.

A whole block of the Nanking Road was roped off, closed to traffic since the second bombing error five days before. Reed turned into airless back streets strewn with filth. Women sat in doorways chattering and fanning themselves in the heat. He flicked one of his last coins to a child with bright, boot-button eyes. A small doubt had begun to nag. Supposing Claud had no work for him? Damn it, he was nearly destitute – he should have kept Sao's twenty dollars.

It was one forty-five when he reached the Bund. Muted sounds of gunfire were carried on the slight breeze up the broad reach of the river. Two weeks of war and we've stopped listening, he thought. Massive stone symbols of permanence faced the waterfront: French Bank of Indo China, Yangtze Insurance Building, *North China Daily News*. And we walk seemingly secure in their shadows.

The Schreiber Building had broad stone steps leading up. He climbed and entered the foyer. The floor was a cool mosaic, the largest in Shanghai, and his footfalls echoed as he crossed to the old-fashioned wrought-iron elevator. It clanked and creaked, taking him up to the eighth floor leased by China Petroleum.

The general office was crowded and busy. He moved along the corridor to the office of the Operations Manager. A slim girl with blue-black hair emerged, files clutched to her white blouse. A friend of Sao's. She glanced at him quickly then lowered her eyes, high heels clicking as she went back to the corridor.

He knocked on the Operations Manager's door then looked in. 'Hullo Claud.'

Claud Biggs took off his horn-rimmed glasses and leaned back in his chair; a long thin man, ageing, shirt impeccably white as though he'd just that moment bought it and put it on. 'I thought maybe I'd seen the last of you.'

'How have you managed?'

Biggs stared at him. 'We've managed.' He lit a cigarette

but didn't offer the packet to Reed. 'You're useful but not essential.'

Claud Biggs had been with the company since 1923, first as plant manager at Hankow, then area supervisor based in Nanking in 1927 – he'd been the last American to leave when Kuomintang troops reached the city and attacked the foreign oil installations. Now he sat at a desk all day, and sometimes into the night.

'What did you come back for?'

'I missed the good life here, Claud – that feeling of belonging, in a humane, well-ordered society.' Reed went to the window. The sounds of gunfire were more noticeable on the eighth floor. 'All this, it must be bad for business?'

'Has your return nothing to do with failure?' Claud smiled bleakly then shrugged. 'Yes. What is happening out there is very bad for business. We can't get near our container depot in the Chapei – Chinese troops have dug in all around it. The area is a ruin.'

Reed could see dust and smoke hanging in the air over Shanghai North. 'They're all crazy. Anything is better than a war.'

Claud Biggs stared, curious at Reed's back. 'You looking for a job?'

He didn't answer directly.'You still employing that Hun pilot for the seaplane?'

'Vogel? Yes, he's still with us – we have trouble with the plane.'

'He'd be better off driving an ox cart.'

'Do you want a job or don't you?'

'I've a couple of things in mind.' Reed tried to sound casual. He watched a seagull planing on a warm current of air. 'Kwang Wha Petroleum needs a maintenance engineer.'

Claud sighed. 'Don't waste my time.'

The seagull slid down the air between high buildings and headed for the river. Reed turned. 'Give me my old job and I'll keep the Stinson flying despite the Hun. And I'll service the trucks whenever I've got time and provided I'm left alone.'

'Wouldn't you like to fly again, Reed? This Hitler fellow – there's a war brewing in Europe and I hear that Vogel is thinking of going home to die for the Fatherland. If I take you on as mechanic, will you fly the Stinson if Vogel leaves us?'

'I'll maintain it, but I won't fly.'

'Why not? I don't understand you.' Claud stared at him. 'You can't be afraid? You used to fly the air mail, St Louis to Chicago.'

'The same route as Lindberg.'

'And you were in the air service in France in 1917–1918.'

'And I flew in the Chaco war – me and Arch Rittenhouse. Now I'm a mechanic.'

Claud rubbed his jaw and continued to stare at him, then shrugged. 'Very well, if you're prepared to settle for so little.'

'How about an advance on my pay, Claud? I need forty dollars and my fare to Chen-chiang.'

'I have to justify every payment. Supposing the Japs bomb your train and kill you – the company's down by forty dollars.' Claud took a notepad from his desk drawer and began scribbling on it. 'That friend of yours, Rittenhouse. I hear he's got his picture on the cover of *Time* magazine.' He tore off the slip of paper. 'The Nanking Express leaves Shanghai West Station at eleven p.m. and the second class fare is eight dollars. I've given you a chit for fifteen.'

'You're a prince, Claud.'

He went to Accounts and they gave him fifteen dollars Mex. Then the lift took him down and he set off along the Bund. It was early afternoon, sun moving over to the west, but he could feel the burning slabs through his worn boots.

He'd got work, and the fare to Chen-chiang, but he needed money for a hotel room for the night, and to tide him over until the end of the month. Briefly he thought about going back to Sao's apartment. He could pretend he didn't know about the shirt, for one last night with her. The possibility evoked an immediate image of Sao's golden thighs, but he scowlingly suppressed it. That was over.

Across the river a large sea-going junk lay half submerged

just off Yun Tseng's wharf. Reed paused, squinting in the bright sunlight. Two small figures were moving on the stern upjutting out of the water. Still watching, he sat on a bench but his thoughts kept returning to the problem. Forty dollars – he'd figured that was about what he needed. He'd got fifteen so now he'd have to find another twenty-five. It would mean approaching the Dane, Dalsager.

A shoe shine boy pestered him so he nodded and stuck his right boot on the box. If he could borrow twenty-five dollars from Dalsager he could get a cheap room at the YM.

The cracked boots shone. He stood and gave the boy five cents. On the other side of the river a launch had moved out from the police pier and was heading towards the half-submerged junk. And Reed began walking again, a puzzled, questioning man, his shoulders hunched.

A squat tugboat dragged a string of barges up river, their wash rippling out to buoys and moored ships, and lapping at the high stern of the sunken junk.

The junk had been there resting in sixteen feet of water for three days, its bows smashed in. There had been no cargo to salvage, and most of the Chinese owner's personal possessions had been lifted and taken off. Bringing up the body had been more difficult.

In the stern, three feet out of the water, a pale, gangling young man was seated by a silt-ruined harmonium. His shoulders and back, unused to exposure, were blistered by the sun and his fair hair was still wet from the river. He frowned, watching bubbles break the surface over the ship's hold. Then a head emerged out of the murky water. Mouth wide, sucking air and grinning, the Chinese sailor held up a dripping umbrella. 'Yun Tseng's!'

The pale young man nodded. 'Enough. Leave it now.' He looked at the approaching police launch, then grasped the tip of the umbrella to haul the sailor from the water. 'Dry off and keep out of the way. We'll try again tomorrow.'

38

He offered no assistance to the launch crew as they secured alongside. An English inspector of the Shanghai Police climbed over the stern. 'Well, well. Russell, is it?'

'That's right. Russell, the spectre at the bloody feast.'

The inspector's pale blue eyes registered faint interest as he glanced round at the shambles of water-logged relics dragged up out of the silt. 'Doing a little salvage work, are you?' And he touched the harmonium with his silver-topped cane. 'That's rather nice. You shouldn't swim in the river, you know, it's filthy for at least twenty miles from the estuary.'

The young man didn't reply and the inspector turned towards the shore. 'You're not thinking of trying to get into Yun Tseng's warehouse, are you?'

'Customs have put a new padlock on the door – they were careful not to give me a key.'

'Quite so. They have the responsibility for its contents now that Yun Tseng is dead. You do see that, Russell?'

'What you mean is, they have responsibility for those six aeroplane engines off the *Star of Asia*.' Russell had a marked London accent that the inspector noted as working class. 'That's what the Japs killed the old man for, isn't it?'

'Vice Admiral Hasagawa has apologized. Compensation will be paid. It was an unfortunate accident, Russell. You must accept that.'

'I don't have to accept anything.' Russell picked up his shirt and began pulling it on. 'The old man's death was a message, clearly understood by Chinese traders – attempt breaking the embargo to help Chiang Kai-shek and you could have a very nasty accident.' He smiled bleakly. 'And Yun Tseng was only the poor bloody agent.'

'Murder in broad daylight, and with the connivance of the Japanese navy?' The inspector managed an impatient sigh. 'There is no case. You are imagining all of this.'

'Am I. See that Japanese freighter moored out there? Its cargo is potash according to the manifest. In fact it's carrying Thermit.' Russell fastened his shirt with clumsy, nervous movements. 'I'll tell you something else about that freighter – there's somebody on there observing us right now.'

'Let us not get too fanciful, Russell.' The inspector stared at the Japanese ship for a moment then turned back. 'You've taken Yun Tseng's death rather hard – it is affecting your judgement.'

'And you could maybe get me declared insane?'

'You must admit that your behaviour has been odd – to say the least.' The pale eyes watched Russell. 'Perhaps you should see a doctor.'

'I'm not crazy!' Russell snarled.

'The consul is worried about you.'

'Of course he is – he wants me on a boat home!'

'Well, let's be honest, Russell.' The inspector's tone hardened. 'You're becoming a nuisance. The Japanese landing is a reality. We have to keep things going as best we can until one side or the other climbs down, and we get peace again.'

'There isn't going to be any peace!' Russell moved agitatedly in the confined space, and the inspector realized that he was lame.

'Even if I thought that I wouldn't say it in public. An old Chinese died when a Japanese gunboat accidentally rammed his junk. Now you must forget it. Off the record, you would be wise to go home to England. But while you're here I want your assurance that you'll cause no more disturbance.'

Russell thought for a moment then nodded. 'All right.'

'And you won't embarrass the Americans again? And you'll write no more of those letters to the Japanese consul?'

'No more letters.'

The inspector's eyes narrowed. It had all gone a little too easily and he suspected that Russell was agreeing just to get rid of him. In that moment he caught a glint of reflected light from the Japanese freighter moored up off Pootung Point. Somebody out there was using binoculars. He couldn't altogether discount the possibility that he and Russell were being watched. He prodded the harmonium with his cane. 'I used to have one of those when I was a boy.'

'The old man used to play it – very badly.'

'Yun Tseng was a canny old devil. He must have been worth a bob or two?'

'He had three useless grandsons,' Russell said. 'I daresay they'll share the business and whatever money Yun Tseng left.'

'But you were like a son to him – so I hear?' And there was the sharp glance again.

'I was just his accountant . . . ' Russell scowled. 'But I want to see justice done.'

'Justice?' The inspector climbed over the stern rail but remained a moment before stepping across to the launch. 'I'm not entirely sure that you are hearing me, Russell. Do be careful. I may not be able to protect you.'

'From what?'

'The consequences of your folly.'

The launch pulled away and yawed, turning, then it moved upstream.

Russell limped along the stern to stare across the water at the padlocked door of Yun Tseng's warehouse. And he reflected on his half-formed plan – folly it was, but it was the only one he had.

CHAPTER FOUR

Reed spent the afternoon sitting in Jessfield Park, he couldn't afford cafés or bars. Twenty cents admission bought a greenness that lulled him, and the distant cries of peacocks. He dozed, though only yards separated him from the traffic of Yu Yuen Road. As evening approached he rose and left, passing the neat, imperative park notices, DOGS AND CHINESE NOT ALLOWED. Another hour maybe, and Dalsagar would show up at the Bukhara. Maybe.

Dalsagar was master of the *I-cheng*, a rusting river steamer plying the Yangtze as far as Hankow. Reed had seen the *I-cheng* moored at the Arnold Bros. wharf, so he knew the Dane was in Shanghai. Dalsager had a small house on the Rue du Consulat, but the etiquette of the situation suggested a meeting on neutral ground.

Reed felt like a tramp, boots dusty again and his shirt sticking to his back. A twenty-five dollar loan would get him a shower and a room at the YM on Bubbling Well Road, and there would be enough left to last him until he reached Chen-chiang. But he was aware now that one of his boots was worn right through the sole.

He turned off into Kiangsu Road, still pondering on his poverty. I'm getting too old to live this way, he thought. I should organize my life – give it a little dignity. Damn it, there's no dignity in worn-out boots.

Some hoodlums were messing up a Chinese pawnshop, tipping the stock out into the street while the pawnbroker wailed. Reed kept walking, it wasn't his affair how the sons of bitches conducted their business affairs. The hoodlums were Dou's men, recruited in the docks for the most part. A few dollars and they bought themselves gaberdine suits and patent leather shoes, and open razors, of course. The pragmatic French had appointed Dou honorary captain of detectives, and crime had dropped dramatically in their district.

Reed reached the intersection near the Commercial Pacific Cable Company and turned right. He was heading for the Bukhara, a Russian restaurant on the Avenue Joffre. It wasn't as sumptuous as Kafka's but the food was better. Reed was hungry, he hadn't eaten since midmorning, but even if Dalsager lent him twenty-five dollars he couldn't afford Bukhara prices. Berdichev, the proprietor, had decorated the restaurant exterior in the extravagant fashion of Kresstoffsky's in pre-war St Petersburg. Beggars hovered, kept clear of the entrance by the boot of a Cossack doorman – he saluted as Reed went in.

There were chess players sitting in the cubicles along one side. Berdichev was tolerant, he allowed his poorer Russian clients a place to sit and even provided the chess sets. There were newspapers in leather folders: *Shanghai Zaria* and *Slovo*, both Russian. And *Deutsche Shanghai Zeitung, Le Journal de Shanghai*, as well as the local English and American papers.

The gypsy dancers were resting, smoking black Russian cigarettes and talking rapidly. Reed picked up the *Evening Post & Mercury* and went to one of the cubicles served by a waiter he knew. He'd noticed Han Yu-lin, one of Dou's lieutenants, seated on the far side of the restaurant with his huge bodyguard. Like Dalsager, Han had a passion for Russian food, though he usually ate at Kafka's.

Reed scanned the paper. The *Evening Post & Mercury* was American-owned so the General Motors strike had got on to the front page, along with the comment that the Neutrality Act was being contravened by China hiring American pilots. Mingled smells of borsch and shashlik distracted him. The waiter was harassed and took time coming over. Bearded, dressed in purple silk, he looked Russian but was in fact a German Jew.

43

'The service here is awful.'

'Go to Kafka's – they've got girls with big breasts and Russian boots. What will you have, Reed?'

'Iced tea, I guess.'

The waiter returned, edging between the tables, a tray balanced on his left hand. He'd been a musician with the Berlin Philharmonic. Now a refugee from Nazism he worked long hours serving food. 'Aren't you eating, Reed?'

'I can't afford Berdichev's prices. Let me know if Dalsager comes in, but don't tell him I'm here.'

He sipped the iced lemon tea and concentrated on the newspaper to keep his mind off food. Five thousand seven hundred and fifteen abandoned bodies buried the previous year by benevolent societies and Shanghai charities. He turned the page. Wreckage, believed to be part of Amelia Earhart's Lockheed monoplane, found off Howland Island in the Pacific. And he paused, attention caught by a short item lower down. JUNK SINKS OFF POOTUNG POINT. But at that moment the waiter passed close and muttered, 'Captain Dalsager has arrived.'

Reed could see the Dane; balding, bearded, impatient, and with thick gold bars on the cuffs of his merchant marine uniform. Wise to give him a little time. He waited until Dalsager was eating, napkin tucked in his collar.

A couple of musicians strummed while the gipsy dancers assumed their expressionless stances in preparation for the dance. Reed crossed the restaurant. There were a few high-class Russian prostitutes on call, who offered an unofficial extension to the service. One of them glanced speculatively at Reed, then looked bored as he moved on.

'Well, I'll be damned!' And he paused at Dalsager's table. 'What a surprise!'

Dalsager's fork was poised. 'I thought you had returned to America?' He looked a little irritated at having his meal interrupted, but curiosity got the better of him. 'Sit down, Reed – for a few moments.' And he signalled to the waiter for another glass. 'Tell me why you came back here.'

44

Reed didn't know, except that it had been a retreat, and how do you tell somebody a thing like that?

'I guess I was homesick.' But an impulse to be honest made him add, 'Maybe this is where I function best.'

'It's temporary, Reed. All temporary. Is that how you feel?'

'I suppose so. I've picked a bad time though, haven't I?'

'You mean the war?' Dalsager finished the kulebiaka and belched softly. 'Have a little wine. This is Shanghai – we're used to trouble. I was here when Chiang Kai-shek staged the coup, there were baskets full of heads hanging from the lampposts. Man is the most savage, ruthless creature ever to walk the earth.' He liked talking and Reed let him. 'In 1932 when the Japanese triggered the last incident, they devastated the north-western districts beyond the Settlement – you could hear their guns twenty miles up river.' He spread melted butter and black caviare on his blini. 'Were you here in 1932, Reed?'

'No.' Reed felt his stomach rumbling. He sipped wine. 'I was in Bolivia – the Chaco – for most of that year.'

'Oh-ho, yes!' Dalsager looked knowing. 'The war between Shell and Standard Oil, a good example of man's ruthlessness.'

Reed didn't really want to talk about it, but he remembered the medal. 'There was no damned oil there. A wilderness, it wasn't worth fighting for. Thousands of miles of burning scrub and desert.' A harsh, dead, thirsty place – Reed scowled. 'We didn't even know who we were shooting at most of the time.' He fumbled in his pocket. 'Say, you might like to look at this medal – it was given me by President Salamanca himself.' Me and half a dozen other boasting, hard-drinking mercenary flyers. 'See, it's twenty-two carat gold. Why, that medal must be worth at least twenty-five dollars.'

Dalsager glanced sideways at the medal and went on eating. 'I have no intention of buying it, Reed. Have some more wine.'

'Well, maybe you'd like to keep the medal as security for a twenty-five dollar loan?'

'You are a nagging puzzle – an odd assemblage of contra-dictions.' Dalsager sighed. 'Why do you ask *me* for money?'

And that was a damned stupid question. 'Because *I* know that *you* know that you'll get the money back.'

Dalsager stared at him, but he was thinking. 'You mended a clock for me – it keeps perfect time. Could you repair a piano – I bought it second hand.'

Reed had never fixed a piano but he knew how they worked. 'I'll do it tomorrow.'

'It is small, upright. I have it in my cabin on the *I-cheng*. I will pay you thirty dollars if you do a good job.'

'No. Twenty-five.'

'But why?' Dalsager had that puzzled expression again.

'Because twenty-five is what I asked you for – you can pay me extra for any parts or materials I need.'

'All right. Twenty-five dollars, and tomorrow night I will buy you dinner in the Bukhara.'

'Tomorrow night I take the Nanking Express.'

'You may die poor, Reed. Doesn't that worry you?'

'Maybe I'll change.'

The young man from the United States consulate tapped on the hotel room door at exactly seven thirty. Linda was still fastening her dress and his precision irritated her.

He had a consulate car decorated with two small stars and stripes pennants – 'It lets these people know who they are dealing with.' A uniformed Chinese chauffeur drove them east along Peking Road towards the waterfront. They were close to the battle zone and sounds of music spilling from the cafés was lost intermittently in the thump of exploding shells beyond Soochow Creek.

'Are they going to keep firing all night?' It was usually quieter after dark.

'The Japanese have landed heavy artillery.' The young man looked at his watch. 'I think we may be a little late for the conference.'

'Why are the Japanese reinforcing their landing if they want peace?'

46

'More bargaining power, I suppose.' And he pointed. 'See there beyond the large Chamber of Commerce building. The Chinese 88th Division is dug in at Shanghai North Station. They're tough regulars – Matsui can't dislodge them.'

General Matsui had revised his tactics. Even though his casualties were less than half those of the Chinese, the cost of pushing through a wasteland of ruined streets and factories was prohibitive. He'd begun the systematic flattening of acres of the Chapei.

Linda had watched the bombardment from high up on the seventeenth floor of Broadway Mansions that afternoon. It was awesome even from a distance, and angry and sick she'd returned to the hotel to write up what she'd seen.

'After a while the smoke covered everything. A large ship – a cruiser would it be? – was shelling from down river, then the bombers came in three waves at sundown.'

'Fortunately there is very little American-owned property in the Chapei. The CPC materials depot, of course . . .'

The mismatch of his train of thought incensed Linda.

Flares arced upwards – thin trails of fire then popping sounds, and brilliant light suffused the northern suburbs. It was the end of the tenth day in the battle of the Chapei.

The car crossed the iron bridge spanning the Whangpoo end of the wild creek. Japanese soldiers were on the far side. Thousands of sampan homes were crowded together in the water below. The car window was slightly open and the foul stench of the creek caught at Linda's throat.

'Whole families live out their lives down there.' The young man closed the window tight. 'Many only come ashore to be buried.'

She couldn't comprehend it. I'm over-civilized, she thought. Liberal, middle class; brought up to believe all people are equal but with a tacit proviso that *we* are rather special. If I'd been one of those creek people I'd surely have died last year. 'Isn't anybody responsible for them?'

'Not really, though the creek is part of the Greater Municipality under Chinese administration. From time to

47

time the British descend on them with disinfectant and earnest advice.' He smiled thinly. 'They listen politely then go about their affairs – they are a health hazard to the whole community. Their births and deaths go unrecorded. Even the Greens leave them alone.'

'The gangsters?'

'Yes. Dou's men – our ugly underworld.'

Linda glanced back at the thousand lights flickering like quicksilver on the dark water.

'I hope you'll enjoy the evening, Miss Bishop.' She felt the slight pressure of his thigh against hers. 'These press affairs are quite lavish. The Japanese go to a lot of trouble. General Matsui is anxious to keep on good terms with the Western powers.'

Linda edged her leg out of range and determinedly continued the conversation. 'What is General Matsui like? I imagine him large, thick spectacles and a great samurai sword.'

'Then you'll be surprised. The General seems to be a humane man – anxious to end the bloodshed.'

'But he brings up heavy artillery. Am I missing some subtlety of Japanese logic?'

'Whatever, it's damned bad form of the Orientals to fight their war on our doorstep. We of the Settlement have to remain aloof from this business.' He frowned to himself. 'You cannot begin to imagine the amount of paperwork the refugee problem has created. It was nearly six before I could get away from the office.'

The car stopped at a barricade and she saw Japanese marines close up for the first time. They held their long rifles casually, but with a suggestion of menace. The young man rolled down the window and held out a pass, and the NCO stared at it then waved them on.

'I guess you're used to press conferences, Miss Bishop?'

'Oh, yes.' A lie – Linda was already beginning to feel apprehensive. What was her journalistic experience to date? Coverage of debates on Church unity. Scandal over church funding in Petersburg, Mississippi – big deal. An interview with H.L. Mencken – she'd been proud of that story. But it had all been before last summer.

'. . .I'll introduce you to Wylie – he's been with Mao Tse-tung in Shensi for the last month.'

Linda was only half listening. Funny the way I've got into the habit of dividing my life into before and after the operation, she thought. Even at that moment she was aware of the scar. If I slide my hand across the smoothness of my dress I'll feel its ugliness. Would her young escort be so anxious to rub knees if he saw it?

The car stopped outside the Japanese consulate. It looked – what? – defensible. Marines stood guard, light from the car head-lights glinting off their bayonets. A white-gloved officer checked the consulate pass and Linda's press credentials as they entered the building. In the colonnaded hall she could hear voices from the reception room. A boy took her wrap. On the far wall hung a full-length portrait of Emperor Hirohito. He looked insignificant – more a dentist than the Son of Heaven.

'The Japanese have their own elaborate etiquette.' The young man led the way into the room crowded with newsmen and a few women. 'They don't like to lose face, so you have to be careful in the questions that you ask.'

Waiters with trays of filled glasses moved among the guests. Everywhere there was food, and people passing each other plates – Japanese hospitality was lavish.

'All paid for personally by the Emperor. I'll get us some champagne.' Her escort turned on his boyish smile. 'Don't go away.'

Some of the press men glanced at her. Linda felt exposed. They all seemed to know each other. There were a number of Japanese – military, she suspected, though they were in civilian clothes. A loudly talking group had their backs to her, very English by their accents and they sounded as if they'd been drinking for some time. One of them turned clumsily, spilling champagne on the skirt of a slender, long-haired Asiatic girl, and he began to apologize. A waiter offered a napkin. The girl raised her knee slightly, dabbing at the damp stain, and her dress, split Shanghai style, briefly revealed her thigh. The man apologized again while he stared. She looked up, freezing him with a glance.

'I can see you're new here.'

Linda turned.

'Y'haven't got a glass.' A large, florid man smiled at her. 'Come with me.'

'I really think I should wait.'

But he'd taken her by the elbow and was steering her through the crowd. 'Don't worry about Jordan – he'll find us. You did come with Jordan, didn't you?'

Linda supposed she had.

'You should never be without a glass – it worries our hosts and they are psychopathically anxious people. Have you ever wondered why?' He scooped a glass from a passing tray and handed it to her. 'I'm Phil McGovern, *South China News*. Now you have to tell me who you are.'

'Linda Bishop.' She glanced around for Jordan.

'I hope you didn't eat before you came. Try a shrimp, they're delicious.'

She shook her head, so he took one for himself. 'All you need in Shanghai is a press card and a place to sleep.'

'When does the conference begin?'

McGovern stared at her in mock surprise. 'This *is* the conference – almost. The Japanese get everybody well oiled then impart the minimum of information.'

A thin, fair man moved across to a window alcove. He'd been in the sun without a hat – and Linda noticed that he had a limp. British, she thought – it's the way they dress. He seemed almost furtive as his eyes searched the crowd.

'I arrived from Canton early this morning,' McGovern was saying. 'The sky was a deep azure blue in the east.'

She saw two of the Japanese who might be military approaching the man in the alcove. They appeared to be checking his identity.

'Ever look at the China coast at sunrise, Miss Bishop?' McGovern took another shrimp. 'It's like being born again.'

Jordan, her young escort, was edging his way across the

50

room – he held two glasses and he looked piqued. 'Hullo, McGovern, when did you arrive? You people are like vultures.' Then he saw the group in the window alcove and scowled. 'Oh God, it's Russell! How did he get in?'

'Isn't he a newspaperman?'

'No, Miss Bishop, he's a lunatic, and damnit, the British were supposed to have warned him off – he's their responsibility.'

The two Japanese were hustling Russell through the crowd. He struggled and Linda heard his voice raised. 'Why have you murdering swine brought *ronin* with you?'

Jordan watched with distaste. 'This is Russell's third embarrassing display – he was evicted from our consulate yesterday.'

'Who is Ronin? He said the Japanese had brought Ronin with them.'

'It isn't a person, Miss Bishop. The word means "without a lord". *Ronin* are terrorists.' McGovern was frowning. 'Officially they don't exist. Unofficially they do the Japanese army's dirty work.'

Russell shouted from the doorway. 'I have a question to ask – a pertinent question!' But they pushed him out.

'He worked for an old man named Yun Tseng who was accidentally drowned. Russell claims it was murder,' Jordan said. 'He has it in his head that the Japanese murdered the old man, and that they intend using terror tactics to capture and hold the capital at Nanking.'

'The capital! But that's two hundred miles up the Yangtze! Could he be right?'

Linda's question remained poised in mid air. A slim Japanese in a grey suit was arranging papers on a table at the head of the room. He wore pebble-lensed glasses in horn-rims.

'The show is about to begin, Miss Bishop. That's Captain Asani, Public Relations Officer.'

She thought he looked like Charlie Chan's son in the movies. The Asiatic girl who'd had champagne spilled on her dress joined him briefly. She gazed around seemingly bored.

51

'And that's Miss Kuang, Pacific Press Services,' Jordan murmured. 'She's a French national.'

'You see how it is with these consulate boys, Miss Bishop. They're all womanizers.'

'Unlike you,' Linda said.

'Oh, I'm the worst possible kind.' McGovern grinned hugely.

There was a sudden shift of attention. Captain Asani tapped a silver dish with a spoon. 'Please. May I have your attention for His Excellency, General Matsui.'

Conversation tailed off. An elderly Japanese officer had entered the room. Painfully thin, right arm held stiffly immobile, he walked to the long table. Newsmen clapped briefly, and he slowly adjusted his spectacles.

'Honoured guests of the Emperor. Great is the burden and sacrifice of our Imperial forces here in Shanghai . . .'

His voice was high and thin. Linda strained to hear him.

'We have come to protect Japanese lives and property threatened by the war lord, Chiang Kai-shek. Our Emperor, divine on the steps of heaven, wishes only peace and harmony.' The General paused and coughed into his handkerchief. 'We have no quarrel with the Chinese people. I am not here to fight an enemy, but in the state of mind of a man who wishes to pacify a brother.'

Linda thought that General Matsui looked sick; cheek bones ready to protrude through parchment skin.

' . . . I urge grave self-reflection by the Chinese people.' And he laboured his points, reading from the notes in his thin, monotonous tone. 'But there is a greater task. Japan will use enlightened methods to convince China of the Emperor's divine mission — all Asians in equal partnership.'

He isn't talking about settling an incident. Linda glanced round, still feeling an amateur among professionals. Somebody will take him up on that, surely? And she noticed the faces of the Japanese. They were all smiling.

The General's speech seemed to have exhausted him, and Captain Asani stood. 'His Excellency apologizes for his poor English. He will do his best to answer questions but regrets that he may have to use me as an interpreter.'

'He understands every damned word that's said,' McGovern growled, and he raised his notepad. 'Excellency, is the incident here in Shanghai a secondary theatre of war to draw off Chiang Kai-shek's troops from the fighting in the north?'

Matsui murmured to Captain Asani who answered for him. 'His Excellency indicates that the fighting in the north of China is quite a separate issue. And he begs to remind you that Shanghai is not a theatre of war. No war has been declared.'

'But a further thirty thousand troops arrived in Shanghai in the last two days.'

'Not so many.' Matsui shook his head and coughed.

Somebody across the room called, 'Your troops are removing merchandise from warehouses on the north side of Soochow Creek.'

'We are not thieves – we are preventing war materials reaching Chiang Kai-shek.'

'But Japanese soldiers are even taking scrap metal from the Chapei ruins.'

'We anticipate an early return to peace. Our soldiers are removing dangerous relics from the battleground. We wish to make the Chapei safe for the Chinese people.'

All the Japanese were smiling politely. Linda felt a sudden icy unease. Harrada, the Japanese Military Attaché, had a handkerchief pressed to his mouth. They are all enjoying a huge, awful joke! What was the question that the odd young man, Russell, would have asked? She was afraid of making a fool of herself in front of the seasoned journalists. But General Matsui was preparing to leave so it was now or not at all. And she raised her hand. 'Captain Asani, will you please ask the General what are Japan's long-term intentions in this area.'

Matsui paused almost imperceptibly over his briefcase. He understood that all right, she thought. But Asani answered for him. 'We have repeatedly indicated that our military operation is confined to the Yangtze delta. A stop line has been drawn . . .'

'Then His Excellency is able to assure us that it is not the intention of Imperial Japanese forces to advance on the Chinese capital at Nanking?'

There was near silence, she could feel every head turned towards her.

The general stared bleakly, then clicked his briefcase shut. But the Japanese weren't smiling any more. And Linda was aware that Jordan had eased back, distancing himself from her. Damn them all, she thought. The whole press conference was a charade.

Captain Asani looked acutely embarrassed. 'His Excellency regrets that he must leave now to attend the bedside of Prince Fushima Hiroyashi who was gravely wounded this morning. But he begs that you continue to enjoy the hospitality of the Emperor.'

The old, sick general passed Linda on his way out. She felt glances in her direction. Conversation resumed. Across the room the attractive Asiatic girl was standing alone, watching her.

'You've rocked the boat.' McGovern grinned. 'Another question like that and Captain Asani might feel obliged to disembowel himself.'

Linda was aware of an odd feeling of unreality, as when a perfectly ordinary dream begins to turn unpleasant. Military Attaché Harrada speared a prawn on a cocktail stick and bit it in half. The Asiatic girl checked her wristwatch against the clock on the wall and a young Englishman discreetly left the loudly talking group and casually joined her. Somebody on the other side of the room laughed loudly – a harsh sound.

'My guess is that you would like to leave now,' Jordan said.

'Yes. Yes, I think I ought to.'

As the car sped back along the Bund she was still uneasy. Poor Jordan – he'd had high hopes for the evening. 'I'm sorry if I embarrassed you.'

He smiled wryly. 'I dare say my career will survive.'

'But I shouldn't have asked that question?'

'The Japanese have repeatedly indicated that they wouldn't go beyond the delta. You made the general lose face by persisting.' Jordan looked out at the distant flashes of guns to the north.

He wasn't trying to press his thigh against hers any more. 'It was because of that young man with the limp, Russell – that's why I asked.'

'What Russell says makes no kind of sense.' Jordan frowned. 'The Japanese already have a costly campaign in North China. Why open another front here, where they are opposed by Chiang's best troops? I've been in Shanghai over five years and I still can't figure the Oriental mind.' He pondered. 'When I went to fetch us champagne I overheard Harrada talking about *tanka* poetry, and when I came back he was explaining to Miss Kuang his technique for shooting robins – can you imagine that?'

'He's revolting.' Linda thought for a moment. 'Miss Kuang – who did you say she writes for?'

'Pacific Press Service, though she does some freelance work as well.' Jordan seemed anxious to change the subject and Linda wondered if he'd tried his boyish charm on her.

As the car stopped outside Linda's hotel, he said, 'I have a strong feeling I started off on the wrong foot with you. I'm sorry.'

'We all do that sometimes. Forget it.'

'I'm trying to be honest now. You really might be safer here in the Settlement, until we see what the Japanese intentions are. I wish you'd reconsider.'

'No. Tomorrow night I'm boarding the Nanking Express – but thanks for your concern.' The chauffeur had opened the car door and Linda paused as she climbed out. 'Listen. The guns have stopped.'

Jordan leaned over and spoke through the open door. 'Our people are being recalled from up river, but the British consul is staying on at Hsia-kang for a while. Let him know where you expect to be if you leave the town.'

'Just in case?' She smiled.

55

'Yes,' he said. 'Just in case.'

Linda entered the hotel and crossed the foyer to the lift. She'd already begun to forget Jordan. Most people did. The lift wasn't working. She pressed the button again and waited, tapping impatiently with the high heel of her shoe. It would have to be the stairs. Five damned floors.

The stairs spiralled up round the lift shaft. A heavy fatigue caught up with her as she reached the fourth floor and she rested a moment, leaning on the sill of an open window. Unease over the press conference remained with her. Why had she gone? – this wasn't what she'd come to China for. She stared out at the night.

I thought it all through in those months of illness. A good job of reporting – useful, but one I could handle. Missions and relief services, I know about them. But it's all turning out bigger, and I'm answerable in some way. She frowned, groping with the thought. I'm answerable because I asked that question.

She remained a moment longer at the window. No flashes or flares beyond Soochow Creek – just a stillness. Perhaps the Chinese troops had pulled back?

CHAPTER FIVE

The bombardment had ended at ten p.m. and now the Chapei was still. Bright moonlight illuminated a wilderness of jagged ruins and twisted railway track. Japanese infantrymen of the "Black" 9th Division picked their way forward, cursing softly as loose brickwork slid away under their boots.

The wasteland was littered with Chinese dead – and dying. They finished them off with a bayonet thrust and went quickly through their pockets. Then, growing more wary, they crawled across the moonlit marshalling yards. Here they were exposed. And they paused at last, kneeling, sheltered in the rubble, and peered across a vast crater.

There was no going any further. Sixty yards ahead loomed the great white block of Shanghai North Station building – six floors of ferro-concrete, its weather end pitted with holes and blackened by shellfire. But it was intact, the standard of the Chinese 88th Division still draped from the shattered wireless mast and beside it a Republican flag brought across the creek that night.

The artillery and naval guns would have to pound it again tomorrow. Tomorrow would be the fourth attempt to capture Shanghai North – the third by the "Black" 9th. At a signal the infantrymen groped their way back to the relative safety of the CPC depot. They could rest for a while. Like animals they huddled in holes and slept fitfully. Some counted the hours as they listened to distant music from the brightly lit city beyond Soochow Creek. And at first grey light the guns opened the sixteenth day of the battle.

*

The faint tremble of gunfire brought down fine particles of dust from the ceiling of Miss Kuang's office.

Pacific Press Services occupied modest premises on the French side of Avenue Edward VII. The exterior of the building suggested slow decline. Kanao Copper Company used the ground floor: dingy offices, worn carpet, a smell of decay. But the upper floors were extensively renovated. The Shanghai branch of Pacific Press had been in operation since 1933 – just after the last incident – collecting and disseminating trade news: imports, exports, changes in shipping regulations, market trends – dry stuff for the business pages of dozens of newspapers and periodicals in the Asia Pacific area. And other information, not for press use, was collected. A Malay half-caste girl operated a telephone switchboard in the reception area on the first floor, and somewhere along the corridor a teleprinter clicked continuously.

Miss Kuang had the best room. Communications from the Tienkin office were on her desk – she had just rendered them into code for transmission to China Special Services Bureau of the Imperial Japanese Army. Item: aviation fuel stocks in the Nanking area. Item: Dutch shipment of military vehicle tyres into the port of Foochow. Item: six Pratt & Whitney aero engines impounded at Shanghai. Miss Kuang's passport said she was French.

She took off her heavy-framed reading glasses and rubbed her eyes. Office hours were her own to decide, but her nights were often demanding. She suppressed a small yawn and went to the window. After the bombing of Wing On's department store she'd noticed a tiny hairline crack in the glass. She pressed it with her finger and spoke without turning her head. 'I had expected the Bureau would send Colonel Takao.' The crack spidered suddenly to the edge of the frame. Would that be bad luck?

'Colonel Takao is seconded to Prince Konoye's staff in Tokyo.' The tall young Asian came and stood behind her at the window. 'I was ordered to take his place – I had no part in the decision.'

'Did you come here directly from Sian, Captain Ohata?'

'As directly as I could. I am using a Dutch passport. There are rigorous security checks at the airports.' Ohata remained behind Miss Kuang, aware of the smell of jasmine in her hair, and her thin, high-necked blouse provokingly proper. 'It seemed wiser to travel by railway.'

'You could have been with me a day earlier if you had taken the Eurasia flight. But you wisely considered the risk unwarranted.'

Already she was playing a game with him. Ohata turned away. 'What difference does it make?'

'How long has it been?'

'You know as well as I.'

'I have not kept count.' Miss Kuang toyed with her jade bracelet and looked out at the traffic on Avenue Edward VII. 'Tell me.'

'Two years. Two years and three weeks.' Ohata paused. 'I have a wife and son now. You understand, of course, that I had no wish to see you again.'

'But perhaps you needed to?' She moved her body very slightly.

He stared at her hips, remembering a lust that drained but left him hungry, and he sighed to himself. 'On the railway journey across Anhwei the plain seemed limitless – it could swallow up armies. I was weary but unable to sleep, aware that the rail tracks led to you. I even wrote a poem.'

Miss Kuang turned. 'And you have it?'

He shook his head. 'You are predictable only in your vanity. With an instinct that you might one day use it against me, I tore the poem into small pieces, and I was not entirely at ease until I had scattered them across the province.'

'But you could recite it to me?'

'No, madam, I could not recite it to you.'

'It is a poem of . . .' She eased closer to him and pretended to ponder ' . . . of restless sleep, perhaps?'

Ohata rested his hands on her waist and felt something like an electric charge. 'And squalid betrayal.'

Miss Kuang smiled.

He pushed her angrily away. 'I've come with new instructions, madam. Tonight you and I travel separately on the Nanking Express. You will leave the train at Changchow and proceed north by road. The Chinese are constructing a boom across the Yangtze east of Chiang-yin. Your task is to find weak points where the boom could be safely navigated by ships of the Ataka class. The area is closely supervised and it may become necessary for you to gain the confidence of the Chinese army officer responsible for security.'

Still smiling, Miss Kuang lowered her eyes. 'We must serve the Emperor in whatever way we can.'

Ohata picked up his briefcase. 'Let us not grace your necessary skills with patriotism. Merchants, Kuomintang officers, Westerners – that English youth, Shanghai gangsters. Your successes are odious . . .'

'Even a captain of Japanese Military Intelligence.'

' . . . and astounding.' Ohata stared at her, puzzled. 'What do you seek?'

Her mouth still curved but the smile had gone. 'Diversion.' She returned to the window.

From his briefcase, Ohata took a canvas belt lined with pouches.

'You will use your Pacific Press Service identity as a reason for interesting yourself in the river traffic at Chiang-yin.'

'Who is the man whose confidence I may need to gain?'

'A hardened expert in counter intelligence. His name is Colonel Tang.'

She turned quickly. 'Colonel Tang!'

'He is dangerous. Work your magic on him only if there is no other way of gaining the information.' Ohata noticed her expression and his eyes narrowed. 'You know him?'

'Our paths have crossed.'

'Would he recognize you?'

'No.' Naked, face painted, standing in line with other whores? 'No, he wouldn't recognize me now.' Miss Kuang put on her glasses, and her expression tightened. 'But I will know him.'

'Even so,' Ohata frowned, 'it might be wiser to ensure that

your paths do not cross again.' He handed her the pouched belt. 'Here are silver dollars to buy whoever you have to buy, and if silver is an inappropriate inducement you will do what you most enjoy doing.'

She felt the heaviness of the belt. 'Have we agents in the area?'

'A Captain Chu Teng of Chinese Maritime Customs is based in nearby Hsia-kang. He is expecting you.'

'I remember Captain Chu – he is afraid of his shadow. Is there nobody better?'

'It is Chu's fear that has kept him alive while others have failed. Zhou Tsa-lin, and the merchant Wei – both were caught by Colonel Tang. Their heads decorate the Chiang-yin South Gate.' Ohata thought for a moment.

'There is one other agent – even I do not know his identity. When you have information on the weaknesses of the river boom you will place an advertisement in the local newspaper, *Jintian*, offering for sale a decorated silver-backed mirror of the Han dynasty. He will reply with the question – do the letters TVL appear in the design? And you will have made contact.'

Ohata began fastening his briefcase in readiness to leave. 'You must complete the task within thirty days.'

'Have you no small word of concern for me?' Miss Kuang smoothed her black hair.

'Concern?' He looked at her with distaste. 'You should survive wherever there are men. But if your position becomes . . .' and he chose the word carefully. ' . . . untenable, you have the bracelet I gave you.'

She fingered the silver of the bracelet. There were two tiny cyanide tablets concealed under the jade decoration. 'I wonder. Is this trinket your insurance or mine? When do you and I meet again?'

'Not until our armies reach Nanking. If by chance we come upon each other at the station or on the train tonight, ignore me.' Weary, he picked up the briefcase. 'Now I have done everything I need to.'

'And we have the whole afternoon, Captain Ohata.' Miss Kuang smiled and took off her spectacles.

The afternoon was humid.

In Chinese City, crowded in disarray between the French Concession and the river, a million people lived out their lives quite separately from the rest of cosmopolitan Shanghai. This was the old part dating back over a thousand years. Russell had chosen to live here. He limped along the Ren Min Lu. His ribs hurt. After being hustled from the press conference the previous night the Japanese had duffed him before taking him to the edge of the English district and dumping him from the moving car.

Temples, drug stores crowded with exotic remedies, a bird market – Russell was barely aware of them. I should get out now, he thought. There were four thousand dollars Chinese tucked inside his passport. A river boat to the *Star of Asia* moored at Li Pai's wharf, and by nightfall the coast of China would be distant lights against a dark sky. What was stopping him?

He limped on towards the North Gate. A dead old man was stopping him. Aero engines! He'd thought Yun Tseng was smoking too many pipes. And then the story about the Japanese freighter with a cargo of Thermit for burning Nanking – the old man had picked it up from one of his junk captains. Madness, or so it had seemed just a few weeks ago.

Just ahead of him a girl in a floral dress examined embroidered handkerchiefs displayed on an open stall. Blonde hair, pale pink skin under her large sun hat. White men and women were not excluded from Chinese City and they came, as tourists usually, hiring a guide at the North Gate. The girl turned and stared at Russell's crooked leg, then she adjusted her gaze as though he didn't exist. He limped past her. Stupid bitch.

Artisans worked in open-fronted shops: jade, ivory, brass, figures beautifully carved in wood, umbrellas. Russell knew them all. Off to the left, the shrine of the Three

Pure Ones. Follow those grim steps to the right and you came to the place of public strangulation.

He left the labyrinth of narrow, ordurous streets and caught a cab. It took him along the Avenue Edward VII and, nervous now, he looked out at the street. Ching Sau Wah & Sons, Dentists, Mai Li Lacquer & Antique Company, Union Mobilière, and there were Yun Tseng's small offices above Maison Ando Beauty Parlour. The old man had seldom visited them – seldom come ashore. At seventy years, and rich, he'd lived on his junk with just four men as crew. Tall for a Chinese, and thin – he'd said it was the opium. Worn and faded blue cotton gown, skull cap, rolled umbrella. Yun Tseng had preferred the junk to his house on Bubbling Well Road, and he'd smoked two opium pipes a day – there was a smell like cinnamon in his cabin.

Russell was aware of a nagging unease in his gut. So I'm doing this for the old man. And what other reason is eating at me? He checked his watch as the cab turned off towards Rue Lafayette. All said and done, Yun Tseng was the only man I could have called a friend, so that will be sufficient reason for now. Nervously he adjusted his tie. He had asked for an interview with the High Dragon of the Green Society.

The tall walls of Dou's garden permitted only a faint stir of air and the guns sounded far off. Russell sweltered in his crumpled white suit – he hadn't known how to dress for the occasion. And he waited two hours, seated on the steps of the long verandah. Distanced from him, other petitioners, all Chinese, were talking softly. From beyond the wall there were muted sounds of traffic.

Earlier, in his rooms above the silversmith's, he'd rehearsed a speech giving reasons why the leader of the Green Society might want to help him, but now the words seemed absurdly inappropriate. Dou's imposing French Colonial villa intimidated him.

A slim Chinese boy squatted, guarding the open doorway. He wore only shorts and scuffed tennis shoes. An automatic pistol was strapped in a holster under his bare armpit. Russell glanced at him from time to time. He appeared to be completely engrossed in a small puzzle toy, but he looked up quickly as an old man with a trowel and hand fork moved across the lawn.

Dou's garden had been constructed by an artist. It mirrored the ancient Taoist principle of harmony with nature. Flowers clustered with studied asymmetry round a series of pools fed by water cascading off a rock: golden-rayed lilies, brilliant campion on slender stems. The old man with the trowel knelt, carefully easing out weeds. Russell watched him. He'd heard a story about one of the gardeners here – a faro dealer in a gambling house in Foochow Road until the Greens broke his hands. Now he tended Dou's flowers.

From the end of the verandah Russell heard a motor mower recede – almost gone – then return. Maybe Dou wouldn't see him? That possiblity seemed slightly prefer-able. Dou would remember that business over the opium shipment – he never forgot an interference in his affairs. And Russell felt an anxious impulse to walk up and down. Instead he tried taking deep breaths. Incongruous across the bright clusters of gently moving colour, he could see a thug with a sub-machine gun patrolling the inner perimeter of the high wall.

Dou Yueh-sheng rarely saw his garden. His day had begun at six a.m., drinking weak tea and reading first the business columns and then the front page of the *North China Daily News*. At nine o'clock he'd been driven across the city in his armour-plated Packard to attend a meeting of Chinese bankers. Mid-day and lunch with the French Prefect of Police for discussion of their respective spheres of influence.

But Dou was getting old. Meetings tired him. In the afternoon he had returned to his villa and rested beside his eighteen-year-old mistress – an actress with the Star Film Company. And the petitioners waited patiently on the verandah.

The ageing gangster was in no hurry at the end of his day. He drank more weak tea and studied the *Shanghai Evening Post & Mercury*, following the words with his finger as men do who have learned to read late in life. He spoke without looking up. 'The man arrived from Loyang this morning?'

'By the eleven o'clock train.' Han Yu-lin sat on the stool next to his master.

'But you lost him?'

Han paused apologetically. 'Only temporarily, Yueh-sheng. We know where he will be later. Before he left the station he purchased a third-class railway ticket for Nank-ing. Then he took a cab to the French district. He must have realized he might be followed – he left the cab at Rue Marcel Tilliot and walked off into the backstreets. It is then he gave us the slip.'

'There could be no possibility of mistaken identity?'

'None, Yueh-sheng. It is the same man – Ohata. He was here in 1932 with the Japanese Mission. His *ronin* murdered the banker, La Zhi.'

The room was darkening and Han went to light the single lamp on the desk, but Dou shook his head. 'Shade it. My eyes ache. This man, Ohata. He must be dealt with, but it is better that we do not make it our concern. Inform our associate in Military Intelligence – what is his name?'

'Colonel Tang.'

'Do it by telephone – do not embarrass him.' Dou paused, frowning, and groped for the newspaper again. 'Here is the name Tang. Is it the same family?'

'Yes, Yueh-sheng. The youngest son by the colonel's first marriage.' Han adjusted the lamp leaving much of the room shadowed. 'The boy died with his company of Shanghai North. The Generalissimo and Madame Chiang Kai-shek have expressed their grief.'

Dou nodded. 'Indicate our sorrow also.' And he pondered the worsening situation beyond the bounds of the Settle-ment. 'What other business do we have?'

'The matter of Lui Yun is settled.' Han indicated to the newspaper. 'Page seven.'

Dou turned the pages and found the report. He studied it carefully. The accompanying photograph revealed little; a bundled corpse under a blanket. It didn't show the broken

65

hands or the stake hammered up the man's rectum. Dou nodded, satisfied.

'There are petitioners waiting,' Han frowned. 'Among them is Yun Tseng's English accountant.'

Dou closed his eyes for a moment, and then he remembered. 'What does he want?'

'He would not tell me, Yueh-sheng.'

'Get rid of him.'

'He says he has an important matter to discuss with you.'

Dou was weary. He wanted the girl to massage his back.

'It has something to do with the old man, Yun Tseng.'

'I will see the others first.'

And Russell waited as one by one the Chinese were sent for. His stomach was in a knot now and he began limping back and forth at his end of the verandah. Maybe there was still time to make an excuse and leave? Like what? A sudden urge to catch the next boat to Australia. He'd strayed too close to the doorway and the slim Chinese boy glanced up from his puzzle toy. He stared at Russell's crooked leg, then shook his head and tapped the automatic pistol strapped under his armpit. 'You stay.'

Russell sat again. It was like being back in the dingy, grey-brick London school, waiting to be caned. He rubbed his ankle where the bone protruded. There had been a proverb on the headmaster's wall, done in tapestry and framed – MAN'S EXTREMITY IS GOD'S OPPOR-TUNITY – he'd never understood it.

The Chinese boy watched him for a moment then offered the puzzle toy. 'You try.'

It shouldn't have been difficult. You moved the toy around in your hand, spiralling a ball bearing up an incline to drop into a tiny hole – there were a dozen variations of the toy in any of the cheap stores. He tried, frowning with concentration, but his hands weren't steady enough and he handed it back. 'Let's see you do it.'

'Goddam easy.' The boy cupped his hand and expertly manoeuvred the ball. 'You want it?' And he held the toy out.

'Thanks.' He felt ridiculously grateful. You could never

tell about people – they were not all as God-awful as you thought. And scowling down, he tried again. Meaningless. It soothed him. The ball bearing popped into the hole. At that moment the last of the Chinese petitioners came out.

The boy grinned and squatted by the door again. 'You go now.'

Han Yu-lin led him into the villa. He'd expected the interior to be opulently Oriental, but the furnishings were a mixture of East and late nineteenth-century West; heavy, comfortable and expensive, arranged with taste. From an adjoining room he heard a radio and the clatter of mahjong tiles. Retreat was now out of the question and he was about to encounter the most dangerous man in Shanghai. A dusty parrot squawked loudly, anchored to its wooden perch. He followed Han along a wide corridor, one side hung with a *k'o-ssu* tapestry depicting mountains and flowers. Through an open doorway he caught a glimpse of an attractive Chinese girl flicking through the pages of a film magazine.

Dou's business room was austere. The High Dragon of the Green Society was seated behind a long, rosewood desk. To Russell he seemed too small and frail to have clawed his way up from the wharves of Pootung. Dou was dressed in a plain blue silk gown. He stared unblinking. An old face – skin stretched across the bones – and framed by the high back of his chair. He wore a ring on each finger of both hands.

He sipped tea and kept Russell standing.

'I know about you. You interfered once in the shipment of my merchandise.' The voice was harsh. 'One of Yun Tseng's junks at . . .' He pondered. 'Chen-chiang.'

There was a prescribed ritual to be acted out. Russell's mouth had gone dry. 'I am grateful for the opportunity to apologize, sir. I had not realized the true ownership of the additional cargo.'

'Yun Tseng was wise, an honoured member of our brotherhood. He corrected you.'

Russell stifled his surprise. He hadn't known that the old man was a member of the Green Society. 'And I honoured

Yun Tseng and acknowledged his wisdom. I accepted his reproach as a son would from his father.'

Dou stared unblinking and sipped tea. 'Yun Tseng told me that you are loyal and worthy of trust, and that you are clever with figures. What do you want of me – employment?'

'Employment?' Russell gaped.

'As the old man is dead, I will give you work.' He gestured to Han Yu-lin. 'Find him something – legitimate.'

'The counting house, Yueh-sheng?'

'Yes.' Dou waved impatiently to indicate that the interview was over. 'The counting house.'

God in heaven! His petition was turning into farce. 'I am grateful, sir, but I don't want work.'

The cold eyes narrowed in wrinkled skin. 'What *do* you want?'

'The Japanese deliberately killed the old man.'

'Unfortunate.' Dou sat motionless, back aching. He was thinking about the girl's hands. 'Yun Tseng was old, as I am old. He would have died soon anyway. The tiger is at our doorstep. If you seek help against the Japanese, go elsewhere.'

'I made a promise to Yun Tseng the day the Japanese killed him. That's why I've come to you.'

Dou leaned forward in his chair. 'They say you are . . .' he tapped his forehead with his finger. 'And now you make a lot of noise.'

'I've protested about the murder.'

'And people who make a noise are sometimes silenced. Better that you do nothing.'

'The promise I made is binding.' Russell tried to lick his dried lips. 'Yun Tseng imported six aeroplane engines for Chiang Kai-shek – that is why he was killed. I must ensure that the engines reach Nanking.'

'Say it quickly.' The old gangster was getting impatient, formality abandoned. 'What are you proposing?'

Something preposterous. Russell kept his hands clenched and talked fast. 'The engines are in a locked warehouse. I need help to get them out – it will have to be done at night.

And I need a boat, like the *Firefly*, to carry the engines up river.'

The cold eyes opened wide. 'You come here and ask for my boat! You would involve me in your absurd plans against the Japanese! They were right about you – you *are* mad.'

'What I propose is just possible.'

'Mad!' Dou stared ominously. 'And you are dangerous!'

Russell's heart was thumping unpleasantly. There was only one card left to play. How would Dou react to losing face? 'I came here, sir, because I understood that you support the Generalissimo.' He looked at his watch. 'But it would be unforgivable of me to take up more of your time. With permission, I will leave the High Dragon of the Green Society to his business of whores and dope.'

Would Dou break his hands – or worse?

Han Yu-lin was poised, waiting for Dou's order.

But the old gangster just sat staring at Russell for a full minute. Then he spoke slowly. 'If you were caught in your madness you would implicate me. So let it be clearly understood. If I provide you with a boat – not my own – and if it is intercepted by the Japanese, you will be silenced instantly and for all time by one of the men I send to accompany you. Do you still want my help?'

Russell couldn't even make a reply. He just nodded.

After Russell had left, the girl came in. But Dou's peace was disturbed and he gestured her to sit at his feet. He stared at the wall and pondered the worried discussion of the bankers' that morning. The whole of the delta could become unsafe, threatened now by events north of the Settlement. He spoke to Han Yu-lin without turning his head. 'You must leave for Nanking on the night express. You will take two letters, deliver one into the hands of the Generalissimo and the other to Dr Kung.'

Han bowed. 'Yes, Yueh-sheng.'

CHAPTER SIX

Night came. Across the city thousands of refugees from the war zone beyond the creek were crowded into Shanghai West Station. Noisy, whole families their belongings bundled up in sheets, they squatted packed together on the platform. Their apparent indifference to time puzzled Reed. They'd brought the reek of the slums. A heavy bandaged old man was resting on his bundle, wife and daughter next to him. The girl looked like a younger version of Sao. Reed scowled to himself.

'Where will they all go?'

'I don't know, Miss Bishop. Up the line to Soochow, Wu-hsi, Ch'ang-chou, Chen-chiang, Nanking – every Chinese has got about a million relatives. There's only one train tonight so I guess some of them will still be waiting tomorrow.' He shrugged. 'Damned war.'

'What war? Nobody has declared war yet. Japan is solving a local problem by peaceful means.' Linda Bishop looked angry again. 'The Emperor says he only wants harmony – don't you read the newspapers?'

'Only the sports page.' He'd spent the whole day repairing Dalsager's piano and he didn't feel like arguing. He wouldn't have felt like arguing about it anytime – the war disgusted him.

Provincial militia in cheap cotton uniforms were on duty in the station. 'They look like sad orphanage boys forced to play soldiers,' Linda Bishop said. Young, some barefoot, rifles too big for them, they edged the crowd back to make a pathway along the platform.

The Shanghai-Nanking Railway dated back to 1908. The

station architecture suggested its British designers and engineers – Reed admired the ugly, ornate ironwork. He could see where two bomb holes had been filled in between the tracks. And he half listened to Peggy reassuring Linda.

'Hsia-kang is nice – you'll like it. It doesn't smell too bad, except in the old quarter near the docks.' She paused, scratching her knee. 'I think I've been bitten already. Are you nervous? Foster will meet you at Ch'ang-chou, he's irritatingly reliable.'

If Peggy liked him he'd be *wonderfully* reliable. Reed smiled to himself.

Now Peggy was frowning. 'Is there time? Can I use the station toilet?'

'Not if you value your health,' Reed said.

'I'm bursting.'

'You can go on the train.' Reed noticed Linda Bishop's quick, forced smile. She was so damned prim sometimes. And now she was asking Peggy if she'd remembered to send the cable to Arch.

Of course Peggy had remembered. Arch was her life, even though she wasn't enjoying it very much. Arch and his goddam womanizing. He asked Peggy, 'Are you okay?'

'Sure.' She smiled, briefly holding him with her eyes, then she looked away.

Two Catholic fathers, long habits roped at the waist, were standing under a hissing gas lamp. They were talking together in French but lapsing sometimes into Chinese. Old and tough – they must have been out here for years. One had a battered suitcase tied round with cord, and the other a rucksack with a mug and blanket strapped to it. They hoisted up their belongings and moved as the soldiers edged back the noisy crowd.

'There's a man carrying a pig!' Linda looked puzzled. 'Surely he isn't taking it on the train?'

'Nobody minds,' Reed said. The pig was trussed up, head sticking out of a sack. The man hawked phlegm for several seconds then spat loudly.

'Oh God!' Linda looked the other way.

71

'Tuberculosis is endemic here – I doubt if God even notices.'

'How would you know what He notices?'

Reed shrugged. He wished he had a drink. There was a bottle in his bag and if the women weren't with him he could get it out and have a swallow. He scowled and tried to think about something else. 'Did either of you ladies bring along the *Post & Mercury*? Pittsburgh may make the National Championship this year.'

'I'm sorry, I didn't buy an evening paper,' Linda said. It occurred to her in that moment that Reed wasn't sure enough of what he wanted or what he believed in to really interest her.

Thoughts of that bottle kept intruding, making Reed edgy. Damned women! He'd stayed an extra day just to accompany them on the train and they hadn't even had the foresight to bring along an evening paper. He wondered how Linda Bishop could look so good at that time of the night and on a Chinese railway station. She was wearing a khaki drill shirt and skirt and a leather jacket. It's a way some of them have, he thought. Hang anything on them and it looks good.

A large thug, head shaved, was shoving his way through the crowd – he used the flat of his hand, easing a passage for the man following. A Chinese. Horn-rimmed spectacles, dark suit, homburg hat, overcoat draped round his shoulders. He looked like a banker.

The soldiers recognized authority when they saw it and even their young officer stood aside. Peggy edged close to Reed as the man passed. 'Does he own the railway?'

'No. His name is Han Yu-lin, he's one of Dou's lieutenants. He has a passion for Russian food – I saw him last night in the Bukhara. I wonder where he's going?'

Linda watched the gangster's departing back. 'Do they have a Green Society in Nanking?'

It was as if Han Yu-lin had known in advance the exact moment to arrive. A shaft of light gleamed down the tracks and the Nanking Express rumbled up from Shanghai South marshalling yards. The locomotive was huge and dirty. A Chinese stoker sweated, face tinged red from the glow of the firebox as he leaned from his high cab and peered back along the slowing line of carriages. Two .50 calibre machine guns with anti-aircraft sights were mounted on a flatcar behind the engine and sandbagged round for protection. Soldiers squatted there or sat with their legs dangling above the wheels. They stared at the crowd with bored indifference.

Reed shielded Linda and Peggy with his back as the refugees surged forward, and their two stringy porters heaved Peggy's trunk and the cases.

'My valise!' Linda started after them as they edged their way towards the rear of the train.

'Let it go,' Reed shouted. 'I'll get it for you when we reach Soochow!'

'Her tablets, Reed! She has to have them.' Peggy had begun to follow Linda, but he caught her arm.

'Get on the train, both of you.' And he shoved his way after the porters.

Shouting refugees were trying to claw their way into the baggage car and soldiers pushed them back with boots and rifle butts. Reed waved one of his ten dollar bills at the guard. 'That bag there – the blue one. Quick – give it to me!'

It was worse going back, and the long line of carriages began to move. He dragged the valise through the crowd then threw it up to Linda.

'Reed, for God's sake!' Peggy held out her hand as he ran alongside, and he hauled himself up as the train gathered speed, rattling out of Shanghai West.

He was wet with sweat and down by ten dollars. Linda Bishop looked penitent, and so she damn well ought to.

'I'm sorry.'

He surprised himself. 'Forget it, Miss Bishop.' He was wondering why those tablets were so necessary to her.

Late finding their carriage, he moved ahead of the two women along the dimly lit corridor. Even first class was full and the air smelled stale. Reed groaned softly to himself.

Han Yu-lin was already seated in their compartment and his smooth-headed thug was standing guard outside.

'We have seats.' He pulled out the reservation tickets, already aware that he was not going to win.

Smooth-head didn't even look. He gestured to Han as if that was sufficient explanation then jerked his head for them to go away. And Reed was on a vaguely familiar spiral, anxiety giving way to outraged justice. 'RES-ER-VATIONS, damn it!'

Smooth-head hadn't understood but he'd bunched a huge fist.

'Let it go, Reed! He'll kill you!'

She was right. And he was relieved that Peggy should drag on his arm. Han must have heard the disturbance but he'd opened his newspaper. A peak-capped guard almost ran along the corridor. 'Sir! Sir! So sorry for the error. This compartment is reserved for Mr Han.'

Reed felt defeated, aware of Linda Bishop just behind him. 'Then you'd better find us another one.'

'First-class compartments are *all* reserved. I will move people in second class.'

'You're crazy!'

The door of the adjoining compartment slid back and a young Chinese army officer stepped into the corridor. He had a lieutenant's insignia on the high collar of his tunic. 'Please.' He bowed. 'Colonel Tang asks that you and the ladies spare him the tedium of solitary travel by sharing his compartment.'

Captain Ohata had used his boots and knuckles to board the third-class carriage at the front of the train. It was jammed full, air already turning foul.

He stood, hemmed around. His coat was too big for him – he'd purchased it in a second-hand clothes shop in Yates Road and it smelled of its previous owner. Ohata rocked with the movement of the train, glad only that he was putting miles between himself and Shanghai. He slid down and sat on his bundle. Those underworld scum, waiting for him when he'd arrived that morning after the long journey from Sian. It must have been at Loyang that he'd been recognized. I'm safe now, he thought, though a doubt remained. Perhaps he would change his appearance when he reached Nanking. His hands were filthy. He licked the blood from his grazed knuckles.

Two hundred miles of cramped travel lay ahead and his head felt thick, eyes heavy. It must be the lack of oxygen. But the stale air wasn't the reason for his depression – it was more deep-seated. It had been with him since he'd left the woman.

They had gone to her apartment above Pacific Press offices. Submission to her slow, calculating lust had drained him. Women were less than men – it was they who should submit. Self-disgust nagged at him. The taint of her was still on his flesh.

Faces appeared unnatural in the weak glow of the single bulb. Some passengers were already asleep on their feet and a child was crying among the cotton bundles. Thousands had already fled from the Shanghai region. Ohata wearily leaned his head back on the carriage wall. We'll push west – soon there will be a million refugees on the move, he thought. He was aware that his sour anger had been triggered by thinking of the woman. She had been on the platform just before the train pulled out: well dressed in the fashion of Westerners. Gold-rimmed spectacles, pigskin attaché case – she could have passed for one of the modern rich Chinese sent to America for an education, rather than a harlot out of Butterfly Row. Even now she was just a short distance from him – back there in the first-class carriage.

Ohata tried to suppress the image of her, forcing himself to think of his wife in Kyoto. But she was a blur, a delicate flower out of focus.

The air stank. Lice had crawled under his cuff and he pondered as he scratched the red marks. This was a long way from Tokyo Military Academy, and the oath they had taken on graduation. We were still clean then, he thought. And the other oath they had taken later – the conquest of

75

Asia for the Emperor. He stared down at his hands. He'd never thought he could become so dirty.

The young officer had left for some purpose and they were alone with Colonel Tang. About forty years old, Reed guessed, though it was difficult to gauge the age of Chinese. His clipped moustache measured the exact width of his upper lip. Head shaved in the military manner, skin a little wrinkled around his eyes – yes, maybe he was older. Two stars on the collar of his well-cut tunic indicated his rank but there was nothing to suggest his function.

'This is good of you, colonel.' Reed took Linda Bishop's valise and put it on the rack. 'Our accommodation was pirated, and I've taken a sudden aversion to the colour of green.'

The other man's eyes registered brief amusement. He sat perfectly upright but relaxed. It was a knack some of them had. Reed had seen peasants sit that way for hours.

Cigarette ends and small litter – relics of the previous journey – were cluttered under the seats. Service on the trains had declined sharply since the beginning of hostilities and the compartment smelled as if previous users had each contributed to its stale mustiness. By sharp contrast the padded head rests were covered with clean, starched, monogrammed squares of white linen.

Peggy had distanced herself from Colonel Tang, but Linda was seated obliquely opposite him. And Reed was a little uneasy – there was something awesome about the man. He felt a need to establish his identity. 'I'm Reed – American citizen. I work for China Petroleum. I'll introduce Mrs Rittenhouse, journeying to Nanking. And this is Miss Bishop, on her way to the mission at Hsia-kang.'

Colonel Tang inclined his head very slightly to each of them in turn. 'You are a missionary, Miss Bishop?'

'No, I'm a writer.' She'd said it with a lot more determination than Reed remembered from that time he'd asked her on the boat, and he wondered if she too needed to assert herself.

'And you are here to write about the Chinese people?'

'Yes – I mean, no. That would be presumptuous of me, wouldn't it? I'm here for only a few weeks – to write about missions primarily. A fund-raising exercise.' She cupped an elegant knee with her hands – a barely conscious trick she'd learned, Reed thought, to shift attention from what she was saying. It was the first time that he'd seen her off balance.

The colonel watched her face. 'There was an American missionary named Bishop in the Hsu-shu district – I think twelve years ago.'

Reed half listened, though part of his mind was preoccupied with the need for a drink.

'That was my father,' Linda was saying. 'He was a good acquaintance of Dr Foster at Hsia-kang. Dr Foster has offered me a roof and bed for a while.'

Colonel Tang nodded, still watching her. 'My headquarters is at the eastern end of the town – on the Chiang-yin Road. Foster's followers are from the hungry dock area.'

Reed recognized inference in the word "hungry". The colonel was saying that Foster's converts were "rice Christians" – in it for what they could get.

'You and Peggy and me – we're "foreign devils", Miss Bishop. Chinese converts to Christianity are called "secondary foreign devils" by their own people.' Reed grinned. 'Missionaries are not universally regarded.'

'But Dr Foster's reputation as a medical missionary stands high – even back home they talk about him.' She had that sharp look again, ready to snap his head off.

Colonel Tang intervened. 'The Chinese people judge religions by their proved ethical value rather than their good works.'

'Really?' Miss Bishop was her cool self once more. 'I understand that General Chiang Kai-shek has become a devout "secondary foreign devil".'

'Yes, Miss Bishop. Since his marriage the Generalissimo has professed Christianity.' Colonel Tang allowed a small polite pause. 'Do you have other contacts in Hsia-kang?'

He was probing, Reed thought.

77

All the lights went out as the train curved towards the war zone north of the Settlement. Linda Bishop's face was briefly silhouetted by flashes of distant guns. 'Have you been to the Chapei battle, Colonel Tang?' There was a glow of admiration in her voice. 'Shanghai Radio reports a single Chinese battalion defending the North Station.'

'A handful of men. They are holding off an entire Japanese division.'

'And the young Chinese officer who died with all his men rather than retreat?' Linda Bishop was asking. 'Wasn't his name Tang also?'

'Yes.'

That single word. Reed was curious.

'I guess it's a common name.' She lapsed suddenly into silence.

The moon emerged from behind cloud, faintly illumining hills to the south. They were clear of the battlefront and the lights came on again. Reed stared out at vague shapes. This part of the country was safe since the ascendency of Chiang Kai-shek, but only five years ago bandits and rebel troops used to raid the villages and even hold up trains.

He could see a building – a temple of some kind on a low hill. Missionaries he'd met claimed that the Chinese had no real religious sense. But everywhere there were shrines; Taoist, Buddhist, or to some local god. A lousy little junk wouldn't put to sea without fire crackers and incantations, and every household revered its ancestors. Maybe out of prudence, like Sao and her rice offering – Reed didn't know for sure. God was an imponderable.

> There was something formless yet complete,
> That existed before heaven and earth.

Reed believed it some of the time.

> If I am forced to give it a name, I call it Tao.

He noticed his own reflected image in the glass of the window; and Peggy asleep now. Linda Bishop had rested her head on the padding. She turned slightly, sensing his

78

interest, and just as quickly rejected it, tucking her skirt over her knees. He felt another surge of irritation. A glance at a girl's legs didn't mean anything. It would be a hot day in January before he needed her.

The door slid back and Colonel Tang's young aide entered. The pair of them talked softly and hurriedly, then they sat in silence as if waiting for something to happen. What was that about?

Pinpoints of light indicated a large village ahead. The train slowed, rumbling into a wayside halt. The Nanking Express didn't usually stop here – Reed had travelled regularly as far as Chen-chiang and he knew this schedule. Nobody alighted and there were no passengers waiting. Flickering oil lamps cast evenly spaced circles of light and between them were shadows.

It was quiet out there.

The track curved and Reed could see the front third-class carriage partially shrouded by steam from the locomotive. 'What's going on?'

The young lieutenant glanced at him quickly then turned away, and Colonel Tang remained staring ahead.

Reed looked out again. A man emerged from the front carriage, pushed from behind. His hands were tied behind his back and he fell clumsily. Soldiers climbed down and hauled him to his feet, half carrying, half dragging him out of sight at the side of the wooden station building.

The others hadn't seen. Peggy opened her eyes then closed them again. Reed watched.

A sudden jolt and the train was moving – light and shadow alternating beyond the window. Reed peered out as they passed the end of the station. Soldiers were grouped in a circle looking inwards and the bound man was kneeling in the dust. A sword arced up.

'What happened?' Linda asked.

'Nothing,' he said. 'It was nothing.'

CHAPTER SEVEN

Sparks and thin wraiths of smoke streamed back from the locomotive as the Nanking Express thundered westward.

Miss Kuang was trapped in her dream, yet knowing it was a dream. She'd boarded a boat; more a large sampan than a junk – a single sail carried it forward. And there were people moving in slow purpose but their faces were smudged, unrecognizable, and they seemed not to know that she was there. Somebody was steering, but to where? Miss Kuang didn't know. The tempo of the wheels changed and she willed herself into waking.

There was a faint greyness of dawn beyond the window and shapes more clearly defined. After Wu-hsi the dining car would serve breakfast, but it would be wiser for her to stay in the compartment. Miss Kuang had witnessed the execution last night, and, numbed, she'd guessed that the man sprawling in the dust was Ohata. It was a mistake to disregard the promptings of intuition – even as she'd lain with Ohata yesterday afternoon she'd had a presentiment. When she'd left the building, she'd passed the dwarf seated on his dirty blanket with his bones, bottles, and divining sticks. He'd called a warning – at least, she'd assumed it was a warning. And then the reason for her unease was confirmed – Colonel Tang was on the station platform. Ohata had pushed his way through the crowd a moment later. Her immediate impulse had been to caution him – fortunately a strong sense of survival stopped her. Somebody was almost certainly watching him even then, so she'd looked the other way. One small slip, and arrest and execution would follow. Or worse – much, much worse. Miss Kuang anxiously fingered her jade bracelet.

She had purchased the French newspaper, *Le Journal de Shanghai*, before leaving the city. It was half open on her lap and she tried again to bring her concentration to it. USA retains Americas' cup. Change of station for the French cruiser, *Lamotte Piquet*. Japanese "Black" 9th Infantry Division in suicidal assault on Shanghai North Station. Her thoughts drifted again.

There were lights far ahead. Wang-ting, she thought, and already she could smell the town. The train passed old ramparts then curved between crowded urban housing. High factory chimneys offered a curious contrast to pagodas and curled tile roofs further back in the hills. Miss Kuang looked out at mounds of rubbish as the train slowed to a stop. The stench was not alien to her. She had spent her first twelve years in similar slums of Huang-ch'iao sixty miles to the north. Bandits fleeing from the war lord, Sun Chuan-fang, pillaged the town; and, family destitute, her father had sold her to the old man who took her by river to Shanghai, there to be sold again to a Japanese brothel keeper in Butterfly Row.

The rail tracks ran parallel with an unpaved street lined with workshops and warehouses: Huberman Mercantile Company, Lower Yangtze Trading Company, Kung Tai Oils, Rodgers & Prior. Miss Kuang could see a lighted, grimy window. Girls were already beginning work – they would labour ten or twelve hours filling jute sacks. Life was brutally short and unsatisfactory for most. A brothel at least offered a slim chance of escape. She'd learned the weaknesses of men and how to use them. It was Ohata who had recognized her talents and put her to work for the Emperor.

She pondered, looking out of the window. Ohata's execution was distressing but she could derive some assurance from what had happened. For reasons she could not begin to guess he'd been done to death hurriedly – and he had still been on his feet as they'd taken him from the train, so it was unlikely that he had implicated her. A day – two – and he would probably have told them everything. Was there any reason why they might yet connect her with Ohata? None that she could think of, but doubt nagged. Miss Kuang allowed herself brief speculation. A totally new identity? Six more months and she could afford it in some style. A boat to Saigon in French Indo-China. A wealthy French husband – she would select him with great care. But beyond that the fantasy hazed. Was there a man whom she would not ultimately despise?

The train began to move again.

Linda felt relieved as the high chimney of the soap factory receded. Why were Chinese industrial slums even more of an affront than those of Chicago? She supposed it was because she'd expected a simpler, nobler way of life even though all she'd read about the towns had suggested otherwise. The pervasive fatty acid redolence of soap oil and the stench of excrement still hung in the air. It's a way we have, she thought, of turning the world into a sort of hell.

She thought of home. There were slums on the far side of the small, New England town, spread along two hundred yards of railway track. But they were distanced from us. For us there was space, and flower pots and lawns, and warm antiseptic houses with modern plumbing. Sickness, when it came, was quickly and expertly managed. I even assumed I was safe. She peered out at the sky. Nobody is – God strikes the innocent and the guilty, young and old, ugly and fair – so you have to concede a harsh equality. Barrenness was more difficult to come to terms with. She'd never thought about children until she knew that there would be none. And sometimes she felt guilty for not having cared enough, mourning the child she would never have. But mostly she didn't think about it.

'China will alter your perspective, Miss Bishop.'

Surprised, she glanced round at Colonel Tang. It was as if he'd read her thoughts. 'Will it?' When she'd woken that morning, he was observing her. There was something uncomfortably intimate about being watched in one's sleep.

'But you must look at China with an innocent eye.'

82

'As the daughter of a Methodist missionary it's maybe too late.' She smiled. 'I'm ridden through with Puritan ethics.'

'I suspect you are less inclined to prejudice than many who come to China. You may realize an affinity for our culture.' The colonel thought for a moment. 'At Hsia-kang where you are going there is a garden. It was created in the fifteenth century by a retired official of the Yung-lo Emperor. You must permit me to show it to you.'

'Thank you.' She felt her face flush. 'That's very kind of you.'

'A garden is incomplete until it is observed.'

Reed said sourly, 'I find it difficult to equate beautifully tended gardens with Oriental contempt for life.' He assumed an expression of innocent questioning that Linda had come to recognize. 'Mind you, colonel, I'm totally uncultured. I've known people completely caught up in the way you Chinese do things, they kind of – lose their heads. Y'know what I mean?'

Linda sensed she was being excluded from an uncomfortable private joke. Colonel Tang was staring at Reed. 'An obsessive interest in the affairs of others can sometimes be quite bad for one's health.'

'Oh, I'd go even further than that.'

Why did Reed have to be so boorish? Maybe to compensate over backing down in the matter of the compartment? Not his fault, though some people had a knack for failure, she thought.

It was almost daylight and work had already begun in the fields. Linda watched. Am I really less inclined to prejudice? Rice requires weeks of back-breaking toil. Women stooped, barely noticing the train as it passed. I'm prejudiced in a culture that discriminates so against women. Do *they* think they are being discriminated against? The women's skirts were tucked round their thighs as they laboured and one squatted to urinate. Linda turned away. What I really lack is love for humanity.

The steward announced breakfast in the dining car and Linda shook Peggy.

Before hostilities the Shanghai-Nanking Railway had boasted of its service but already everything was makeshift, cutlery greasy and cloths stained. Incongruously, each table had a small flower in a delicate glass.

Linda noticed Han, the gangster, seated alone.

'I feel as if I'd spent the night on a train.' Peggy looked her thirty-five years; hair lifeless and lines round her eyes. '*And* I've been bitten – I told you I would be.' She scratched her thigh through her skirt. 'Insects know who to home in on. It's Ch'ang-chou next stop, and you get off. This is our last cup of tea together.'

'I promise I'll miss you.' Linda meant it. 'Shopping will be very boring – I'll just go out and buy exactly what I planned to buy. And I won't drink tea at one thirty in the morning. And I'll sleep in a nice tidy room.'

'I'll miss you too.' Peggy looked wistful. 'I haven't had a girl friend since I left the dance act.'

'But you'll see Arch soon.'

Peggy pondered, toying with her teaspoon. 'I think he's been having another woman on the side while I was gone.' She shrugged. 'I suppose it's the way with men – married life gets boring for them.'

'You've trailed around the world for him! Men are rats!'

Peggy balanced the spoon on the rim of the cup. 'It's not entirely his fault. It used to be good with us – physically. But now he can't . . .' she tailed off. 'If you see what I mean. Maybe it's me – and he has to try with other women just to find out?'

That explained the tightness around her mouth when Arch's name was mentioned, and Linda felt slightly ashamed at wanting to draw back from Peggy's confidence. 'Arch should take you home. I *mean*, for God's sake! He shouldn't even be here – our government ordered all the American flyers to leave China. You'd both stand a better chance of – of getting it right if you went home.'

'Oh, Arch wouldn't break his contract – with him it's a matter of professional pride. He says if you're a mercenary you have to be twice as honourable as everybody else.'

'Honourable! That's rich! And what about *you*? Damn it, Peggy, this is 1937! Women do have certain rights, you know.' But Linda was already aware that reason wouldn't work. Women like Peggy were drawn to self-sacrifice by the Arches of this world – or to vagrants like Reed. 'I'll worry about you – now promise you'll write to me.'

'I'll write. And thanks, I've wanted to talk to *somebody*.'

But she didn't feel she could talk to me until we were ready to part company, Linda thought. And that's a pretty sad reflection on me as a friend.

Colonel Tang's young aide entered the dining car. He glanced around as if searching for a vacant table and then joined Mr Han.

Peggy and Linda argued about who should have the privilege of settling the last bill. The young officer seemed to be deferring to Mr Han – he started to write something in a pocket book but Han stopped him and tore the page up. Linda wondered, was the aide here in the dining car because Colonel Tang didn't wish to be seen talking to a member of the Green Society?

On their way back along the swaying train, Peggy stopped off at the toilet, and Linda saw Reed standing in the corridor just outside their compartment. Unshaven again, he was staring at the flat countryside. She didn't really want to talk to him but suspected that he was waiting for just that purpose so she joined him at the window. 'The colours are different, aren't they? Perhaps that's partly why Chinese paintings seem slightly unreal to me.'

'It's to do with the light.' He lit a cigarette. 'Things aren't always the way we see them.' And he exhaled slowly, smoke fanning out across the window glass. 'You're a long way from home, Miss Bishop.'

Linda sighed. 'All right, let's have it. What are you really trying to say?'

'The colonel – and all that crap about a garden and you making it complete. I'd be very careful of that guy if I were you.'

'Isn't it remotely possible that he genuinely wishes to

85

show me an ancient Chinese garden? You keep assuming women are foolish, helpless creatures.'

'No. I don't think you are foolish or helpless.'

They both paused, staring out of the window as the young officer came back along the corridor and entered the compartment. Then Reed spoke earnestly. 'All those questions last night. Your cultured Chinese colonel is probing, Miss Bishop. Be careful what you tell him. And if he asks you again to go and look at gardens with him, make some excuse.' And he nodded as if they were now in agreement.

Linda was amazed. 'I don't *need* this from you! I really don't need advice from some . . . some *drifter*!'

'People are killed on that guy's say-so. My guess is he's Chinese Military Intelligence and they are a tough bunch.' Reed stared at her. 'But you do what the hell you like.' And he turned and went back into the compartment.

It made no sense. But then neither did it make obvious sense for a Chinese colonel to be in some sort of liaison with a prominent Shanghai gangster. Linda bit her lip. Reed's warning was honestly meant. Why was she so abominably rude to him? She groped with the question. It wasn't just because his manner grated. She was half aware that her impatience was triggered by a small, nagging fear – maybe she hadn't got enough time to resolve the questions of her life? Last year death had been close behind, and was still insufficiently distanced.

The train slowed, rolling into Ch'ang-chou station. Billboards displayed patriotic posters alongside a Coca-Cola advertisement. Even this far west there were refugees with bundles. A boy was selling newspapers but Miss Kuang couldn't hear what he was shouting so imperatively. She watched as first-class passengers climbed down from the exit near her window. Some haggled quickly and confidently with the porters. Others, strangers to the city, stared around uncertainly. A ragged vendor moved along the platform holding up oranges to the passenger windows. Three fingers were missing from his hand. He wheedled, '*Shuigo.*' Miss

Kuang shook her head and surveyed the crowd. And yes, Chu Teng of Chinese Maritime Customs was waiting for her near the entrance to the station. She could almost sense his anxiety as he bought a newspaper and scanned the front page, a fat man with a drooping moustache. He peered at the train, looking for her, and Miss Kuang was aware of bad vibrations. Chu Teng, afraid of his shadow, and an unknown agent whom she could only contact by newspaper advertisement. And they had already lost Ohata. The thought triggered her memory of the dream, but she didn't know why. A boat. I was on a boat, and I was afraid.

Colonel Tang walked towards the station exit with his young aide. Miss Kuang felt safer, but she remained seated by the window. The tall American girl climbed down from the train and glanced around, seemingly confident and anxious to get started. Why would the girl who had asked embarrassing questions at the press conference be travelling in the same compartment as Colonel Tang? It could be mere chance, but Miss Kuang filed the question in the back of her mind. Sometimes patterns emerged out of seemingly coincidental elements. Two other Westerners had alighted. A girl, slightly older – overdressed but with good legs. And a man – she'd noticed him at Shanghai West. Now he was singling out a porter. Miss Kuang appraised him. Slouch shouldered, battered leather jacket, heels of his boots worn down. A rugged man, perhaps an inch shorter than the tall girl. And he was probably American, she guessed. There was a sureness about Americans, quite different from the polite audacity of the English. He had the look of a man puzzled by his life.

There was always a twenty minute stopover at Ch'angchou. The three on the platform stood talking, as though waiting for somebody, and Miss Kuang waited also, curious about them but reluctant to allow herself to be recognized by the American girl. A middle-aged Westerner was edging towards them through the crowd. White-haired, he wore one of those absurd collars still favoured by some of the missionaries; and he appeared to be concerned, frowning as he shook hands with each of them.

Now, Miss Kuang thought, while they are in conversation. She left the train and signalled to a porter, then she detoured slightly to pass behind the four. Captain Chu Teng of Maritime Customs saw her approaching, but she indicated that they should keep walking.

'Do not talk now. Have you a car? Pay the porter quickly.'

She glanced back while he fumbled for coins. The white-haired missionary was holding a cable form and speaking hurriedly to the overdressed girl.

Captain Chu Teng hoisted up Miss Kuang's bags. Although fat, he was strong. 'It is dangerous,' he muttered. 'Too many people who may recognize me. But there was nobody reliable to send.'

'Your face will give you away, Captain Chu. Compose yourself. Try to look happy.'

His mouth turned up in a travesty of humour. 'There have been many arrests. And worse – Colonel Tang is back.'

'Smile, Captain Chu.'

Ohata executed. And now arrests.

'I had not anticipated that events would move so quickly,' Chu Teng muttered. 'Nanking was bombed this morning!'

Dr Gerald Foster, medical missionary at Hsia-kang, handed Peggy the cable. 'Nanking was bombed this morning. Your husband is right, Mrs Rittenhouse. It will be safer for you at the mission for a while.'

Reed watched Peggy staring down at the cable, and his first thought was uncharitable: Arch doesn't want her in Nanking.

'All those weeks of travel, and to have got so close!' Peggy looked defeated.

'Buck up. At the mission house we'll find things to keep you busy.' There was a slight edge of impatience in Foster's tone and Reed wondered if he found visitors a nuisance.

'Was the air raid bad?'

'It seems so. The Japanese hit two of the city hospitals. I picked up the early morning news broadcast on XMHA. Captain Rittenhouse's cable arrived at the mission an hour later – it follows that *he* must be all right.'

Sure he's all right, Reed thought. The son-of-a-bitch is indestructible. Arch is one of those heaven-favoured people who can always count on a large measure of luck.

'Now the worry begins.' Peggy's voice was flat. 'It's a bitch, isn't it? Another few hours and I would have been there.'

'Well, at least *I'm* in luck.' Linda squeezed her arm. 'I'll have somebody to go shopping with.'

The whole situation was beginning to depress Reed. 'I'll fetch your trunk from the baggage car,' he said. But Peggy stopped him. 'No. Stay with me a minute, will you?'

'Sure.' He wished the engine's clanging bell would sound so that he could get back on the train. 'Sure I will.'

'And Dr Foster and I can sort out the trunk.' Linda began steering him away. 'Do you mind, doctor? . . .'

Peggy waited until they'd moved along the platform. 'What do you think?'

'I don't think anything. Why should I think anything?'

'Oh, just for once, Reed; as a friend. Just this one time tell me what you think Arch is up to.'

'Now why should he be up to anything? Y'have to assume he's genuinely worried for you, Peggy. Y'have to start from there.'

Han was stretching his legs, walking the platform and paring an orange with a small penknife. His bodyguard was just behind him.

'I can't look at you,' Peggy was saying. 'You know what I'm thinking. There's been a gap between Arch and me, and it's suddenly widened.'

'It's not that bad, Peg. You'll see.'

Han jerked his head and the bodyguard went to the newsboy and bought a paper. The work NANKING was big on the front page.

'You know what? It's a pig's eye being a woman.' Peggy sniffed.

'You're certainly all woman. I'll grant you that.'

'Am I?'

'You know it,' he said.

'My battered self-respect needs shoring up. In Cuba you wanted me, didn't you?'

'Yes.'

'And you still do, once in a while, don't you.'

'Yes.'

'You won't just leave me here – you'll come and see me?'

He held her. 'I promise.'

'I wish you could like yourself as much as I like you.'

'You're crazy,' he said gently. 'That's a stupid thing to say.'

And the cool Miss Bishop returned with Foster – she had her firm, in-control expression, glancing away as Peggy stood back from Reed and dabbed her eyes with her handkerchief. 'The trunks are on their way to the Metropole. Why do so many Chinese hotels have conventionally Western names?

Questions – questions. Reed remembered that she'd called him a drifter and he decided he'd seen enough of her for a while. The train was blasting steam. He hugged Peggy again and let her go. 'Got to leave you now.'

Han and his thug were climbing aboard.

'Dr Foster – nice t'meet you.' Reed shook his hand. 'And Miss Bishop – I wish you luck.'

'I think I was ungrateful.' She smiled. 'Thanks for looking after us. You did a good job.'

Maybe she was not so bad after all. He climbed up as the train began to move out of Ch'ang-chou station, and waved to them. Peggy waved back, but Linda Bishop just raised one hand very slightly.

CHAPTER EIGHT

Autumn is the season of storms. A typhoon spent itself blowing north before it reached the coast, but Shanghai caught the lashing rain. When night came the wind lessened but the rain continued to fall heavily. It ran through Russell's hair, soaking his collar. Lighted traffic hissed past on the Rue Lafayette. He could hear Hungarian music from Joe Rareira's bar – it would go on spilling out until dawn.

Russell had thought he was late crossing into Frenchtown. The heavy flashlight thumped his hip as he limped along. Margot's brothel. He'd never been in there – the girls were imported from England and France, and only champagne was drunk. He crossed the road and continued to Avenue Joffre, then waited under a street lamp opposite the new casino. I didn't even bring a razor, he thought. And I'm not late – just nervous.

This end of Avenue Joffre was shabby, peopled largely by White Russians. It looked like the outskirts of St Petersburg before the Great War. Shops and shashlik restaurants had pictures of the dead Tsar, and names in the old orthography. How suddenly warm and familiar they all were. He wouldn't see them again for a while, maybe never – Russell pulled up his collar. I could be seated comfortably in a steamy café, drinking tea and reading a newspaper, he thought.

A Russian girl with an elderly man walked slowly past. She wore a white belted raincoat and a scarf over her long blonde hair. Father and daughter, Russell thought. They'll probably walk this way tomorrow, and where will I be? He watched them and felt lonely. The girl was carrying a shopping bag. Maybe I could have got to know her?

Wet rubbish choked a drain under the lamppost and a small lake was forming, extending outwards into the road. The next five hours – that would surely be the worst? If he could get through the next five hours. He stirred the rubbish with the toe of his shoe and water gurgled down the drain.

A black Citroën slid out of the traffic, pulled in at the kerb just beyond the street lamp and the rear door opened. A Chinese face grinned back at Russell through the rain. It was the boy from Dou's verandah. 'Goddam wet.'

He climbed in next to the boy and the car moved away before he'd closed the door. Windscreen wipers flicked back and forth and rain blurred the lights of traffic ahead of them. He tried to relax. They were heading towards the French quay. The Chinese boy was wearing black trousers and black roll-neck sweater but still the same worn tennis shoes. 'You want gun?' He groped behind the seat and lifted out a Belgian automatic pistol.

'No. I might kill somebody.'

The driver laughed harshly. 'He's Lao. I'm Mazurov.' He turned his head briefly – a Slav, mouth too large for his face and yellow stumps of teeth. 'We'll do the killing.'

'With luck we won't have to kill anybody.'

'You bet.' Lao grinned.

Mazurov drove past the fragmented wall of the Chinese City. And I won't see that again for a while, Russell thought. Five minutes and we'll be at the steps. His anxiety had reached his stomach. Who was it the old man used to chatter his prayers to? Shang Di, the great god and universal provider. What should I ask for?

'We do as you say.' Mazurov glanced round quickly, then turned south along the French quay. 'But only so long as you know what you're doing.'

'How will you know if I know what I'm doing?'

'I'll know.' Mazurov rolled down the window and spat.

Lights from lamps along the quay flickered like quicksilver in the dark river. The Whangpoo was two hundred yards wide at this point, flowing its last ten miles to

Woosung and the Yangtze estuary. Mazurov stopped the car at Bouchard's steps and switched off the lights.

Russell felt sick. He wanted to go on sitting there in the soft leather and the warmth. Instead he climbed out before the others and peered at the river. The rain would be an advantage, obscuring visibility. 'We cross without lights. I hope somebody brought the crowbar.'

Lao rummaged in the car boot and found it. He swung it whistling round his head. 'Smash a goddam skull – more or less.'

'We'd better get on.'

A Chinese was waiting for them with a frail sampan – it felt unstable as Russell stepped over the stern. And that was all he needed; the rocking motion as they crossed the dark rain-swept river triggered a surge of nausea. He leaned over the side and vomited. Mazurov sniggered softly. 'And we haven't seen a Jap yet.'

Russell wiped his mouth with his sodden handkerchief. He was cold and sweating but he felt better. They were nearly across, the piers and go-downs of Pootung shadowy. Sparse lights illumined moored ships moving slackly on the incoming tide. And there was rubbish in the river – bundled shapes half submerged. The sampan slid under a hauser and bumped gently against the stern of a junk, *Fushan*.

In the near darkness Russell could just discern the axial rudder. The junk reeked. They pushed the sampan round to where the downward curve of the gunwale was only three and a half feet out of the water. Two Chinese already aboard had heard them. 'What colour are you?'

'Green.' Lao hauled himself over *Fushan*'s side and Russell and Mazurov followed.

With the flashlight shielded, Russell made a quick inspection. The *Fushan* was old and filthy; high mast slightly forward of midships and a foremast right up in the bows; mat and batten sails reefed slackly. Stench from the bilge mingled with the reek of stale fish. 'God Almighty!' He knew little about boats but this one was clearly ready for scrap.

Lao, the Chinese boy, followed him. 'Has good engine.'

He felt his way up to the stern. Mazurov held a hatch open and flicked the light down at the diesel – that looked old as well. But somebody had done some thinking for them: there were four full drums of diesel fuel. And in the deckhouse – it was really just a shelter open at the front – there was a box of dried fish, water casks, cans of food, palliasses. British Admiralty charts of the Yangtze as far as Nanking were in a folder – they were dated 1905 but they were better than the map he had rolled up in his pocket.

Lao watched. 'We go yet?'

'No. We wait for the tide to turn.'

He looked at the opened folder and the boy peered curiously at the chart. 'Like dragon.' And he traced the course of the Yangtze with a grubby finger.

'Yes. We have to get our hands on the aeroplane engines then take this rotting junk ten miles down the Whangpoo to the estuary, here, and all the time we'll be a possible target for the Japanese warships. Then we sail along the dragon's body to its head, here at Nanking.'

Lao nodded. 'Jap ships on dragon's tail?'

'Probably.' He couldn't think of any reason why they shouldn't be. 'There's a boom – a sort of a barricade across the river at this point – Chiang-yin. The Japanese can't get beyond there. Maybe we can't either.' He'd worry about that if they ever got as far as the Yangtze.

'Han said we'd have weapons.' Mazurov searched among stores piled haphazardly to find the wooden box. He lifted out a .45 calibre submachine gun and grunted with disgust.

Lao took it from him and grinned. 'Like the movies – br-r-up!'

'It'll be no use at any distance. But *this* . . .' Mazurov carefully, almost reverently, fondled a Mannlicher rifle. 'This is no toy.'

'I'm no good with either.' Russell relieved Lao of the submachine gun and gingerly replaced it in the box. 'We'll need some protection for whoever steers. Take the palliasses and stack them round the stern bulwark – it will be better than nothing.'

94

Mazurov didn't like taking orders, but he went with the boy.

They settled down to wait for the tide. The two sailors were vague shapes, squatting amidships under a tarpaulin awning. A wick set in oil inside a tobacco tin gave them a tiny flame. There were sounds of a rat scuttling over the planks.

Russell watched the river with growing concern. *Atami* wasn't on schedule. The Japanese gunboat could make sixteen knots – certainly more than *Fushan* with its worn diesel. If it turned up at the wrong time they were done for. The cold rain had eaten into him, sapping his resolve. He went into the deckhouse for some shelter but kept his eye on the river.

Mazurov had lit a storm lantern and shaded it. The boy smiled to himself as the Slav loaded the Mannlicher. Mazurov's hands were large and ugly but his movements were precise. He filled the magazine and spoke to Russell as he slid an extra cartridge into the breach.

'Is there money in this for you?'

'No.'

'Why are you doing it?'

Decision after a lifetime of compromising – a sort of test of himself? Because retreat from the promise he'd made to the old man might be just a little worse than dying? How did he really know why he was doing it? So he gave the easy answer. 'Chiang Kai-shek needs aeroplane engines. Why are you helping?'

'Because Dou says so.'

'Do you do everything Dou tells you?'

Mazurov shrugged and squinted along the barrel of the rifle. 'Dou owns me.'

'He kill a girl, so to speak.' Lao's white teeth showed. 'Dou fix it with French police. Mazurov cut up lots of girls.'

Russell looked at the ugly hands. So it was probably Mazurov's job to dispose of him if the Japs intercepted the junk. He checked his watch again and left the deckhouse. On the Bund side of the river high tower blocks, brightly lit, stretched away to the north and west. *Fushan* was slack on its moorings, the tide was on the turn and the gunboat *Atami* still hadn't shown up. They couldn't delay any longer. He called to them, 'Douse the lights.'

Lao joined him. 'Now we go?'

'Yes.' And he took a deep breath.

The elder of the two Chinese sailors remained by the clacking diesel. Its noise could surely be heard as far as the Bund! Russell peered through the falling rain. The stern light of a small vessel moved ahead of them as Mazurov worked the tiller, turning the junk down river along the Pootung shore. The French cruiser, *Lamotte Piquet* was moored in the deep channel – Russell could hear the music of a party somewhere on board.

A wide creek led off from Shanghai Marine Motor Works on the right. Now he could count the go-downs. Yun Tseng's half-submerged hulk had been moved by the port authority that afternoon. The warehouse was ahead, just a short way from the Customs house on Pootung Point. He signalled to Mazurov to pull over. The Chinese sailor cut the engine and they bumped gently alongside Yun Tseng's wooden jetty.

Now it really begins – no possible retreat. Russell scanned the dark expanse of river and listened, picking out familar sounds. Traffic on the Bund. A siren. Muted thump of guns to the north. Fear sharpens the ears – he was acutely aware of the lapping sounds of water against timber and the hissing of rain. The clock chimed on the Shanghai Customs Building across the river.

Mazurov was edgy. 'What are we waiting for?'

'Shut up and listen!'

Russell had heard another sound. The gunboat was approaching from round the point.

'Get down!'

They lay flat. *Atami*'s searchlight probed ahead as it followed the curve of the river. Would the Japanese notice that *Fushan* hadn't been there last time? Russell's heart thumped. Mazurov was sprawled next to him and he wondered how the Slav would make the decision quickly to cut his throat and dump him overboard.

The searchlight flickered along the jetties and *Fushan* lifted in the wash as the gunboat passed up river. Eighteen minutes and it would be back.

'Quickly!' Russell led the way, running up the jetty.

He had the old man's keys but Customs officers had changed the padlock on the warehouse door. 'Crowbar!'

He wedged it under the iron hasp and levered, hands trembling. Damn! He couldn't move it. The Slav leaned on the crowbar with him, grunting, and the hasp gave suddenly, screws splintering out of the thick wood. They slid the heavy door back. At least four minutes gone.

The warehouse was dark, cluttered with the old man's merchandise, and Russell wasn't sure where the engines were. 'Look for six large wooden crates. And a trolley – we'll need a trolley.'

They searched with flashlights, moving round the mounds of jute sacks. Lao found the crates, bigger and heavier than Russell had remembered. Moving one of them was alarmingly difficult. They used the crowbar, levering the crate and edging the trolley under it. One – it would only take one! They manoeuvred along the narrow gangway and out through the door. Thank God for darkness and rain. Russell sweated, his muscles already aching. The jetty sloped and it needed all their strength to slow the trolley. Metal-rimmed wheels ground into the planking. He got in front, pressing his back against the crate and easing it to the side of the *Fushan*.

'Now lift, damn you!' Eight minutes before the *Atami* would come back. And they lifted, straining their backs and arms and stomachs to lower the first engine into the bowels of the junk.

Dragging the trolley they ran back into the warehouse, no longer caring about noise as boxes crashed over in their haste. Another crate was levered up onto the trolley and wheeled out to the jetty. *Fushan* settled lower in the water as the second engine lay alongside the first. Three minutes left before *Atami*'s return run.

'We've got to get away from here!' Mazurov peered up river.

'No! One more!' Russell could barely move the trolley on his own. Lao hesitated then pushed from behind.

The others followed, kicking aside the tumbled warehouse

97

goods. Mazurov cursed, and went on in a blasphemous frenzied monologue as they took the strain and lifted once more.

As they reached the warehouse door Russell heard the gunboat coming back. They forgot the limitations of strength, running the trolley down the jetty and hoisting up the crate. A beam stabbed the night, flicking along the shore. And the crate was poised.

'Push the bitch over the side!' Mazurov shouted.

'No! Lower it.'

But halfway lowered, Mazurov let go. The crate crashed down and one of the Chinese seamen shrieked in pain. There wasn't even time to look at him.

'Start the engine!'

Diesel clacking, *Fushan* wallowed away from the jetty and out into the current. Russell stared back frantically. It was as familiar as the nightmare when you can move only slowly from imminent danger. The searchlight probed insistently, following the general direction of their sound. And Mazurov leaned hard over, turning the junk along the high dark side of a steamer moored in midstream.

'For God's sake what are you doing?' Russell shoved him aside and seized the tiller as the junk's fore rigging snagged on a steel hauser. Reefed sail and timber crashed down onto the deck. 'We can't outrun the gunboat – we must lose it! Hide! Over there among other ships.' *Fushan* yawned sluggishly and turned back towards the Pootung shore.

The brilliant white light from the *Atami* scanned, then fixed on them. Russell shielded his eyes, and heard a shouted order in Japanese through a loud-hailer. He wondered if Mazurov would kill him now – just in the moment of interception. But the Slav was shouting to Lao, 'The rifle! Get it!'

A minute – maybe a minute and a half and they would be among the dozens of anchored ships. The Japanese shouted again across the dark water and almost immediately a machine gun crackled. Bullets splintered *Fushan's* high bulwark. No time to wonder if they'd all be killed – Russell steered for a gap in the crowded junks. Narrow, they might just save themselves.

The gunboat was close behind them, its engines loud. The machine gun crackled again ripping through timbers. Russell felt a searing burn across his cheek. Mazurov steadied the rifle on the guard-beam and fired repeatedly at the searchlight. And the light suddenly went out leaving Russell blind. He gripped the tiller and mouthed, 'Shang Di, Shang Di, Shang Di.'

They slipped through the gap.

The old Chinese seaman shut off the engine and they drifted almost silently among high ships' sides. Lao caught at mooring ropes slowing them alongside a seagoing junk.

Somebody shone a lantern down and Lao hissed in the dark. 'We do business for Dou!' The lantern went out.

They waited. The rain fell down.

Atami's engines throbbed close by as the gunboat cruised slowly along the perimeter of moored shipping, and voices called in Japanese. Three – four – five minutes. The gunboat turned and searched again, then the engine roared, wash rippling along the junks, and the sounds receded.

Russell was still holding the tiller, fingers clenched tightly. Slowly he let go and gave a long sigh. 'Allow the Japanese to get well clear.' It was then he realized why his cheek was burning. A bullet had nicked the bone just under his eye. And Mazurov was very still, humped over the guard beam with the rifle under him. Russell shielded the flashlight and shone it on the Slav. There was blood on the deck.

'Mazurov!'

Mazurov groaned but didn't move.

Lao slithered up next to him. 'Hurt bad.' And he lifted Mazurov's legs and pushed.

'Hey! Wait!' Russell whispered.

'No use now.' The boy's white teeth showed. 'Finished more or less.' And Mazurov fell clumsily over the stern and splashed into the river.

It was a relief, watching that bundled shape drifting out and slowly sinking.

Now that the gunboat had gone, storm lanterns glowed along the high side of the big junk and faces peered down. Russell felt very tired, like a battery suddenly drained, barely enough energy to move midship. The injured Chinese sailor was still lying with half his foot trapped under the third engine crate. He'd pushed the handle of his knife in his mouth and was biting on it. They levered the crate and the other seaman dragged him out.

What to do with him? Russell rubbed the rain from his eyes and stared down at the pulpy mess. All the toes were crushed. He gently eased the knife handle from between the clenched teeth and bound the sailor's foot with rags – they were dirty but he had nothing else. And all the time the man's eyes were on his face. Perhaps he anticipated the same end as Mazurov. 'I make no sound,' he murmured.

'You did well.' Now he was just a liability. 'If we can get you onto that junk, will they look after you?'

'They look after him.' Lao spoke rapidly in Chinese to the faces above them – Russell heard them threatened with Dou's displeasure. A rope end flopped down onto *Fushan*'s deck.

'I climb.' The sailor balanced on his uninjured foot and tested the rope. He was glad to be getting out. Russell pushed a wet fifty dollar bill into the man's shirt. 'Go on. Get going.'

They watched him haul himself up, and over the junk's side. He waved briefly and the old seaman waved back.

Now they were just three – soaked men, and cold. Rain splashed on the wooden crates. Lao rubbed his sleeve over his face and looked at Russell questioningly. 'Staying is bad as going?'

Ten miles to Woosung. With luck the rain and darkness would hide them from the Japanese ships and they'd reach the Yangtze before first light. Russell nodded. 'Yes. Staying is bad as going, more or less.'

CHAPTER NINE

The road was bad after the rain. It was really just a section of field wide enough to take two bullock carts – or these days a cart and a bus. The battered Ford slithered, wheels spinning every few yards. 'It's better after the sun has been up for a while – it bakes the mud hard.' Foster frowned and changed down the gears again. He'd offered no explanation why it had been necessary to start so early.

Another twenty minutes of slow, jolting movement, and Linda felt numb. They'd stayed overnight in Ch'ang-chou so that Foster could confer with the surgeon at the English hospital, and they'd risen at the awesome hour of four. Now Linda's back ached with the effort of maintaining balance. She'd given up on the scenery. My first close-hand look at real China, she thought. It was flat and featureless; wet fields stretching off in all directions. But there was a range of hills to the west.

'There were bandits out there when I first came,' Foster said.

'Not now, I hope?'

'No. Kuomintang troops moved in and slaughtered most of them – stuck their heads on poles.' He frowned again. 'Having the army here has been a mixed blessing – they'd be better employed fighting the Communists.'

Linda hadn't expected a missionary to say a thing like that and she was slightly shocked. Chiang Kai-shek had fought five campagns against Mao Tse-tung and the losses on both sides had been horrendous. But who counted the Chinese dead? She stared, puzzled, at Foster's back. His long, white hair was tied together with a piece of tape.

There was no doubting his concern for the Chinese. The floor at the back of the car was cluttered with boxes that he had collected at Ch'ang-chou – drugs, dressings, seeds for his rural project. Nothing for himself – nothing personal. Foster's life was work. 'It's very good of you to let us stay at the mission.'

'You can probably make yourselves useful.'

'I hope I won't be there long – no offence,' Peggy said. 'Arch should be able to find me somewhere nearer Nanking. Don't you think?'

Foster concentrated on his driving as though he hadn't heard the question. 'There was an article, and a photograph of Captain Rittenhouse in the Nanking paper – what? – two or three days ago.'

'The consul will love that.' Peggy frowned. 'Arch should keep himself out of the newspapers.'

It's a way some people have, Linda thought. She'd seen pictures of Arch – large-jawed, handsome, with the look of a man able to take on the world single-handed. Somebody had called it the X factor – news reporters are drawn to such men. Could it really be that Arch Rittenhouse was impotent, as Peggy had suggested? Linda's knowledge of physiology was pretty basic. One brief sexual affair – not particularly uplifting. It wasn't much to base a judgement on. Of psychological reasons for male inability she knew only what she'd gleaned from novels.

Ahead of them, old white walls reflected sunlight, and beyond were green-tiled roofs. 'Is that Hsia-kang?'

'Yes, that's it.'

Of course, we can't smell it yet, Linda thought.

The dirt road led to a gateway, its massive timber doors open. A watch bell hung over the gate. To the east and within the compass of the wall a hill jutted up, cluttered with houses.

'It's an outcrop of rock. Four thousand years ago the river used to flow this side. We had a French archaeologist stay awhile last year – he was full of stories. He said Marco Polo visited here.' Foster shrugged as if it was unlikely, or of no significance even if it was true. 'We have a population of about six and a half thousand – there's been no exact count for over thirty years.'

Linda could see funnels and the high masts of junks.

'A lot of them are stuck here because of the boom across the river at Chiang-yin – it is supposed to prevent Japanese warships coming beyond the delta. But small boats with shallow draught find a way through at night; traders whose livelihood depends on getting up the Yangtze. It's dangerous because Colonel Tang's soldiers are trigger happy.'

'We met Colonel Tang on the train.'

'So, he has returned.' Foster ground the gears. He drove under the massive bell of the Moon Gate, and they were suddenly caught up in what appeared to be a blaring carnival. It was vivid colour after the green sameness of the plain.

A wide, unpaved street was crowded with people – they all seemed to be shouting. The shops, built mostly of wood, were open at the front – dead poultry hung from rafters, and bunches of nameless white roots. Some of the traders squatted in the dust, their wares piled around them. And there was rubbish, and offal buzzed by flies. Pyramids of oranges and water melons. There were padded jackets and blue cotton gowns draped over bamboo frames. Tea houses overflowed into the street. Inevitably it smells, Linda thought.

Foster edged the Ford between bicycles and laden donkeys. Further on beyond the market, he nodded to his left. 'Court House and Post Office.'

But Linda was wondering about the ragged soldiers strung out in single file, and shuffling westward. 'Aren't they going in the wrong direction?'

Foster adjusted his wire-rimmed glasses, and smiled thinly. 'Which is the right direction?'

'Well – the war's the other way.'

'Then maybe they're doing the smart thing.'

The car reached the waterfront – a tiny imitation of the Shanghai Bund. Junks and steamers crowded along its seven hundred yards. A gleaming white gunboat with a Union Jack painted on its canvas awning was anchored off shore. 'The British are stuck here too.' Foster seemed to find that amusing.

He made a right turn along a narrow street flanked on one side by warehouses. Linda caught a glimpse of a temple. 'Taoist,' Foster said. 'That's the opposition.'

They followed a perimeter wall of yellow brick. 'And this is home.' He turned through a narrow entrance and stopped the Ford in a dried mud compound. 'Hsia-kang Mission welcomes you.'

Foster was a self-contained man whose imagination (Linda wasn't sure that he had much) never seemed to mesh with her own. If he found his visitors a nuisance he never showed it. And Linda discovered that the mission was a place where she could work. It was built largely of the same yellow brick that had been used for the compound wall, and it had a tin roof. There had been extensions: an annexe and school room by the previous incumbent, and a small hospital with an out-patients dispensary by Gerald Foster. The chapel, also of yellow brick, stood separate at the north end of the compound.

The bungalow was comfortable though the furnishings were sparsely masculine. Shu, an ancient and arthritic housekeeper, was quartered in the annexe. Foster had been alone since his wife's death two years before. An assistant sent by the Methodist Foreign Mission Committee in Chicago was found drowned after only three months, and his replacement hadn't yet arrived. Helpers, usually students from the University of Nanking, came and went. There was a trained nurse at the mission when Linda and Peggy arrived – Mayling – she shared the annexe with Shu. But the others had left no trace except for photographs. Linda found snapshots in most rooms; Chinese faces smiling or serious, stuck in the corners of mirrors or pinned curling to the wall, as if Foster valued them, but not sufficiently to put them in an album or inscribe a name and date.

Linda tentatively offered to help out in the dispensary in the mornings. She soon regretted it. Ulcerated limbs and foul, fevered breath left her guiltily sickened. Fortunately another nurse, Wu Guo, arrived off a river steamer from Nanking with his wicker travelling case, and Foster suggested to Linda that she spend time with the children instead.

It was a puzzle. She watched Peggy out of the corner of her eye. Some women have an immediate way with children, as though they had a dozen of their own. Why did she herself find it so difficult to relate to them? Linda washed a small face then turned her attention to the little girl's hands. Even if it was possible, she couldn't imagine ever becoming a parent – Peggy, yes, but not her.

The death of Foster's wife had left the mission school without a teacher and he had turned the classroom into an unofficial orphanage for a dozen waifs – nine were girls abandoned by their parents.

'Girls are a liability,' Peggy said.

'But it's unforgivable – can you imagine abandoning your own child?' The small, soapy hand slithered out of Linda's.

'Even *my* father thought a girl was just a mouth to feed.'

'The world's run by men for men.' As she dried the hands Linda noticed lice in the child's hair – it was difficult not to draw back. And there's the paradox, she thought. I feel for people, particularly children, in an abstract way. Faced with the reality of running noses or floods of tears I'm really not much good.

Foster began his day early – he was always working by the time Linda and Peggy breakfasted. Each morning a queue formed at his out-patients dispensary and he handed out medicine and advice and performed minor surgery. Serious cases were sent with a note to the English hospital in Ch'ang-chou.

He'd given Linda the use of his study in the afternoons. She'd already typed and sent off two three-thousand-word articles on the work of the Hsia-kang Mission, but they hadn't really satisfied her. She'd got the burning itch now to

105

write something bigger, and a third article, on the social consequences of the Japanese invasion, interested her far more. The material was all around. But there were problems with it. And this stuff wasn't what she was being paid to write – she ripped it out of the typewriter, but started again.

Her preoccupation with the article meant that she didn't see so much of Peggy. And for half an hour each day, Mayling, the nurse, gave her a lesson, pointing at objects and naming them in Chinese or holding up her fingers and saying the numbers. It was slow work – the tones baffled Linda. It was a relief late each afternoon to take a walk as far as the market area. Usually Peggy came with her.

' . . . and I had this strange dream,' Peggy was saying. 'I was on a boat but I didn't know where it was going. It wasn't exactly a nightmare, though I didn't like it – I was a bit scared.'

'It's indigestion. You eat too much before you go to bed.' Linda still had the language lesson on her mind. 'Did you know there are four different meanings to the word "*ma*"? It's a matter of tone. I thought I was saying "hemp" but actually I was saying "horse".'

'No, that's "ma",' Peggy said, and she frowned at a street vendor's rice flour cakes. 'I eat too much. I mustn't eat so much.'

'Perhaps you're compensating. I've *lost* weight – a couple of pounds.' Linda kept a careful check. 'It must be the heat.'

'The hot season is really over now.' Peggy glanced at her. 'You're all right? – taking your tablets?'

'Dr Foster has given me some more. I'm fine.' She'd felt off colour on only one day since she'd arrived at the mission and, God knows, that wasn't bad. And the town was peaceful, she preferred it to Shanghai.

'But sometimes I think it's too peaceful,' she said. 'Back there in the east, armies are slogging it out on the delta. And I keep remembering that press conference I attended in Shanghai. I asked General Matsui a question – I felt like a real journalist then.'

An open sewer spilled its filth into the Yangtze. Warehouses of Butterfield & Swire, Jardine Matheson, Peter

106

Maihofer, extended west along the waterfront. The two girls turned off and walked towards the market. Seen from the Hsia-kang Bund they were an attractive pair. Bare brown arms and legs, and flimsy sandals – their step was light. Sunlight reflected off their floral cotton dresses and white, wide-brimmed hats. They were still young.

'I've got a mystery for you,' Peggy said. 'You know Dr Foster's wife died two years ago? Well, it was suicide.'

'Suicide! Who says so?'

'Wu Guo, the male nurse. He says all the Chinese know about it.'

'That guy is a dreadful gossip. I wouldn't believe *anything* he said.'

'I'm just trying to make your life more interesting. I mean, for God's sake, there's nothing to do here, is there?'

Linda felt sorry for Peggy, stranded in this Chinese backwater by a husband who seemed totally unconcerned. No, that wasn't quite fair – Peggy had received a letter from Arch only yesterday. She'd read it and said nothing.

Sidewalk shops offered ivory, herbs, and sandalwood. They'd reached the fringe of the market in Yibai Street. A woman with a child carried pick-a-back fashion was seated outside a cheap restaurant – she was preparing to behead a chicken. Linda wanted to brush flies from the sleeping child's eyes.

'You'd think somebody would tell them about trachoma, wouldn't you? Or you'd think that flies equals disease is so obvious it doesn't need saying. They lack common sense.'

The woman cut off the chicken's head. Everything would go into the pot, even the claws and beak. She smiled at the two girls, and Linda suppressed a puzzled distaste. I guess *I* lack charity, she thought.

'There's some yellow silk at that place by the Moon Gate.' Peggy edged through the crowd.

'Okay.' Linda sighed to herself. 'Let's go and haggle.' She suspected that Peggy's compulsion to spend was yet another way of compensating for a distant husband. 'But we'd better not stay too long. Foster gets a little edgy if we're not back by the time Shu serves tea.'

'He's gone off with his medical kit so maybe we'll get through tea without his sharp eye – I'm scared to drop a crumb.'

'You don't like him all that much, do you?'

'Do *you*?' Peggy shrugged and bit her lip. 'It's not that. It's that I don't really want to be here. I ought to be with Arch, but sometimes I wish I could just go home – to South London.'

Sometimes the small, sad hopes of people, for warmth and love, filled Linda with anger against the God she wasn't sure existed. It was unfair that He should create them with this need, and then so often let them carry it unfulfilled to their graves.

Near the Moon Gate they came upon the old man said to be over three hundred years old. 'I don't believe it,' Peggy said.

Nobody could remember when he hadn't been there; blind, motionless, seated on an old blanket. Linda wondered who brought him to that place each day. And was it worth being alive and so old?

'You can see he's not a day over 250,' Peggy said.

They came away without the yellow silk. The sun was going down and there was a suggestion of autumn in the air. Linda felt limp from pushing through the crowd, and anxious to return to the mission for a shower and tea. 'I have a recurring nightmare of smelling like one of those women who gut fish on the quay. Showering has become an obsession.'

'Maybe *you're* compensating for something.' Peggy smiled maliciously.

As they neared the mission, they heard dull, distant thumps. That was the second time this week. Japanese planes were bombing the river boom at Chiang-yin. Three more thumps. The planes were too far off to be seen and the sounds, familiar now, passed almost unnoticed.

Tea had already been served in Foster's study and old Shu clucked disapprovingly. Linda went off to shower.

Water cascaded over her. It was the only shower in the

mission and Dr Foster had imposed a two-minute rule. A fussy, busy man, he gave his attention to everything, from surgery to the bean crop in the mission garden. His coarse soap was in the dish. Linda speculated about him. She'd needed more tablets. How to explain that sudden and totally unexpected revulsion as he'd examined her? He had, after all, done a brisk, professional job. And had he noticed her disgust? She thought she'd concealed it, but perhaps not quite enough. Foster was a puzzle. Wealthy – or so Wu Guo the male nurse said. The rural project was paid for out of his own money; and although the Mission Committee back home had financed the building of the dispensary, Foster had equipped it. Yet he had only one suit, brought out for occasions like the visit to Ch'ang-chou. The rest of the time he wore faded drill, knotted tie supporting his trousers, and Chinese sandals.

From the study Linda could hear static, voices, music, static, as somebody shifted the radio waveband. Then a snatch of "Good Old Shanghai" – XMHA played it half a dozen times a day.

As she rubbed the towel across her belly she felt the ugliness of the scar. It's *only* a scar – that's all, she told herself. Lots of people have scars. Peggy has one on her thumb. And Reed has a scar under his jaw, white where the stubble of his beard doesn't grow. He was coming from up river to visit them and that would at least keep Peggy interested for the day.

The XMHA news broadcast began as she dressed. ' . . . and with the fall of Shanghai North Station, the Chinese defenders have lost their last foothold across Soochow Creek . . .' Had Reed found himself another Chinese girl to sleep with? It was people like him who gave America a bad name abroad. As Linda went along the passage to the study she noted the British announcer's perfect diction, 'General Matsui's assault troops of the "Black" 9th have broken through into the suburbs. Japanese troops now control a large area north of Shanghai, including Ta-ch'ang, Wu-sung, and Pao-shan at the mouth of the Yangtze River . . .'

Dr Foster hadn't heard her approaching, she could see him through the open door. Map spread, he was following the advance of the Japanese 9th Division.

'It doesn't sound good, does it?' She hadn't particularly wanted to join him for tea but now he'd seen her. 'Japanese planes bombed the boom at Chiang-yin again this afternoon – Peggy and I heard them. Do you think the Japanese army could get this far?'

Foster took off his wire-rimmed glasses and rubbed his eyes. Then he stared, almost as if he disliked her. 'They are just ordinary men – human beings like ourselves – Miss Bishop.'

CHAPTER TEN

Fifty-six miles of dirt road linked Chen-chiang and the smaller town of Hsia-kang, and Reed had to take it easy because years of potholed tracks had ruined Greta's suspension. He hadn't given the truck that name, it was there on the cab door when he'd bought it from a Swedish couple in Hafei two weeks before.

It was going to be a fine day – his jacket was slung on the seat next to him. But already there was a suggestion of autumn in the air – something that told you to enjoy the feel of the sun on your skin because all too soon a bitter wind would howl out of the north.

Greta roared lustily and Reed tried to guess where the hole was in the exhaust system. Close up to the silencer probably, that being the most difficult place to fix it. There was a universal law and he'd come to understand its working.

Greta was a fifteen-hundredweight pick-up truck, or so it was described on the registration document. The engine and chassis had started life in Detroit, and seen from directly in front the machine was recognizably a product of Ford. But if you shifted your perspective very slightly you began to have serious doubts.

He'd paid fifty dollars for the truck – the Swedish couple were going home after nearly twenty years. They'd bought it from a Chinese trader who had modified the body to take a maximum load – it now extended eighteen inches either side of the cab. Tarpaulin was stretched over a frame enclosing the rear, and laced down on the tailboard.

Off to the right Reed could see the hills, their tops still

hazy with the morning mist. A Japanese bomber had crashed on the far side the previous day. It triggered thoughts of Arch who had his pictures in *China Weekly Review* after shooting down his fourth enemy plane.

Three attempts to contact Arch, and the son-of-a-bitch hadn't replied. It was a way Arch had, and he'd turn up out of the blue and look faintly surprised that you could be offended, and pick up the conversation again as if you'd never really been out of his thoughts – who knows, perhaps you hadn't? But there were one or two things that needed to be discussed; like why his shirt was in Sao's apartment for instance. Reed brooded to himself. The truth of the matter was, he'd stopped thinking about Sao within a week of leaving Shanghai – well almost. And it was just a matter of principle that Arch should be made to know that he hadn't entirely got away with it.

The dirt road was heavily rutted and he changed down gear, registering almost subconsciously that the lever didn't slick in as smoothly as it should. Another job. There was the Stinson float-plane to keep serviced, and three CPC trucks based almost permanently at Chen-chiang.

Reed scowled to himself. When would he find time to fix Greta properly? He'd done a decoke late last night, and changed the head gasket, cutting a new one from thin hide. But the truck needed a re-bore. And he'd have to make two new leaves for the nearside rear spring. He rehearsed the job in his head.

A cloud of brownish-yellow dust followed the pick-up truck. Reed never considered its appearance: the flaked paintwork and rust, the iron bar covered with bits of motor tyre that served as a front fender, the split leather bench seat seeping kapok and horsehair. But he knew from the sound how each mechanical part was working or failing – some part of his brain switching from piston to crankshaft to linkage to differential, visualizing each in turn. His need for expression was almost fulfilled by daily improvisation and constant adaptation of his mechanical skills. Hell, stripping down the engine of the Stinson – that's how he'd been able to forget

112

Sao in one week. But this ability to sink himself – in Greta's electrics, or the inner workings of Sven Dalsager's piano – was also his ruin. Ambition, or at least some rough plan for the future, always got lost, pushed down the list of priorities. It was his satisfaction to save things, restore them, make them work smoothly again.

The great Tao pervades everywhere, both on the left and on the right.

He could see the white walls of Hsia-kang about four miles off. A bus stirred up the dust as it started on its journey south. Reed passed it, grossly overcrowded, its roof piled high with baggage, bicycles, crates. And then he was entering the town. There were heads on poles over the West Gate. Silk banners floated above shopfronts, and he could smell the kerbside restaurants, and the offal and the excrement. How did the fastidious Miss Bishop find all this?

He knew, in all honesty, that although he'd come to this town for Peggy's sake, it was because of Linda Bishop that he'd shaved, found himself a clean shirt, and washed his neckscarf. And thinking about this he began to resent her again. Different she might be, but not as damned smart as she thought she was. Or as sure of herself. Remembering her at the ship's rail on their journey across the Pacific he was able to say with certainty that some large doubt nagged at Linda Bishop.

The traffic had come almost to a stop, edging round an ox cart. The ox had sunk to its knees and the owner was kicking it. Students were using the hold-up to collect for war relief. A girl walked quickly along the line of vehicles, smiling and shaking her tin. Reed gave her his loose coins.

He followed the instructions sent by Peggy, though he assumed from the handwriting that they'd been written by Linda Bishop – firm, each letter perfectly legible. And he came to the narrow street, and the Taoist temple, and the yellow brick wall of the mission compound.

Linda saw Reed arriving. She waved but didn't go over to talk to him. What, in God's name, was that pile of junk he was driving? He should be ashamed, for letting down the entire Western civilization.

When he walked into the mission he said, 'You're looking fierce, efficient, on top of things, Miss Bishop.'

It was going to be a bad day.

She'd been struggling against the feeling since she'd got up that morning, and it seemed altogether wiser to keep out of the way. She went to the kitchen to help Shu dole out soup.

It had been arranged – and Linda had made the offer with the best of intentions – that she would look after the children on her own while Peggy and Mayling rode with Reed to Chiang-yin five miles to the east. Reed was supposed to be delivering or collecting something. And it wasn't merely that she wished to avoid him – that possibility had been examined under the microscope and rejected. Peggy was to have a break, that was the intention. And Mayling. It was just a bit galling that they should take the offer for granted and assume she really preferred to stay at the mission.

'It will probably be a bit boring.' Peggy put on her wide-brimmed hat and examined herself in the mirror. She was wearing make up for the first time in days, Linda noticed. 'All they've got at Chiang-yin, love, is one traffic policeman and the boom across the river.'

'Have fun.' Linda kept the resentment out of her voice and went off to look after the children. I don't even like children all that much, she thought. Except once in a while I miss the one I'll never be able to have. She got out paint and paper; messy to clean up but it kept them involved longest. Children are anarchic – I'm sure I never was. She was determinedly kind and patient, turning her pique onto Reed. Fancy driving around in that awful wreck – he'd helped Mayling up into the cab as if it were a Cadillac.

Moving among the children, Linda felt disturbed. The war had marked them. They chattered and laughed, but there was violence in nearly all the pictures they painted. Bombs and fire and destruction. One child sat alone, staring at blank paper. When Linda dipped a brush in colour and handed it to her she just held it listlessly. And Linda felt guilty. She was only filling in time with them and would go away and live a quite separate life.

Tired of painting, they grouped around her and sang songs taught them by Mayling – Linda knew them now though she didn't understand all the words. The small girl was a worry, she just sat there staring at the floor. She had retreated into herself, to somewhere that was safe. Maybe she couldn't get back? Linda took the girl onto her knee. The other children sang a song about the goddess who would come in a boat and find them when they were lost.

Reed's noisy truck returned earlier than Linda had expected. Shu came to look after the children, so Linda went to Dr Foster's study where the others were drinking tea. Peggy had a migraine, eyes red-rimmed, and Mayling was dosing her with aspirin.

Foster seemed impatient. 'Aspirin will be of little use. Yours is an allergy condition, Mrs Rittenhouse – search your memory and find what triggers it.' And he drained his cup and went out.

He's so useful to the human race – far more so than me. How can he be so lacking in sympathy, Linda wondered?

'I guess I'll go and lie down in the dark.' Peggy rose. 'I'm devastated, Reed. Promise you'll come again?'

He kissed her on the cheek. 'If you'll cut my hair one more time.' He smiled at her.

It was odd, that small feeling of being excluded. Linda stacked the cups on the tray and Peggy left. Mayling was asking Reed about the shot-down Japanese bomber.

'Where did it crash? Oh, how I would love to see it – and the men who flew in it so *brave*!'

'Hell, I don't know about that. They were just trying to get home, that's all. We'll go out there and take a look at it if you want?'

'Now I have compelled you to ask me.' Mayling embarrassed easily. 'I must not take up your time.'

'You want to see it? That's what we'll do. It's only five miles out of town.'

Does he sleep with a Chinese girl?

Like Mayling, Linda was curious about the crashed bomber. And Mayling said, 'You come too, Linda. It will be exciting.'

'Yeah.' Reed glanced at her casually as if he didn't much care one way or the other. 'You could write a little story about it.'

Write a little story! But she chalked that up as an unintentional insult. 'Okay. I'll go and get my camera.'

They left almost immediately because the autumn days were short and Reed would have to drive back to Chenchiang. Linda's suspicions about Reed's truck now seemed valid. 'Did you deliberately remove all the springs?'

'It just needs fixing,' he said.

'I've been in the town long enough to forget how bad the country roads are.'

'Chiang Kai-shek's government has built some good ones but there isn't enough money.' He shrugged. 'Things get done slowly. Much of the budget goes on the army. The Japs have been at the back door since '31. Chiang has fought five campaigns against Mao and the Communists. Before that there were the war lords to crush or coerce.'

'Shouldn't Mao Tse-tung and Chiang co-operate against the Japanese?'

'I suppose so.' Reed didn't seem very interested.

'They've surely got to do that if they are to win?'

He scowled to himself. 'It's not my damned war.'

She thought, with banner headlines about the bombing of Nanking, Reed will pick up a newspaper and turn to the sports page. He only has opinions about small things. Yet that assessment didn't quite fit.

'Tell us about yourself. Where did you come from?'

'What d'ya want to know that for?' He frowned at the road.

'You have this very irritating habit of answering a question with a question, Reed. C'mon, tell us about your family and when you were born.'

116

'It's boring stuff,' and he shrugged. 'If you *must* know, my father was a judge in Petersburg, Iowa, and . . .'

'What!'

'Petersburg – it's on the Cedar River.'

Linda was astonished. 'No, no! Say that again about your father being a judge!'

'Judges are just like other people. I mean, there's no magic in it – he was no better at running his life than anybody else.'

'But didn't he want *you* to take up law or something?'

'No. It was already decided, the day I was born, that I'd go to medical school. There was only one doctor in Petersburg then – that was my uncle, and I was going to inherit his practice.'

'Well, here you are a mechanic, so what happened?'

'I actually *got* to medical school, in Chicago. I was there for one whole year – that was 1917. Then we went into the war . . .' He shook his head. 'I wanted to see it all. Two other guys were planning to go up to Canada and enlist in the Royal Flying Corps and I was going with them. They never went in the end, and I joined our own air service. I went to France.'

'And that's when you met Arch Rittenhouse?'

'That's right. We flew together.' Reed lapsed into silence.

And they'd gone off to another war in South America. Then Reed had given up flying and become a mechanic. She was really no wiser now than she was when she started. Linda paused in her thoughts, watching three naked children in a drainage ditch. They were washing a slab-sided water buffalo – it stood patiently while they scrubbed at its back and splashed. The country was peaceful, and still warm. It was good to be out. And good to be away from Peggy for a while – the thought surprised her.

She hadn't been really free of the mission and its routine since she'd arrived in Hsia-kang. There had been one other small outing. Linda had visited the Chinese garden with Colonel Tang. He'd just driven into the compound without any prior notice. A few polite questions about how she was

117

getting on at the mission – that was all he'd asked. She couldn't believe that her answers could have been of much interest to him. But it didn't matter because the visit had acquired another significance.

Mayling was explaining to Reed that Hsia-kang gangsters were buying up rice and hoarding it against the inevitable shortage. Linda started to listen, but her mind drifted back to the Chinese garden and its path winding to the manmade lake. Perfect. And distanced by four hundred years from the life of the town. Colonel Tang knew each vista, pausing repeatedly so that she could discover them for herself. 'A garden is a microcosm in which a man may construct his own small world.' To what purpose? She hadn't been able to ask the question. An artificial Eden separated from the larger world by only a stone wall? Manmade order out of nature's disorder. Perfection painfully preserved for four hundred years – and there was only one certainty. Sooner or later the garden would be overwhelmed – swamped by that world outside. The ultimate futility of man's labour dragged at her heart. We might just as well be standing in a wilderness. 'Why do we struggle so hard?' And she'd shrugged hopelessly. 'We're so insignificant in the end.'

'You may never find meaning in your life, Miss Bishop. But while you zealously search you are not insignificant.'

She thought about Colonel Tang's reply as Reed's truck carried them further from the town. If only one could *feel* that significance.

Mayling was still talking about the Hsia-kang gangsters. 'The magistrates take no action against them when they are brought before them.'

'Probably getting a kick-back,' Reed grinned cynically. 'They're just respectable gangsters. And that reminds me,' he glanced sideways at Linda. 'Han Yu-lin – Dou's lieutenant. You remember him?'

'You mean the guy who took our compartment on the train from Shanghai?'

'That's him. He's staying at the same hotel as me.' And Reed began explaining how Green Society influence extended up river even to the Generalissimo's headquarters. 'I just wonder what the hell Han is doing in Chen-chiang.' He looked puzzled.

Linda decided in that moment that Reed was quite a good looking man. I never noticed it before, she thought. Not handsome – his nose must have been broken at one time. Slightly hunched he was like a boxer or a stevedore, and sometimes like a hobo tramping through the rain. And once in a while his face was interesting – more so than the thoughts in his head. How had he come by that white scar under his jaw? What would it be like to go to bed with him? The thought surprised her, and, tingling, she suppressed it and stared out at the country again.

Mayling was saying that the whole crew of the Japanese bomber had escaped, right under the eyes of Chinese soldiers – they'd even carried their wounded gunner with them. Her eyes shone. 'Such heroism.'

Already the story was turning into the stuff of legend, and Linda had begun writing it inside her head. The damaged bomber had force-landed on rising ground in full view of farmers working in their fields, and the pilot hauled the gunner from his turret. As Chinese militia from the nearby village approached, a second bomber landed on the uneven slope and rescued the stranded crew, wounded man and all.

The flyers hadn't had time to destroy the crashed bomber. There it was, on the side of the slope ahead. And there were tyre marks, and a deep gash in the soil where the port wing had snagged when the undercarriage collapsed. Two ragged militiamen stood guard to stop looters and memento hunters. The bomber was much bigger than Linda had expected, and sinister even in its stillness. Villagers and townspeople had come to look at the wreck before it was carried away from public display in Nanking – they milled around, amazed and staring.

'There's a hole here – would that have been a piece of a shell?' Linda stood shadowed under the starboard wing smeared black behind the motor. The bright red Rising Sun symbols made her uneasy. She walked right round the

119

wrecked plane, climbed onto the collapsed wing and peered through the viewfinder of her camera at the gunner's turret. Click. There were ugly holes below the plexiglass and she supposed that was when the gunner had been wounded. Click. Suddenly she didn't like what she was doing. She was like one of those vultures in Shanghai, photographing the dead. When she turned, Reed was watching her.

She felt slightly ashamed. But even so, it would make a good story – she could write it honestly. 'Do you suppose Captain Rittenhouse might have shot this one down?'

'I don't know.' Reed shrugged. 'What makes you think that?'

'The way everybody talks about him – the hero stuff. And getting his picture on the cover of *Time* magazine. He begins to sound like Superman.' Linda knew as she said it that she was really just probing.

'Arch ain't Superman.'

Mayling had found the tyre marks of the second bomber and she called to Linda and Reed. They came and looked.

'There were thirty of our soldiers shooting at it,' she said.

Reed looked dubious. 'I wouldn't be too worried with thirty Chinese militia shooting at me. No offence, Mayling, but it's when they're trying to hit something *else* you start worrying. And that's fairly easy ground to make a landing on. I don't see those Japs as heroes.'

'I so want to believe that the enemy can behave well – that they are not all ruthless and heartless as we are told.'

'If I'm forced to think about it,' he said, 'what *about* those militia – half starved, worn out weapons. They're pretty ignorant, but they know that they are always the losers. If a Jap bullet doesn't get them, disease or malnutrition probably will. Five of them were killed when that second bomber strafed them. To do their best in those circumstances calls for solid endurance – I rate that more than courage.'

Linda had even thought of a title for the story, and Reed was beginning to ruin it. 'That the Chinese soldiers have great endurance doesn't detract from the courage of the men who got their wounded comrade out of the turret, and the courage of the pilot who put his plane down to save them.'

'If you want to think of them as heroes . . .' He shrugged. 'That bomber was on its way back from Nanking. Hospitals, the slum districts, the university – they don't give a damn what they hit.'

'You keep shifting ground,' Linda said. He'd killed that story stone dead – she couldn't possibly use it now. 'I thought you said you didn't think about the war?'

'That's right, I don't.' And he shut up, seemingly barely interested, until both girls had seen enough. For her part, Linda had decided that figuring out his motives was too tiring. It isn't that he's wrong about that bomber, she conceded. It's just that he has a different kind of thinking process. Now he'd gone back to the truck and she guessed he was getting himself a drink.

The sun was low in the sky as they started back. When they reached the town there were glints of light in the shops, even though a black-out was supposed to be in force. Near the magistrates' court a boy was selling *Jintian*, the local Chinese newspaper, and Linda stared curiously at the girl folding the paper into her briefcase. That was the second time she'd seen her in this street. What was her name? Kang? No. Miss Kuang of Pacific Press. Maybe she was living around here?

Reed drove through the market area to the waterfront, then turned off for the mission. When they reached the compound the children were playing under the single gnarled tree. Old Shu was seated on the steps, watching them. One child, the small girl who never spoke, was standing alone a short distance from the others.

Linda climbed down from the truck and walked round to Reed's side. 'It was good of you to take me.'

'I hope you enjoyed it.'

'Yes. It was nice to get out.' And she paused, not quite sure how to say it. He'd started the engine again, frowning to himself.

'I was a little bad-tempered. I'm sorry.'

'Women get broody.'

'Gracefully put.' She wished she hadn't bothered.

His frown deepened as he listened to the engine. 'Damned exhaust system needs renewing. Gotta go now.'

She watched the truck turn out of the gate. Broody!

Reed was thoughtful all the way back to Chen-chiang. There was enough daylight to get him ten miles without using the headlights. No part of the day had gone quite as he had expected. He couldn't say that his latest encounter with Linda Bishop had been an unqualified success. Why had he got himself into an argument over that Jap bomber crew? He groped under the fascia for the bottle of rye wrapped in a rag. One drink – that was all. And slightly worried about his need, he slid the bottle back. That would have to do until he reached the hotel.

It was nearly nine o'clock when he did, and dark. Waiters were discreetly clearing cutlery and preparing for tomorrow's breakfast, but they set a place for Reed.

The hotel was for birds of passage, like himself: Chinese, English, French, American, Danes. Even Russians, from the newly built airfield a few miles to the south-west. Their fighter planes were being trucked over the Gobi desert for the defence of Nanking – Stalin had an interest in seeing that the Japanese didn't win too easily. And framed portraits of the Generalissimo and Madame Chiang Kai-shek looked down from the dining room wall.

Reed ordered pineapple chicken, a soup, and a Chefoo beer to go with it.

There were only a few late diners in the room. Han Yu-lin, lieutenant and business expert to Dou and the Green Society, had a table to himself in the corner. Chopsticks poised, he frowned down at the *South China Daily Herald* opened and neatly folded by his plate.

A waiter hovered, noticing that Reed had finished the Chefoo beer. He gave up the struggle and ordered rye whisky.

Han Yu-lin was preoccupied with the business page. He

barely noticed Reed, and he'd lost interest in his meal. The price of gold had risen quite sharply. Rothschild were quoting 34.80 US dollars an ounce. He scanned further and noted the price of silver on the London Metal Exchange.

For thirty of his forty-six years, Han had been in the service of the Green Society. In his younger days he'd worked on the Shanghai streets: protection, extortion, cracking skulls for Dou. He'd made a little on the side and Dou had chastised him then used his business skills. For over a decade he'd been an administrator, and trusted in so far as the High Dragon trusted anybody.

A waiter brought rice wine. Han gestured to him to remove the remains of the meal and sat pondering the two tasks given him by Dou weeks before.

On his first visit to Nanking, he'd conveyed to the Generalissimo private assurances of support from Chinese bankers and merchants in Shanghai. A sum of thirty million dollars was agreed. Further visits, to Finance Minister Kung, had provided Han with opportunities for his second task: the transfer of Green Society bullion from banks along a possible line of Japanese advance up the delta. Su-chou, Wu-hsi, Ch'ang-chou. And now Chen-chiang – he'd removed it all. The figures were in his head, he committed little to paper. 3936 taels of silver and 906 of gold, safe now in the vaults of the Mercantile Bank of China on Nanking's Jianye Road.

Han was weary from his journeys. The railway service had deteriorated rapidly under the pressures of the war, and twice his trains had been strafed by Japanese fighter planes. Now that the second task was completed, he was free to return to Shanghai. But a sudden reluctance had overtaken him. And here in Chen-chiang, with communications disrupted, he had a breathing space. He was virtually out of Dou's reach – or so it seemed to him. The thought made him glance quickly round the dining room.

Han drank more than he would normally, enjoying the slight numbness of his head. The business page of the newspaper was still open on the table and the gold figure of

34.80 kept flickering across his thoughts. What of the silver? 3936 taels would weigh as much as two men. He calculated its worth at the London Metal Exchange price of twenty-two pence a troy ounce. Difficult to move – weight disproportionate to its value. But the gold? That was different.

Han scanned the room again, it was almost empty. Foreigners – the American who drank too much, and two worried oil men in deep discussion. A Chinese, neatly business-suited. Han studied him discreetly. He could never be sure that Dou hadn't planted somebody to watch him.

Thirty years, and he'd never seriously contemplated defection from the High Dragon's service. His life was comfortable; a small villa in Frenchtown Shanghai, a Packard automobile, a mistress young enough to be his daughter – she'd been a gift from Dou. Beautiful, educated in France, accomplished in the sensual arts – he'd suspected that she spied on him but accepted this as part of his life. And it was not burdensome. These days he was seldom asked to take physical risks. He could spend afternoons at the racetrack – aware that Dou knew how much he won or lost – and his evenings at Kafka's. But looking back, he couldn't remember when he'd last slept entirely at ease. There was always the risk of unforgivable error, or changes in the Society's power structure.

Han scribbled calculations on the margin of the newspaper. 906 taels of gold – approximately seventy-five pounds in weight. It was just portable. He speculated. In the normal flow of events the gold would be released only on the written authority of Dou. But there was a contingency plan agreed with Dr Kung. If Nanking was seriously threatened by the Japanese, Green Society deposits would be withdrawn from the vault of the Mercantile Bank of China and moved with government bullion to Hankow.

At 34.80 an ounce the 906 taels were worth forty-two thousand US dollars. There were places where a man could live out his life quite comfortably on such a sum. Not in

China of course, and Dou's agents would find him even in Saigon, Macao, or Manila. But America maybe? Or France – his mistress talked of Paris sometimes as though it were a dream city. Or England – Rothschild's figure for the London market was seven pounds six shillings and three pence an ounce.

He tore the margin from the newspaper and put it in his pocket. Obviously he had no real intention of defecting – the risks were terrifying. It was just a game to play inside his head. But the thought remained as he went up to his room. Supposing he could find a way of getting Dou's gold out of China?

CHAPTER ELEVEN

Only the mast and stern of *Fushan* showed above the high reeds. Tide low, the hull gently touched yellow silt. Russell woke and shivered.

Somebody was pumping – he could hear the rhythmic clank, and water gouting over the side. He stayed for just a moment more, sprawled face down on the aero engine crate. Smells of Lao's cooking mingled with the pervasive stench of stale fish, so it must be Tzu who was working the pump. How long had he been asleep? Russell turned his face and peered at his wristwatch. Four hours!

The axe was in his belt, digging into him as he rolled over onto his side. How could he have slept for four hours? He rubbed his rugged stubble of fair beard, and the wound under his eye twitched. I'm getting careless, he thought. Or maybe I'm just running out of steam. Usually, when it was his turn to rest he would just sit and doze, his back to the bulwark in the high stern so that he could wake and in the instant see down the length of the junk. I won't bloody well last out if Tzu sees that I sleep soundly. Now the white-haired Chinese seaman was coughing again and resting on the pump handle.

Far out in the river, Russell could see smoke from a ship's funnel. It was difficult to estimate *Fushan*'s position with accuracy – mile after mile of reeded shore and the villages all alike. The river had a sameness that disturbed. He frowned to himself and touched the scarred flesh under his eye and the twitching stopped. A damaged nerve maybe? He went towards the stern. Late yesterday the river had narrowed, both shorelines visible, and that should show on the map.

His movement disturbed the rat; long, nude tail, fast, it

126

scuttled over sacks. Russell pulled the axe from his belt and hurled it and, tail flicking, the rat disappeared into a gap in the planking.

Tzu laughed. 'Rat belongs – you no get him,' and he relapsed into another fit of coughing then spat. 'Ten years he live on junk. He get you first.'

Russell slid the axe back in his belt. 'They don't live that long.' But he didn't believe it. The rat knew each of them – knew when to run, knew when they were tired. It was as old as the devil.

'He get you, and Lao.' Tzu resumed pumping. 'He not get me.'

'As you say, old man.' No, the lung sickness would get Tzu – it was endemic among junk crewmen. Russell went to the sheltered part of the stern. Which was worse, rotten fish or the smell of Lao's cooking?

The boy was squatting on his heels by the paraffin burner. His shirt, bleached by the sun, was split across the shoulders. There was only one cooking pot and every meal had the same nauseous taste. 'Hash, so to speak.' He stirred the soggy grey mess with a flat stump of wood. 'You hungry?'

'Why don't you try leaving out the fish?'

'Fresh – Tzu catch it with line.'

'From the bottom of the river? – I'll bet it stank even as he pulled it out.' Bones, tail, even the head of the fish had probably gone into the pot. Russell rummaged and found the British Admiralty chart.

'Gives it flavour.'

Russell unrolled the chart. It was out of date, surveys made years before by a coast inspector of China Maritime Customs. He ran his finger across, finding the point where the river narrowed. They'd carefully avoided contact with other shipping. Wise, but they had no news. The previous night they'd seen lights of ships half a mile out, and later they'd heard boats running ashore at Paimou Inlet – he suspected that the Japanese had made another landing. Their purpose he could only guess at – to link up with Matsui's "Black" 9th pushing west from Shanghai? Maybe those Japs had moved parallel with them inland and were ahead somewhere. There was no precaution against that – except to keep *Fushan* going, at dusk and very early in the morning before the Japanese scout planes were active.

He left the chart and peered towards the far off northern shore through a gap in the reeds. 'Did you notice that the river is narrower?' If he'd guessed correctly there was a mud fort a few miles further on.

'We near village.' Lao drew the piece of wood from the pot and licked it. 'I hear girl call. Someone answer.'

'You should have woken me.'

'You need sleep. Better we get out of here.'

'Not yet.' Progress was painfully slow and he was anxious to put more miles between them and the Paimou Inlet, but there was still too much light. 'We'll wait for near sundown.'

The boy wrapped a rag round the iron handle and lifted the pot off the burner. 'Cooked now.' And he slopped the mess into three wooden bowls.

Tzu usually ate alone in the bows but today he stayed. 'Good!' He nodded approvingly. 'Needs more fish.'

Russell forced his down – there must, after all, be some food value in it. 'Old man, do you think we could manage eight miles?'

Tzu looked blank then scooped into his bowl with his fingers. Miles didn't mean much to him. 'Mud fort. We get there tonight, maybe.'

So he was right about that. Russell examined the sky. The high cloud was barely moving and the air was still. Hot season over, the temperature dropped rapidly near the end of the day. 'There's no wind. We'll have to use the diesel.'

Tzu looked around and sniffed. 'Wind come soon – first little, then much.'

'If you say so.' Tzu could tell hours before what the weather would do. He'd sailed with pirates when he was young and fit, and he knew the Yangtze, even the turbulent rapids above Ichang. 'We'll start as soon as the sun is low.'

Tzu licked his bowl. 'More money is due to me.'

More in his pocket and he'd desert – not that there was

any money to spare. 'I've told you, I have to save what we have to bribe our way round the boom at Chiang-yin. You'll get money when we reach Nanking.'

But the old man shook his head. 'More is due.'

'Why do you want money?' Lao scraped his bowl over the side. 'You are earning the gratitude of Mister Dou.'

Tzu recognized the veiled threat. He shrugged and went off to urinate in the river.

The sun was lower in the sky but it was still too early to move. 'Another twenty minutes,' Russell said. He took out the puzzle toy and frowningly tried to roll the ball bearing up the curved incline. What a stupid, soothing game. Why did Lao always win?

They took turns. Tzu watched, contemptuous. 'I know man in Foochow. He make things disappear.'

'I know man in Shanghai – a nobody, poor. He raise the dead.'

'I see man in Wu-hu – make lightning from his fingers.' But Tzu was lifting his shaggy head and listening. 'Boat!'

They lay quite still and waited, watching the river through the camouflage of reeds. After a while Russell heard faint splashing sounds. A girl paddled a sampan in the slack current near shore, and she paused, her small craft drifting as she looked at *Fushan*'s stern exposed. Then she paddled on.

Russell sighed slowly.

'Pretty.' Lao continued to watch her.

And Tzu wiggled his finger obscenely. 'River girls all the same.'

'She saw us and she'll tell somebody.' Russell stared at the sun still bright above the horizon. 'We'd better leave now.'

They used long bamboo poles to edge *Fushan* away from the reeds. It was heavy work with just three of them. Sweat stained Russell's ragged shirt. They needed the power of the huge Slav, Mazurov, left for dead in Shanghai's fairway. And Tzu was right, a breeze began rippling the surface of the water, so they unreefed the tattered sail, and Tzu took the tiller, steering them out into the broad expanse of the river. Nearly ten miles across at this point – you could lose a small junk easily. But Russell felt exposed, uneasy, wishing the sun would go down.

The breeze stiffened, swaying the high reeds, and a great flock of wild fowl lifted off. The worn sail strained. Russell kept checking the shore against the chart. He'd travelled in old Yun Tseng's junks many times along the river, but he'd never before concerned himself with the intricacies of navigation. Tzu had it all in his head, but Russell didn't trust him.

Water slopped along *Fushan*'s sides. Russell watched. He couldn't be sure that a Japanese gunboat wasn't somewhere ahead. Three – four days before, from their concealment in the reeds, they'd seen the *Kotaka*, grey, large, sister ship of the *Atami*, steaming up river. Lao came and squatted next to him. 'We reach Nanking soon?'

'Two weeks.' Russell thought for a moment. 'Maybe a little longer – it depends on what awaits us.' There was the boom to cross or get round. Maybe the approaches were mined? His gut stirred, ready to ache again. I'll worry about the boom when we get there, he told himself.

He'd been worried all his life. Mostly about nothing of real importance – he'd come to see that since trusting his life to the rotting timbers of *Fushan*. And he suddenly remembered the darkness – he'd worried about that as a boy, hiding a candle and a match under his bed. Fear was a shameful thing – grandfather found it and laid into him with a stick. The grammar school – now *there* was a worry. And having a bad limp and what the other kids shouted. It had been worry about failure after going to work for the City tea importer. Night school to study book-keeping and accounts – I never had the nerve to do anything more enterprising, he thought. Accepting the offer to work in the Shanghai branch had been a huge step – how did I ever make it against grandfather's predictions of failure? I should have pushed that drunken old man down the stairs, it would have been no great loss to the world.

Lao watched another junk far off to their right. 'Nanking as big as Shanghai?'

'No, not as big. Where did you learn to speak English?'

130

'I pick it up.' The boy shrugged. 'Yates Road jail. I was little. They make me servant to governor's missis – she was Jesus lady.' He grinned and sang –

> And we shall dwell, when life is past,
> With angels round Thy throne at last.

'Marvellous.'

'I know prayers to God Almighty.'

'Good. You can say one for me. What else did you learn?'

'Read and write more or less. Look after Jesus Lady's kids.'

'She must have been very trusting.' Russell scanned for red marker buoys where he thought the chart indicated that the bank had extended.

'Learn to cook.'

'She didn't teach you very well.'

'Food damn good. How we get back to Shanghai?'

'I don't know. We may not be able to for a while. Does it matter to you?'

The boy shrugged. 'I have girl so to speak. Nice – not brothel girl. She work as servant in Han Yu-lin's house.'

'Han – Dou's business man?'

'Yes.'

'I'll do my best to see you get back to Shanghai, if that's what you want.'

'You have woman in Shanghai, Russell?'

'No.' He'd had one once, afraid all the time of losing her because of his limp. 'No woman.' The last time he'd seen her she was riding along Bubbling Well Road in a Daimler. Being made to feel ridiculous was an effective antidote to love – if that's what it had been. It was just after that brief glimpse of her that he'd entered the service of Yun Tseng. And it was odd. That old Chinese had been like the father he'd never had. 'Never let a woman possess you, Russell. *Buy* one for what you need. They use their bodies because they have little minds. They do not have souls.' And where was the old man now? Body smashed – thin bones broken like sticks. He was maybe sailing some other, far off sea.

131

'Go and make us more tea, Lao.'

'You bet.'

'And boil the bloody water this time.'

A little wind, then more, just as Tzu had said. The mast was bending – two hundredweight of spar and stretched sail depended on it. They were doing well. Another ten minutes or so and the sky would darken – they'd be safe again. The river curved, he could see a small village on the point. The mud fort should be on the left bank.

Wind flecked the water. He could hear a noise from further on – like a wasp. What the hell was that sound? Tzu was high in the stern and he waved and shouted.

A white floatplane appeared from round the point, flying low over the river and straight towards the junk. Russell stared and his mouth went dry. Japanese! 'Turn to the shore!'

They were half a mile or more from the protection of the reeds and *Fushan* lost momentum as they turned. Russell ran to the diesel but Lao was already trying to start it.

The floatplane climbed and turned.

'They've seen us!' Russell seized the crank. He jerked it and the engine coughed, then stopped. The plane snarled past only a few feet off the water, and the observer was peering down at the junk's deck cargo. It went out of sight beyond the bend – wasp sound receding. And then it came back, the deep red glow of sunset on the underside of its wings.

'They're going to attack!' Russell hauled on the crank again and the engine began its reluctant thumping tempo.

The plane snarled in low, its single forward gun firing, and the pilot kicked the rudder from side to side, steering the stream of bullets into *Fushan*'s rotting timbers and splintering the wooden cases. Russell opened the throttle wide. He heard Tzu's harsh cry as sail and battens crashed down.

Sodden sail canvas dragged in the river. Tzu had abandoned the tiller and the junk slewed round in a half circle.

Russell shouted to Lao, 'Get Tzu steering again then go

back to the diesel.' He pulled the axe from his belt and began hacking at the tumbled mass of rigging. Please, Shang Di, don't let us heel over.

Tzu was doubled over but the boy kicked and shrieked at him. 'Get up! Dou will tear out your heart!' And he went on kicking him until he took the tiller again.

The Japanese seaplane came at them once more before *Fushan*'s churning propeller drove them straight into the shore. The bottom scraped sand and Lao shut off the engine. Frantically they dragged armfuls of reeds over the junk's sides to disguise its shape. Tzu was shouting and coughing. 'Take me to village!' Trailing blood, he crawled across to the diesel and tried to crank it.

Russell hauled down more reeds. 'Go and help him.'

'Goddam right – I fix.'

The plane flew back, banked, turned, but daylight was fading and after a while it climbed steadily towards the darkening eastern sky.

Russell sank down on the deck. They knew what they were looking for – murdering bastards. The junk was a shambles of fallen rigging and shattered timber. Then he remembered Tzu.

The old pirate was stretched out on his side, like a dog run down in the street. One scarlet hand grasped the diesel crank. He was quite still, skull split open and blood and flecks of brain seeped from the hole. Lao stood over him with the axe.

'For God's sake! Why did you do that to him?'

'Merciful release so to speak.' The boy wiped the axe on the dead man's trousers.

'Maybe we could have saved him!'

'No. Tzu hurt too bad – make trouble for us.'

Right, of course. Tzu would have betrayed them for money if he could. And what would they do for a man wounded in the stomach? Russell stared at Lao and a doubt began to crawl across his thoughts. Perhaps the huge Slav, dumped overboard at Shanghai, wasn't the appointed executioner after all?

'We manage.' The boy was watching his face and he handed him the axe. 'You safe right now. We both safe.'

Russell slid the axe in his belt. 'We'd better get rid of Tzu.'

The dead man was light; skin, bone and sinew. Had Tzu speculated about his own end? Maybe this was better than slowly coughing up bits of his lungs. Every life is complete, fulfilled in its own way. Russell lifted the head and shoulders and Lao let the legs slide over the side. The small red eyes of the rat watched from a dark recess. Tzu's body plunged among the reeds but the split head remained above water, mouth open, as though the old pirate was about to ask for more money. Lao pushed down hard on the face until bubbles ceased popping to the surface.

To the west a blood red line streaked the skyline and already stars were appearing above *Fushan*'s broken mast. What the hell am I doing here in a place so unnatural to me? Russell wondered.

The boy rubbed his hands on his trousers. 'I make tea.'

At Paimou Inlet, eighteen miles down river from where *Fushan* rested, Japanese troops had made a landing the night before. They moved westward, with the river to their right and General Matsui's "Black" 9th Division far to their left. As dusk came the path of the 9th Division was clearly marked by long, red smears along the horizon.

The 9th had burned every town and village along their route, from Ta-ch'ang in the Shanghai suburbs to Ch'ang-shu – Sergeant Kimura had lost count of how many. His was one of the forward and flanking companies, thrust out like a shield around the head of the division. His clothes stank of sweat and smoke, and he was weary.

Here was a good place to rest. Kimura walked through the thin grove of trees. Twenty-four hours – they needed that time to kill the lice and wash their clothes. He'd been in the army since he was twenty, first as a conscript then eight years as a regular, and he could recognize clear signs of stress throughout the company.

Kimura began his nightly inspection of the rifles. 'Clean it. Oil it. Your rifle is your best friend.'

All of us disgraced last year. Kimura found a rifle with a soiled breach and he cuffed the man's head. Thirty per cent casualties among us, the highest in the division. It has made us fatalistic, and barbaric. Assigned first in attack after attack, how long before our disgrace is erased?

Kimura's inspection of the rifles was interrupted by a summons to the company commander, Captain Hashimoto. To confirm their rest? Kimura wanted to believe that, but as he returned through the grove of trees he was aware of a small foreboding. Hashimoto was a man of enormous vanity. He'd served under the captain in Manchuria, then followed him recklessly into the army mutiny last year – they'd brought Tokyo to a stop for four days. A piece of madness.

A dimmed storm lantern illumined the interior of the tent. Hashimoto was stripped to the waist, washing in a canvas bucket – a fastidious man with an eye for the girls. Water dripped from his moustache. 'At ease. Have you eaten?'

'Yes, sir.'

Hashimoto rubbed his face with a towel. 'And you are rested?'

Such concern for his well being? Kimura felt wary, more so when Hashimoto offered him a cigarette. He took it, bowed, and put it in his pocket.

'We must look after each other, Kimura, for the girls back home.' It was the captain's habitual joke, intended to secure the bond between them. They were both thirty-one years old and had joined the army the same year. And they were both from the same city, though Kimura was from waterfront slums and Captain Hashimoto's family owned a fish canning factory.

'Battle fever has propelled us this far, Kimura, but the men need something to lift their morale. Morale is of paramount importance.'

Kimura maintained an expression of polite interest,

135

wondering if he had been summoned for another lecture in psychology. The captain interested him – he even felt grudging respect, but he didn't understand him.

' . . . so we are entered into a contest – a race . . .'

Kimura's foreboding sharpened.

'A display of extraordinary endurance and courage will clear us of disgrace. I have issued a challenge to the company commanders of the entire regiment. Our honour is at stake, Kimura. We must be the first unit to reach the second stop line.'

Kimura stared. 'Sir, the second stop line is at Hsia-kang, seventy miles away.'

'Sixty-seven. We must move rapidly. You may be sure that General Matsui will be watching with great interest. Tell the men to be ready to move an hour before dawn.'

Pointless to question the order, Hashimoto was hungry for prestige. Kimura saluted and went out into the night. What were the odds now? He was weary of calculating them.

CHAPTER TWELVE

From the window of the mission washroom, Peggy could see gulls – twenty-five, maybe thirty of them spinning on the wind. As if on a signal they abruptly alighted, crowding along the apex of the Yashima warehouse just beyond the compound wall. Arch should arrive in – what? – about two hours. The reminder brought a fresh wave of anxiety. She sunk her hands into the large sink and began scrubbing again; children's clothes, towels, sheets.

The washroom had become a morning refuge, out of the way of Foster – he frightened her a little. And Linda didn't look in all that often, Peggy had noticed. Linda wasn't particularly domesticated and had a barely concealed distaste for anything soiled.

The wringer was old and clumsy. Peggy cursed Foster softly as her fingers caught in the rollers. Always salvaging – he must have found this bloody thing in the river.

Two long cords were strung out between the wall of the washhouse and the single, gnarled tree. Peggy hung wet sheets next to already drying shirts and stood back. There was solid satisfaction in a line of clean washing, she thought. Inside the bungalow Linda's typewriter was clicking, and there were soft sounds of digging beyond the corner of the bungalow. Foster's two garden boys had been hard at it since eight o'clock in the morning. They were digging slit trenches in readiness for the long-awaited air raid.

Hsia-kang hadn't been bombed yet, though Chiang-yin to the east and Shen-kang ten miles south were both left burning the previous week. Mayling said it was because the Japanese had an important spy in the town and didn't want

137

him hurt. Peggy pushed back a strand of damp hair and looked up at the sky.

Almost every day enemy squadrons passed over, usually on their way to Nanking. They came back, formations less tight sometimes where the Chinese fighter planes had thinned them out. At least she didn't have to worry about Arch up there today.

The sounds of digging ceased for a moment then began again. Gerald Foster came round the side of the building. He seemed in a hurry. But then he always was.

'Ah, Mrs Rittenhouse – I'm glad I've found you. We now have two slit trenches near completion. I fear there is already a little water in them but they should offer us protection.' He glanced at the line of washing, eyes resting fractionally on Peggy's underclothes, and he looked quickly away. 'If the warning should sound you must go immediately to the nearest trench and take shelter.'

'I'll certainly do that.'

He nodded and looked at the gulls swept up on the wind. 'It's fine drying weather – you've done well today. And your husband – he arrives early this afternoon?'

'Yes. He said he was catching the CNAC flight to Ch'ang-chou.'

'Be sure that you tell Shu – she will set an extra place for dinner.'

'It's very good of you. I don't know how long Arch will be able to stay.'

'He will surely want to eat. You're looking tired, Mrs Rittenhouse. Are you well?'

'I'm fine.' She started unpegging some of the dry clothes because it allowed her to move away from him. 'Honestly, I feel fine.'

'I'm glad to hear that.'

'And I'll certainly remind Shu about an extra place for dinner. Thanks again.'

He stared at her, expressionless. 'Don't work too hard, Mrs Rittenhouse.' And he turned and went into the bungalow.

Foster was clearly a good man, though a bit cold. Why is it that I don't like him near me? she wondered.

Anxiety over Arch's impending arrival was getting to her again. She sought out Linda in the study.

'Give me five more minutes.' Linda looked up then down again.

But Peggy was too nervous to keep quiet. 'Wu Guo says Dr Foster's wife swallowed morphine.'

Linda frowned slightly.

'That's how she *did* it.'

'Did what?'

'Killed herself.' Peggy watched Linda. 'I envy you, love. I was never clever. At school I couldn't spell. Or multiply. Seven times eight – that used to throw me into a panic.' She knew that Linda wasn't really listening. 'Fifty-four.'

'What?'

'Seven times eight.'

'It's fifty-six. But you're good with children – much better than me.'

Peggy stretched out an elegant leg and examined it critically. 'I was a passable dancer.' Good, in fact, though never good enough for a West End show. Good enough for a professional company touring Midlands towns. "Cheryl's Girls". Always on the move, cheap boarding houses and low pay. 'We did a whole year in Australia – clap anything there, they would, providing the costumes leave nothing to the imagination. Then we went to Jamaica – can you imagine that!' An exciting life at twenty, but getting flat and stale at twenty-eight and your figure going a bit.

Linda looked up. 'I've nearly finished.'

'Don't hurry. I'm fine.'

Peggy rose and went to the window. 'You ever think that your life is sort of shaped by chance?'

'It's crossed my mind a couple of times.'

'I mean, there we were in Kingstown and the nightclub went bankrupt – the owner had been speculating in bananas and we had the biggest all time glut that year – they were letting them rot. We didn't even have the fare home. And

139

somebody said "Let's see if we can get a work permit for Cuba, it's only a hundred miles." And I said "Okay" – just like that, on the spur of the moment. So five of us went in the end. If I'd had the fare home I wouldn't have gone. And I wouldn't have met Arch and Frank Reed bootlegging. Funny, isn't it? – the way things turn out.'

'Yes.' Linda stared at her. 'It's funny.' Then she briskly pulled the typed page from the machine and read a fragment aloud.

'"But we break no international treaty if we respond to the overwhelming needs of ordinary Chinese people. Drugs, ambulances, trained medical personnel. For the immediate future these will be more important to China than our particular brands of evangelicalism and education."' She stared at it for a moment. 'It's not what the committee in Chicago wants, but I'm beginning to think I can't write that other kind of stuff any more. What do you bet they'll replace me?'

'You've asked me that three times in three days. Do you really want to stay here?'

Linda frowned. 'I suppose it would be a relief if the committee orders me home. But the war's getting closer and I'd feel like a deserter.'

'Deserter? From what? What a crazy idea. This isn't our war. Japan is nothing to us.' Linda was difficult to understand sometimes – always getting impassioned or angry about things.

Linda was sealing the article in an envelope. 'I'll post this when I go to the cable office. Arch arriving soon?'

There was that surge of anxiety again. 'Yes. I'd better go and make myself beautiful.'

She'd nearly reached the door and Linda called to her. 'Are you *very* nervous?'

'Yes.' And she shrugged. 'Habit.'

'Remember, *you* have rights as well as Arch.'

Linda tidied the desk for Gerald Foster and put the cover back on her typewriter. New resolution – I'm going to stop giving useless advice. Peggy will do what she has to do, and reasoned argument just doesn't enter into it. This was a tendency Linda noted in others but as yet failed to see in herself.

She went to Mayling for her daily lesson. Mayling had the small, withdrawn, orphan girl on her lap. She wrote Chinese characters and made Linda copy them.

'Post office?'

'No, no!' Mayling laughed. 'Journalist. Like you.'

It was incomprehensible. Each character was a little picture. She could now haltingly ask for basic things in shops, and sometimes grasp fragments of conversation, but the language was beyond her. And I'm not used to feeling stupid, she thought. It's a lesson in humility.

Halfway through the hour she heard movement, and voices in the passageway outside – one unfamiliar.

Arch Rittenhouse had arrived.

She was filled with curiosity, but continued copying the strange symbols and repeating back words to Mayling until the lesson was over. And for God's sake why do I feel nervous at the idea of meeting Arch Rittenhouse? He's nothing to me – just another man who takes and gives little back.

There was a leather hold-all in the passageway, bulky, scuffed, decorated with fading steamship and air line stickers, and an officer's peaked cap with the blue and white sun badge of the Kuomintang army had fallen from the hatstand. Raffish, the wire had been taken out of the crown. Linda picked it up and looked at it, then hung it on a hook. And in the strange way of things her image of Arch was already changing. She was suddenly aware of her shapeless sweater and baggy slacks. Damn it! she told herself, I don't care what he thinks of me, and she went into the room.

He was seated with his back to the door, and Peggy and Foster were facing him. Linda was immediately aware of the largeness.

So this was Arch; flyer, war hero, thorn in the flesh of American bureaucracy. And impotent?

'The roads are full of refugees. I counted six dead on the

way from Ch'ang-chou – stripped of everything. I guess the poor devils died of exhaustion. What's your impression of the local situation, Dr Foster?'

Even Foster seemed a little wary of Arch. 'The central armies are still intact and they are between us and the Japanese. I think Hsia-kang is safe for the time being.' He looked round and saw Linda. 'Captain Rittenhouse, you haven't met our other guest.'

Arch stood and held out his hand. His bulk was alarming. 'I've heard a great deal about you, Miss Bishop – from Peggy.' And he bowed, an almost quaint, outmoded gesture that surprised her. Then he sat and resumed the conversation with Foster.

'The regular army on the central front is being reinforced with peasant militia recruited a thousand miles to the west – have you seen them, doctor? Half die before they ever meet a Japanese. As soldiers I would put no faith in them. I can't see that the delta can be held.' He took a silver cigarette case from his tunic pocket. It was large, ornate, slightly vulgar. Peggy must have bought it for him, Linda thought.

'Assuming the Chinese continue their present strategy of trading space for time, I would think you have a couple of weeks.' He frowned and lit the cigarette. 'That's just nice time to arrange your departure.'

'I'm a little more optimistic, captain.' Foster stroked his white hair. 'The Japanese have said they only want a settlement of the Shanghai matter. I can't see them pushing this far. What would be the point?'

Arch nodded politely, and Linda had the strongest impression that he was one of those people who are quite sure of their opinions and merely go through the motions of consensus by debate.

'Even if the Japanese army fails to advance this far, their air force will bomb all these towns. I'm grateful to you, Dr Foster, for looking after Peggy, but I want her to go home to the States for a while.'

'America isn't home for me.' Peggy stared angrily at him. 'I won't go without you, Arch.'

142

'I can't leave, Peggy, you know that. Neither can you stay here. And Nanking is a worse proposition because of the daily bombing. So it's either the States, or south to British Hong-kong – I could maybe get down to see you from time to time.'

'But you wouldn't!' Peggy's mouth tightened. 'All these weeks before you could get *this* far!' She stood and began putting tea things on the tray. 'We both know I'd never see you if I'm in Hong-kong.'

Arch leaned back in the chair, resting his head and briefly closing his eyes. He was very tired – Linda experienced a sudden, puzling shift in perspective.

'We have to weigh what we want against what is possible, Peggy. If you go to Hong-kong you could stay with Harry and Martha – you like them.' And he stopped abruptly. 'We'll talk about it later.'

Peggy was tight-lipped, picking up the tray. 'Yes, we'll talk about it later.' And she went out to the kitchen. Foster frowned at his hands. Linda tried to think of a not too obvious reason for going to her room.

'I'm scheduled for stand-by first thing tomorrow.' Arch was still leaning back, like a man used to seizing what rest he could. 'But I guess I'd better stay overnight if I may, doctor?'

'You are of course welcome.'

Arch rose to his feet and the room seemed too small for him. 'Who has a telephone? I'll have to let the base know what I'm doing.'

'There's a phone at the cable office – that's probably the nearest.'

'I'll show you the way,' Linda added quickly. 'I was going there anyway.'

He nodded. 'Give me a few minutes with Peg, will you?'

Linda went to her room to change – she could hear Arch and Peggy arguing softly in the next room. She put on a shirt, and a jumper because the weather was turning cooler. And should she wear high heels? Yes. She didn't want to crane her neck looking up at Arch Rittenhouse.

She waited on the verandah. He came down a few

143

minutes later, pulling on the crushed peaked cap and adjusting it at a slight angle – a barely conscious gesture.

They followed the narrow street past the deserted Yashima warehouse. Children were playing a game with smooth pebbles but they ran screeching to Arch and begged for coins. He took out his loose change and scattered it.

Linda had begun to regret her offer to act as guide. She didn't know what to say to him, so she didn't say anything. Only sixty paces separated the mission from the Taoist temple – its stone tiger and dragon deities stared at the street. The front area was swept clean of rubbish and animal droppings. An elderly black-gowned monk sat under the eaves. His hair was done up on top of his head with a shuttle of wood. He dozed, eyes half closed, but nodded as they passed him. '*Ni hao.*'

'*Ni hao.*'

'You ever go in there, Miss Bishop?' Arch glanced back.

'Not yet.'

'Why? Does it scare you?'

'Certainly not!' She'd seen two Westerners trying to pose the old monk for their snapshots. They'd talked too loudly and made her feel ashamed to be white. 'I'm just not too sure that we should intrude, that's all.' She paused, regretting that she'd said something that might prompt Arch into argument but impelled now to go on. 'Dr Foster says Chinese religion has disintegrated into mere superstition – I'm not sure about that either.'

Arch didn't answer.

Some people had a way of gaining an advantage just by keeping quiet.

Wrong. Arch was thinking. He looked up at high cirrus streaking the clear blue. 'Those clouds are made of ice crystals. Or perhaps they are the thoughts of God. Which would you prefer to believe?'

The question surprised her. But he went on without waiting for an answer. 'Taoists deal in mysteries. Who wants a world that can be completely explained? Are you staying on in Hsia-kang, Miss Bishop?'

'Staying on?' She was still trying to catch up with clouds and the thoughts of God. 'I don't know. I'm expecting instructions from the mission committee in Chicago. I suppose you think I should go home?'

He tilted his head, looking down at her. 'Not necessarily.'

'But you think Peggy should go back to America.'

'You're a free agent. I'm responsible for Peg's safety – she was already on the boat when troubled flared up in Shanghai otherwise I would have stopped her.'

Was that what Peggy was to him – a responsibility? Somebody to be packed off to a place of safety while he got on with his own life?

They'd turned off at Yibai Street at right angles to the river. It was the town's spine, lined with shops, the only street with paving. A rain water drain ran under the uneven slabs and gushed into the Yangtze. Arch paused, briefly interested in a potter squatting outside his shop, then he walked on. Linda nursed her indignation. Peggy had dragged five thousand miles to be with this arrogant ox, and he just wanted to be rid of her. He hadn't even thought to buy her a present.

Wrong again.

An elderly Chinese was cutting leather on a block. There were belts, bags and sandals hanging from bamboo poles, and Arch was examining the workmanship. After a few minutes' deliberation he picked out the handbag that Linda would have chosen for herself. 'How much?'

The old man pushed his wire-rimmed glasses up on his forehead and fingered the bag. 'Twenty-five dollar.'

'Fifteen.'

Linda watched Arch haggle then settle for twenty-one. He looked awkward holding the bag in his large hand.

'I'll carry it.' She adjusted the strap to fit over her shoulder. 'Peggy will like it.' Though it isn't the one that Peggy would have picked. She wondered again at the mismatch of Peggy and Arch.

They reached the cable office and it was crowded. Arch waited to use the single telephone booth and Linda joined the slow-moving queue for the counter, refugees, most of them. The air was foul. A young woman turned away from the counter and Linda recognized her – the Chinese girl from Pacific Press Service. Miss Kuang saw her but gave no sign as she edged her way out.

Government proclamations covered the walls, and some carried quaint English and French translations:

The Nationalist Government of the Republic of China politely warns that river passengers proceed in an easterly direction at their own risk. Enemy mines have erupted the vessels of many flags.

Were Chinese mines less impartial? She reached the counter and the clerk began thumbing through cable forms awaiting delivery.

It never ceased to amaze Linda that a cable should actually reach her here in Hsia-kang, though in fact the Chinese postal and cable services were remarkably efficient. Her hands trembled slightly as she took the form and went out to the street to read it. Arch was waiting.

'What does it say?'

'"Return home via Hong-kong."' She bit her lip. 'They couldn't make it plainer.'

It wasn't just the blow to her ego. There's a contrariness in human nature, she thought. Last night, unable to sleep, she'd half hoped for a good excuse to go home. But now, ordered to return, she knew for sure that she wanted to stay. 'I wrote some good stuff for them.' She began walking. 'Even though it wasn't exactly what they wanted.'

He adjusted his step to hers. 'You could stay and write for somebody else.'

Freelancing in this vast, alien country? 'The consul wants me out as well.'

'And you don't have to do as he says.'

Not if you're Arch Rittenhouse. He'd taken her arm, steering her out of the path of an ancient, open-topped automobile. A British naval officer off the gunboat, *Aphis*, was seated in the rear. He glanced first at her legs, then at

146

Arch. And Linda felt a sudden, surprised satisfaction. Arch was bigger than any man they passed.

He released her arm. 'Do you mind telling me why you don't want to go home, Miss Bishop?'

'I'm a writer, it's as simple as that.' Even as she said it she knew that that was only a part of it. Life was short. The ugly scar, curving round her bowels and bladder was a permanent reminder of time seemingly squandered. What had she done up till then? Nothing. 'Ernest Hemingway says you can't be a writer until you've been in a war. I want to write about something important – worth while . . .' Her mind groped then she let the thought tail off. 'Is your excuse for being here any better?'

His shrug implied a world of difference. 'I'm a professional. And I don't have time to be too introspective about what I do.'

He'd made her motives seem small and she felt stung. 'But you're just a mercenary – a man who kills for his pay.'

'There was a time when the profession of mercenary was considered honourable.'

'Hardly so today. And how does Peggy fit into this medieval notion?'

But Arch had paused, frowning up at the sky.

'What is it?'

He shook his head. 'Listen.'

Linda could hear only the sounds of the street: pedlars, children, a trundling, wooden-wheeled cart. Then a sudden awful roar. A twin-engined bomber streaked low over the houses. Bright red disc markings on the wings – it was trying to evade a fighter plane close behind it. The noise was terrifying, and Arch pushed her into a doorway and hunched over her as the first bomb shrieked down. The earth shook and she knew she was mortal, clutching Arch as two more bombs rocked the houses.

The planes were gone as suddenly as they had appeared.

Glass tinkled and bit of debris clattered down. Somebody shouted. A brief, awful jolt, and then the world was back to normal again.

147

'It's okay.' Arch held her, and she was aware of the leather smell of his jacket, and the pressure of him, and her own heart thumping.

Slowly she let go of his shoulders. But he held her for a moment longer, then stood back, staring at her. 'It was just a stray. Unloaded its bombs to gain height – I doubt if it will reach the coast. Are you all right, Miss Bishop?'

'Yes, I'm all right.' Her arms felt bruised. It was his hands, she thought. Smoke was rising over warehouses on the waterfront – the other two bombs had fallen in the river. 'We should get back to the mission.'

'Yes. They'll be worried.' He continued to stare at her. 'Peg will be worried.'

And now he is aware of me, Linda thought as she turned away. That's what I wanted of him all along.

They hurried past the Taoist temple. Corrugated iron sheeting, lifted by the blast from the Yashima warehouse roof, littered the narrow winding street. She felt no reluctance as he took her hand to help her over them.

'It must be awful in Nanking – bombed every day.' A brief smile of thanks and she released his hand.

'You become accustomed to it,' he said.

'Even so, it must drain you.' Words. Words unrelated to what was going on inside her head. I'd forgotten that feeling of knowing I'm alive. I'd forgotten what it's like to have a man want me.

CHAPTER THIRTEEN

The wooden slums burned easily at this time of the year. Smoke irritated Sergeant Kimura's eyes. He could feel the heat from the blazing row of shops, and showers of sparks flew up into the night as a roof collapsed. The town had fallen to them without a shot being fired, gates left wide open. Ishiwara's company had found some of the people hiding in the fields, but the provincial levies and most of Chu-tang's population had fled at the approach of advanced units of the "Black" 9th. Our reputation goes before us, Kimura thought, and that is all to the good. He would rather they reached and took Nanking without a fight, but he knew it would not be like that.

The air shimmered in the heat.

The street was deserted, just Kimura, and the angry crackling of flames. He could hear men shouting, and in gaps between the houses he caught glimpses of them. They stumbled around under piles of loot – discipline was getting slack in some companies.

A thin, scabrous dog followed him at a safe distance, frightened by the fierce transformation of the town. Kimura's bowels churned again and he felt a wave of nausea.

The men of his company were gathered at the intersection of the two main streets. Some were asleep where they squatted. He called them to attention and they formed up in three ragged lines for his roll call. The mangy dog, exhausted, went down on its belly and watched, whining softly. Near dawn, sky still dark. Kimura could have read off the company roll by the red glow from the burning warehouse, but he knew all the names by heart. Two men were slightly drunk and overburdened, their tunics stuffed with cheap rubbish they'd stolen. Kimura took it from them and threw it aside. 'You want something to carry to Nanking? I will find you something.' And he gave one the heavy 7.7 machine gun and the other a box of ammunition. The men of the company laughed.

'We await the captain.' Kimura stared around. His gut stirred once more – it was the dried fish they'd eaten, his had tasted sour. He gave the order for the men to break off but told them to stay put. Captain Hashimoto had said they were to move off earlier than the other units, but that was before he'd found the girl.

Imperative necessity forced Kimura to cross the street and enter a ruined house. He relieved himself, emptying his bowels. He groaned softly then pulled up his trousers and returned to the men. Still no sign of the captain. They squatted and smoked – some of the younger ones had again fallen asleep. To the east the first pale light revealed the skyline. Kimura left the company and went to the house where Captain Hashimoto and Lieutenant Kadota had taken the girl.

Hashimoto was pulling on his boots. 'I hope you have rested, Kimura, we have a hard day ahead of us.'

The girl appeared to be asleep.

'We are ready to move, sir.'

'Have we rations enough?' Hashimoto splashed water into a bowl and soaked his face and hands. 'We are well ahead of the main column – they will be unable to keep us supplied.'

'Each man has enough rice for three days, sir, and I have checked their water bottles. I have also redistributed the available ammunition – there is sufficient.'

'You are a good NCO, Kimura.' Captain Hashimoto paused and listened, head tilted. 'Our bombers.' He smiled and slapped Kimura's shoulder. 'We'll win this war in three months. Bring my map case.' And he strapped on his sword and revolver as he left the room.

Kimura heard the bombers droning over. He was curious and pulled the blanket from off the girl. She was naked, face bruised, and she stared up at him with terrified eyes. He threw the blanket back over her and walked out.

*

150

The Japanese bombers attacked Chen-chiang early in the morning with the sun behind them as they arrived. Twenty minutes and it was all over. Soldiers were digging in the new mounds of debris, and there were fire hoses strung out all over the city.

The raids were beginning to affect the hotels. There wasn't enough fresh food, and electricity was off for much of the day. Han Yu-lin prodded at the breakfast set before him – it was barely cooked. High in the service of the Green Society, he was accustomed to good living and the indifferent meals filled him with distaste. He pretended to eat but watched the door, waiting for the American, Reed.

The windows were boarded over since blast from the bomb in Kiangsu Road had shattered all the glass, and now with broad daylight outside the dining room was unnaturally lit by dozens of candles. Few of the tables were in use. There were still Western oilmen and engineers hanging on, and earnest looking members of relief agencies. The tall Swede with a Red Cross armband; a Belgian priest seated with the Australian; and there were two Danes in dark suits – Han had discovered that they were arms salesmen, he made it his business to find out about people. And where was Reed? Sleeping off an excess of drink perhaps. Han poked the breakfast again then gave up in disgust and turned to the newspaper.

It was really just a double sheet, hastily printed and full of type errors – the newspaper offices had been bombed last week. The Generalissimo's speech was reported word for word – Japan's advance would be broken, there could be no alternative to eventual victory. It had ceased to interest Han.

He had bought a map – it was tucked inside the double news sheet. Until yesterday stealing the Green Society gold and defection from Dou's service had been an elaborate fantasy – strong enough to delay his return to Shanghai but not hardened sufficiently to impel a decision. Purchasing the map had been the first concrete step along that path, and if Dou so much as suspected . . . Han hastily suppressed the thought.

Yesterday, the idea of escape had begun to seem too dangerous. He'd gone to the bookshop in Flower Market Street and asked for maps. South to Wencheng, clearly that was the way he would have to go, and then a coastal junk to Shanghai. But the old shopkeeper had mistakenly unrolled the wrong map. Fukien province. And there it was: Foochow, the seaport on which his fantasy had pivoted. It must be an omen. He knew in that moment that he must commit himself to escape or forget it forever. He'd made polite conversation, discreetly inserting identifying phrases, until he was certain that the old man was not a member of the Greens, then he'd bought the map. The decision was made.

Han looked towards the door again. Why hadn't the American come for his breakfast? He opened the news sheet and cautiously examined the folded map. Within the period of transfer of government bullion there would be the better part of one day to help himself to 906 taels of gold – it was all stored together in the vault of the Mercantile Bank of China in Nanking. He'd thought it through very carefully. Before Dou could learn what he had done, he would be on his way to Foochow. A new identity, and he would go to Europe, or possibly America, nothing to connect him with his past.

Han adjusted the cuffs of his shirt. Gold studs on soft linen. His suit was immaculately cut and padded to give his slight build a suggestion of bulk. After years as financial adviser to Dou he would be able to pass himself off quite easily as a businessman. Businessmen were, after all, gangsters in good clothes who arranged for others to do their dirty work. For a long time now Han's dealings with businessmen had been elaborately formal. Not so in those early years when he'd dispensed terror for Dou. He remembered the Su-chou banker: soft-fleshed, fat and vomiting as they'd unwrapped the mallet and bamboo stake and placed them on his desk. That was years ago. Now Han was respectable.

He glanced up quickly.

Reed was walking across the dining room to his usual table. Eyes puffy, it was obvious that he had a hangover. Han recognized tell-tale signs. Lack of concentration – Reed was staring blankly at the menu. Now he'd closed his eyes and was touching one eyebrow with his fingertips. Han watched with amused contempt. He delayed until the waiter brought coffee to Reed, then he rose and crossed to him.

'Mr Reed. May I join you?'

Reed blinked and focused. 'It's supposed to be a free country. You do what the hell you like.'

Han smiled. It was difficult to adjust to the directness of Americans, but then they had no culture of their own. Han sat in a chair that allowed him a view of the doorway. 'I would prefer not to be seen talking to you, Mr Reed, so I will say quickly what I have to say. In the not too far distant future I will need an aeroplane – a private aeroplane – to take me on a journey from Nanking.'

'I don't fly any more.'

'I am prepared to offer a substantial sum.' Han noted the flicker of interest in the American's eyes.

'Just supposing we had an aeroplane, where do you want to go and what sort of substantial sum are we talking about?'

Promise him anything – I'd never pay him, Han thought. 'I will give you 5,000 American dollars for my safe arrival in Foochow.' And he smiled. Now he had the foreign devil's undivided attention.

Reed sipped his coffee. 'I assume that for that kind of money we would have no official authorization for being in the Foochow area with a floatplane. Why do you want to go there?'

'My reasons need not concern you, Mr Reed.'

Reed shrugged. 'The plane we are talking about belongs to China Petroleum. I merely service it.'

Han sighed inwardly. Reed was a contrary person. 'But you *could* fly it. And the China Petroleum Company will soon cease operations on the Yangtze. We have time, Mr Reed. I am asking that you ensure that you and the floatplane are ready for me in Nanking on a day I specify.' He paused, frowning and pretending to consider. 'If you feel that the flight from Nanking to Foochow is particularly risky, I could increase my offer to, say, 5,500 dollars?'

Reed's eyes narrowed sharply. 'I think your offer smells, Mr Han.'

'And I think you should think about it.'

'You'd better try somebody else.'

'Is your rejection final?'

'Yes.'

Han rose and smiled thinly. 'I hope you do not later regret it.'

Reed watched Han's departing back. Five grand. It could set him up. But he'd be crazy – wouldn't he? – to make any kind of deal with a guy like Han.

And he sat there for another ten minutes, brooding, and waiting for the coffee to clear his head. He was so rich, of course, he could afford to pass up 5,000-dollar offers. Almost nothing saved, he was living from pay cheque to pay cheque. And I'll have to slow down on the drinking, he thought. But already he needed the first one of the day. I'll start saving – next month. Brice, CPC's area manager, hadn't said anything about closing down yet. Reed rose, left the dining room and collected his coat.

As he passed the reception desk on his way out, the clerk handed him a message – it had been telephoned through from the cable office. MEET ME TWENTY HUNDRED AT GOLDEN DRAGON. ARCH.

So the son of a bitch is still alive. Three times he'd contacted the Chuyin air base and had no reply from Arch. Reed screwed up the message and stuffed it into his pocket, then he began walking.

The hotel was in the British Concession, avoided by the Japanese bombers as far as they were able, so the results of the early morning air raid weren't apparent to Reed until he'd crossed over into the Chinese part of the city. A street was roped off because of an unexploded bomb. Detouring, he saw soldiers shoring up the front of a ruined store – its twisted neon sign still hung crazily over the paving. Further on a cinema advertised *Sing-song Girl* with a huge gaudy poster. Reed had seen the film in Shanghai last year. He started guessing why Arch might be coming to Chen-chiang. Halfway between Hsia-kang and Nanking, Arch must be on his way to or from Peggy.

Chen-chiang straddled the Grand Canal. It had a population of over a hundred and fifty thousand and back in the Sung

154

Dynasty it had been the capital of China. There were large quays capable of accommodating sea-going ships – Reed could see Dalsager's river steamer mooring up at Pai On Wharf, and the British gunboat, *Aphis*, trapped this side of the boom. Reed turned off into Rice Market Street.

It was a noisy mix: ancient run-down buildings alongside new banks and office blocks. Foreign sailors had made it their own, and the Chinese had obliged with bars, brothels and taxi dance halls. The street led southwards to the railway yards, a bewildering network of spurs, loops and sidings, and a broad creek that emptied into the Yangtze – it was here that Reed worked.

In 1932, CPC had leased frontage and a corrugated iron shed from the China Merchants' Steam Navigation Company, and they constructed a wooden ramp to run their floatplane down into the water. Reed had been there much of that time, with monthly visits to the CPC depot in Shanghai until recently. He'd got the Stinson floatplane hauled up in the shed: a long rusting structure with a storeroom and an office at the far end.

The shed interior was an ugly cavern. A scarred wooden bench along one side, lifting gear suspended from a beam in the centre. A battery of four metal clothing lockers was next to the sink in one corner. There was a generator – useless now because they'd run out of fuel. But the centre of the shed was taken up by the Stinson floatplane, resting now on its trolley.

The machine had a beautiful line. It was one of four brought out, brand new, to operate the first air mail service in China. CPC had purchased it in 1932. That was when they'd hired Reed – he'd fitted the twin floats.

He had one drink from the bottle he kept in his locker, he hissed inwards. It was good stuff. He took out his shapeless overalls and pulled them on. The day really began in that moment – war, Han, Arch, the omissions of his life and the guilt, all took their subordinate places. Reed's attention centred on the plane.

He worked with rapid precision, tools seemingly extensions of his hands. And he frowned to himself. The current problem

155

was the pilot, not the engine. How to get it into the Hun's head? There was a diminishing supply of aviation spirit so they'd had to use fuel of higher octane than the Stinson's Whirlwind engine was used to. All right for short periods but the plugs could foul, and he'd cautioned the Hun to lean the mixture every now and then to burn off the deposits of lead. Now he'd got a new difficulty. The Hun leaned it excessively and he'd burnt out a valve.

Such was Reed's concentration, he barely thought about the bottle while he worked. The need was there again as he finished and prepared to screw the cowling back on. Brice, the area manager, had arrived and was standing watching him. 'What the hell you doing with that engine?'

The voice jarred and Reed felt instant irritation. He peered down at Brice from his high place on the trolley. 'What d'ya mean what am I doing? I had a burned out valve.' His dislike of Brice was constant.

'You should have stopped by the uptown office on your way here,' Brice said. 'We're finished – kaput. There's no way the company can get tankers through up river until hostilities end, so we're all being paid off.'

Reed rubbed his hands on a rag, and nodded slowly. 'What about the plane?'

'What *about* it?' Brice looked belligerent. 'There's no aviation spirit left – how much have you got in the tanks?'

'Enough to fill a cigarette lighter.'

'If we abandon the goddam thing intact the company loses the insurance. You'd better wreck it.'

'Wreck it!'

'Yeah. Drain out the oil and run the engine until it seizes. Do it tomorrow, before you collect your severance cheque from the office – you get a full two months' pay.'

Reed looked at the Stinson again then scowled at Brice. 'Two months' pay? What about passage money home? We're all supposed to get a free passage or money in lieu. The company promised us that.'

Brice stared at him. 'That's for permanent staff recruited in the States. You left of your own free will, then returned to

156

China and Claud Biggs gave you a job. That makes you local labour, so you don't qualify.'

'But damn it, I *was* permanent staff, four-five years, and I never had any passage money paid me!'

'I don't make the goddam rules.'

Reed detected Brice's unspoken satisfaction at being able to deprive him of two hundred dollars. 'Claud wouldn't have done this.'

'Then take it up with *him*.'

'I damn well will – soon as I see him.'

But Brice was looking impatient again. 'I've got a lot to do, Reed. I'll see you tomorrow.' And he turned away.

Brice had his own ways of interpreting the rules, and they were far now from appeal to Claud. And he knows it, Reed thought. Even so, I should ask to see those rules written down.

It was early afternoon and he didn't know what to do with himself. His last job for CPC was finished. The Stinson was ready to fly again, but there was no gas for it. The shed would stand idle, like all CPC's installations along the lower Yangtze. In Shanghai and New York and London, speculators would note the drop in CPC share prices, then turn to the main news or the sports pages.

He got out of his overalls, washed, then took one drink. The prospect of wrecking the Stinson depressed him, and he thought again about Han's offer. Who would have aviation spirit for sale? He ran his eye over the aeroplane's sleek shape. Stretched canvas, patched in places; and a replaced wing strut, grey instead of red because he'd never found time to paint it. All the hours of work that the Stinson represented, how could he smash this beautiful, tired machine?

Reed left the shed and walked back the way he'd come. Normally he would have stopped off at the Fragrant Breeze for a Chefoo beer and a sandwich but today he didn't even think about it. There was the question of where to go next. Damn it, he'd come back to China because he was unable to make a decision about his life, and now he was being edged towards options, preferences, alternatives once again. South to Canton, he supposed, then a boat home – he could put off a decision until he reached San Francisco. But even so, without passage money he'd have to count every dollar. I should have started saving as soon as I came back here, he thought. And then he remembered that Dalsager's ship was moored up at Pai On Wharf. Dalsager might be persuaded to take him on as crew as far as the southbound railway at Wuchang.

No roots or real purpose. No place I particularly want to go. Reed slouched along Rice Market Street. Sell the truck and I'll make twenty dollars if I'm lucky – nobody will buy it because of the gasoline shortage. Reed was conscious of being nearly thirty-nine and as poor now as when he'd first come to China. Seen from the inside, maybe all men must count their lives a failure? But there are times in each day when I'm happy, he thought. I can make things work smoothly. What is success anyway – money in the bank? Your name in lights?

For among the creatures of the world some go in front,
      some follow;
Some blow hot when others would be blowing cold.

He reached Pai On Wharf. Dalsager's ship, the *I-cheng*, was leaking wisps of steam from its single black funnel. There were red rust streaks on the hull – it needed a coat of paint. The house flag of the Chang Seng Steamship Company hung limply at the stern.

Stevedores chanted monotonously as they unloaded huge, sagging sacks under the eye of the *compradore*. Like ants they seemed able to shift much more than their own weight. Most of them were barefoot. And how did they see their lives? Reed went on board.

He found Sven Dalsager in his cabin. Tunic off, he was making tea on a small burner.

'Iron Buddha.' Dalsager concentrated as he heated the delicate teapot. 'Taste it, and other teas seem lifeless. I buy it from that place on Avenue Foch in Shanghai. You should try it. There isn't a Chinese on board who knows the correct way to make tea. Surprising, isn't it?' And he glanced up briefly. 'What do you want, Reed?'

158

'How's the piano?'

'Fine.'

'That's good.'

Dalsager sighed. 'Let us try again. What is it that you want?'

'CPC is finishing – along the Yangtze at least. I'm being paid off, and I thought you might be able to use me as far as Wuchang.'

'CPC finishing, eh? They can't get their tankers up river because of that damned boom. And I'm stuck this side.' Dalsager poured into fine porcelain cups. 'Taoists believe that tea is an important ingredient in the elixir of immortality – what do you think of a proposition like that?' He offered Reed a cup. 'I have a full crew.'

'Maybe you've got something else that needs fixing?'

Dalsager pondered, sipping his tea, fingers splayed out like a duchess. 'You are an embarrassment to me, Reed. You undercharged for your work on the piano.'

'Give me a free ride to Wuchang and we'll call it quits.'

'If you sell your services cheap, does it mean you have a low opinion of what you are offering?'

'Maybe it means that I think everybody else is overcharging.'

Dalsager sipped and peered into his cup. 'It has a delicate bitterness, note the after-taste, Reed. Be on board no later than mid-day Friday.'

Reed walked back to the hotel, and it was now well into the afternoon. On the third floor corridor he passed Michel Boulin of the French hospital. 'We were hit again in this morning's raid. That's the second time.'

'Didn't I tell you not to let them paint a red cross on the roof? – it's a direct invitation. Are you going home, Michel?'

'I shall stay as long as I can.'

Reed went to his room and spent ten minutes under a tepid shower. People like Michel aways stayed, but there were far more expatriates leaving. Three Socony engineers had gone, their table in the dining room suddenly empty two days ago. And the Britisher down the hall, on his way to Hong-kong.

He shaved carefully because he didn't want any hobo or drifter comment from Arch. The tri-motored Eurasia Junkers roared over, its noise trembling the shaving mirror. Reed held the razor poised. There was no denying he was looking forward to seeing Arch again, despite the business with Sao. Twenty years we've known each other. He stared into the mirror and finished shaving. God, where did all those years go? He'd seen Arch turned into a war hero by the press then rejected as a politician. And after flying the air mail he'd joined in Arch's plan to make a fortune bootlegging – hell, we didn't do all that well at it, we weren't crooked enough. Then the Chaco war with Arch trying to be a hero again and make a name for himself. And now China. And it looked as if at long last Arch might get to be famous.

Reed dined early. Han Yu-lin was in the far corner and facing the door, *North China Daily News* open next to him at the business page. He gave no sign of recognition. And Reed probably wouldn't have noticed – he was having the usual small struggle over what he should drink. A compromise in the end. He had a single whisky and followed it with a Chefoo beer. That would have to do until he saw Arch.

It was dusk when a rickshaw took him to the south end of the town. The rider loped along, bow-legged, riding on the shafts when he reached the slight downward gradient of Ox Street. The sun had gone during that short journey. Reed paid off the boy with twenty cents and a five cent tip, and he walked the rest of the way.

The Golden Dragon was one of the three best restaurants in Chen-chiang, though Reed never ate there. The speciality of the house was duck marrow soup prepared by an old man who had cooked for the Empress Dowager at the turn of the century. There was an American-style bar set off at the side through a bead curtain; it was used by technicians and pilots from the civil airport a half mile beyond the south wall. Travellers paused here on their way in and out of the town, and younger members of Chen-chiang's Western community came because someone had once said it was different and rather exciting, though apart from the food and the girl who sang it was really quite ordinary.

Reed sat in a recess and ordered whisky, and felt the familiar knot of anticipation until the glass was in his hand. Brice was at the end of the bar. He was in conversation with a tall, fair-haired man.

The wall of the recess was decorated with signed, framed photographs – nobody Reed had ever heard of. He drank slowly, trying to make the first one last. From the restaurant he could hear the Chinese girl singing a folk-song.

Brice and his companion were leaving but he paused when he saw Reed. 'Where were you this afternoon? I tried to get you at your hotel – about four fifteen.'

Reed didn't answer the question. 'What did you want?'

'The company just might come up with fifty bucks towards your passage money – it depends on a number of things.'

He went on hurriedly. 'I've changed my mind about the Stinson. I want it down the slip and in the water first thing Thursday morning. Can you do that?'

'Where are you going to get aviation spirit?'

Brice looked wary. 'Don't worry about the fuel. The Hun and I think we can get some. We'll take the Stinson to Nanking – the company may need it there.'

Reed was intensely curious but he didn't show it. 'Okay.'

The tall, fair-haired man with Brice said, 'Don't I know you? Yes, I surely do. We met at the Del Monte, celebrating Chinese New Year. You were with Captain Rittenhouse and his wife.'

Brice added grudgingly, 'This is Fletcher, YMCA. He's just back from the States.'

'Oh yes, I remember you,' Reed said, though he didn't. 'Did you come through Shanghai?'

'Three-four weeks ago.' Fletcher talked about how the war was affecting the International Settlement. Reed only half listened. He was wondering where Brice was going to lay his hands on enough aviation fuel to get the floatplane to Nanking.

' . . . and there was a shoot-out on the river the night I reached Shanghai from Yokohama. Some thieves with a junk broke into a warehouse and took three Pratt & Whitney engines. They fired on a Japanese gunboat and killed the First Officer – now the Japs are searching for them . . .'

The Chinese girl was singing the marching song of the

Second Army Corps. She always performed in the restaurant but Reed had never actually seen her.

' . . . and General Matsui has declared a new stop line.'

'What happened to the old one?'

But Brice was impatient to go. 'Don't forget, Reed – the Stinson has to be in the water by first light Thursday morning.' He almost hurried Fletcher out of the bar.

Reed stared at the swaying bead curtain. Han Yu-lin has made Brice an offer! He was sure of it. He forgot his good intention and swallowed down the first drink and signalled to the boy for another.

Alcohol dulled the sharp edges of his thoughts. He could see the commander of the local Chinese garrison drinking at the bar. Rumour had it that he was in love with the girl singer of the Golden Dragon.

He wasn't happy about what Brice intended to do. The Stinson would be quietly scrapped or sunk in Foochow as soon as Han's purpose was served, of that he was sure. He didn't give a damn whether Han Yu-lin succeeded or failed, or what might happen to Brice and the Hun for that matter. But he cared about the plane. It deserved an honourable end.

The bead curtain parted and Arch Rittenhouse entered, six feet two of him, crushed peaked cap with its blue and white Kuomintang badge, battered leather flying jacket, hand-made English shoes. Reed waited for Arch to see him.

Arch glanced round. His eyes narrowed and he came over to the recess. He moved very lightly on his feet, like a boxer. 'It's been – how long, Frank?'

He sat relaxed and pushed his cap back on his head. There were women in the bar and they glanced at him. He was still a handsome man – maybe just a hint of sag under the heavy jaw and wrinkles forming around his eyes. 'I've visited Peggy at Hsia-kang and I was anxious to see you, Frank. So I arranged to stop over on my way back.' He took out a cigarette and slid the ugly silver case across the table. 'I've missed you. Did you have a good time back home?'

'There wasn't much work.' Reed flicked his lighter and held the flame for Arch. 'I got taken on at the Seversky plant on Long

162

Island for a couple of months. They're building the most beautiful plane you've ever seen.'

Arch blew smoke up at the ceiling. He had a way of listening carefully but all the time evaluating, working on his own thoughts. 'This obsession with screwdrivers and wrenches. You should be flying.'

Reed frowned. 'I don't think so.'

'You don't think.' Arch smiled. 'That's exactly your problem. How I used to envy your skill.'

'I'm a mechanic, Arch.'

'You've lost sight of what you are. It's something we have to talk about – later.' He changed the subject. 'I must have just missed you and Peggy at Shanghai. I was ordered back to the Chuyin air base for the defence of the capital.'

'Peggy told me.' And he'd spent that last night with Sao – that was the other topic for later. 'How is it over Nanking, Arch – what are you flying?'

'A Curtiss Hawk – it's outdated.' Arch frowned slightly. 'The game is getting much faster. Trying to out-turn the new Nakajima is non-habit-forming. But skill and experience count.' He grinned. 'I rely on cunning, and I get as much sleep as I can.'

But he's tired, Reed thought. This isn't the Chaco with minimal opposition.

A girl had entered. Sable draped her shoulders. She stood hesitantly at the bead curtain. English, Reed guessed, they all looked sort of – what? – English. Twenty or twenty-one, with long blonde hair and attractive eyes. She had a young man in tow, he was wearing a dinner jacket. Seeing Arch, she crossed to their recess. 'Captain Rittenhouse! And so far from base! *And* you are in the newspaper again.'

Definitely English, her accent was impeccable.

'Daphne.' Arch stood and shook her hand. 'I haven't seen you in Nanking. I assumed you'd gone to Hong-kong with your aunt.'

'Aunt Clare went – with her dogs and a bundle of Agatha Christie novels.' She smiled down at herself. 'But you know me – always the last to leave the party. Uncle insisted in the end.

I'm staying at Kao-tzu.' She looked up again quickly. 'That's quite near your base.' She didn't bother to introduce her young man. 'And you, captain? Have you been up there, clawing the enemy from the sky over Nanking?'

Arch smiled as if amazed by her. 'Yes. I've been up there.'

'Modesty is so becoming in a hero.' She was waiting for him to invite her and the young man to sit.

'This is a friend of mine – Frank Reed. We haven't met for a long time and we have things we must discuss. Do you mind, Daphne?'

'Yes. I mean, no.' She smiled and bit her lip, clearly disappointed. 'No, of course not. I told you I'm at Kao-tzu. The number is 283. Repeat that.'

Arch grinned. 'Two eight three.'

She smoothed her hair with her finger tips. 'You'll telephone me?'

'Of course.' He squeezed her arm. 'Next week some time.'

The pair moved to the bar. Daphne glanced back at Arch then began an animated conversation with her young man.

'Nice kid.' Arch signalled to the boy and pointed at the empty glasses.

But Reed felt sour. 'You giving her English lessons?'

'Oh, come on now, Frank.' Arch's eyes flickered with amusement. 'I take her out once in a while – God, I'm old enough to be her uncle or something. We have conversations. She tells me how mixed up she feels and I talk to her about responsibility to her family, and about her future. It's difficult for kids – there are no absolute values any more. I feel for them, Frank, if we have another war.'

'Where d'ya meet her?'

'A party somewhere. She's the niece of the British consul. She really should have gone home.'

Arch had a way of attracting the young. It was his certainty, or so Reed supposed. 'What are you doing about Peggy?'

Arch looked wearied by the question. 'Exactly what I told her. She'll have to go south to Hong-kong.'

'And you, Arch – what are you going to do?'

'I must stay and honour my contract despite all these

protests from Washington.' Arch had switched his mood, and tense now he leaned forward. 'The Japanese plan to dominate the East, and ultimately that means direct conflict with the United States. By remaining here I am making a statement to the people back home. We've got to get all the neutrality legislation reversed.'

Arch meant what he said. He'd stir the bureaucrats and shake up the isolationists. But Reed knew that there was a measure of self-aggrandisement in him. Twenty years ago somebody had said Arch was a hero, and that's what he was going to be. And it was as if Arch had read his thoughts.

'We only have one life, and we must make it count, Frank.' He sipped at his drink, taking it slowly. 'I feel my life must have some high purpose or what was the use of being born? I've tried to make Peg understand that.'

'I don't think she'll go along with being packed off again, Arch.' Peggy was a loving woman with very ordinary needs. She'd never grasped what made Arch tick. Why had they ever married?

'You know how very fond of her I am.'

'You've got a funny way of showing it. All this stuff about concern for her, but you've got something going with young Daf over there.' Reed had begun to dislike himself.

'That was unworthy of you, Frank.'

'You were having it off with Sao while I was gone. I found your shirt.'

Arch didn't even bat an eye. He just sat there staring at him. 'Wrong.' Then he clicked his fingers at the bar boy and pointed at the glasses again. 'I'm not sure who you are getting self-righteous about, yourself or Peg.'

'Are you saying you didn't sleep with Sao?'

'You left her – went home without saying for sure you'd be back, so why is it important to you?'

'You're shifting ground, Arch – you're very good at that. I don't know why you didn't do well in politics.'

'Sao was sleeping with Winstanley at CPC before you left.' Arch leaned back, impatient now. 'Didn't you even suspect what was going on? She was after bigger game than you.'

It was probably true – he recognized that as soon as Arch had said it, and his dislike of himself turned to mild disgust for being a dupe.

'And in all honesty, Frank, can you blame her?'

Daphne and her young man were having an argument. They got up to leave and as they passed the recess she smiled. 'Good luck, Captain Rittenhouse. You *will* telephone?'

'When I can, Daphne.' But this time he only looked up briefly, as if she was just an acquaintance. And Daphne was stung. She turned quickly and pushed through the beaded curtain. The young man paused, staring angrily at Arch. Arch looked up coolly. 'Is there something I can do for you?'

He hesitated, then followed the girl.

'You've really confused her now,' Reed said.

'The young sometimes take themselves too seriously. Forget about that.' Arch had switched mood again. 'Let's talk about you. You've become a nobody – even Sao knew that. And you're drinking too much. I want you to come in with me – I've had a word with Colonel Chennault about your experience and he seemed quite impressed. You're a flyer, not a mechanic. Flying is the only way you can ever *be* somebody. The Chinese Air Force needs skilled pilots with combat experience. You'll have a contract and a temporary commission as lieutenant, and you'll get seven hundred and fifty dollars a month. It will be good for you. And when we go home you'll have a clear idea of where you fit in.' Arch pondered briefly. 'For my part I intend running for public office – people will listen to me next time.' And he paused. 'What do you think, Frank?'

Reed stared at him incredulously. 'Me fly in another war! After the Chaco? That was a dirty business.'

'I disagree. We did an honest job of work.'

'No, Arch!' he interrupted. 'What we were paid to do was wrong, and we should have backed out of it. I don't want any part of another war.' He swilled down the whisky in one gulp.

Arch watched him, concerned. 'Of course, if that's how you feel about it. It was just an idea.' He glanced at the empty glass gripped tightly in Reed's hand. 'What will you do?'

'I've got passage on a boat as far as Wuchang. I'll go south by rail to Canton, then home.' He suddenly didn't much like the feel of being first into the lifeboat even though departure was being more or less forced on him.

'That's probably wise.' Arch finished his drink and glanced at the clock. The local garrison commander went into the restaurant as the girl began a love song.

'I'll get us another drink.'

But Arch shook his head. 'No, Frank. I have to catch the commercial flight at six tomorrow morning and I need sleep.'

'Just one – for the road?' He regretted he'd asked – it was the kind of appeal that drunks make to excuse their last two or three. 'No. Go and sleep, Arch.'

Arch stood and straightened his cap. 'I'll worry about you. Write to me when you get back to the States.'

'You never damn well answer, but I'll write anyway.'

Arch reached the bead curtain, but he paused and turned. 'I had a dream – three times. We're walking along a shore – you, Peg and me ahead of you. There's a girl in a boat – she's beckoning to me. What do you think it means?'

'I don't know, Arch. Dreams don't have any meaning.'

CHAPTER FOURTEEN

One small window high up. The bleak office made her uneasy – Miss Kuang shifted on the hard bench. There had been no time for skilled make up. She took a mirror from her bag and examined herself. Tired – she'd had the dream again and then she couldn't sleep. Black-framed spectacles partially hid dark shadows under her eyes. A sudden, unequivocal summons at seven in the morning and only five minutes to put her clothes on. The difference between arrest and invitation to assist Colonel Tang was perhaps slight. Why had she been brought here? Captain Chu Teng of Maritime Customs was her weakness – his fear could have led him to a foolish slip. The Hsia-kang assignment was beginning to wear Miss Kuang down.

The middle-aged army major came back into the room, and she put her mirror away. He glanced at her Western-style clothes then ignored her, hastily scooping files from the cabinets and dumping them into a sack. For destruction? During the last few days Miss Kuang had noticed several indications of withdrawal of the army. There were provincial conscripts encamped beyond the eastern wall, but a regiment of seasoned regulars of the "Generalissimo's Own" 88th Division had marched straight through Hsia-kang in the direction of Nanking. And government supply dumps at nearby Chiang-yin were being emptied.

Her speculations were interrupted by an orderly calling her name. He led her along a narrow corridor. Miss Kuang took deep breaths to calm herself. Was it possible that Colonel Tang would recognize her after all this time?

She was shown into his office, it was as sombre as the room she had just left.

The colonel was reading from a sheaf of typed pages. He glanced up. 'Please sit.' He indicated a chair set back four paces from his desk, then resumed reading.

Miss Kuang felt exposed, seated there in the centre of the room. Perhaps the colonel was merely pretending to read? She crossed her legs to gauge his response, and he looked up from his notes.

'I regret that I must encroach on your time, Miss Kuang, but we have a war that is not going well for us. I am hoping you are able to assist me.'

So it wasn't arrest. 'I was surprised by your summons, Colonel Tang – so early in the morning.' He looked no different from that other time ten years ago – a handsome, expressionless man.

'You are a French national?'

'Yes, by blood on my father's side. I was born in Indo-China.' A lie, but nobody could ever fault the background created for her by the Special Services Bureau.

'What do you know of the junk captain? Chen?' He was watching her face.

She was unpleasantly surprised. 'Captain Chen? I have met him only once. He sought me out and offered me a story for Pacific Press – at a price. He claimed to have information about a vessel called the *Fushan*, and its stolen cargo.' Her version of that encounter was near-true but with a few omissions. 'The story was of no interest to Pacific Press and I did not buy it from him.'

'*Fushan*?' The colonel stroked his jaw with his finger. 'Chen has dealt in other information, useful to the enemy.'

'Am I suspect?' And she smiled, suggesting the absurdity of the question. 'I am sure that if you produce Captain Chen he will confirm my account of the conversation.'

'Chen has been murdered. The motive appears to have been robbery.'

'But how terrible!' Miss Kuang feigned shocked surprise. Ideally Chen's body should have washed down river. 'I must

169

confess I am relieved that Pacific Press had no dealings with him.' She cupped her knee with her slim hands. 'Are you familiar with our company, Colonel Tang?'

'I am becoming interested.'

Yes. He was becoming interested.

'I must assure you, colonel, that although we aim to assist financial and business interests in a wide area of the Pacific, we identify strongly with China. I would be happy to provide you with a copy of any information that has passed through my hands while I have been in Hsia-kang.'

'I have already seen copies of every cable you have sent since your arrival, Miss Kuang.' He smiled.

And still he had no idea who she was. Miss Kuang remembered sullen, resigned, over-painted girls, their breasts exposed; and police of Shanghai Greater Municipality ensuring respectful silence while Colonel Tang walked slowly along the line. He had been searching for Ohata even then. And it mattered nothing to him that the brothel girls of Butterfly Row were virtually slaves; bought, sold, degraded, mutilated sometimes. The thought of humiliating Tang was rich.

'I wish I could do more for China,' she said. 'Madame Chiang Kai-shek is an inspiration to all Chinese women. How else might I help, colonel?'

'You must soon consider your arrangments for departure.'

So the Imperial armies were getting close. But she couldn't leave yet – not until she had handed over the map of the boom defences to the unknown agent. 'I would of course do as you instruct, Colonel Tang, though I would prefer to stay long enough to be . . . of service.' The timing on the last two words had, she hoped, suggested a number of interesting possibilities. And now there was a recognizable glint in the colonel's eyes.

He pondered. 'It is not essential that you leave immediately. I assume that you occasionally hear things – you move around among the foreign traders and businessmen. And if you are approached by others, like Chen, I would be interested to know what they say.'

He had correctly assessed her potential. 'Information is sometimes given me unwittingly. And young men seem impelled into indiscretion merely to impress.' Miss Kuang adjusted the hem of her skirt – a provokingly prim gesture.

'Then we have the basis of an arrangement?'

It had all gone a little too smoothly. 'But how should I contact you with such information?' She pretended to consider. 'You could perhaps call at my hotel?'

'It could be embarrassing for you.' The colonel looked faintly amused. 'The hotel is owned by the Frenchman, Fourcade. There is a rear entrance and Fourcade will say nothing if I use it.'

'You have wisely assumed my inexperience in these matters.'

The audacity of her scheming astonished her. Miss Kuang left the colonel's headquarters and walked towards Yibai Street. He was of course far too clever to be taken in by her pretended patriotism or innocence, but vain enough to believe that she found him attractive. Miss Kuang felt light-headed. She would use him, then humiliate him.

She reached the northern end of the market area. A column of carts moved along Yibai Street from the South Gate. Wounded from the delta battles were passing through almost daily. And they stank. Scarecrows shuffled along beside the carts, thin cotton uniforms in rags and mostly without boots or rifles. The crowds stared pitying, curious. Some handed out food purchased in the market.

A ragged soldier, head and face wrapped round with a foul dressing, clung blindly to a rope trailing from the rear of a cart. Sometimes he stumbled but he never let go of the rope.

Miss Kuang was able to observe the scene with indifference. Men suffer because they are brutish and stupid. There was nothing new in human misery. Soldiers were the remembered scourge of her childhood, moving back and forth across the province. Her mother ravaged and butchered in front of her – that particular image was now blurred, as if seen through the heat of a fire.

171

She was sure that the straggling procession was part of a "strategic withdrawal" of the Chinese Central Army. She could only guess at the speed of the Japanese advance. And Miss Kuang's task was near complete. The map of the boom defences had been drawn for her by Chen, the junk captain. Until the moment the paid thugs pushed his head under the water he had believed she was shipping opium through the boom for Dou.

Miss Kuang edged her way towards the centre of the market. Will I ever be safe? she wondered. After I have finished this part of the assignment. After I have dealt with Colonel Tang. After Nanking. The words of the Fu Kay practitioner in Shanghai nagged at her – 'When we have no body, how can misfortune or disaster befall us?' Yesterday she had visited the small temple behind the district law court and sought the future in *chow chien*. Asking the question once again she had selected a rolled-up paper on which was written an answer. It was even more ambiguous. 'You will need a boat to cross the river.' Experience suggested that the meaning would emerge sooner or later.

She paused at the stall of the bloated Korean who sold ivory, and pretended to examine his work. Chu Teng of Maritime Customs came here each day in case she needed him. Was she being watched? Miss Kuang resisted the urge to glance round. The colonel did not yet suspect her – but a small doubt remained. Tonight he would come to her room, of that she was certain. Her flesh tingled.

Chu Teng was approaching. She could see him over the heads of the shoppers. She picked up a delicate box and studied the pattern worked into it. What if Chu Teng was questioned on some trivial matter? His fear could be her downfall. Ideally the fat captain of Customs should suffer a drowning accident, but paid murderers were unreliable – she couldn't chance another body being found.

Chu Teng went to the other side of the stall. His movements were nervous – he must never be exposed to questioning, Miss Kuang thought. She replaced the ivory box and allowed her fingers to touch his. Even afraid, he was

172

easy to arouse. She made the tactical decision to take him to her bed that afternoon.

'The junk, *Fushan*, was sighted five miles beyond the boom,' Chu muttered, and his fat lips trembled. 'I do not know what to do.'

'It is quite simple,' she soothed him. 'Have the crew arrested and leave them in their cells until the town falls. The Japanese navy will arrange a hanging, and you will receive credit for preventing the aero engines from reaching Nanking.'

He glanced anxiously around then nodded.

After draining his lust she would provide Chu Teng with the means to take his own life. Miss Kuang smiled at him.

Colonel Tang left his headquarters shortly after Miss Kuang. He noticed that the eating house opposite was closed. Prudent men with a little money had left.

His orderly was waiting with the black, armour-plated Buick – it had been abandoned by the war lord, Wu P'ei-fu, after his defeat in the civil war a decade earlier. Bumpers crumpled, sagging suspension, the automobile had had a succession of military owners, and two changes of engine before its most recent inheritor had defected to Mao and the Communists.

Colonel Tang watched the streets – an old habit. But the girl, Miss Kuang, was on his mind. Half French by blood? He doubted it. Yet he had no reason to suspect the rest of her story – Pacific Press seemed respectable.

The letter writer was missing today. And the boy who cleaned shoes. A funeral procession for Chen, the junk master – another small mystery. Colonel Tang was aware that somebody was pre-empting information and anticipating his moves.

The Buick edged round the column of wounded and was briefly caught up in a fresh exodus of refugees moving towards the Moon Gate. Only a week ago Hsia-kang was swollen, with people sleeping in the streets. Now it was emptying. Refugees trudged straight through leaving only the sick and the old.

The armour-plated car swept into the mission compound. It was a puzzle to Tang that his own people should adopt the faith of the foreigners. Christianity was an alien religion, yet there were Chinese who embraced it wholeheartedly; the Generalissimo and Madame Chiang, all the influential Soong family, the old war lord General Feng who baptised his troops with a hose.

As he climbed out of the Buick he observed the long queue outside the dispensary. Foster had his uses. As he walked towards the steps of the bungalow the tall American girl was opening the door.

Linda had seen the car arrive. Carelessly dressed, and now aware of it, she tried to tidy her hair with her free hand. Her left arm supported a child of perhaps two years – blue-black hair and large, frightened eyes, and it occurred to Colonel Tang that Miss Bishop was ill at ease with children.

'I'm astonished, colonel. Is this a social call?'

'Unhappily no.'

'Please come in. We can probably arrange some tea?'

'No, thank you.'

He resents missionaries, but he quite likes me, Linda thought. He's a bit like a handsome uncle that you feel pretty safe with but are not entirely sure about. 'The situation seems to be getting worse?'

'Quite so. I must speak with Dr Foster.'

She hitched the child awkwardly onto her shoulder. 'He's very busy – in the dispensary.' She hoped the colonel would come up with some other option. 'I'm typing angry letters for drugs – he doesn't have time to write them.'

'I must speak with Foster *now*, Miss Bishop.'

'Yes. Well . . . Right, I'll tell him.'

She left, carrying the child. Linda was amazed how quickly the colonel could get her into a state of uncertainty, like a schoolgirl badly prepared for a lesson. And she looked like a slattern and the child had rubbed her runny nose on her shirt. Linda glanced at the small face – perhaps she was getting a cold. 'And you weigh a ton – d'ya

174

know that?' The quicker Mayling took her off her hands the better. 'I'm going to put you down.'

The child understood no English, but she stretched up her hand to be held and trotted along beside Linda to the dispensary.

Foster adjusted his wire-rimmed glasses, and, frowning, he scrubbed his hands. 'What could that man want of us? It's disturbing – everybody knows he is in Military Intelligence.'

He went to the study, and not wanting to seem an eavesdropper at the door, Linda took the child for a walk.

How do parents cope, with months, years of that tiny stumbling pace? 'I don't know what we're going to do with you, baby.' They still hadn't got a proper name for her. Today she was dressed in clean cotton trousers and a smock – Mayling was giving her extra attention.

Linda led her past the slit trench, now a foot deep in water. The blast of a boat horn startled gulls, they flew in a wide circle and the child followed them with her eyes as they settled again on the abandoned Yashima warehouse.

'Birds,' Linda said. 'Big birds.'

They were jostling for space along the exposed ridge timber and some perched on the bare rafters. Linda stared. Nobody had replaced the corrugated iron sheets blown from the roof the day the Japanese plane had jettisoned its bombs on the town. That was the day Arch had held her. No direct word from him – but what had she expected? And she'd just got used to the idea that that afternoon with him had been all of it – and maybe just as well – when he'd enquired about her in a letter to Peggy. Had she found another reporting job in China? Peggy read the innocent question out loud. Then she'd glanced up quickly, her eyes sharp. Peggy was no fool. And since then Linda had been slightly wary, avoiding mention of Arch.

But how could one casually read sentence from a letter warm her so? It made no real sense. Linda walked with the child, up past the single tree and the lines of washing. I'd been feeling low, she remembered, worried, and afraid in case I was getting sick again. You can go for days – weeks –

working mechanically and wondering about its worth, physically tired for no reason you can think of. Then something as simple as a man asking about you, aware of you as a person, and the world looks quite different. I was suddenly not tired and I liked people again.

The child stopped and stared.

'Yes, darling, it's a pussy cat.'

So I'm not so very different from Peggy. Or the readers of the sentimental novelette? All the ingredients of romantic fiction were there in that encounter with Arch. Linda wasn't happy with this inescapable assessment, and in the dialogue inside her head she argued that if Arch was of some importance to her right now it was because of her need for certainty. Not only was he the biggest man she'd ever met, he was the only one who seemed sure of what he was and where he was going.

Bombers droned over, very high today on their way to Nanking. The child knew the sound and clutched at Linda's thigh, hiding her face. Linda picked her up again. There were rumours that the Chinese army was in full retreat. And where did that leave Peggy and her?

She took the child indoors, and pausing outside the study she heard Foster's angry voice. 'I suspect you are overstepping your authority, Colonel Tang, and I cannot accept what you say.'

The colonel replied softly and Linda wasn't able to hear what he said. She went to the doorway of the bungalow and waited for him.

'Colonel. May I ask you one question?'

She thought he might be angry after the exchange with Foster, but he didn't appear to be. 'Only *one* question, Miss Bishop?'

'I really have several. Are you able to say how far off the Japanese are?'

He walked as far as the slit trench and there he stopped. And he took up a handful of soil and ran it through his fingers, like a peasant. 'Thirty miles – perhaps less.'

'That close!' It didn't seem possible that they could have

176

moved so fast. 'But the defence line, colonel. You'll stop them?'

'Unlikely.'

'But you're surely going to try?'

He shook his head. 'Of the hundred methods of military strategy, to run early is the best. We trade space for time. We are already outflanked – our professional army could be lost here and it is needed ultimately for the stand east of Nanking. There will be a holding action at Hsia-kang but the town will have to be abandoned. I have told Foster that his mission must close. You have two days and you must be gone.'

'Only two days!' Linda bit her lip. 'That's kind of sudden! Mrs Rittenhouse and I had planned to go next week.'

'The Japanese have passed their own stop line. They are no longer guaranteeing the safety of foreigners.' He paused. 'I want you all to reach safety. It is best that you go directly west by road, or follow the course of the river.'

'Yes. Yes, of course.'

The child sensed Linda's tension and began to cry, knuckle pressed to her mouth.

'Is the girl an orphan?' Colonel Tang peered at her. 'Or abandoned? Girls are often seen as a burden to their parents.'

'Abandoned. I can't have children.' Linda was astonished at herself. She hadn't meant to say that.

'Where did you find her?'

'I didn't. She was found on the wharf by Mayling – a Chinese nurse. We don't even know her name.'

Huge sobs shook the child and she coughed.

Colonel Tang frowned. '*Bu keyi.*' He brushed a tear from her cheek. She stopped crying and stared back at him.

Now how did he do that? Neither Peggy nor Mayling could soothe her once she really started to cry.

For a moment the small girl and the colonel continued to stare at each other. A last gulp and she yawned, rubbed her eyes and dozed on Linda's shoulder.

'Call her Suyin.' He turned towards his battered automobile.

'That sounds a good name.' Linda wanted to ask him if he

177

was remaining in Hsia-kang until the Japanese came, but she decided that perhaps she shouldn't. 'Tell me, colonel. Do you believe in purpose?'

'More questions? Men behave purposefully, so I must assume a purpose.'

She watched as the car spurted gravel and roared out of the compound. A small, token defence and we're going to let the Japanese take the town – Linda had got into the way of 'we' and 'our side'. We can't just keep retreating. Where the hell does it end? And Peggy and I can't go south now – it would mean crossing the Japanese line of advance.

We'll have to go westward. With the child at her shoulder, Linda walked back to the bungalow.

Peggy had seen her talking to Colonel Tang. 'What did he say?'

'The Japanese are only thirty miles away. We have to leave.'

'For Nanking?' Peggy stared at her.

'Yes.' Linda nodded. 'I guess it has to be Nanking.'

And to the east, advance units of General Matsui's "Black" 9th had reached Sha-chou. They circled to the south leaving the town for Nakajima's 16th Division.

The advance hadn't been uneventful; they had encountered the Chinese rearguard several times. And skirmishes with straggling groups had led to fierce, inter-unit rivalry. Ishiwara, who commanded the 3rd Company, claimed to have slain eight Chinese in individual sword combat. Captain Hashimoto was close behind with a claim of seven.

Sergeant Kimura ensured that the men were fed, then he swilled soup and watched from a respectful distance as Hashimoto cleaned the curved blade of his sword. Young officers could indulge themselves in these Samurai exploits. He, Kimura, had far too much to think about. And he had noticed that one of the captain's 'valiant adversaries' was a boy of twelve or thirteen, struck down from behind in the act of fleeing – quite legitimate as the boy was in uniform, but hardly worthy of a shouted *Banzai* from the man. Kimura

178

dipped hardtack in the soup and ate hurriedly. Soon they would have to move again.

The captain oiled his sword blade and slid it into its scabbard. Kimura seized the moment, and throwing the dregs of soup aside he went to Hashimoto and saluted and bowed.

'Sir, it is necessary that we decide what to do with the two badly wounded who are unable to keep up.'

'Wounded?' Hashimoto wiped the scabbard, he wasn't really listening.

'Two of our men, sir, barely able to walk.' It was all well and good for the captain to play warrior games, but an infantry company didn't run itself.

'If they delay our advance they must be left behind until the main column reaches here.' Hashimoto strapped the sword to his waist. 'We must be first into Hsia-kang, Kimura, or remain disgraced.'

'If we leave our wounded the Chinese civilians will kill them, sir.'

'They have rifles. Ensure they have food and water for two days.' Hashimoto tied a white silk scarf at his throat. 'Alert the company, it is time that we moved.'

'Yes, sir.' Kimura remained expressionless. He'd tried. The wounded must take their chance.

The company moved on over flat country. Late in the afternoon they encountered opposition of a sort – perhaps a dozen Chinese. They'd dug in among some distant trees and they opened fire with their rifles much too soon. Bullets whistled hopelessly wide, and even Kimura laughed with the men. Then, turning, he was struck low in the buttock.

It was painful, and humiliating – some of the men were grinning. Others might assume he had been running away. Kimura cursed softly. The almost spent bullet had gouged an ugly wound. He got the corporal to extract it and apply a field dressing, then hitched up his trousers. He could walk, with difficulty. And that he must do or be left behind.

Now they were advancing over rice fields and low hills, no more towns between them and Hsia-kang.

CHAPTER FIFTEEN

Fushan wallowed sluggishly on the end of the tow rope. The weather had turned cold, or perhaps it was just that Russell was very tired – he huddled in his old raincoat. All that careful planning; and the Customs boat had slid out from shore minutes after they'd edged the junk through the boom. Russell rose slowly and limped to the pump. Either they'd had very bad luck or Customs knew they were coming.

The two armed Chinese put on board by the river inspector watched idly as he began pumping. He scowled at them. Unless he pumped, the stinking junk would flounder unmanageably. And it was no good asking Lao to do it. The boy was curled up, sleeping like a dead man – he needed rest. So Russell worked the pump handle, and *Fushan* was dragged along in the wake of the Customs launch, tow rope alternately tightening and slackening.

The two guards lounged on the packing cases. They chewed sunflower seeds and spat. Russell became angry. Sweat ran into his eyes and his tired muscles flagged. 'Hey, you!' he called.

They stared, surprised.

'Come and pump – *mashang*!'

Maybe it was his appearance – eyes red, sunk into his bearded face, and the ugly still-raw bullet gash on his cheek. They looked at each other cautiously then came over to take turns with the pump. Exhausted, Russell huddled down in his old raincoat again. He stared listlessly at the mirror fastened by Lao to the stump of the mast – it was supposed to deflect bad luck but it clearly hadn't worked.

They were being towed towards the Hsia-kang Bund. Russell could see the Customs flag over a white brick building half a mile away. Lao stirred, then sat up quickly. Russell didn't know anybody who could wake as fast as the boy.

'Where they take us?'

He nodded towards the pier. 'It will be all right. Chinese Maritime Customs are on the whole fair and reasonable. We'll get help.'

The boy looked for a moment, then he shrugged. 'Nobody cares goddam.'

'*We* care!' Week's on this stinking boat, dragging those engines up river. 'You see. *Somebody* will listen – they can't all be as stupid as that river inspector.'

Lao took the stub of a cigarette from the pocket of his torn shirt and smoothed it with his fingers. 'You make the inspector angry.' He scratched a match with his thumbnail, lit the stub and handed it to Russell. 'That also stupid.'

'His man hit you and I protested!'

'Mistake. Important he shouldn't lose face. You shout at him.'

The boy took back the stub of cigarette and sucked in smoke. 'Mustn't shout. You smile. Maybe I fix him later.'

'Pardon me, but I feel a little unsure for *my* neck when you say things like that.'

Lao assumed an expression of shocked innocence. 'We friends, Russell!'

'Then I'm sure you'll forgive my unworthy suspicion.'

The launch slowed, slackening the cable, and bumped alongside the Hsia-kang Customs pier.

It was strange to be standing on firm ground again. Russell kept bracing his legs, unconsciously anticipating movement. 'What do you make of this, Lao?' He watched people hurrying by. 'All the time we were being shot at and near drowned, the world was going on its own way.'

'Girls.' Lao smiled and stared around the Bund. Further on a few women squatted on bundles, waiting with their men for passage on the junks moored off shore. At the Rapid

Steamship pier there was another queue for a dull red rusting hulk. I wouldn't want to trust my life to that, Russell thought. And on the Bund there were militia; straw hats, straw sandals, tattered uniforms a dozen shades of green and hung about with a strange mix of leather and canvas accoutrement. They loafed in groups as if they didn't know why they were there.

Heavy guns sounded far off to the east.

Russell hurried along the pier, Lao behind him. 'We'll see somebody in authority.'

'Do not make him angry.'

They were led into a small office. There were pictures of Sun Yat-sen and the Generalissimo on the wall. A European in a crumpled white suit looked up from behind his desk. He told the Chinese clerk to fetch a chair for Russell but ignored Lao. 'My name is Surganov. You may sit.'

Russell declined, he felt a growing unease. A Russian! This is why they were brought here instead of Chiang-yin. White Russians were men without a country of their own, they had no claim to the protection of extra-territoriality. Surganov would do as he was told by the Chinese river inspector.

'State your name and where you have come from.'

'Russell. We've sailed that junk from Shanghai, and I wish to protest . . .'

Surganov waved his pen. 'Not yet.' He wrote briefly on his notepad.'You were caught after you had breached the boom at Chiang-yin. You were in possession of a detailed map of the river, but you had no documents for the vessel or its cargo.'

'Of course I've got no bloody documents!' This was the third time Russell had told the story and he was getting edgy. 'The junk isn't mine and the cargo is stolen!' He felt the slight pressure of Lao's elbow but he went on anyway. 'I tried to explain to that river inspector . . .'

'You had on board a Thompson gun, a repeating rifle and pistols. The river inspector insists you were attempting to elude arrest.'

'He's an idiot – or worse! We are trying to reach Nanking with three valuable aero engines for the Generalissimo.'

Surganov shook his head. 'Our river inspector believes that the engines are worthless – a cover for your real intentions. Enemy agents have repeatedly attempted to find weaknesses in the boom. You will be kept here until Captain Chu Teng arrives to conduct a full investigation of your case.'

'Investigation! But the Japanese are only – what? – two, three days away at most!' Anger welled in Russell. 'You and this Captain Chu Teng plan to hold us here until it's too late! In God's name, why?'

Lao bowed to Surganov. 'If I may address your honour? Our employer grows impatient if we delay.' And his eyes opened wide in an expression of wonder. 'Like yourself, he is very important man. Lot of pull so to speak. His anger spills over everybody, like wrath of God.'

'Employer?' The Russian looked wary, pen poised. 'What is this man's name?'

Lao lowered his voice. 'We have great privilege to serve Mister Dou of Shanghai. Mister Dou does big favour for the Generalissimo.'

Russell felt incompetent. He should have left all explanation to the boy.

Surganov put down his pen. Two, three days and the Japanese would be here. Dare he ignore the threat of this little Shanghai thug? With luck he would be on his way to Nanking with his family by the time Imperial troops captured Hsia-kang, but how safe would they be? Dou's filthy fingers stretched everywhere.

The guns thumped in the distance.

He read through the notes again, looking for a way out. There was Captain Chu's emphatic written instruction that *Fushan* and its crew were to be detained. What might be the outcome if he, Surganov, let them go? A trumped up charge in a Chinese court and no protection for him – his loyal service would count for nothing.

Russell read anxiety in the Russian's face. 'Mr Dou

provided the means for us to get those aeroplane engines to Nanking. Who will be blamed if they fall into Japanese hands?'

And that was sufficient. Surganov jerked his head at the clerk.

'Get out.' He toyed with his pen. 'I cannot release you without the authority of Captain Chu. But I will ensure that Colonel Tang of Military Intelligence learns that you and the engines are here.' He paused. 'And you will inform your employer of my co-operation?'

Russell nodded. It would have to do.

Lao smiled at the Russian. 'You are man of honour – more or less.'

The Russian stared at him.

And the faint thump of guns brought fine particles of dust down from the ceiling.

The gunfire was still a long way off, more felt than heard. Earlier in the day Linda had thought it was distant thunder, and she'd noticed the mirror shimmer while she was dressing. It was the first real intimation that the war was getting close. By mid-afternoon the wind shifted round and the guns were barely audible.

Dr Foster had talked that morning with a junk captain heading up river. Linda walked along the Bund with Peggy and Mayling – she'd decided that they should at least take a look at the man's ship.

'We must keep our options open. And you can't possibly stay here, Mayling.' Linda couldn't see why the Chinese girl was soul-searching at a time like this. 'You've got to come with me and Peggy.'

'Linda's right, love. Reed will take the three of us out – honestly, he won't mind an extra passenger.'

'You make it seem so easy – merely a matter of packing a bag. And I could not leave without little Suyin – she has nobody.'

Peggy straightaway said, 'Then you've got to bring her as well. We'll look after her between us. Right, Linda?'

184

'Sure.'

Peggy responds immediately, so why did I hesitate over the child? Linda asked herself. I *did*, for just a fraction of a second. She didn't know why, except that she was wary about taking responsibility for other people's lives. If I say yes then I'm committed to them. Peggy shares wholeheartedly while she's with people; anything of hers is theirs also, but she forgets them as soon as she moves on.

'The three of us and little Suyin will have to be gone by tomorrow mid-day.' The name, given by Colonel Tang, fitted the abandoned girl so well that Linda suspected it really belonged to her. She pulled up her collar against the cold wind along the river. People got to look like their names. Arch. Didn't that fit him exactly? He couldn't be a Charles or John or Alan.

'I shall be so pleased to see Reed,' Peggy was saying.

Some people seem destined forever to be referred to by their surnames. Linda thought hard, but she couldn't remember Reed's Christian name.

There were a few moored ships but almost everything over the size of a sampan had left. Linda noticed a small battered, dismasted junk tied up at the Customs pier. Its cargo of three wooden crates seemed excessive for its size and it sat low in the water. A young Chinese Customs officer was climbing over the side. He glanced, interested, at Mayling as she walked by.

'It's unfair,' Peggy said. 'I spent twenty minutes in front of the mirror, and Mayling doesn't even wear make up.'

'We ought to think seriously about passage on a junk. The roads to Nanking are sure to be congested.'

'We don't do *anything* until Reed gets here. He'll have his truck.'

Her faith in that drifter was boundless. 'We need at least one other possibility – we can't count *entirely* on Reed.'

'Hundreds, maybe thousands of Chinese will be overtaken by the enemy.' Mayling bit her lip. 'It seems wrong for me to leave.'

'What are you saying? That you shouldn't get in the

lifeboat because it won't carry everybody? You can't save Suyin unless you come with us.'

But Linda recognized the mechanism of Mayling's guilt. A mission school in Nanking – her father had taken her there each day while other girls were treated as chattels by their parents and put to work in the mills. Then sent to the Institute of Hospital Technology to train as a nurse – it had separated her from her childhood friends. Mayling spoke English most of the time. Without the sponsorship of the foreigners and their Christian mission there would have been no education or training, no status. And no guilt.

'Dr Foster is remaining behind. He is quite determined.'

Colonel Tang might decide otherwise, Linda thought. But she said, 'I suppose the Japanese wouldn't harm an American missionary, and maybe it's better that some British and Americans stay – as observers.'

'Why? This isn't our war!' Peggy looked mystified.

Mayling took no part in the argument. Peggy and Linda often disagreed these days. An underlying antagonism? She preferred Peggy – loud, untidy, loving, sometimes outrageous. Linda was very determined, and interesting, but concerned with her own thoughts. Now she was walking half a pace ahead, as if distancing herself from Peggy's opinion. It was a way she had. What of that awful scar low down her body?

Linda was trying to resist her nagging doubts. We were crazy, she thought, we should have left last week. A cold wind rippled the river. She wasn't all that sure she wanted to risk getting out of Hsia-kang on a Chinese junk – they were an easy target for enemy planes. And she knew she was hoping Reed would arrive with his truck, though she didn't have a lot of faith in him.

The late afternoon sky was darkening as they reached the China Navigation wharf. Huge sliding doors open, the warehouse was crowded and noisy. Four men using rapid hand signals were selling off merchandise that the owners were unable to move up or down river. The press of people was frightening. A grinning Chinese lurched out under a high burden of green greatcoats.

'What can he possibly do with all those?'

'Sell them to somebody who can turn them into something else.'

'But they look like army stock. How are they able to sell army greatcoats?'

Mayling shook her head. 'Linda, you are always asking questions I cannot possibly answer.'

The crowd spilled outwards and almost merged with another crush of people trying to board a sea-going junk moored at the wharf's edge – it looked rotten, low in the water.

Colonel Tang was watching the crowd from high up on a wooden platform used by the *compradore*. The Chinese with him was dressed in a smart Western-style suit. Linda saw soldiers mingling with the people, and when the colonel nodded they moved in on two men and took them away.

Just after that, Tang noticed Linda; and climbing down, he edged his way towards the three girls.

He's a handsome man, Linda thought. 'Colonel! Is shipping also your concern?'

He bowed. 'I am sorry, young ladies, I cannot recommend passage on this particular vessel.'

Chinese sailors with clubs were spaced along the junk's side, regulating the passengers up one gangway – they paid as they boarded and tried to find somewhere to sit on the overcrowded deck. Westerners in the press of people still trying to board were waving handfuls of dollar bills. The sailors let them through.

'They make me feel ashamed to be white.' Linda stared angrily. 'What must the Chinese think of us?'

'Perhaps what they have always thought.' Tang gestured. 'What you see here is the beginning of a general exodus.'

Chinks of light were appearing in the windows and shops of Yibai Street, and he glanced round. 'It is not safe for you here now that darkness approaches. I will walk with you towards the mission.'

'The Japanese must be close, colonel. Will you have to stay?'

'For a while. I have work to do.'

'Tracking down the enemies in our midst? Oh, I'm sorry, I guess I really shouldn't ask.'

'There *are* enemies, even here in Hsia-kang.'

Linda watched as a company of ragged militia trailed past on their way to the East Gate. 'They are boys, and they look so sad.'

'They have come all the way from Szechuan.'

'So far, to fight for a place they've never even heard of?'

'They fight for China.'

'They have no greatcoats,' Linda said.

Stars were already appearing in the darkening east. 'There's one up there for everybody.' Peggy peered up. 'You have to pick out a star for yourself but you mustn't tell anybody which it is. Arch told me that. His is over there – somewhere in Orion.'

Linda didn't really believe in that sort of thing but she found herself searching anyway. Supposing by some chance she picked the same star as Arch Rittenhouse? She could see a red glow along the horizon – perhaps a burning town. The stars were infinitely remote. 'Compared with them, what are we? Sometimes I feel I'm nothing.'

'Is your Western religion no comfort to you?' Colonel Tang glanced sideways at her. 'Does it not promise you the personal concern of your God?'

Linda was aware again of the sudden loneliness. Nobody really knew if He existed.

Peggy stared around. 'Look how clear the sky is! Reed says the nearest star is four light years away – whatever that means.'

Reed says, Reed says. Linda felt a stab of irrational anger. 'I hope he has a practical plan – *if* he gets here.'

Peggy stopped and turned right round. 'Reed will do his best for us.' Then she walked on with Mayling. By the time they reached the narrow winding street leading to the mission, Peggy and Mayling were a dozen yards ahead and deep in conversation, and she was alone with Colonel Tang.

'Why did you delay leaving Hsia-kang, Miss Bishop?'

'It was part accident, part . . .' She shrugged. 'That junk at the China Navigation wharf – we don't even know if it will make it to the next town up river. Everything here is much less certain. So it's a sort of match, you see? Me feeling temporary, against this war-torn background. That probably makes no real sense?'

'You feel that your life is that unsure?'

Linda usually avoided talking about last year. 'Let's say I've become more aware of the tenuous hold we have on life.' She paused at the stone beasts outside the Taoist temple. 'Is this where you find answers? I still haven't figured out what Tao is.'

'Easier to say what it is not.' The colonel entered the temple and Linda followed him. 'Tao is the way – the natural order of things.'

'You make a religion of that?' She found herself whispering.

'It makes more sense as you grow old.'

The interior was lit by fat, guttering candles. Floor slabs were worn, but new white stone blocks had been morticed into the smoke-blackened side wall.

'Three times the temple has been all but destroyed; once by earthquake. Tai-ping rebels burned it in 1853 – they thought of themselves as Christian, you see.' He smiled to himself. 'And in 1927 the temple was badly damaged by shellfire when General Chiang Kai-shek's troops reached the delta.'

Candles burned in front of a shrine, and small offerings were grouped on a low stone. Five red beads – Linda wondered who had put them there. For a moment she wished she was alone in the cool, semi-dark interior. She could say a prayer, and maybe Somebody would hear. 'Why the scraps of paper there?'

'They are messages. The priest will burn them and their essence will reach the next world.' The colonel turned away. 'Some Tao concepts are puzzling – disturbing even. Some of it is superstition.'

Linda paused at a scrolled text open on a table. Beautifully

189

worked with a brush the symbols were perfect in themselves. They don't even need to have a meaning, she thought. Colonel Tang translated for her:

> There was something formless yet complete
> That existed before heaven and earth;
> Without sound, without substance,
> Dependent on nothing, unchanging.
> All pervading, unfailing.
> One may think of it as the mother of all things
>   under heaven.
> Its true name we do not know;
> "Way" is the by-name we give it.
> Were I forced to say to which class of things it
>   belongs I should call it Great.

He stared down at the text as if he had forgotten that Linda was there.

CHAPTER SIXTEEN

It was the hour of doubt, neither night nor morning. Reed stared up at the floatplane still mounted on its trolley, and he sipped the coffee – it was yesterday's heated up again. At this hour the mind should be buffered with alcohol; failing that, it was better to keep it busy. He threw the dregs across the floor of the shed and took his overalls from the metal locker.

Last night's determination not to drink was already making him edgy. Three young women to be brought out of Hsia-kang – he should never have agreed. He scowled. Why couldn't Arch rescue his own wife? And, damn it, he'd just got used to the idea of going home, and was even beginning to enjoy it. There was his free passage with Dalsager as far as Wuchang to consider as well – he'd lost that now for sure.

But Reed had to acknowledge that he'd fairly successfully evaded responsibility for others up until now. There's some kind of balance, he thought. You don't get away with everything. And he tied a piece of string round the waist of his overalls. This one last job, then he'd drive as fast as he could to Hsia-kang.

He walked right round the hauled-up Stinson, still staring at it. He had a little over an hour maybe before Brice and the Hun arrived. They had fuel hidden somewhere, or they were bringing it with them. They'd take the floatplane to Nanking for Han Yu-lin of the Green Society, and they would use it then scrap it.

A plan to disappoint Brice had been moving around inside Reed's head since the accidental meeting at the Golden Dragon several nights before, though he'd put off making a decision. Now it was crunch time, but he needed that fifty dollars Brice had promised him.

The floatplane and its trolley weighed well over a ton. Normally it took two men and a diesel-driven winch to move the plane down the slip and into the water. Today it would be just him, and no winch because the remaining diesel fuel had been taken for the trucks. Aviation spirit, motor spirit, diesel, paraffin – they were all becoming scarce, drying up as the military confiscated stocks.

He unhooked the tackle for lifting out the Stinson's engine. The damned thing was heavy. He fastened the hook to the trolley then dragged the gear to the rear of the workshop and wound the chain over a beam. He'd never done it this way before. All those student calculations: efficiency, velocity ratio, distance moved by effort. He secured the chain, leaving himself sufficient slack. Arch would have calculated it all; he did it by eye and feel.

He levered under the wheels with a crowbar, and felt his muscles straining as he edged the trolley towards the slip. Thirty minutes gone. The last part had to be done in near darkness because of the blackout. He opened the heavy doors fronting the river and the cold morning air chilled him.

Should he now drill a series of holes in each float? They would slowly fill with water, but Brice would have paid him the fifty dollars before the plane became obviously unflyable. It was a good plan – the meanest, lowest trick he could play on Brice. Again he delayed decision.

Levering, he noted the amount of chain left to him – the trolley reached the edge of the ramp and slid over, jerking up the remaining slack. And it held. The first grey light silhouetted the wireless mast down river. Brice and the Hun would be here soon.

Reed worked as fast as he could, letting the load down the slip a little at a time. With several feet to go he lost his grip. The tackle rattled and the burden plunged down, splashing into the river. He released the trolley and secured the floatplane – it bobbed gently.

Should he wade in and drill those holes? How large and how many to ensure that it stayed afloat for half an hour? – another student calculation. Small lights of a car were moving along the

192

waterfront towards CPC's mooring. Reed stood there, staring at the Stinson. It was such a beautiful machine, he knew he couldn't sink it. He went back into the shed.

Brice arrived. He glanced around suspiciously then opened the heavy doors a crack. 'So you managed it on your own.' He peered down the slip for a moment then closed the doors.

'How about the fifty dollars?'

'I did my best for you, Reed, but the Nanking office would only sanction thirty.' And Brice peeled off three tens from his fat roll.

'You're a lousy bastard, Brice. Y'know that?'

'I don't make the frigging rules.' He held out the notes. 'Do ya want them or not?'

Reed took them. All that use of his expertise. He felt like a dupe – a loser. He should have drilled those damned holes.

'You can get going, Reed. There's nothing more for you here.'

'I'm going.' The gasoline was stashed somewhere and Brice didn't want him to see it. Reed collected up his tools and washed his hands.

'I'd offer you a lift, but there's not room – we've got a lot of baggage. CPC stuff,' Brice grunted.

They would pick up Han Yu-lin in Nanking and take him to Foochow, that was the baggage. 'I don't need a lift, I've got my truck.'

'Yeah, well, good luck.' And Brice was already turning away.

Reed slung the toolbox in Greta's rear and drove off through the British district. He crossed the Grand Canal and took the road east to Hsia-kang. That's the second time Brice has made an idiot out of me he told himself. Dalsager was right – I'll die poor.

After an hour he saw a long column of men moving ant-like towards him. A mounted figure led them, and when they were closer he saw that the elderly officer was riding a small, long-tailed pony – his toes in the stirrups were near to the ground. His men swung along in single file, strung out for half a mile along the straight road, Kwangsi infantry, they were the best of the provincial troops. Their boots were worn thin and their uniforms were in rags. Some were carrying two rifles and a few wore regulation steel helmets of German pattern. Most were bare-headed, heads shaved, faces drawn to the bone. Why were they going west instead of facing the advance of the "Black" 9th Division? Perhaps they'd been withdrawn for a rest? Reed immediately rejected the idea – Chinese soldiers were among the worst treated human beings on God's earth. No, they were part of a general retreat, and he was the only man moving in the wrong direction.

> Mine is indeed the mind of an idiot . . .
> I seem unsettled as the ocean;
> Blown adrift, never brought to a stop.

Reed was within eleven miles of Hsia-kang when an oncoming convoy of battered army trucks drove him off the hard surface. He braked, then opened the throttle wide as the off-side wheels slipped sideways and down. Too late. Greta slid nose down into the drainage ditch and settled slowly, water covering the headlamps and seeping in over Reed's boots. He scrambled out, and up the ditch and cursed at the sky. 'What are you doing – ganging up on me?' Now he really did need a drink. Even if he had the means to haul Greta from the steep ditch it would take hours to dry her engine and get all the silt out of her.

Refugees were trailing past with their carts and belongings but they barely glanced at Reed and the drowning pick-up truck. And could he blame them? Nobody gave them lifts and they didn't expect anything. When lorries approached they stepped aside and kept walking, eyes down. There were two or three thousand years of surviving in that kind of disinterest. He dragged his leather bag and the toolbox from Greta's rear. Eleven miles.

The guns were firing off to the east, but their sounds, echoing off the low hills seemed all around. Reed slouched towards the town – already the toolbox felt as if it weighed a ton. Young women were waiting for him to get them to safety, and he was going to turn up with just a box of tools. The wreck of the truck wasn't his fault yet he couldn't evade the awareness of failure. He shifted the toolbox onto his shoulder and he knew he wasn't

194

going to throw it away. The tools reassured him – they were essential to his image of himself.

The walls of Hsia-kang were visible by the time he reached the road fork where the main track led south to Ch'ang-chou. When he neared the town gates he saw zig-zag trenches, dug by the militia and already abandoned. The defence, if that's what it was supposed to be, now seemed concentrated along the walls. Heads, grotesque on their bamboo poles, decorated the gate arch and, droll, they grinned down at Reed as he entered the town.

Early that morning, Linda had willed herself into waking. With dawn light, the single tree and the compound wall visible beyond the window were uniformly grey. Fragmentary images from her sleep slipped away as she sat up, but her heart was thumping. It was nothing – just a dream. The few remaining impressions were not in themselves frightening. She peered at the luminous dial of her wristwatch then pulled her nightdress over her head. She had known she was old, alone by a lake – or was it a river? But it was the boat, somewhere out there in the mist, that she didn't like to think about. Skin goose-pimpling, she dressed quickly. Dreams had no meaning.

The two bags were packed, ready since last night, and the portable typewriter was on top of the trunk. Nothing left to do. Linda folded her blankets, aware that she was doing it for the last time. She looked around to see if she'd forgotten anything then went out to the kitchen.

The mission was quiet. Even old Shu wasn't up yet, and no birds were singing in the compound – it was as if the strangeness of the dream was rubbing off onto her waking day.

As she took down mugs for tea she heard Mayling's light step along the passage. A new day began and the dream substance slid back into her subconscious.

The Chinese girl looked even more attractive when still half asleep. 'Our last night here – it feels strange, doesn't it?' She rubbed her eyes. 'Little Suyin woke me three times, then I stayed awake until four, worrying about her.'

'For heaven's sake, why? Suyin's managing.' Linda couldn't

195

really comprehend Mayling's anxiety. 'That child can keep going longer than you or me. And she'll eat anything you put in front of her.'

'That is because she knows what it is like to be hungry. Did you know that Suyin cries in her sleep?'

'She'll get *over* it.' Linda checked her watch against the clock. 'Tell me, Mayling, did you ever dream you'd grown old?'

'No. In all my dreams I am the age I am now. Why are you asking?'

'Oh, it's nothing.' And she shrugged. 'How do you feel about two fried eggs?'

'I'll help.'

'Okay, set the table.'

Foster came in, looked at his drugs in the refrigerator then went out to the chapel. Linda knew he just sat there – she'd seen him. And whether he prayed, or waited for some kind of guidance, she didn't know. Or maybe he just goes there to get out of the way of three women?

She cracked eggs into the frying pan, and Mayling switched on the portable radio. XMHA Shanghai put out music early in the morning – the first news broadcast was at six. Today it was local music, recorded at the Canidrome Ballroom the previous evening. Buck Clayton sang "Good Old Shanghai", and the brass section blared.

'We'd better call Peggy.'

'I'll make her a bacon sandwich, though how she can eat it at this time of the morning I don't know.'

The three of them sat at the kitchen table, eating and exchanging opinions about what they should wear, and when Reed would arrive. There was a shared awareness that this day was going to be important in their lives. It was a good feeling, Linda thought.

'Why are you smiling to yourself?' Peggy asked.

'I was just thinking. One day I'm going to write a book about us – all of this.' Linda turned up the volume of the radio as the news broadcast began. The League of Nations had passed a resolution condemning Japanese aggression.

'Much good may that do anybody.'

Shao-chou had been bombed at dawn, and the Japanese "Black" 9th was reported to be into the outskirts of Huapshih.

'But that's only fifteen miles west of here!'

'Twelve.'

'Why is that army division called the "Black" 9th?'

'I don't know.' Mayling shivered. She was uneasy. 'It will be difficult to keep ahead. They are so close.'

'Reed will take care of us,' Peggy said.

'You would expect Dr Foster to be anxious, watching the town emptying. But he remains very calm and patient with everybody.'

'It's because he's staying,' Linda glanced at the clock again. 'It's only when you've made the decision to go that waiting around makes you nervous. Wu Guo says it's the same with being bombed – you start to lose your nerve when you take to the air raid shelter. He and Dr Foster and old Shu will be too busy to be afraid.'

'Dr Foster is mad,' Peggy said. 'Can you see the Japanese allowing him to just carry on as usual?'

'They'll be here by tomorrow.'

Linda rose and went to the window. It was light out there now. She looked across to the entrance of the compound. Some time tomorrow, Japanese soldiers would walk cautiously towards this house. She turned back to the others. How cold it had suddenly become. 'I wonder when Reed will get here?'

They expected him around the middle of the morning but noon came and went and he hadn't arrived. Foster sent Wu Guo to Colonel Tang's headquarters to ask if there was room on an army transport for the three girls and the child, but Wu Guo returned shaking his head – most of the vehicles had already left.

Linda sat on the verandah. There were only the old and sick in the queue outside Gerald Foster's dispensary. Others, unfit to take to the road, had come to camp in the compound, hoping that he would protect them when the Japanese arrived. And they were relying on Reed. She bit her lip.

Sounds were different today; no cars or trucks beyond the compound wall, no calls of street traders, no clacking of machinery in the silk mill. A dog was howling, locked in some-where, and the thump of the guns was closer. The genial voice of Shanghai Radio predicted cold weather. Then Linda saw Reed walking through the gate. All he had was a box and a bag.

An unreasonable anger seized her. She'd really begun to believe he *would* rescue them, and he turned up here on foot with nothing but a damned toolbox!

Reed paused in his slouching walk, putting the box down for a moment. Seeing her he raised his hand as if acknowledging that he'd brought nothing with him but a talent for failure.

He began talking – explaining – before he reached her. 'I ended up in a ditch. I tell you, those Chinese army drivers are crazy!'

She forced a smile. 'A truck like yours – you *deserve* to be driven off the road.'

And what the hell do we do now? she wondered.

A panic had seized the town that morning, and those who the previous night had been determined to stay, suddenly bundled their possessions together and took to the road or the river. Now there were no civilians to be seen on the Bund. Soldiers sat in their sandbagged machine gun positions and waited for Japanese aeroplanes. Some of the militiamen had deserted in the night. Tide low, a few hulks were settled on the mud, and the rusting steamer. Moorings were empty, apart from *Fushan* and a launch tied up at the Customs pier.

Colonel Tang hadn't reached the battered junk until mid-afternoon. He frowned and prodded one of the engine crates with his stick. 'Captain Chu of Maritime Customs believes that you are working for the Japanese navy.' And he looked round at Russell. 'Captain Chu says these engines are outdated, no use; part of a trick to get you to the boom so that you could map it for the enemy.'

'If Captain Chu really believes that he is a complete fool. The engines were impounded in a warehouse in Shanghai. We took them from under the noses of the Japanese and it is our intention to get them to Nanking.'

'And you say Mister Dou of Shanghai gave you the junk?'

'The crew also. There are just two of us left. The others were killed or injured.'

Colonel Tang stared at him. 'Why would you, a foreigner, invite such danger and antagonize the Japanese?'

Russell sighed. For the first time in his life he wasn't going to give in to the negative side of his nature. 'I made a promise to an old man,' he said.

'Aeroplane engines for General Chiang Kai-shek? Your story is unlikely.'

'We've been hounded all the way from Shanghai! You can see we've been shot at!'

'But by whom?' Tang gestured to his aide to open one of the crates.

It took time to find the crowbar; and Russell sat dejected, staring up at the sky. Sometimes he speculated that maybe the three crates and his journey were a task imposed on him by Somebody up there; every obstacle a test of his will.

A soldier pressed on the crowbar, and the lid groaned and lifted.

The aero engine was straight from the factory, gleaming new and smeared with grease. 'You see here, this metal tag,' Russell said. 'Pratt & Whitney "Wasp" – they are fitted to China's latest fighter plane.'

A single spent bullet was lodged in a cooling vane of one of the cylinders. The lieutenant prised it out and handed it to the colonel. 'Sir, it is seven-point-six – Japanese.'

Tang toyed with the bullet for a moment then put it in his pocket. An officer was reminding him of the time and he nodded. 'You may leave at first light tomorrow, Mr Russell.'

'So you believe me! Why can't I leave today?'

'Tomorrow, Mr Russell.'

Russell was in a black mood, he'd spent the previous night on a bug-infested mattress in a stinking cell. 'If you release my crewman, let us have some food, and timber to make repairs, we could be several miles up river by nightfall.'

'I will see that your crewman is released.' Tang was preparing to go.

'We've already lost two-days!' All Russell wanted was to get Lao out of jail and leave Hsia-kang behind him. He tried the magic again. 'I'm sure Mister Dou would appreciate your co-operation.'

Colonel Tang just stared at him. 'You leave tomorrow. And there is a condition. You must take some passengers – people from the Christian mission here.'

'I can't do that! Those engines are *important* – I haven't got time to worry about passengers!'

'Three young women and a child.'

Russell slapped his forehead with the flat of his hand and gestured hopelessly at the open deck of *Fushan*. 'Damn it, there are no – no facilities for women!'

'I am not offering you a choice. Be realistic – you need a written authorization from me if you are to proceed further up river. And you need stores. I may even find you some diesel fuel.'

Women! For God's sake! They sapped his confidence – he was never sure of himself when women were around. 'You're blackmailing me!'

'Quite so.'

Colonel Tang was tired. And he was gratified to have resolved two problems at one stroke. Russell was obviously innocent, though as mad as his fellow countrymen. But how to explain the actions of Captain Chu Teng of Maritime Customs?

Russell tried one last protest but he knew he wasn't going to win. Colonel Tang gestured wearily and left.

Daylight faded but the gunfire continued into the night, rever-berating in the empty streets and off the high buildings fronting the river. At dusk a reconnaissance patrol from Hsia-kang had encountered an advance unit of Japanese infantry.

Colonel Tang stood at the window of Miss Kuang's dar-kened room and watched shell bursts on the low ridge beyond the town. Orange and yellow, and smoke. Like dragons' breath, he thought, and remembered the festivals of his child-hood. Banners and offering fires, and the great monsters with

200

grotesque heads winding and writhing through the streets – he had thought they were real. The gongs and sputtering fireworks to frighten away demons. He had believed there were hungry ghosts, unleashed through the gates of hell. What did he believe now?

Miss Kuang called softly in the darkness. 'Come back to me.'

But he stayed at the window. When the Empress ruled in her corruption, he had believed in constitutional assemblies. Later, naked force seemed the answer and he came to believe in the Kuomintang and Chiang Kai-shek. Then there was comradeship – they had crushed the war lords and fought the Japanese in 1932. They had harassed Mao Tse-tung's peasant army because there had to be conformity. But there were always too many problems, too many necessary compromises. It had all needed ten years of peace. He needed ten years of peace.

'Why do you stand there? What do you see?'

'Dragons' breath,' he said.

'We still have two hours.'

He came and lay beside her on the bed, and stared up at the ceiling lit intermittently by the distant flashes. 'I have arranged safe conduct for you. You will be taken down river under a flag of truce with two other French nationals at mid-day – they are both priests, and there is a Belgian nun. At Chiang-yin you will transfer to a Japanese freighter bound for Shanghai.'

Miss Kuang did not intend going that far. Tomorrow she expected to dine with the Japanese General Matsui and his staff. She pulled back Tang's tunic and ran her fingers over his bare chest. The muscles were hard. An old scar under his left nipple excited her. She took his hand and rested it inside her thigh. Middle-aged. An adequate lover – no more than that. His ardour was short, easily drained, and he returned to his thoughts. Yet he had casually mastered her. The experience was quite new to Miss Kuang.

She lay in the darkness and stroked his body. This would be the last time. Tomorrow evening, when she dined with the staff of the 9th Division, Colonel Tang would be either a prisoner or

201

dead. The humiliation she had promised herself for him no longer seemed relevant.

Miss Kuang pondered as she watched the flashes on the ceiling. She would not risk her life to save his, yet she would prefer that he didn't die. Strange that it should come to this after only two nights together. What did she really know of him? His son was killed in the Chapei fighting. As a boy he lived in Yunnan province. He smoked Tiger cigarettes. Once snared, men usually bored her, but now she found herself trying constantly to follow Tang's thoughts and join in them. Earlier in the day she had allowed herself a brief fantasy – another darkened room, far from the war, and where nobody expected anything of either of them. And time. Perhaps I would never tire of him? she asked herself. And I would play no elaborate games.

She leaned up on her elbows. 'Will it be necessary for you to remain in Hsia-kang?'

'No.' He groped in his pocket for his cigarette case. 'The defence of the town is in other hands.'

She felt a small flicker of relief. So he probably wouldn't die here after all.

'I must ensure that the foreigners at the mission leave at first light. They will take their chances on the junk, *Fushan*, and reach Nanking as best they can.' He struck a match, and her body was golden in its flare. 'And there remains one other task – Chu Teng, a captain of Maritime Customs.'

Miss Kuang froze then quickly recovered. 'Chu Teng?'

'Have you picked up any information on this man?'

'I have not heard that name.' It would be wiser to say no more, but she needed to know. 'What has this captain of Customs done?'

'I am not sure. He is under arrest.' The colonel blew smoke into the darkness. 'Perhaps he is just stupid. When I have seen the *Fushan* leave with its troublesome cargo of foreigners, I will question him.'

Miss Kuang continued to run her fingers over her lover's chest. That fool, Chu! She didn't dare enquire further. Chu had cyanide now but supposing he lacked the courage to swallow it! Her mind raced ahead, exploring the ominous possibilites. If Chu was questioned before she left, and he told something – everything . . .?

She slid her body across Tang's. 'We have only an hour left to us. And if I go to Shanghai we will probably never meet again. Why does it have to be so? Let me stay here until you leave.'

'Why do you talk so foolishly? You would not be able to travel with me, and it is too dangerous for you to remain – Matsui's infantrymen will not pause to ask you if you are half French.'

She arched her body up from his in case he should notice the rapid pumping of her heart. 'But why must I go to Shanghai? I could leave at first light with the other foreigners boarding *Fushan* and you and I could meet in Nanking?'

She waited.

He didn't reply.

And she knew instinctively that if she touched him she would lose the game. So she stretched out on her back. 'If I reached Nanking I would wait for you.'

'Quiet, woman,' he said. 'I am thinking.'

CHAPTER SEVENTEEN

The cell had a barred window high up in the wall permitting Chu Teng a small, narrowed view of the night sky. The rest was darkness. He could hear rats scurrying in the dirty straw covering the cell floor, and the sound fed his fear. Chu lifted his bare feet onto the board and squeezed back into the corner.

The board rested on bricks at each end. Opposite, and next to the heavy wooden door, was a latrine bucket. Chu had used it three times, emptying his bowels, but the sick spasms persisted. Pride, lust and greed had brought him to this – a grey despair crawled across his thoughts and it seemed to him now that it had always been there, dormant, waiting for this night.

They had taken away his tunic as well as his shoes. Chu Teng shivered uncontrollably and hugged his knees with his arms. All men must come to death in the end, but perhaps he could still save himself for a while longer – tell everything and offer to find out more?

The rats scratched in the blackness.

He was clutching at empty hope – no dignity left, it had peeled off him as they'd stripped him of his uniform.

'I was a captain of Maritime Customs,' he said aloud.

Now he was nothing. And no one could save him from a shameful, degrading end. No sons to honour him, he would join the hungry ghosts.

One task remained.

Chu eased himself off the board, and, still shivering, he felt in the straw, running his fingers along the base of the wall. A loose stone? – no, it was too soft, crumbling as he squeezed it. He tried the far wall, drawing back in horror as a rat scrambled across his hand. Then he found a hard fragment of brick. Groping back in the darkness, he knelt on the board and scratched the name – KUANG – large in the plaster of the wall. Now it was done. She too would pay.

Nobody would perform the prescribed rituals. Chu prayed to his ancestors and begged for ultimate forgiveness. Then he sat, calm once more and feet drawn up, watching the barred window for the first suggestion of morning light. The poison capsule was sheathed in silk and glued to his skull. He fingered in his thick hair and prised it loose.

Hell awaited him.

He crushed the capsule in his teeth and gripped the board with all his strength.

With the first grey light, Reed reached the Customs pier. He had only the tool kit and his scuffed leather bag.

The Chinese boy pointed. '*Fushan*. Good boat.'

'What did you say your name was?'

'Lao.' He grinned through split lips.

'What happened to you?'

'Customs men ask questions. Amateurs.' He spat into the river.

'I'm sailing with you and Mr Russell. My name's Reed. Let's look at the junk.'

Fushan was low in the water. It was some time since she'd been pumped dry. Reed could see that the three wooden crates were a heavy burden for that sized vessel. Fresh stores, some planed timber and a twenty-foot smoothed-pine spar had been dumped on top of the crates. There was a guard huddled in the stern shelter. He pinched out his cigarette and slung his rifle on his shoulder, glad to be relieved. 'You sail in this?' And he surveyed the stinking junk and tapped his head to indicate their madness.

'You tap tomorrow,' Lao said. 'If you still have head.'

Reed turned his gaze on the stern shelter – it would barely keep the rain off. 'Where did the junk come from?'

'My employer provide.'

About forty feet, Reed estimated, but narrow at the waist where the beam measurement was used to assess cargo capacity. The slippery decking was inch-and-a-half pine, rotting in places. He could feel the slight tilt, she was down by the head. Reed could only conclude that the gift of the junk had been an elaborate Chinese joke. He had serious doubts. 'How the hell did you and Russell manage to get all the way from Shanghai in this hulk?'

'Sea goddess, Ma ku, on our side. And Jesus Christ-which-is-in-heaven more or less.' The boy grinned. 'But Russell driven by a devil. I look after him for my employer.'

'Who *is* your employer?'

'Small man. Lot of pull.'

Reed examined the shelter. Open to the air on one side, it was crowded with charts, sacks, damp blankets, a dirty cooking pot. They must have lived like pigs. He wondered how the fastidious Miss Bishop was going to react to the stench and dirt.

It was getting light but the sky was heavy with rain clouds.

'That drum of diesel fuel – who gave us that?'

The boy's white teeth showed. 'Colonel Tang and I have discussions – he get the drift.'

You couldn't even buy the stuff it was so short. 'Your employer, the small man – does he have a lot of pull with Colonel Tang as well?'

Lao assumed a puzzled expression as though he didn't understand the question. He tilted his head and listened to the guns. 'Japs will come today.'

'Yeah, they'll probably burn the town before nightfall.' Reed scowled to himself. And this god-awful excuse for a boat was their only way out. The boy held a flashlight for him and he climbed down to look at the four-stroke engine. It was old. He rubbed the metal plate and read the maker's name – Stuart Turner, 1918. He felt for play on the shaft.

'Goes most times,' Lao said. 'Bilge pump not so good.'

The pump was old as well, of Chinese design, sturdy, probably made by a back-street smith. Reed tried it. A long metal arm, waist high, worked up and down to activate a

206

suction barrel, but the linkage was worn from excessive use. He opened the well, and lying flat he peered with the flashlight for several minutes. The bilge was deep in foul water, and the lower part of the barrel was rusting – bits came away in his fingers. Sooner rather than later they were going to have trouble with that pump. 'What a bitch,' he said.

'Who have you got down there?'

He raised his head and turned. Miss Bishop's perfect ankles were only inches away.

'My word, Reed, aren't you the early bird? I thought I'd be first on board.' She set down her baggage. 'Two cases – I had to abandon my trunk. And one typewriter – I thought I'd sneak it on before that tight-lipped young man, Russell, becomes anxious about the weight.'

'I've already got him figured as crazy.' Seen from Reed's position, Miss Bishop had an interesting body. She was wearing a suede leather jacket, and a scarf over her head and round her neck. Her shoes were expensive, and sensible if he could bring himself to be honest about them.

'Do you really think this junk will stay afloat?' She looked around frowningly. 'It doesn't seem that ship-shape and Bristol fashion.'

She, on the other hand, did. He rose, wondering again at her ability to look attractive for an unlikely journey. 'Crisp as the morning – you must have slept well, Miss Bishop. And no, I'm not sure this junk will stay afloat.'

She stared at him. 'I worked half the night with Wu Guo in the dispensary and worried the other half. Aren't junks supposed to have a mast or some damn thing to hang the sail on?'

'That's right. The drum of diesel fuel won't last us. We're gonna have to put up a sail somehow, and it looks like none of us knows much about boats.' He groped in the toolbox for a wrench. 'We have another little problem. I hope you can swim. The bilge is deep in water and our cargo is likely to take the junk to the bottom of the river.' He scowled at the crates. 'Russell must be some kind of nut, hauling those

207

damned things this far.' All the British were crazy, he thought.

Linda bit her lip. 'One thing I've noticed about you, Reed, you're unfailingly negative.'

'Just a realist.' But she was almost right – he'd condemned the journey before they'd even begun. He started dismantling the head of the pump.

Linda turned, peering at the low hills to the south of the town, and the bubbles of smoke from shellfire. 'Hsia-kang's last day – I suppose the Japanese will gut it?'

'That's what they usually do.' But now he was regretting his perverse compulsion always to assume the worst. 'Hsia-kang has probably been burned half a dozen times in the last hundred years – the Chinese will rebuild it when the war moves on.'

'Can they? Yes, I suppose they will.'

'And this old junk,' he added forcefully. 'Tougher than it looks – that's another thing the Chinese have been building for thousands of years.' He rapped the timber with his fist. 'They know how to build junks.'

'And this one will get us to Nanking?'

He hesitated almost imperceptibly. 'Yes, Miss Bishop. The junk will get us to Nanking.'

'You sound like a used car salesman.' She watched as he worked the pivot loose from the pump fulcrum. 'What are you doing?'

'This pump's been used so much it's shaking apart.' He cursed softly as the spanner slipped. 'I'm gonna replace the worn washers – pack this spindle out tighter so there's less sideways play.'

She didn't understand. But he felt that her anxiety had eased so he went on talking casually. 'Arch would do it differently – he's got a mind like a slide rule.' And he fingered a cigarette from the crushed packet on his shirt pocket. 'You've met Arch?'

'Yes. I've met Captain Rittenhouse.'

'Arch would calculate the maximum theoretical height of the water in the cylinder – stress on the pivot, stuff like that.

208

In the Chaco war Arch always used less fuel than anybody else – he'd figured the precise throttle settings for the gas we were using. He never ran short.'

She didn't say anything.

'I'm pragmatic, like the Chinese.' He laid out bits of the pump. 'I do it all by eye and guesswork.'

'And does it work?'

'Usually. Not always.'

Two Japanese seaplanes were circling under the dark rainclouds.

'I assumed Captain Rittenhouse would be good at anything he did.'

She'd said it lightly but Reed had the impression that Linda Bishop was attempting to prolong discussion of Arch. 'I can seal a radiator with ox dung – Arch can't do that. I'm an acknowledged master with ox dung.'

She smiled patiently. 'Do you see any future in the ox dung business?'

'By temperament and experience I'd say I'm well suited to it.' Reed grinned as if it was a joke, but he half meant it.

Lao was squatting, watching the aeroplanes, but he stood suddenly and listened. 'Motors coming.'

Reed could hear only distant gunfire and the two planes circling. The first drops of rain fell. A moment later a Dodge truck painted drab army green crunched along the Bund. A large, black, gangster-type car followed, and Reed observed it curiously.

Mayling was helped from the back of the truck by Dr Foster, then Peggy passed down the child. And the four of them stood there, uncertain, partly sheltered from the rain. Russell climbed from the back of the truck, and limped as soon as his bad leg took his weight. He hustled the other four along the wooden pier. Reed thought he looked angry.

'Reed! For God's sake!' Peggy climbed over *Fushan*'s side, unintentionally favouring Lao with a view of her knees. 'There isn't room to swing a cat!'

'Oh, you'll like it,' he said. 'Wait till you see the sun deck.'

Colonel Tang and an attractive Chinese girl had emerged

from the black car. They stood talking for a moment then walked quickly towards *Fushan*. The girl was well dressed and carried a slim leather valise. A soldier followed her with baggage. The colonel was in a hurry, speaking rapidly to Russell before the Englishman boarded the junk.

'Here is written authorization for you to proceed up river. I advise that you make every effort to reach Cooper Bank before stopping. The River boom at Chiang-yin is not yet breached but General Matsui's 9th Division will be beyond Hsia-kang by tomorrow.'

They were moving fast! Reed felt a small surge of alarm. He helped the Chinese girl as she stepped across the gap into *Fushan*; and her eyes sought his briefly, questioning, before she let go his hand. She joined the others, searching for space on the cluttered deck.

'Miss Kuang is a French national – a representative for Pacific Press Service,' Tang was saying to the scowling Russell. 'It is very important that she reaches the safety of Nanking.'

Important to whom? Reed assumed she was Tang's mistress. You'd *have* to be a colonel to afford a woman like that.

And Foster had resumed what was clearly an on-going argument. 'I shall protest when we reach the capital, Colonel Tang.'

'There is insufficient time for me adequately to express the gratitude of this miserable town and its people.'

'You have driven me from my mission!'

'Pardon the correction, Dr Foster. Not one square inch of Chinese territory is yours. Please board the junk immediately.'

'There are sick, destitute, abandoned, with only a male nurse and an old woman to look after them!'

But the colonel had ceased listening. Head back he watched the two seaplanes as they circled in the rain. 'Think yourself fortunate that you do not have to witness what happens here.'

Dark, ominous clouds were building up. One of the

210

planes banked sharply, slid down the air then dived to drop its bombs on the centre of the town. The pier trembled with the shock wave. Rain spattered the crates as they cast off and Russell clambered aboard. The propeller churned and *Fushan* moved slowly out into the vast, melancholy river.

She was low in the water; only a foot of freeboard. Lao was at the tiller. Reed could see worry nagging at Russell as he surveyed the cluttered deck, and his six passengers crammed uncomfortably, watching the receding shore.

Miss Kuang was in the stern looking back as *Fushan* turned up river. She raised her hand briefly to Colonel Tang. Reed wondered about the gesture. Would those two ever meet again?

The colonel was a small figure on the pier. He pulled up the collar of his greatcoat and walked back to the car. Wind lifted paper rubbish, scuffing it along the deserted Bund until it became soaked by the rain blown almost horizontal across the broad sweep of the river.

Within minutes the open deck of *Fushan* was running with water. Rain blew in through the open side of the stern shelter, soaking the four young women and the child huddled together. Reed rubbed rain from his eyes and peered ahead as the junk, bow down, headed towards Nanking.

Riding through Hsia-kang's wet, empty streets, Colonel Tang speculated on *Fushan's* chances of reaching the capital. Watching the junk's wallowing passage, he'd begun to doubt. Perhaps he should have insisted that the women remain until mid-day then cross to the Japanese under a flag of truce? Too late now, their journey had begun.

The driver detoured round Yibai Street where a bomb had fired the district courthouse – it flared uncontrolled and black smoke fanned out in the blustery rain. The two Japanese planes had gone. And at the back of Colonel Tang's mind there was a question – why hadn't the town been bombed before? Unless there was something or some-body here valuable to the enemy.

In the market area soldiers were dragging up an ancient field gun for the defence of the town's eastern gate. At mid-day hostilities in the area would cease briefly and the gate would be swung back. The last of the foreigners were to leave – two French priests, a Belgian nun, and the Danish archaeologist. Colonel Tang had deleted the name of Miss Kuang from the list of those expected by the Japanese truce party. He thought about her again. A sensual enigma – he had never been sure what she was thinking except in those few minutes before her desire was slaked. And once, when she thought he was asleep, she had stroked his face with her fingertips.

The car reached headquarters. There remained the task of interrogating the fat captain of Customs and he went immediately to Chu Teng's cell. Chu had fallen off his plank bed and lay face down in the dirty straw.

Colonel Tang rolled the body over with the toe of his boot. The rats had already been at work. He squatted on his heels and forced open the clenched mouth. Cyanide – he could smell it. He stood again and rubbed his hand over his jaw. To kill himself over a stupid mishandling of the junk and its cargo – how to explain that? He would probably have released Chu today. The suicide made no sense. Unless – unless Chu knew something else – something important – and feared for what he knew?

The colonel turned to leave, then noticed the characters scratched large in the plaster above the dead man's bed: KUANG.

He stared. The jigsaw pieces slotted together. Miss Kuang had been playing an elaborate game. He knew now why she had been so anxious to leave before he questioned Chu. She had outwitted him, made him ridiculous. And the colonel's jaw tightened. The game was not yet over.

CHAPTER EIGHTEEN

The wake of *Fushan* washed briefly over the sandbar then merged again with the river. Nearly five miles separated the north shore from the south.

The breeze had shifted and Miss Kuang could smell land. She'd found a place to sit alone, squeezed between the two furthest engine crates. She watched the gulls. A pair – they had followed the junk all the previous day. Sometimes they alighted on the bows but seemingly not for rest. Wings wide-spread and barely moving, they could stay in the air for hours. They were always close together, Miss Kuang had noticed. Now they planed effortlessly astern.

She glanced round as Reed edged past her carrying a coil of heavy rope. 'Elegant, aren't they? You ever wonder how they do it?' He watched the gulls with her. 'They're riding on a cushion of air close to the water.'

'Are they? How clever of them.' Reed seemed knowledgeable about birds. 'I have not seen gulls so large.'

'Some are bigger.' He stared at them, a faint smile on his lips. 'Seen them on the east coast of America with a wingspan well over five feet.' And he moved on.

Reed had repaired the pump and was attempting to rig a sail. A useful man to cultivate, Miss Kuang decided – one couldn't be sure how this voyage might turn out. She had observed him carefully: usually easy-going but sometimes argumentative, occasionally unreasonable. But Reed had a rough charm, unlike Russell who appeared to make the decisions. Russell was shy of women, no doubt because of his limp. He talked to other men when he had to, but the only person he seemed comfortable with was Lao, the little Shanghai thug. All things

213

considered, the junk journey was not as bad as Miss Kuang had thought it would be in those first two days, swept by rain and sleeping fitfully to the sound of perpetual pumping.

She pulled up her coat collar. The wind was cold, rippling the water. Autumn was running into winter. She felt safely enough distanced from Hsia-kang to begin weighing her prospects. Captain Chu Teng of Customs was probably dead, and she must assume he might have implicated her. Colonel Tang? Possibly dead also, and safer for her if he was. Though the fantasy remained, surfacing unaccountably whenever she was alone – it could all have been different, both of them outcast together in some far-off place. Chance was never that kind.

Miss Kuang stifled her irritation as Peggy called. It seemed to be the brassy English girl's self-appointed task to find work for her. This time it was moving the stores to the newly-built men's shelter and putting them into dry sacks.

She took up her end of the load and moved awkwardly with Mayling who felt impelled to work harder than the rest of them. Mayling was easy to understand: a 'rice Christian', guilt-ridden because of her divided loyalties, and compensating for her guilt by worrying endlessly about the child, Suyin. Miss Kuang allowed Mayling a little more of the weight until they reached the men's shelter. It was a series of bamboo frames with a tarpaulin covering.

Linda Bishop argued politely with Peggy about how the perishables should be stored.

'It makes more sense to stack them here.'

'But they're more get-at-able lower down, love.'

'That damned rat will agree with you.'

The two appeared to be good friends, but there was a tension between them that Miss Kuang had sensed since the outset of the journey – she kept a mental note of affections and antagonisms; they could sometimes be useful.

She left Peggy and Linda to their argument, and instead of returning for more stores went further forward to the toilet – a bucket within a bamboo and canvas shelter in *Fushan*'s bow, not quite high enough to conceal the user's head. This did not

214

worry Miss Kuang unduly. Let the excessively modest Linda Bishop endeavour to hide her natural functions. The American girl was a puzzling mix. And probably apprehensive of men – she and Reed seemed at war much of the time. In the makeshift toilet, safe from requests to help with this or that, Miss Kuang watched the two seagulls. With a small effort of imagination she could envisage *Fushan* as they saw it; tiny, fragile in the immensity of the great river.

Her thoughts were interrupted by the now all too familiar clanking sound. Somebody was pumping again. *Fushan* had a bad leak. There was a gap, thin but long where the planking had separated, and it was below the waterline near the bow. Water, yellow with silt, gushed from the pump faucet and back into the river.

'Reed says you are much stronger than you look.' Linda squatted next to Lao as he worked the lever up and down. 'He also says you are a gangster.'

Lao grinned at her and went on pumping.

She eased her back against the stump of the old mast. 'Dear God, I'm bushed.' Her hands were chapped, skin cracking between the fingers. She examined them with distaste. How long did it take to get scurvy? She had wanted something significant to write about but hadn't figured on this much discomfort.

'How did you and Mr Russell manage the junk all on your own, Lao?'

'Five of us start. One hurt, we leave him behind. Two die, so to speak.'

'That's awful! How did they die?'

'They have accidents.' He rested for a moment.

'Here, let me take a turn.' Linda rose wearily. 'One hundred strokes of the pump – you can count.'

He nodded and wiped the sweat from his face. 'I pump whole goddam Yangtze through this hull.' He peered round at the sky. 'We lucky up to now – no Jap planes. Better when we have sail, we go faster.'

'You're supposed to be counting.'

The twenty-foot spar lay almost horizontal, one end resting

on the stern shelter and the other heeled up against the old stump. Reed was attaching stays and running them out along the decking. Linda wondered how he proposed to raise the spar vertically. East Hartford Yacht Club was never like this. The thought evoked a memory of home and safety; crewing occasionally and clumsily on long, warm holiday weekends.

'God's teeth!' She rested on the pump handle and stared down at her blistered hands. 'It must be a hundred by now?'

'Sixty-six.' Lao's white teeth showed, and he took over again.

Linda stuck her hands under her arms to warm them. 'There's a strong rumour, Lao, that Mr Russell got the *Fushan* from Mr Dou of Shanghai, and that you work for Mr Dou?'

'Dou?' He looked puzzled, as if hearing the name for the first time.

He wasn't going to talk. The Green Brotherhood probably slaughtered garrulous members. Linda edged sideways and sat herself next to one of the crates to get out of the wind. Now that she'd stopped pumping she felt cold again. It was debilitating, this constant exposure to the weather.

Reed called to her. 'Miss Bishop, I could do with a little help *if* you're not too busy.'

'I *am* busy. I'm busy trying to keep from freezing to death. If you want me to help lift that tree trunk you can think again.' But she went anyway.

Reed was working by eye. He'd secured the rope stays and shrouds to the mast head and was laying them out in some order of his own. The engine crates were in the way and he cursed softly. 'We'd be better off if we dropped them overboard.'

'Aren't they the real purpose of our journey?'

'Only in the mind of our crazy captain.' He re-arranged the order of the ropes. 'I saw a Chinese do this once, but I can't remember . . .' He frowned and rubbed his jaw. 'When we get the damned thing up I'll have to think of four different things at once. I'm not even sure we can raise it and hold it steady against the movement of the junk.'

'You're doing fine – for an ox dung man. Diesel engines.

216

Pumps. Reluctant paraffin burners. Mind you – and I have to say this, Reed – a horizontal mast could be a bit of an embarrassment when we sail triumphantly into Nanking. Maybe the problem requires a slide-rule mind? What would Captain Rittenhouse do?'

It was an innocent bantering question. She hadn't thought why she'd said it until she caught the sudden enquiry in Reed's glance. She turned her head away.

The mast was almost ready. Russell listened to Reed, then told Linda and Peggy to take the tiller and hold *Fushan*'s bow into wind so that the junk wouldn't roll. Reed began to organize everybody.

'He's a great fixer-upper,' Peggy said. 'He can fix up anything, like motor cars and leaky roofs.' And she smiled. 'The only thing he can't fix up is himself.'

'That's not so rare,' Linda said.

Reed had lashed bamboo poles to form a rigid apex secured upright to the deck. He passed a rope over the top and fastened it to the head of the new mast where it rested on the stern. And he held up his hands, fingers crossed, and nodded to Russell, Foster and Lao in the bows. They hauled on the freed end of the rope. Would it work? Linda bit her lip, willing them to succeed. And the mast came up, a foot, two feet, with Reed steadying it. They heaved again. The bamboo poles curved under the strain. Fine spray came over the bows. The new mast swayed, then it was upright against the stump and Reed held his arms around them while Lao lashed mast and stump together.

'Now the wedges – quickly!' Reed gritted his teeth.

Lao hammered in wedges while Russell and Foster tightened the heavy stays.

'Well done!' Linda clapped her sore hands. 'You're not just an ox dung man.' She had an impulse to hug him but instantly rejected it. 'Don't look too pleased with yourself – it's your turn to pump.'

Russell slapped the new mast with the flat of his hand. 'You've done it, Reed.' He looked round at him. 'You're a very useful feller.'

'You're not going to listen to me,' Reed said, 'but we'd make better progress without those damned aero engines.'

Russell smiled. 'That's right. I'm not going to listen to you.'

Even with its new rigging, *Fushan* had an odd appearance. They used a single lug sail braced with battens, but it was smaller and squarer than the original. The bows were low under the burden of the cargo, suggesting that she might slide under, and the cramped men's shelter in the waist resembled a makeshift tent.

With a fair breeze *Fushan* moved faster than the diesel could have driven her, but the sail made more work for them for it needed constant attention. A slight shift of wind or change of course and the junk heeled, or the sail flapped lifelessly.

'Think of the fuel saving.' Russell ate hurriedly as he stared at the map. 'Ta-kang. That's about fifteen miles. We can maybe get fresh water there.'

He's barely aware of what he's putting in his mouth, Linda thought. She noticed Peggy filling his bowl again. 'We've got enough water, love, so where's the fire? Why don't you rest more?'

Peggy's attitude to Russell puzzled Linda. Sometimes, when he was irritable, she mocked him savagely. But she did things for him that she wouldn't do for anybody else.

'He drives himself too hard.' Peggy stooped and scooped up Suyin. 'You'd think Dr Foster would make himself a bit more useful. Russell could do with all the help he can get.'

Suyin pulled herself loose and peered around, uneasy, until she could see Mayling again.

'I've never seen him shirking.' Linda didn't really like Foster but she felt sorry for him. He'd brought along a prayer book, and he'd try and read it for a while each day. His glasses were broken and it was difficult for him. 'I think he feels lost. He can't fit in yet.'

Peggy's aversion to Dr Foster simmered. 'He keeps nicely aloof when there are decisions to be made.'

'Oh, c'*mon* Peggy!' Close confinement was making them bitchy. Linda fastened the tarpaulin across the entrance of the shelter and blew on her hands. Do the men discuss us the way we discuss them? she wondered. Everything smelt of damp in this shelter. And so did they. How long before she got a shower again? 'You seem very concerned for Mr Russell?'

Peggy shrugged and assumed a blank expression. 'Men! They all need propping up. It's not that I fancy him. I *mean*, I've got enough to worry about with Arch.' And she changed the subject.

Linda lay back and pulled the damp blanket over herself. Yes. There was Arch. She felt guilty by inclination.

The wind dropped when night came but there was sufficient moon for them to steer by. Russell divided them into three watches, and Lao started the diesel.

Linda shared the early morning with Reed and Miss Kuang. The shore was a black, undulating line against the faintly lighter sky to the east. The compass indicated that the river was curving south again. Linda used the flashlight to peer at the chart. 'There should be an island ahead.'

Reed had the tiller. 'We should see it a little after dawn.'

There were pinpoints of light inland – villages maybe. Huddled in her coat, Linda sat near Reed and watched them. Little farms. Did they know the Japanese were coming? She dozed, then woke suddenly to find it was grey morning.

Reed was holding the compass in his free hand. Patchy mist drifted and Linda was startled by the tops of trees seemingly jutting up out of the river ahead.

'It's Hound's Tongue Island,' he said.

Miss Kuang was still curled up under a blanket.

'You shouldn't have let *me* sleep as well.'

'What did ya dream about?'

'Did I dream?'

'You seemed afraid,' Reed said. 'You muttered something about a boat coming for you.'

'I don't remember any of it. Strange, isn't it – that country we go off to each night? We must spend much of our life there, but we usually forget it entirely when we wake.'

The mist rolled along the water.

'It's difficult to judge distance in this stuff.' Reed corrected course. 'The chart shows shallows where the silt has built up,

219

but it's years old — I don't know where Russell got it from. Sandbars can change their shape. And there are no markers — I guess the Chinese removed them because of the Japs.' He peered at the island. 'There's a white house.'

'And a tree nearly at the water's edge. Like on the Willow Pattern plate. But it's not a willow or a cherry tree. And we don't have a pair of runaway lovers on board, do we?' The mist had thinned, and Linda could see a sampan tied up at a rickety pier. 'Isn't there supposed to be a tyrannical mandarin in the story — the girl's father? He's going to make her marry an old, ugly duke when the peach tree blossoms. Right? But the pair of lovers escape in the little boat to the island and live happily ever after.'

Reed frowned, trying to gauge the distance between the junk and the shore. 'The story is really about the journey of the soul. Get it? That's why there are two doves in the pattern — they're symbols. The boat bears the souls of Hung heroes to the Isle of the Blest. It's a common belief; a boat, a journey. The Egyptians believed in the boat, and it's in Norse legends. And the Greeks: you pay the ferryman a coin to carry your soul across the river — I forget the name of it.'

'The Styx. You amaze me, Reed. I thought you only read the sports pages? You don't really believe all that stuff, do you?' Cold common sense defeated her and she was unable to retreat into the comfort of the ancient story. 'I mean, a boat to the hereafter. It's a bit too cosy.'

'Is it?' Reed frowned in concentration and steered the junk away from the shallows. 'I didn't say I believe it, but neither do I find it cosy.'

'Doesn't it make more sense to reject all the legends and myths?' She was hoping that he would come up with an acceptable option.

But he just shrugged. 'I thought you were religious?'

'Why wouldn't I have doubts?'

'Well, *your* lot know where they are going,' he grinned, 'don't they?'

'Why do you always sneer?' She turned away.

'Who's *sneering*! What did I say?'

Miss Kuang went through the motions of waking, though in fact she had heard every word.

The island ahead was shrouded in mist again. Linda shivered and pulled up her scarf. If there was just one thing she could believe in.

By mid-morning when the sun had burned off the mist, the Yangtze had widened and they were unable to see the northern shore. Planes flew over towards the west, too far off to be identified. Reed was pumping again. He'd counted to two hundred and was sweating despite the raw wind. Two hundred and five – two hundred and six . . .

Sandbars, mudflats and reeds – the river was low at this time of the year. A bamboo landing stage, sections bound with rope, pushed out across the mud – seemingly from nowhere. Reed hadn't seen a living soul along the shore. The Yangtze opened at the passage of the junk, and closed behind it. Sometimes he felt that they had become a living part of the river.

> Great Tao is like a boat that drifts;
> It can go this way; it can go that.
> The ten thousand creatures owe their existence to it
>   and it does not disown them.

Of the eight adults on the junk, Reed was the least concerned about their isolation. Two hundred and twenty – two hundred and twenty-one . . . Keeping *Fushan* going had become an end in itself. A brief purpose. Two hundred and twenty-two . . . This damned pump won't last out if we work it so hard, he told himself. Russell would have to be told. One whole day to find the leak and repair it, and take the pump apart and fit a new pivot.

From the shelter behind him he could hear the women talking, particularly Linda Bishop – her intonation was precise. 'Do you think we could ask Mr Russell to give some thought to the toilet arrangements? Trailing up to the bow and encountering that Chinese boy with his trousers down was embarrassing – not for him I must add, he merely grinned at me.'

It was odd. Linda Bishop didn't irritate him any more. How

221

had that come about? Reed didn't know. Long limbed, a little too thin – he wondered what she looked like undressed, and for a while he was unwilling to suppress the image. Girls like her – he'd always avoided them. They were a royal pain with their principles and matters of conscience. But now he frequently found himself speculating about Linda Bishop's body, and he even had arguments with her inside his head.

He had a rest. It took a little longer each day to pump *Fushan* nearly dry. The cool Miss Bishop was hanging out some washing on a makeshift line in the stern. He had to admit that close daily proximity with her was one more reason why he didn't care much about how long the journey took. Not that he'd want to get stuck with a woman like that. No, that wasn't what he had in mind at all. But questions of how to arouse her interest crossed his thoughts each time he noticed the movement of her lips. She could be damned touchy, though – like early this morning, snapping at him over nothing. It was odd the way he'd felt closest to her then.

Reed peered around. They'd seen only a few distant junks since the Chinese naval launch had come alongside yesterday to check *Fushan*'s passengers and cargo. And the naval officer told them that the boom at Chiang-yin was breached – somehow the Japanese had got hold of a detailed plan of the defence, and a gunboat was through. A new line of blockships had been sunk at San-chiang-yin ahead of *Fushan*. They should encounter it this evening. Reed began to pump again. He tried to feel himself part of the river, but instead became angry. 'Hey, Russell! How about somebody else taking a turn?'

'Sure.' And Russell took the pump himself and worked it vigorously. 'We've got to make our best possible speed. Give some thought to rigging another sail, will you?'

'We need to make repairs before you start thinking about more sail. Damn it, Russell, this pump needs attention for a start. See, the pin here – it's badly worn . . .'

'We're not stopping,' Russell interrupted, 'unless we have to.'

222

'That doesn't make a whole lot of sense. The leak just slows us down, so does the cargo.'

'So do the passengers.' Russell stared at him, and the nerve below the scar on his cheek began to twitch.

Reed felt his hackles rise. 'Three Pratt & Whitneys aren't likely to win or lose the war, for God's sake! As things stand, if we hit bad weather again you'll have to let them go over the side!'

'I'll make that decision, if it ever becomes necessary.' Russell's jaw had tightened. 'You just worry about the sail, eh?'

'I'm keeping this goddam boat afloat, Russell!' He turned away in disgust.

Peggy followed. 'You could go a little easy on him.'

'Me! Go easy?' Reed leaned against the rail. 'Why the hell is he doing this anyway – you ever stopped to wonder about that? It isn't *his* war. I think he's crazy.'

'And you, me, the rest of us are normal?' Peggy shook her head incredulously. 'Mayling talks in her sleep, about guilt and God. We've got a Shanghai gangster. Foster just sits and stares at the river. And that Kuang girl – I reckon she's a crook, or a whore, or both. And who in their right mind would call *me* normal? Trailing across China after a man like Arch.'

'You're the most normal person I know. But you missed out the cool Miss Bishop. What drives her on?'

'I thought I knew. Now I'm not sure.' Peggy frowned to herself.

'Why does she take those tablets all the time?'

'She's been cut by a surgeon – it looks awful. But she never talks about it.'

'I didn't know.' All those questions, and the camera and ever-ready notebook. What was the answer she really sought?

Lao shouted. They were encountering wreckage and he was staving it off with a pole. Large pieces of timber, a waterlogged sail, a bamboo cage full of drowned chickens. A corpse badly burned.

'That's San-chiang-yin ahead.' Russell squinted into the setting sun. 'We're approaching the second line of block ships.'

'And soon the light will fade,' Reed said. 'We should anchor, then try crossing in the morning.'

'No.' Russell shook his head. 'Remember there's a Japanese gunboat behind us. We've got a chart, and the deep channel runs straight. We'll pick our way between the block-ships and be clear of here by daylight.'

In a way it made sense – once across that second barrier they'd be safe from the gunboat. But Reed felt uneasy. He squatted on the bow.

For another hour they saw floating debris, and he counted four more bodies, then the way was clear again.

Late in the afternoon, it would soon be dark. And there was heavy cloud. There would be no moon tonight. Then Reed saw a funnel and masts jutting out of the water. They'd reached the boom. *Fushan*'s slowly turning propeller held them almost motionless against the sluggish current. No boat had come out from San-Chiang-yin to intercept them.

'What do you think?' Russell limped forward to join him. 'I'll steer. You stay in the bow and signal right or left?'

Reed didn't like the idea, but he nodded. 'Okay, we'll try it.'

Foster and Lao stood ready with poles while Reed lay face down, his head over the bows. The junk moved slowly forward to the double line of sunken ships. They'd been filled with concrete, towed out, and then holed. It was strange: those snapped off masts like broken teeth and the river rippling round the superstructure of an old cargo steamer. And there were sounds, like tapping and deep groans, as if people were trapped inside that submerged hull.

Fushan scraped along drowned rigging. Reed saw wire cable looped over a partly exposed spar, then down, then up again. He remembered the badly burned corpse. 'Russell! The ships are mined!' And he signalled frantically to the left.

Russell hauled the tiller round. There was a terrifying grinding of wood on metal and the junk lifted, tilted sideways, then slid free. They were across.

Fushan drifted, and Lao was already leaning over the side and peering down for damage. They didn't need to search. As

Russell pulled back the cover of the trunk they could hear water gushing into the bilge.

'God in heaven!'

Even pumping continuously they were unable to suck the water out fast enough. The light faded rapidly, and it began to rain, soaking through Reed's shirt and chilling him. Russell got them in a chain, passing buckets back from the bilge. Bend, scoop up water, straighten. *Fushan* groaned. What they ought to do was beach the junk.

Foster and Lao were working the pump lever between them. *Fushan* wallowed, deck tilting down at the head, and Reed struggled to keep balance. The river was vast and black. Linda took the heavy bucket from him. Rain streamed through her hair and her shirt was sticking to her. She wouldn't be able to keep this up.

He snarled, 'It's no good, Russell! Run the goddam junk on the mud!'

'Not until it's light enough to see! We could wreck it!'

'Morning is hours away! Lighten the ship, damn you, or we'll all drown!'

They threw the stores overboard, then their own baggage. In near darkness Reed saw Linda lurch to the side and drop her typewriter in the river.

They bailed and bailed.

The tilt of the deck alarmed Reed. Stoop, lift. He stared angrily as Russell groped, roping the three crates tighter to stop them from sliding. 'There's damned near a thousand pounds set right over that leak, Russell. Those engines could drag us down!'

'Soon it will be dawn!'

'We'll probably drown!'

Crazy! Reed leaned for a moment, resting. And the others toiled, arms and backs straining with fatigue. There was the first grey light. *Fushan* had been carried upstream on the tide and was over a mile from the shore. How many of them could swim that far? Reed wondered. Their movements had become clumsy. Linda Bishop looked ill. The bucket slipped from her grasp, bounced down the deck and over the side. And Reed caught her as she lost her footing and clutched at a stay. Cold and soaked through. For a moment she was limp, compliant in his arms, and he felt again the surprise that is never a surprise. Perhaps he held her too tightly, for she resisted, pushing back from him. 'Let *go* of me!'

Stung, he let her go.

She sank to her knees, head drooping, and held onto the stay. Water broke over the bows as the river threatened to engulf them but the others had stopped bailing. *Fushan* could sink any minute – just slide under! Reed turned his anger on Russell. 'We're gonna have to topple one of those crates overboard – d'ya hear me? And I mean right now!'

'No!' Russell clenched his fists. 'It's getting light – we'll steer for the shore!'

'We'll never get that far! You'll lose the junk, the engines, *and* your passengers!'

Lao snaked up and took his place beside Russell – he had a heavy spike in his hand. But Reed's bitter anger welled over and he didn't care. 'One engine has to go, Russell. Are you gonna do it, or do I?'

Lao jerked the spike up, pointing it at Reed's throat, but Russell stopped him. 'All right. Do it.' His thin shoulders sagged.

It took all of them except Mayling crouched with the child to lift the crate and push it over the side. And Russell watched, defeated, as it up-ended and sank like a stone.

CHAPTER NINETEEN

The Japanese gunboat *Ataka* had groped its way cautiously as far as Hsia-kang and was anchored off the Bund. Repeated attempts to make wireless contact with General Matsui's advance infantry units had come to nothing – co-operation between the army and navy was never good. A landing party was despatched.

Sergeant Kimura watched as *Ataka*'s longboat bumped and slid along the side of the Customs jetty. A naval lieutenant reached across to the ladder and climbed up.

Kimura knew why he'd come. *Ataka*'s captain wanted to know who controlled the shore west of the town – the white-liveried naval officers feared to lose their boat. Pain nagged in Kimura's wounded buttock and everything irritated him. He slept only in brief snatches and he'd become savage and morose. He feared the humiliation of returning home with such a dishonourable wound. Would anybody believe that a soldier shot in the backside could be serving the Emperor loyally?

Much of Hsia-kang had been gutted. The impeccably dressed lieutenant glanced round, curious, then stared at Kimura's ragged uniform and unkempt beard. Kimura implied an insult with his slow and extravangantly rigid salute. What would the navy look like if it had to do a little real fighting? 'We are of the 116th Regiment, 9th Division, sir. If you will follow me I will take you to Captain Hashimoto who commands our company.'

'The 116th Infantry?'

'Yes, sir. The first to support the naval landing party in the Chapei.' Kimura was reminding the officer that Japanese marines had been unable to do the job, but the other man was remembering that units of the 116th had been disgraced in 1936. He followed Kimura along the riverfront. A woman, eyes closed and legs spread wide, lay under an army cape. Her shape was surrounded by dried blood.

'Was your company the first to enter Hsia-kang, sergeant?'

'Yes, sir, we forced the East Gate.'

'You have served the Emperor well.'

'That is our function, sir.'

The officer paused to peer at a neat row of five decapitated corpses. 'What is this?'

Kimura stared straight ahead of him. 'Captain Hashimoto has killed these enemy soldiers in individual combat, sir.' It was, of course, obvious that two of them weren't soldiers at all but middle-aged peasants. He observed the officer's expression of distaste. He could think whatever he wished – how often had the army pulled navy chestnuts out of the fire?

They continued along a narrow winding street to a Taoist temple. Kimura paused briefly to bow to the elderly monk standing under the eaves, then he moved on – he'd begun dragging his leg. What news might the naval officer bring from down river? Kimura hoped for a lull in the fighting – time to rest his wound. Time to fit out the company with new boots and winter coats. And it was good here – they had comfortable quarters for a change. He led the officer into the mission compound.

Ataka sailed again an hour later – Captain Hashimoto had politely conceded minimal information to the navy. *Ataka*'s captain was cautious as he headed slowly up river. He'd heard unconfirmed reports of another barrier further on.

Twenty minutes bailing, ten minutes rest. Linda lost track of time. She noted dully that the sky was blue between clouds. As she passed the bucket back from the trunk well, Miss Kuang waited for her to stretch before she took the weight. Some know best how to survive.

Linda rested. Her hands were bleeding, skin white and

dead-looking from long exposure to the water. Dear God, she was so tired. Where were they? Reed was checking the map against the shoreline, and he called to Russell. 'There's a large village about eight miles further on, but I don't know if we can make it. Russell?'

Linda started bailing again. Russell didn't answer. He'd barely spoken since they'd pushed the engine over the side the previous night.

'Are you listening? We're taken in so much water we're barely moving, Russell.'

'You seem to be running this bloody junk, so try making the decisions.'

Peggy snapped, 'Oh, for God's sake, Mr Russell! Have you given up?' Her hair straggled lifeless and she wiped the back of her hand across her eyes. 'I thought we had men on board.'

Russell stared at her for a moment. 'Thank you, Mrs Rittenhouse. I'll apply myself to the problem.'

Linda passed up another bucket and tried to straighten her back. Giddy, she felt the panic of no longer being quite in control, and she sat abruptly and pressed her head to her knees. Reed had seen, and he stood over her. 'You okay?'

She nodded. 'I'm fine. I'll bail again in a minute.'

'Wait till you've rested.'

'I've told you, I'm *all right*!' Why am I snapping at him? She'd felt confused about Reed since last night when he'd saved her from falling.

'Well, *fine*!' he said, and turned back to Russell. 'Eight miles to the village of Tan-tou-chen. Or we could run the junk onto a sandbar, repair the damage, then pump her out.'

'*Fushan* could be stuck until spring when the river rises.' Russell shook his head. 'No, I don't think we could risk that.'

Linda lifted her head. 'You could try fothering the leak.'

They looked at her.

'I heard about it when I used to sail sometimes. My cousin . . .'

Russell interrupted gently 'Don't you worry about it, Miss Bishop. You take a rest.'

She was ready to drop. But more, she was angry. 'You

could at least listen, damn you! You stretch sailcloth over the leak and nail it or something.'

Reed saw immediately what she was getting at. 'Pressure of water on the leak holds the sail against the hull. Yeah, it might work,' he added cautiously.

'Well, don't bust a gut in your enthusiasm,' Linda said.

'Somebody will have to get wet.' Russell limped to the bows and peered over. 'And it had better be me. Stop the diesel.'

Fushan drifted, and they gathered in the bows as Russell pulled off his coat and shirt and poised, shivering in the cold wind. He was so thin, Linda thought, and not strong – he shouldn't be doing this.

· 'If you drown yourself, Mr Russell, I'll kill you,' Peggy said.

Lao passed a rope round Russell's waist but paused before tying it. 'I go?'

'I've already told you. No.'

'Hey, Russell.' Reed looked uneasy. 'I'm more practical – how about I go?'

But he isn't insisting, Linda thought.

Russell shook his head and peered down at the dark water, then he took a deep breath and jumped over the side.

Air bubbled to the surface, then Russell's head emerged – he was gasping as though plunged in ice. They passed sailcloth down to him and he kicked as the weight of the wet cloth took him down. Bubbles plopped intermittently – then nothing.

He was so clumsy. Linda watched anxiously. She was vaguely disappointed in Reed for letting Russell do this.

'He's been down too long!' Peggy clutched at Reed's arm. 'Pull him up, for God's sake!'

Lao kicked off his shoes ready to jump, but Reed had dropped the rope and he dived over the side. It was a smooth, beautiful movement, Linda thought, as if the decision and action were one. And she waited, fascinated, for Reed to reappear.

Foster hauled on the rope and the two heads bobbed to

230

the surface. Russell rested a moment, then they both kicked down again. Linda saw the sailcloth tighten.

It was done.

Lao, angry, leaned over the side to help drag Russell out. 'I don't have to kill you – you kill your goddam self.' And he pulled Reed out as well.

Shivering violently, Russell allowed Peggy to rub his gaunt body. 'What you need is a good slug of whisky,' she said. 'Hey, Reed, is there anything left in your bottle?'

Linda went to fetch the bottle from Reed's toolbox and noticed with surprise that it was almost full. She paused, staring down at it. He held me, because that's the way he is with women, she thought, but I shouldn't have snapped that insult.

She took a blanket and draped it round him. 'Tell the truth, Reed. You stopped up that leak with ox dung, didn't you?' And she rubbed his leg – it seemed just bone and hard-packed muscle. 'How come you're such a good swimmer?'

'Us drifters have a few inconsequential talents.'

'Yes, but I *mean*, even a non-sport kind of person like me could see you're good. That was special – your speed. Like an instant reflex.'

He didn't answer, and she rubbed the other leg and went on determinedly. 'Sometimes you're a puzzle, you really are. I had you pegged as one who takes a month to decide whether or not to shave.'

'It's a way women have, of assuming they know every damned thing about a man.' He walked off to the shelter.

She called after him. 'And we were getting on so famously!'

Had I assumed I knew all about him? Linda lowered herself slowly, squatting her back to the mast. I don't even know myself. When Reed held me, soaked through and cold, I felt safe. I wanted to go on being held. Reed – Arch Rittenhouse. For just a moment I had them mixed up inside my head, and I wanted it to be Arch.

She ached all over, aware of an immense lethargy. Energy

231

had drained from her quite suddenly when the immediate danger of sinking had passed. With scarcely room to move and no way of shutting off the voices of the others, she tried closing her eyes and pulling her collar up over her ears. If only she could sleep. And then write – she'd feel better if she could write. The diary she'd so determinedly kept going since leaving America was hidden under her blankets – no entry since the time she'd tried to describe Arch Rittenhouse. She guessed it was guilt, and slipped into an exhausted state of half-sleep – aware of voices and movement around her, and of her emerging thoughts. One day, if we're ever judged, we'll have to answer for the sins we would have committed if we'd had the chance. And she jerked into wide-awakeness. If we get to Nanking I'll avoid Arch.

The junk limped the eight miles towards a shabby collection of shacks fronted by wooden jetties. A few stone-built houses with green and yellow tiled roofs up behind the waterfront dwellings and further along the shore there was a white pagoda flanked by trees.

As *Fushan* approached the jetties, Linda could see that the village was larger than it had first appeared, but flat, straggling off to the south and east. Only two junks, little more than sampans, were tied up on the waterfront.

The diesel stopped and *Fushan* scraped alongside a wooden pier. Children gathered from nowhere, and a few adults. They peered at the junk, and Russell addressed them in Chinese. 'Our boat is damaged. We seek permission to make repairs here at your excellent village.'

They chattered together and seemed to ignore him. Some of the children ran off and the small crowd settled down to watching the junk and its occupants. Linda was angry. How could they be so callous? She went and sat in the stern to shelter out of the wind. Mayling handed her tea and she cupped her hands round the mug. 'We've survived, but I'm too tired to care.'

Nearly every personal possession had been thrown overboard. Suyin was clutching at dry beans spilled on the

232

floor. Grunting with her small efforts she picked them up one at a time and held them up to Mayling.

'Thank you, darling. All of Peggy's clothes, except those she was wearing. And her shoes – all gone.'

Miss Kuang lay on her back, eyes closed.

Linda looked around listlessly at the few remaining possessions. 'Are we covered by Lloyds?'

Mayling frowned, uncomprehending.

'Joke.'

I didn't mind losing the case with my clothes, or my camera, Linda thought. But the typewriter – that's something else. It's like losing part of myself. And she suddenly remembered her tablets – they'd been in the case! A small panic seized her. How necessary were they?

Miss Kuang spoke without opening her eyes. 'Soon we will be in Nanking, Linda. We will manage for this short time.'

'Yes. And we won't have to sleep in this awful little shelter any more.' It was slightly disconcerting the way Miss Kuang seemed sometimes able to read her thoughts. 'Have you noticed how the insects emerge after dark? We must have struck just the right combination of dim light and foetid dampness for them to flourish. A huge beetle dropped on me the other night.'

Miss Kuang opened her eyes and prised an insect off the tarpaulin with her fingers. 'They leave me alone.' Her jade bracelet slid down her smooth arm.

Something was happening outside.

An old man had arrived. He looked important and was dressed in a green silk robe. Linda regretted her uncharitable thoughts about the villagers – they'd clearly understood Russell and sent the children to fetch their head man.

Russell spoke to him for several minutes, and he nodded gravely. The children became noisy and he clicked his fingers at them. They were instantly quiet. The adults strained to hear what was being said, but they drew back when he looked round.

'How do you get to be as impressive as that?' He could cope with anything, Linda thought – flood, famine, the Japanese, death.

'Age and the absence of passion – how the hell do I know?' Reed grunted. 'Faith in himself, maybe – a man is pretty much what he thinks he is.'

The old man left, with children holding his hands and clinging to his gown.

Russell came back on board. 'His name is Sung Chao-chi. He says we can stay as long as we need. He gets news from travellers and he thinks the Japanese army is two or three days behind us but he can't be sure. Half of the villagers have already left.'

'What about help with the junk?'

'Sung says he might be able to find somebody who knows about boats. He apologizes that his house is too small to accommodate us for the night and he suggests that we go to the inn.'

One night in a warm, dry place. I'd put up with cockroaches – even mice, Linda thought.

'Sung will arrange to replace our lost stores at a reasonable price. But there's nowhere around here where we can take a boat this size out of the water.' Russell looked weary. 'So how do we get at the damage to *Fushan*'s bow?'

'The hole is a couple of feet below the waterline.' Reed pondered. 'Those two remaining engines must weigh twelve hundred pounds. If we lift them off and pump most of the water out . . .' his eyes narrowed. 'No. We'll just pump *some* of it out. And we'll shift all the weight to the stern. Alter the trim and water will shift sternwards as well. Maybe the bow will rise sufficiently for the boat-repairer to get at the hole.'

'That's good.' Russell stared curiously at Reed. 'That's very good.' He pulled his coat off. 'We'd better make a start.'

The Chinese on the jetty watched while the first of the two remaining crates was unshackled and tilted on its side. Foster cut wooden rollers and they edged the crate towards the rear. Already the deck was less sharply inclined.

When the second crate passed the waist of the junk, water in the bilge swilled back into the stern. The trim shifted rapidly and they had to haul on the crate to prevent it running away with them. Water overflowed into the diesel compartment and the stern sank lower.

Peggy wiped the back of her hand across her forehead and stared at the excitedly chattering Chinese. 'You'd think they'd offer to help – they're supposed to be on our side.'

'No. We're supposed to be on *their* side,' Foster said. 'The world doesn't revolve around us.'

They moved everything movable aft of the waist, and the bow came up another three inches. Reed clambered onto the jetty and stared at the junk. *Fushan*'s stern was pushed down into the mud. 'We'll pump again.'

After another fifteen minutes he leaned over the bow and pulled away the sail cloth repair. The hole was above water. And nearly half the day had gone.

Lowered in a rope sling, Reed examined the damage. He braced his feet against the hull. God's teeth, how had they managed to stay afloat?

The water was up round his waist, freezing him. He scowled, prodding the timbers with his pen knife. Two of them were soft – they'd have to come out.

'Good afternoon.'

A Chinese youth with thick spectacles was smiling down at him. 'I am boat-repairer.' A gold tooth showed. 'Allow me to examine, please.'

The youth didn't look like an artisan, more a student, Reed thought. He was still smiling as he pulled off his drill trousers and sat himself in the sling. 'Lower, please.'

They lowered, and he peered myopically at the hole then snapped off one of the broken timbers to feel behind it. 'The rib is sound. Pull up, please.'

Reed was curious. This little guy knew his job – you could always tell. He nodded to Russell.

'When could you start?' Russell frowned anxiously. 'We can pay you.'

'I will begin repairs immediately.' The boy's gold tooth showed again. 'I will make no charge except for materials; wood – cedar if possible – copper nails, cotton for caulking.'

Reed was caught up, intrigued by the skills required. He assisted, anticipating what the boy would do, and offering the tools: augers, adze, claw, caulking-iron. Two of the villagers had a fire going under a hot box, and Reed learned how to steam new planks to shape. He lost himself in the work, forgetting his aching back, and the sting of Linda Bishop's seemingly instinctive rejection of him last night.

The boat repairer worked fast but it was clear they weren't going to be able to leave until the following day. They decided to do as Sung had suggested and spend the night at the inn. The old man would send two of his grandsons to guard the junk.

'That boy is going to a lot of trouble for us.' Linda watched the boat-repairer.

Reed noticed that she had washed and combed her hair. 'The Chinese are generous people.' Dark shadows under her eyes merely made Linda Bishop more palely attractive. 'They owe us nothing, God knows.' He was trying out a new theory inside his head that the poor are more helpful than the rich. 'They have nothing but they want to help. I hear that thirty of their young men were roped together and taken for service in Chiang Kai-shek's army only last week.'

'Why didn't they take the boat-repairer?'

'He went and hid until the recruiting squad left.'

'He wants something from us – that's why he's working so hard.'

'I thought *I* was supposed to be the cynic?' Reed remembered her in the white dress standing at the rail of the *Star of Asia*. 'You were wide-eyed and credulous when we sailed into Shanghai. What happened?'

'I thought we were trying not to irritate each other? My guess is that he wants to sail to Nanking with us – there's no great ethical issue at stake. He'll ask Russell at the inn tonight. Have I got a bet? We'll make it merely fifty cents as you're so sure I'm corrupted.'

'Okay. Fifty cents, and you'll see just how wrong you are.'

'What do you eat at a Chinese inn? At least I'll have no problem about what to wear – I've only got the clothes I'm standing in.' She frowned to herself. 'I did put on some lipstick.'

He'd noticed. And her hair looked good like that; long and loose.

'I borrowed the lipstick from Miss Kuang – she only threw half her baggage overboard. A small lapse of memory, I guess. And I hope you're going to shave, Reed. One of you men must surely have saved a razor? This is our big night out and I don't want to be seen with a bunch of hoboes and . . .' She'd just stopped herself from saying 'drifters' '. . . and strolling players.'

'Why would I bother?' he said, and noticed with sour satisfaction that he'd scored a hit.

Linda bit her lip. 'Maybe I'll ask Lao to escort me.'

'And we were getting on so famously.'

The youth had caulked the seams in the planking and covered the repair with white lead. At his smiling suggestion the villagers shifted the cargo back and pumped out the bilge. He told Reed that the junk was at leasty forty years old. Some of the timbers were from another junk, certainly older.

Sung's two grandsons arrived to guard the *Fushan* for them and Reed asked casually about their helper. Apparently, his name was Mu. They said he'd grown up in the village and worked on the boats. Because he was clever, the old man had taught him to read and write.

Reed was even more curious and said so to Russell. 'Don't you think it's just a bit odd? – that boy has ducked out of military service and nobody here seems to resent it even though their sons are taken. He's lived in a foreign mission and nobody resents that either.'

Russell was frowning down at the chart. 'I'm sorry, Reed. What did you say?'

Reed finished washing in cold water, and smoothed his hand over the stubble on his jaw. Without a razor between them, the beard would have to stay. There were oil stains on his trousers and his boots were scuffed and worn through. He scowled. 'What do you say, Russell – we could pass for a couple of tramps?'

Russell looked up questioningly. The pale yellow light of the storm lantern made his face appear even more gaunt.

'I was saying, we look like hoboes.' Reed pulled his leather jacket on. 'It's just an attempt at conversation.' Crazy bastard, he thought. A lonely man with a purpose, and a limp. What did it feel like to limp through life? He made a big effort. 'Y'know, I have to hand it to you, Russell. Getting two of those engines this far. Yes, sir, you've got a will of iron.'

Russell stared at him for a moment. 'I suppose it must seem like that.' And he went back to measuring miles on the chart.

End of conversation. Reed left the shelter. He found Miss Kuang on her knees, searching along the planking between the engine crates.

She looked up quickly. 'I have lost my bracelet – somewhere near here, I think. I had it a short while ago. The clasp must have come undone . . .' She tailed off and resumed her search along the planks.

'I'll look with you.' He sensed her anxiety. 'Is the bracelet valuable?'

'Only to me.'

They groped, feeling in the cracks.

'We're not having a lot of luck, Miss Kuang. When we reach Nanking you could perhaps get another one?'

'There are few like it.'

They lifted scraps of timber left by the boat-repairer. Reed saw silver and jade reflecting in the beam of light. 'You can stop worrying.'

'Thank you so much.' There was unmistakable relief in her eyes.

He'd seen a bracelet like that before – you unclipped the jade and there was a sort of secret hiding place underneath. 'I'm glad we found it.'

'I've worn it for a long time. I felt unlucky when I thought it was lost.'

'I'm the same,' he said. 'I've got an old five-centime piece – from France when I flew in the Great War.'

'And has it brought you luck?'

'I don't know. How can you know for sure? I'm still alive so maybe it has.'

'Yes. We are alive.' She was close to him and he felt something like a small electric charge.

The other women were emerging from the stern shelter, looking slightly self-conscious, groomed as best they could. Peggy had found a piece of ribbon for Suyin's hair.

It was, in fact, Foster who had insisted that they should invite the old man, Sung, to eat with them. The invitation was extended to others who had helped repair the *Fushan*. So what had begun as a duty somehow turned into a social event.

Half the villagers had assembled ouside the inn on the edge of the village.

Peggy was appalled. 'God's teeth! We didn't invite them *all*, did we?'

Reed shook his head. 'Most have come to watch.'

The kitchen was a mud-brick fireplace in a long room; warm, lit by smoky oil lamps. Over the fire hung bunches of garlic and onions, and strips of pork dark with insects. Linda stared. 'Reassure me, Reed. We're not actually going to eat that?'

'The heat of the cooking kills the germs. And we ask for boiling water to wash the bowl and chopsticks. It doesn't offend them – they think it's one of our strange religious customs.'

The old man, conscious of his status, arrived exactly two minutes after the foreigners, but with a gift of melon seeds for their journey.

They sat on wooden benches at a trestle table. The innkeeper insisted on serving them himself though his children and fat wife worked for him. The meal took time to prepare. Children crept in and squatted along the wall, waiting to see how the foreigners ate. 'Big nose.' And they giggled.

'I'm concentrating on how hungry I am.' Linda Bishop determinedly avoided looking at the spitoons.

Steaming bowls of rice, vegetables and pork were placed on the table.

'You gain face if you can eat a lot,' Reed said.

Lao picked dexterously at the bowls. 'You pretty good with chopsticks – for a foreigner.'

Lao had been ready to kill him last night on the listing deck of *Fushan*. 'And you're quite handy with a spike.'

'We friends again, so to speak.'

'Okay, we're friends. Do you know a man named Han Yu-lin? – he's a business associate of Mr Dou of Shanghai.'

Lao pretended to ponder. 'I have heard name.'

'Would you advise anybody to do business with Han Yu-lin?'

'Han very common name in China.' Lao returned to eating as if the topic was closed, then he said, 'Some men wear good suits – silk shirts. They still cut you up.'

'Is this a private conversation or can anybody join in?' Linda Bishop was making a fairly adequate job with the chopsticks.

'Lao was offering me advice.'

'How to keep head on neck.' Lao was convulsed by his own joke.

For the first thirty minutes the boy who had repaired the boat ate in silence but, hunger satisfied, he leaned back. 'What is your honourable name?'

'My miserable name is Reed.'

The boy smiled, enjoying the game. 'To where do you travel in your splendid junk?'

'Our contemptible junk is bound for Nanking.'

'The bastion of Kuomintang government. You will be safe within the city walls.' He belched softly and produced a packet of Chinese cigarettes. 'I would very much like to go to Nanking.'

Reed accepted a cigarette, and didn't look at Linda though

240

he knew she was smiling to herself. 'You would have to ask Mr Russell. He is responsible for our insignificant lives.' He dragged on the cigarette and coughed. 'God in heaven!' Saltpetre and scent. They were the worst you could smoke and only a complete addict would persist.

Russell looked up when he heard Reed mention his name. 'Our young friend would like to travel with us.'

The boy added, 'I have no money, but I would bring my own food. I would be useful to you.'

Russell looked tired again, calculating additional weight and diminishing deck space. 'How can we refuse you? Yes, please join us.' He had the beginnings of a gut ache and only half listened to the conversation. And he'd lost his appetite. Any changes in his arrangements, however small, triggered the same latent anxiety – it was with him each night when he lay twitching and dozing. Anxiety is a habit. If only he could drain himself of tension.

'You're supposed to be enjoying yourself.' Peggy was watching him. '*And* you're not eating. At least drink some wine.'

If he drank too much he'd be in no fit state tomorrow. 'I've had enough.'

'Oh, for heaven's *sake*! It will relax you – don't you ever relax? You're not *alone* with that old junk. You've got Lao and Reed.' She smiled, white teeth perfect. 'And me.' Then she turned away as the old man proposed a toast to the worthy strangers from the West.

Russell remained aware of Peggy sitting opposite. She was leaning forward as the wine was poured once more. Her breasts were tight against her shirt.

Russell had felt embarrassed in her company since the second night out from Hsia-kang when he'd made his way to the stern to refuel the diesel – there'd been a light in the girls' shelter and he could see through a small gap in the tarpaulin. Peggy Rittenhouse was half undressed, washing. Frozen, fascinated, he'd stood there in the darkness. Then somebody inside pulled the tarpaulin together. The image was still sharp.

He changed his mind and drank more wine, feeling the slight numbness in his head. When he'd first met her he'd thought her blowsy and overdressed, and slightly coarse. He still thought that, but now he couldn't stop looking at her. And all the time he wondered how she saw him. Her accent, similar to his own, stirred memories of London and belonging – grimy streets, a permanent debt at the corner grocer's, and a warm kitchen smelling of food. Sometimes when she talked he could almost imagine himself back there. In sudden, brief flashes she was beautiful, but he knew if he told her that he'd sound like a fool.

Lao passed the bottle to him again. 'It okay. I watch.'

The wine was smooth on the tongue but it burned inside. And the noises of the inn began to confuse him. Peggy was explaining to the boy who had repaired the boat that she was English but married to an American. Her eyes seemed to be saying something entirely different, and Russell wondered muzzily about Arch Rittenhouse, air ace and friend of Chennault. He retreated within himself as Peggy linked arms with Reed to drink to free China. Let her flirt with other men, he had things to do.

In the morning he had no recollection of how he'd got to his mattress. Lao must have put him there and stretched the blanket over him. He had a thick head and felt sluggish. The others were stirring. Reed was washing at a pump in the yard. They'd spent the night on the inn floor or lying on the tables, as travellers do in China, warm in sleep and dry for the first time since leaving Hsia-kang.

Still muzzy, Russell negotiated a price of essential stores replaced by the innkeeper and Sung, the old man. He tried to buy diesel fuel but there was none for sale.

At mid-morning the boat-repairer came aboard *Fushan* with a small bag of food and books. Stores loaded and bilge almost dry, they cast off and moved out into the river once more. The villagers gathered to watch them leave and waved and clapped. Russell wished he hadn't drunk so much. He saluted the old man, tall in the small crowd.

'Isn't it different,' Linda Bishop said. 'Just twenty-four

hours ago I thought them callous and indifferent, and I hated them.' She remained there in the stern, waving occasionally until the figures on the jetty were too small to see.

The junk passed Chen-chiang and even from a mile and a half Russell could see the damage along the waterfront; wrecked steamers, a huge crane tilted over. But there was no smoke to suggest that the bombers had been there that day. Head clearing, Russell felt an odd, unaccustomed sensation of well-being. We're going to get there, he told himself, and I'll rid myself of this burden. I'll go home, and I won't bother to find a job for a while. I'll sit in London parks, and in the cafés of Notting Hill. Maybe I'll find myself a girl? The image of Peggy intruded and he forced himself to think about the journey to Nanking.

'What will you do when we reach the capital?'

'I shall travel on, to the west.' The boat-repairer was working the tiller.

'You're not prepared to fight for Chiang Kai-shek?'

'No. I will go to Shensi Province to join the 8th Route Army.'

It had begun to add up: the travelling, the books in the bag, the hiding from recruiting squads. He was a Communist. The 8th Route Army was made up of Mao Tse-tung's veterans.

'Chiang Kai-shek is China's past,' Mu said. 'Comrade Mao is the future.'

'You have a long journey ahead of you.'

'I will get there.'

Russell didn't doubt that he would.

With the approach of darkness the timbers of *Fushan* were covered with white frost. They anchored the junk in shallow water up river from Chen-chiang. Another twenty-five miles to the capital – they could be there by tomorrow afternoon. And this might be their last supper together in the junk. Russell left the others in the women's shelter and took his bowl out on deck.

He ate looking out over the stern. The sky was crowded

243

with stars and the river lapped softly along the hull. Voices from within the shelter seemed an intrusion in the immeasurable mystery of night. Russell gauged their optimism but made no attempt to follow what was said – until Peggy spoke.

'After I've phoned Arch I'll go to the Imperial Hotel on Sun Yat Sen Avenue. I'll ask for one of those suites with a marble bath, and I'll lie in it for two hours.'

There was that sharp image again.

And then they were arguing again about where to stay, as if they expected Nanking to be perfectly intact. Russell pondered – they were a strange mix. After Nanking they would scatter over the world. Would anything ever seem as important for him as this had been? He'd done it for Yun Tseng but mostly he'd done it for himself.

He heard Reed's voice. 'Hey, where's our crazy captain?'

Russell didn't mind. He'd done what he set out to do – the rest didn't matter. And anyway, he knew that despite their bitter wrangling, Reed half envied him. It was an entirely new experience for Russell.

At that moment Peggy came out and stood with him at the stern. 'Sometimes I think you avoid me. Do you, Mr Russell?'

'How can any of us avoid the others on a junk this size?'

'You're evading. You *know* what I mean. You always go to somewhere where I'm not.'

'I'm sorry, I've had a lot on my mind: the engines, the boat. And you, of course – all of you,' he added quickly.

'That was close – you nearly admitted it. I always know where you are – I can feel your eyes. And I turn and you look away.' She laughed softly, white teeth perfect. 'I'll bet you'll be so glad to get me off your junk?'

That was also true. But in a way . . . 'In a way I'll be sorry.' And he knew instantly that he'd made a tactical error.

'Will you? Tell me why?' She moved close to him – her breath steamed. And for Russell the conversation had suddenly turned into a minefield.

'You've been very good . . .' he groped. 'All of you.'

'Yes?' Her voice was warm, intimate, just for him. She turned her face up to his. 'Tell me how good I've been.'

'Lao and me – we might not have managed . . .' He groaned inwardly. He sounded like a fool! And he retreated into more words. 'Those engines – they're a gift, y'see? – a gift for the general. Unless I get them to Nanking, all this will have been a bit of a waste, won't it?'

It wasn't an answer that she'd wanted. He felt her drawing back, disappointed in him, and he panicked, gabbled. 'This is the first time in my life I've done something important. And I daren't . . . I daren't think about anything else.'

'You have to take a few chances in this life. Goodnight, love.'

He stayed there feeling like an idiot. Not only had he failed her, he'd broken his own set of rules. But somewhere at the back of his thoughts there was anger, at her for casually provoking the situation. What did she want with him, anyway? Her husband was famous and an air ace. He limped to the men's shelter. It made no difference. After tomorrow he probably wouldn't see her again.

In the morning as soon as the mist thinned, they sailed out into the deep channel. There was no wind and the diesel thumped slowly, pushing the junk up river. Small villages dotted the shore, and wooden stages. Every square foot of land was cultivated. Russell could see refugees, ant-like, heading westward towards the capital. There were low mountains to the south and the mist still clung to their summits. Then, far off, he saw the great white wall of Nanking.

CHAPTER TWENTY

The fifty-foot-high ramparts followed no regular pattern. Seventy-one miles of brick and rammed earth encompassed Nanking. The city had no clearly defined centre. Government offices, gracious palaces, temples, consulate buildings spread themselves along Sun Yat Sen Avenue running like a spine through the city. Within the wall to the south, slum villages had expanded, touched, fused together. The railway from Shanghai ran parallel with the northern wall then curved into the dock area beyond River Gate on the north-west rim.

Han Yu-lin was tired and edgy. Bombers from Taiwan and the Japanese mainland had raided on four consecutive nights. The mid-day raids had become a matter of routine - so punctual that the traders closed up business at eleven forty-five, a few minutes before the sirens sounded.

Black dots appeared in the eastern sky – the planes always came in from the same direction, and unloaded their bombs on the dock area of the congested slums. Twenty minutes and they tightened up their formations, wheeling eastwards once more. The last bomber was hit smoking as it plunged towards the river. Pathé newsreelmen followed it down cranking away for the edification of American cinema-goers. And the 'All Clear' sounded.

Han Yu-lin emerged from the foul air of the crowded department store basement and found a restaurant in Jianye Road. Already the paving outside was crowded again as Nanking resumed business. Han sat near the window. He was beginning to look shabby; his expensive suit needed pressing and the hotel laundry service was returning his shirts unironed. Things were not going well. Each day changes in circumstances required makeshift readjustments to his scheme. He sipped tea and watched the street. Ambulances clanged through the traffic on their way to the worst hit districts; and army trucks followed, packed with civilians recruited to dig in the bomb rubble. Nanking had the feel of a city under siege. Han checked his watch. Twelve thirty-five. He looked through the window to the Mercantile Bank of China opposite. Some of the staff were leaving for their mid-day meal. Han watched for the faces of those he knew had access to the bank vaults. The fat man was early today – he'd altered his routine! Han frowned, pondering the consequences of chance.

His plans had started to go wrong the day he learned that Dou had left Shanghai. But then what should he expect? That was the day the bomb had cracked the mirror in his hotel room. Bad *fung shui*. Almost immediate replacement of the mirror had failed to reassure him – who could tell what evil might have entered in that brief time? And that was the day that Brice and the German pilot had failed to turn up with the aeroplane. Now Han would be forced to use one of the ships of the convoy to make his escape.

The original plan had been bold and simple but it had hinged on one shaky component. The removal of Green Society gold must coincide with the transfer of government bullion – there was no other way that Han could take possession of it without inviting suspicion – and this in turn was dependent on the departure of Chiang Kai-shek's administration to Hankow. But how could Han have known that this would take so long? The strongest rumours suggested that the Generalissimo would leave within the next forty-eight hours, but Han suspected that he would still be there when the Japanese were at the city gates. It would have to be done by the 10th, he thought, and before the convoy of ships left for up river. And he'd need a tough Brother in case of trouble.

He paid and left the restaurant and still pondering his problem he walked towards the Street of Steps. The city was

bracing itself – indications were everywhere. Garish patriotic posters exhorted the population to resist. New ration
scales to take effect if a state of siege was proclaimed were
displayed on every hoarding.

A short-sighted beggar assumed Han was a Westerner
and clutched at his sleeve. Han kicked him briskly in the
knee. The beggar shrieked but Han didn't even glance back
– he had seen a face he knew. Perhaps his luck had changed
for the better. He pushed through the crowd, following the
slight figure of Lao.

Reed had slept late. He'd slept late every day since the
Fushan reached Nanking. He leaned up on his elbow and
peered hard at the bottle on his bedside locker – there was
only a third left. 'Go on. I'm listening.' Could he really have
drunk that much last night? 'You say you left Lao at . . .'

'A cheap eating house on the Street of Steps.' Russell sat
for a moment on his own bed. 'I went to the headquarters of
Nanking Military District to see a Captain Yang, but when I
returned to the eating house Lao wasn't there. I waited an
hour then came back here.'

'And he's not in his room?'

Nervous, Russell rose again. 'That's the first place I
looked.' He went to the window and opened it. 'The air in
this room is stale. Why do you lie around, Reed?'

'Because, unlike you, I have no lofty purpose. I can sleep,
Russell, without being plagued by guilt and soul-searching.'

'I don't think you're as happy with yourself as you sound.'

He was touchy, and lost without the little gangster. Reed
scratched. 'Lao probably saw somebody he knew – he'll
show up later.'

'He doesn't know anybody here . . .' Russell frowned out
at the untended lawns ' . . . except us.'

'Now that's where you're probably wrong.' Reed gave up
the struggle and took his first drink of the day. 'Yes, sir,
every Chinese has got a million relatives. One of the girls
might have seen him,' he added. For three days they'd all
been boarded together in the Agricultural College. Foster

had arranged it – he already had work here in the relief centre. 'Did you find anybody who would take those two aero engines off *Fushan?*' Reed only asked as a gesture of interest – he didn't really give a damn about them.

'Perhaps. Perhaps I have.' Russell continued to frown out at the lawns. 'It was my fourth attempt. I've tried General Headquarters of the Chinese Army – they wouldn't let me in. And the offices of Military Transport near the old Ming Palace. And the Military Engineers' barracks – they're too busy. There are no trucks available, or men – they're overworked clearing bomb rubble from the streets. Then I found this fellow, Captain Yang, at the headquarters of Nanking Military District, and I threatened him with Dou's displeasure if he didn't help.'

All that leashed tension – Russell's ceaseless activity was like an unspoken reproach. Reed couldn't enjoy lying in bed. He sighed and pushed back the blankets. 'Close the damn window, will'ya? What did this Captain Yang say?'

Russell hunched his shoulders. 'There's something going on there at Military District. General Tsai Tin-kai left in a big hurry with Walter Stennes – their car nearly knocked me down.' He turned, still frowning. 'Captain Yang said to come back tomorrow. He might find a spare truck and half a dozen men to lift the engines out of *Fushan.*'

'He might – he might.' Reed stripped off his vest and began washing at the small sink. 'You've done your best, God knows. Why should you care any more?'

Russell glanced at him as if the question didn't even warrant an answer. Reed mentally shrugged – what could you say to the guy?

Russell sprawled out on his own bed and stared unseeing at the ceiling. 'Lao and me, we dragged those engines all the way from Shanghai, but the Kuomintang military act as if I'm asking a huge and impossible favour just for them to take them off my hands. I begin to wish I could give them to Mao Tse-tung.'

'You take it all too damned seriously!' Reed started to shave, his face covered with soap. 'Nothing matters *that* much. To stay sane in this world you need to take a long-term view. Fifty years from now, that's – what? – 1987. Chiang Kai-shek will be dead and so will Mao Tse-tung. Some other war lord will be ruling China. And Japan? It'll have reverted to a fourth-rate power – just you see.' He got carried away. 'America will probably be running the world by then.' He noticed again the grey streak in his hair. 'One thing is certain, Russell: what's happening here in 1937 along the Yangtze delta will be forgotten by most everybody.'

Russell wasn't listening, and Reed found himself wondering briefly what Linda Bishop would look like in another fifty years. Elegant. She'd look elegant. 'Who'll be President of the United States in 1987, Russell?' and he grinned. 'Somebody like Arch Rittenhouse, I'll bet.'

At what point had mere irritation and an interest in Linda Bishop's body turned to – to what? Damn it, he didn't know. She'd rejected him – that was part of it. But only part of it.

Thinking about her had become a habit.

Russell was restless and began pulling on his coat. 'Fifty years' time. If we live that long we'll be old men weighing our lives. And what will they have amounted to?'

Reed had a strong feeling the conversation could become depressing. 'There's a convoy of ships with British gunboat escort leaving for up river on the 10th. We've got to be on one of those ships, Russell. We reach the southbound railway at Wuhan. Wuhan to Canton, then we get a boat – leave the Orient behind us. What'll you do, go home or try some other place? I wouldn't mind trying Canada.' He frowned at himself in the mirror. This is the role he'd always enjoyed playing; the loner on his way again, self-sufficient, all his belongings in one bag. And another part of him the admiring spectator of his own performance. He wasn't sure he cared for it any more. 'Where the hell'ya going?'

'I'm going to take a look at the *Fushan*.'

'It's safe – and chained up, for God's sake! You've got to

cross the Safety Zone and walk half a mile along the docks!'

'It's better than sitting around. Maybe Lao went there.' Russell reached the door and turned. 'And I feel more at home on that junk. Our lives were real for a while.'

That was true. And he hadn't needed a drink. Reed nodded. 'We're invited to the theatre tonight – seven o'clock. You, me, Peggy, Miss Bishop, Mayling, Foster, Miss Kuang – guests of Arch Rittenhouse.' And he avoided looking at Russell. 'Peggy hopes you'll come.'

Russell smiled wryly. '*Does* she now.'

Reed didn't know what to do with his day, so he walked to the south-west side and looked for a bar. He entered the first one he saw, and learned there that Brice was in Nanking.

The Shining Star Drama Company had fled south following the Japanese seizure of Peking, and the players were giving their final performance in Nanking before commencing a tour to raise money for war relief. The company was already famous, and nearly a thousand people packed the university auditorium. Reed was two rows behind Arch and Linda Bishop. Because of the crowd they'd had to sit quickly where they could, and Reed felt sour.

Electricity was off since the mid-day raid and the stage was lit by acetylene lamps. Men with two-string fiddles, a flute player, and a percussionist with drums, gong and cymbals sat to the right. Although Reed's ear had never completely attuned to the five-note scale he recognized the melody from other plays he'd been to.

Not only am I sour, I'm becoming ridiculous, he thought. Shaven, bathed, boots cleaned. And all because Linda Bishop was going to be there. He'd even let Mayling trim his hair – it was long now, well over his collar. Mayling was seated beside him; she murmured that the actor with the blue-painted face was the villain. And that, presumably, was why he was dressed as a Japanese officer – Reed's mind drifted, unable to concentrate on the players. Russell concerned himself with those damned engines; and the others were busy helping Foster, or sending cables and making complicated arrangements for getting home. But he'd done nothing purposeful because he had no plans beyond boarding a ship on the 10th. No plans at all.

Though the music was old, the play was new. With elaborate gestures the blue-faced Japanese officer indicated his base desire for the innocent Chinese girl. Two rows ahead, Arch said something to Linda Bishop. Her head inclined briefly towards him and Reed felt a stab of jealousy. There was something between her and Arch – he didn't know what it was but it sparked whenever they were within a few paces of each other.

'Blue face' ordered the girl's father to be buried alive. There were groans from the audience – the girl's virtue was at stake. How do we get caught up in a story so flimsy? Reed wondered. Even Miss Kuang was absorbed, lips slightly parted, as though the survival of innocence was important to her also. The hero, in a plain soldier's uniform, arrived in time to save the girl and her father, and the audience indicated its approval as 'Blue-face' grovelled.

There was a short break before the main play of the evening. With all the windows heavily blacked out the air had become stuffy. Mayling talked to Reed. 'Colonel Tang is in Nanking – Peggy caught a glimpse of his car today.' Reed made the necessary exclamations of interest but his attention was still on Arch and Linda. Was Peggy, now seated further back with Foster, watching them also? And perhaps Mayling sensed the question.

'Captain Rittenhouse is very tired. You see? It is there in the set of his shoulders.'

'Is it? Yes, I guess it is.' Mayling was always surprising him. Reed studied Arch's back – it was obvious now that she had mentioned it. Arch tensed, then relaxed. He seizes what rest he can, Reed thought. He used to do that in the Chaco war and in France in 1918 – he was good at it, falling into a chair and instantly going limp. But he didn't need rest so much when we were in France. We were young then.

Arch appeared animated again, leaning sideways and talking rapidly. Reed was aware of sudden concern for him.

> Stretch a bow to the very full,
> And you will wish you had stopped in time . . .

The players began *The Fisherman's Revenge* with a cacophony of sound. Reed knew the ancient plot. A meeting, a misunderstanding, a quarrel, danger, reconciliation. And it was as if his concern for Arch had somehow spilled over into the story. Reed sat forward in the seat, watching as the actress mimed a journey in an imaginary boat, steering with a little oar as the current carried her faster and faster. The boat could not sink – he knew that but he was nevertheless afraid.

The play ended, and after applause there were patriotic speeches to send the Shining Star Company on its way. Reed's attention flagged again. His need for a drink triggered memory of the bar that morning, and the question, Brice was still in Nanking, so where was the Stinson?

Speeches ended, the audience filed out into the cold, clean air. Linda had left Arch to Peggy. That's damned decent of her, Reed though ironically. The streets were moonlit, no chinks of light from the buildings around the university. They walked the short distance back to the Agricultural College; Peggy with her hand looped in Arch's arm, and the others behind. Russell had separated himself, limping on his own, but Arch insisted on including him in the conversation.

'What does it feel like to be a notorious pirate, Mr Russell? I hear the Japanese have put a price on your head.'

'They don't need excuses to kill people.'

'They say they'll *hang* you.' Arch smiled. 'What you did was remarkable.'

'I wonder if it was worth all the trouble. Nobody seems to want those areo engines.'

'Does that really matter? You outwitted the Japanese and you've become part of the legend that will defeat them. That's surely more important. Resistance is built around legends.'

And it was the stuff of life for Arch, more important than truth, Reed thought. Supposing the newspapers hadn't made

Arch into a hero in 1918, would he have gone home and settled in his father's law firm? Reed didn't know.

Linda Bishop was asking if the play they had just seen, about the girl in the boat, was based on a legend.

'It's all the Chinese have got right now,' Arch said. 'Limitless numbers of men, and legends. And the Generalissimo.' He paused, smiling. 'It has just occurred to me, Miss Bishop. As a writer you may care to see Chiang Kai-shek in the flesh? I could arrange it.'

'Yes – I'd like that very much.'

She had seized the opportunity immediately. As they made their arrangements Reed suspected that Arch had worked it all out carefully beforehand. He wasn't inviting his wife. 'It will just be press and the civic leaders, Peg. And anyway, I don't think it would interest you.'

If Peggy minded, she didn't show it.

When they reached the college, Arch hugged Peggy briefly. 'I'll see you the day after tomorrow, Peg.' And when she held onto him he smiled. 'Don't worry, I'll be okay,' and turning, he said, 'Walk with me to my car, will you, Frank?'

Why the feeling of foreboding?

The car was parked at the International Gendarmerie Headquarters. As they walked Reed let Arch do the talking.

'I haven't thanked you, Frank, for getting Peggy out. I suspect Gerald Foster isn't up to a crisis. And Russell is neurotic, poor guy. The burden probably fell on you.'

'No, that's not true.' He couldn't let Arch's assessment pass. 'It was Russell's drive that got us to Nanking – he's all nervous energy.'

But Arch shrugged, ending the matter. 'I'll get in to see Peggy off when the convoy sails; and I'd be grateful if you would stay with her and Miss Bishop as far as Canton. I have faith in you, Frank. More so than you have in yourself.'

Faint moonlight illumined the bombed ruins of the Universal Bazaar. An anti-aircraft gun had been set up on the flattened rubble and Reed could see lighted tips of cigarettes as the gunners kept their night vigil. There were crates of anti-aircraft shells stacked against a fretted wall still bearing a Coca-Cola advertisement.

'I hear you're gonna be on the Generalissimo's staff, Arch?'

'That's right. I'll have the ear of the press and I'll be able to influence public opinion back home.' He frowned slightly. 'The job carries the rank of lieutenant colonel so I'll be able to send Peggy enough to live quite comfortably.'

'Lieutenant colonel!' Reed shook his head incredulously. 'You always thought big, I'll grant you that. All those times we drained sumps, cleaned carburettors, flew booze out of Cuba. You always had big plans.'

'And the Chaco?' Arch smiled. 'I thought we'd come back loaded, and with big reputations.' He looked up at the night sky. 'It's good to make something of one's life, Frank. I'm going to shake them all back home; the head-in-the sand isolationists, the observers of legal niceties who block aid to China, the speech-makers who prove by weight of words that America shouldn't re-arm. There are people in Sacramento who want me to run for Congress when I go back, but that won't be for a while.'

'If you're moving west with the government, couldn't you let Peggy stay in China with you?'

They had reached the car and Arch leaned against it. 'I've thought long and hard, Frank. And I've reached the conclusion that Peggy would be better off without me – I mean permanently. She'll have money – I've seen to that.'

He'd somehow known all along that Arch would do this. Reed was suddenly sick of being a human being. 'Have you told her?'

'No. I'll tell her the day after tomorrow.'

'You're a lousy son-of-a-bitch, Arch.'

'It's in Peggy's best interests.'

'You're doing this in Peggy's best interests? That's the worst kind of self-deception!'

Arch tensed then let his shoulders sag. 'You've never been able to forgive me, have you?'

255

'For *what*, damn it?'

'All of it. France and the medal they gave me – my picture in the papers. Peggy, Sao – the girls who turned to me instead of you. And you lost your nerve, Frank – back there in the Chaco. You'll never forgive me for that. And you make some kind of virtue out of not flying any more. *That's* the worst kind of self-deception.'

He stared at Arch. It was true. It was all true.

Far off to the east a flare arced up, popped, and slowly burned out as it fell.

'Early warning.' Arch bit his lip. 'You're still the only real friend I ever had, and you are important to me. Do you believe me?'

'Yes.' He was tired. 'I guess I believe you.'

'I'll see you the day after tomorrow.'

'So long, Arch,' he said. 'Take care.' But he couldn't bring himelf to shake Arch's hand.

The car sped off towards the east of the city. He watched the winking tail lights until they disappeared.

Beyond the eastern ramparts of Nanking there are tombs, low hills and temples, then a bleak winter landscape of resting rice paddies and small, mud-walled villages. The fresh provincial levies had formed a defensive line five miles from the city. The flat land is criss-crossed with waterways and time-worn tracks, but in winter it has a brown sameness that disturbs. The town of T'ang-shan, some fifteen miles further east, had been taken that night by the 116th Regiment of Matsui's 9th Division. Resistance had been unexpectedly determined and they'd had to send a radio signal for artillery fire on the wall.

After the long advance from Shanghai the infantrymen's boots were worn out and they were short of food. Ragged and filthy, they moved about in the red glare and drifting smoke, bayoneting the limp bodies of Chinese defenders. Some looted and others searched for girls. Most of the population had fled three days before.

Sergeant Kimura watched the engineers as they planted

explosives in the square towers supporting the south gate. The rest of the town would burn. He stuffed half-cooked rice into his mouth. The remaining civilians were now assembled and separated – men into the empty jute mill and locked there. The women squatted, huddled together outside the outer gate – forty or fifty of them, mostly old. Kimura ignored them while he ate.

He was unable to sit. The wound in his buttock had opened again and festered, staining his trousers. The pain was constant but humiliation prevented him from reporting sick. I can finish the campaign, he thought. There are no towns left between here and Nanking.

A roar of flame signalled the firing of the jute mill. It burned for ten minutes, sparks flying up into the darkness, then the roof fell in.

Kimura threw aside the empty bowl, and limped off along the outside of the town wall to examine the effect of the artillery fire. Barely marked! The shells had merely poked the surface. Mind jaggedly alert, Kimura stared. Packed earth and brick, that was all, but they were twelve feet thick. From behind him he heard the long, high shriek of a girl, but the ramparts still held his attention. They'd had to scale them like medieval warriors, the disgraced companies sent in first – over sixty of the 116th Regiment dead before they'd managed to plant the flag on the top. It would be Nanking soon and those walls were twice as thick and three times higher.

CHAPTER TWENTY-ONE

In the south-eastern district of Nanking they were clearing debris from the mid-day bombing and it was difficult to get through the narrow streets. Acrid smoke drifted over the roofs. Water from a dozen fire hoses gushed like a river down Ju-bao Street, swirling rubbish over the slatted drain covers.

Russell picked his way across the flood and limped to the palace of the long-dead silk prince. Today he was allowed to enter merely by mentioning Captain Yang's name. But the atmosphere in the decaying palace had changed; he sensed it as he crossed the marble entrance hall. The ache began in his gut. He'd made up his mind he was going to hand over those engines – they'd been bought by China and they weren't his responsibility any more.

Movement on the wide staircase was mainly down. Yesterday his presence had caused glances but today nobody noticed him. It was two twenty – he was ten minutes early.

A broad gallery extended round the stairwell of the first floor. Why all the mess? Straw from wooden crates had spilled over, kicked along the thick carpeting, and soldiers were taking out telephones from the rooms nearby. The huge, framed picture of General Chiang Kai-shek was being unscrewed from the wall.

Russell paused a moment then went on. Yang would have to take the engines now! He reached the third floor. It was quiet, no movement up here. And at Captain Yang's office he stopped. Empty. File drawers open, desk cleared, and only a few scraps of paper littering the polished floor.

Russell began mouthing obscenities; mindlessly repeating

them over and over. The Kuomintang didn't deserve to win. Mao and the Communists wouldn't have passed up those engines even though they hadn't got any aeroplanes – they would have spirited them out of the city and kept them safe for another day. What a *waste* it had all been!

He thought of trying other offices, but the silence on that upper floor suggested it would do no good. On his way down he was jostled by soldiers carrying curtains and typewriters, and out in the courtyard there were trucks, and a mountain forming; piled desks, chairs, carpets, filing cabinets, all awaiting loading. Was that stuff more important than engines?

Water from the hoses still flooded the street. Russell splashed his way across without caring that his feet were soaked. 'All that way for nothing,' he snarled aloud. 'I've dragged those engines all the way from Shanghai!'

People were glancing round at him as he limped on, but he didn't care. He missed Lao. Why had the little sod gone off like that? 'We came all that way.'

Russell had thought he was used to being alone, but now his isolation weighed on him. His bad leg hurt and he wished he was back on the *Fushan*. That had been the most significant time in his whole life. And Peggy had been there every day. I'll go home, he thought. I'll just go home. I should have done that in the first place.

The street led to a Confucian temple, and ahead, beyond the squatting traders and bamboo-framed stalls, someone was banging a gong. A lunatic – he could see the man now. Rags hung from his spindly limbs as he danced. The traders had stopped business while everybody stared. Stooping low, the man beat the gong then arched his back, shouting something. Russell was suddenly aware that the dance was merely a preamble, and another man was standing motionless in the background. Masked, very tall, he wore a long leather coat of some ancient pattern, and his hands rested on the hilt of a heavy broadsword.

The dancer fell to his knees and began tapping the gong softly. As Russell edged through the crowd, the leather-clad man flicked the great sword up and spun it over his head. It hissed through the air then arced like a reaper's sickle; left, right, left, right. And Russell perceived the purpose. The invaders were to be cut down and Nanking saved, just as the virtuous warriors of antiquity had resisted oppressors. The ritual lasted several minutes and now the masked swordsman was motionless again.

The crowd applauded.

Russell felt the warrior's eyes on him. He was an alien, not one of them. And others turned to stare as well.

Still angry, he limped away, aware that their eyes followed. 'Do I care what they think of me? Let them try that sword out on a bloody Jap tank.' And he'd got to stop talking to himself – it was a sure sign of madness.

Some of the shops along the pot-holed street were closed, owners gone up river, but a religious store displayed hexagonal mirrors and charms, joss sticks and calendars. The smells of a cheap Chinese eating house hung in the air. Russell glanced through the window, then stopped in his tracks. Beyond the smudgy glass he could see Lao seated at the counter with another man. They appeared to be deep in conversation but Lao glanced up and recognized him.

He should have thought before pushing through the narrow door. Lao was already making his exit via the kitchen.

'Hey! Wait!' Russell followed, blundering into a fat woman gutting a chicken. Steam billowed from a huge saucepan, and the startled, sweating cook shouted as he pushed past him and ran limping into the alley at the rear.

Lao had turned and stood facing him. 'No good, Russell. You go that way – no questions,' and he gestured up the alley.

'Where have you been?'

'You go now. No questions.'

'Damn you! I thought we were friends? Just tell me . . .'

'Now too late.' Lao stared.

In that moment Russell knew that somebody was behind him and he started to turn, but a heavy blow on the back of his neck made him reel. He stumbled then sank to his knees in a mound of rubbish. There was a roaring in his head and his vision greyed. A hand pulled on his hair, dragging his head back. Faces peered down, then the hand released him.

The rubbish stank. A scraggy dog circled cautiously and as Russell tried to stand it bared its teeth, so he stayed on his knees for several minutes. The roaring sound faded and he felt sick. Slowly he stood, holding onto the wall. His right arm and hand hung uselessly. The end of the alleyway seemed immeasurably far off, but he reached the street. A tram clanged by.

People glanced in his direction but did nothing. Two chattering Chinese girls stepped round him, glanced back, and went on. A beggar clutched at him and thrust out a tin. By the time he reached the Bank of China, Russell was able to walk without touching the wall, but his head ached and his right arm and hand were still numb. The rickshaw boy looked wary and wouldn't take him until he'd fumbled clumsily in his pockets and held up money. Then he was carried back across the city to the Agricultural College.

Dr Foster peered into his eyes with a tiny flashlight. Face close up, he looked strange to Russell – glasses repaired with wire and slightly crooked. 'The numbness in your hand and arm will probably wear off, but you must lie still for at least two hours.'

Peggy came into the room and stared at him. 'God Almighty! What happened to you?'

'He needs to rest. I'll look by again later.'

'I'll sit with him.'

Russell lay flat on his bed. The headache had eased but the numbness in his hand persisted. Peggy fetched some sewing and sat facing him. 'Were you robbed?'

'No.' He couldn't bring himself to tell her that Lao had been there. 'Probably just an angry Chinese – they've got no reason to like us.'

He stared up at the ceiling, and he supposed she wasn't very interested in the morality of the West's exploitation of

China. 'Did you ever read those park notices in Shanghai? "Dogs and Chinese not allowed." We'd hate them, wouldn't we, if it was the other way round?'

'I don't think about it.' She'd started on the sewing – a child's dress or something. 'Why don't you go to sleep?'

'Too much on my mind.' He'd seen her fall asleep just sitting on *Fushan*'s deck. It was a knack some people had, of shutting off. He wished he could do it. 'You don't have to stay here with me. I'm all right now.'

'Don't you want company?'

'If you have nothing else to do . . .' He wanted her there, but solitude was more comfortable.

'I hate being on my own. I play the radio loud, or I sing.' She paused from sewing. 'I get nervous if I'm on my own for long. I like people round me – you know? – and everybody jolly.'

He nodded seriously, assuming that what she'd said was important to her, though he was unable to understand it. 'What would you like to talk about? How about London – you ever miss it?'

'Sometimes.' She went back to sewing. 'Just recently. I've missed London just recently.'

'What season do you miss – spring, summer?'

'*I* don't know!' Peggy stared at him as if he'd asked something strange and unanswerable. 'I miss *places*. Battersea Park Road. Hammersmith Palais on a Saturday night – you ever go there? Oh, sorry!'

Cripples don't go to dance halls. 'No. I never went there.'

'How about the Shepherds Bush Empire? Oh, I *really* miss that!'

Russell smiled to himself. 'I'll buy it for you.'

There were sounds outside in the passage – a child's voice, and then a woman speaking softly. Peggy listened, needle poised. 'It's Miss Kuang.' And she frowned and began sewing again.

Miss Kuang had astonished herself by offering to look after Suyin. Already she was regretting it – generous gestures invariably drained one's time and energy. Within minutes of Mayling's departure, the child was looking anxious.

'Mayling?' And she began peering round the furniture.

It seemed wiser to use Suyin's search to fill the hour or so until Mayling's return. So they walked the corridors of the Agricultural College, the child trotting ahead and pointing at doors and cupboards for Miss Kuang to open. Most of the students had left weeks before, carrying the college equipment and trudging westward to set up again in Szechuan province. Miss Kuang passed empty lecture rooms.

She was worried. The Imperial armies – Nakajima's 16th, Yanagawa's 114th Division and the "Black" 9th – were only two or three days from the capital, but there was no way for her to make contact with them. Ohata would have dealt with that, but Ohata was dead – executed by Colonel Tang.

They paused briefly for Suyin to peer at butterflies, wings spread, trapped in time within a glass case.

And where was Colonel Tang? Miss Kuang wondered. She had dreamed of him again last night; they had walked hand in hand along the dark margin of a lake – or was it a river? And I was afraid, she thought. A dream of mist-covered water had returned persistently since she had reached Nanking. The fortune teller offered no explanation. Whatever he'd seen with his sightless eyes he had kept to himself.

Through the glass panel of a door she could see Dr Foster prodding gently at the ribs of an old man. 'No, Suyin, we must not go in there. Let us try this way.' A smell of soup and unwashed bodies hung in the air. The relief centre at the Agricultural College was one of three – its organizations had arisen out of charitable work undertaken by British, German, French, and American residents during the previous months of bombing. Consular officials and most of the foreign businessmen had left the city, and their elegant houses and bungalows were taken over, absorbed along with the Agricultural College into what was now being declared a noncombatant "Safety Zone". Miss Kuang was cynical enough to doubt whether Japan would accept this piece of Western arrogance.

That morning, in response to a covert message, Miss Kuang had crossed briefly to Pukow. The intermediary, a dockworker, had told her that she must go to the Imperial Hotel at mid-day on the 10th, and then wait for instructions. But she would miss the convoy, it was assembling now in the fairway; a British Lumber Company ship, a CPC tanker, the *Valdemar*, and Captain Dalsager's creaking river steamer – the *I-cheng*. The ships, escorted by British gunboats, would sail without Miss Kuang on the morning of the 10th. She could only assume that her mysterious contact had made arrangements for her safe transfer to Japanese hands. But her unease persisted. What more could they require of her? The Imperial navy wanted Russell – they proposed to hang him. But she was paid by Special Services Bureau of the army, uninterested in naval affairs.

Miss Kuang returned with Suyin along a familiar passage that took them to Linda's room. Linda looked off-balance – almost unwelcoming as she stalled them for a moment at the door. 'But this is rude of me – come in and sit down. I've got time.'

'Suyin and I are wearying of each other's company.' Miss Kuang sat gratefully, and she glanced quickly round the room. An empty cardboard box and coloured string. A new dress draped ready on the bed. 'You are proposing to go out?'

Linda hesitated almost imperceptibly. 'I'm going to the reception at the tomb of Sun Yat Sen – Captain Rittenhouse has arranged it for me. The Generalissimo will be there,' she added quickly.

Miss Kuang had a sudden sharp insight. Linda was about to do something foolish. 'And you'll be back later?'

'Yes, of course.' Linda glanced at her curiously.

Suyin, tired now, was close to tears.

'Come, Suyin.' Miss Kuang picked up the coloured string from the floor and tied the ends together to make a cat's cradle. 'First a house.' How strange that after all the years and all the things that had happened, her fingers could still remember the ancient game. 'Then a dragon – see there, his head and tail. Now a boat.'

The string came apart.

She stared down at it as sudden images from last night's dream welled into her consciousness. There was a boat. And she had been afraid.

'Miss Kuang, are you okay?'

She looked up at Linda. 'Yes – yes, I'm perfectly all right.'

Linda looked relieved. 'For a moment I thought . . . Say, it's getting late – I'll have to get ready. Are you sure you're well?'

Miss Kuang stood and picked up Suyin. 'I'm quite well.' But there is danger ahead for me, she thought, and for Linda too. And she tried to hang on to the fragment of her dream, but it slipped away, back to somewhere deep inside herself.

'Take care, Linda,' she said.

There was only an hour to get across the city. Linda changed into her new dress, fumbling with the zip. Now she was nervous. And it would have to be high heels – Arch was the tallest man she'd ever walked beside. A last, quick look in the mirror. How did she see herself? Ordinary and rather selfish after all that moral posturing. And the second-hand typewriter was reflected there – a reproach. She couldn't bring herself to write. And it was because of Arch.

Foster's orderly had managed to find her an ancient motor cab. Beyond the Artillery Barracks the built up area thinned to parkland. She hadn't been this way before. The wall at the Tai-ping Gate looked massive – there were machine gun positions all along the top. Inside the wall and to her right, a hill-top fort with ancient guns pointed beyond the city.

She peered in her bag. Ferrous sulphate tablets and cab fare money. Notepad and three sharpened pencils. But where was the lipstick?

Out of Nanking, the road ascended the lower slopes of Purple Mountain. Linda applied the lipstick, aware of the driver watching in his rear view mirror. There's no art to find the mind's construction in the face – she felt slightly ashamed. All this careful preparation was for Peggy's husband.

The cab driver pointed to a distant building fronted by a gate. 'Hung Wu sleep there.'

'Thank you,' and she looked. The hills were dotted with tombs. And beyond, where the ground fell away to the east, there were Japanese soldiers pushing on towards Nanking. They wouldn't see them for a couple of days, but they were coming.

Further on, a blue and white pavilion faced the southern slope – Kuomintang colours. The cab was approaching the final resting place of Sun Yat Sen, father of the Chinese Republic. It was from here that Chiang had decided to make his farewell speech. There were dozens of vehicles parked outside the three-arched gate. Linda paid off the cab driver.

'You want I wait?'

'No.' She wasn't going to think or plan beyond seeing Arch. 'Thanks, but no.' And she walked towards the gate. Already three o'clock. Other latecomers were hurrying, some had umbrellas because of the fine rain. Linda stopped suddenly and stared. A large, battered saloon car was parked off to one side on its own, mud-splashed, bumpers dented. It was Colonel Tang's. So he'd got to Nanking after all.

Linda followed others, up a tree-lined walk to the second set of gates leading to the pavilion. Eight sections of broad steps led up to the mausoleum, and by halfway she was weary. Soldiers were at the head of each section to protect the Generalissimo and his staff. God in heaven! She paused for breath. But it was impressive. Yet more steps stretched ahead, and when Linda reached the top she was wet and windblown. Life being what it was, Arch Rittenhouse would probably find her looking like this. And inside the building, more officers stood around, and members of the Kuomintang government. A large, florid man was walking towards her.

'Well, well! It's Miss Bishop, isn't it? Phil McGovern, *South China News*. We met in Shanghai, remember?'

'The press conference. Yes, I remember.' That was a

lifetime ago. She took a brief look round to see if she could see Arch. 'You got me a drink and you told me who everybody was.'

McGovern allowed himself an appreciative glance at her figure. 'I can tell you who some of these are. See – there. Walter Stennes, military adviser to the Generalissimo, and the man behind him with the glasses – that's Dr Kung, Finance Minister and a sharp dealer.' He grinned. 'There's nothing to drink here but I'll buy you one later.' McGovern had a staccato delivery. 'Over there. T.V. Soong, Premier and brother of Madame Chiang. He holds Dr Kung in complete contempt – but then, doesn't everybody.'

'Where is General Chiang Kai-shek?'

'Preparing himself. This is to be one of those symbolic gestures he favours.'

Linda peered around. So many people, yet so much space. 'Do you know a Colonel Tang, Military Intelligence?'

McGovern's eyes narrowed. 'I saw him a few minutes ago.'

The ceiling high above bore the Kuomintang flag. Extracts from the 1912 constitution were carved into the walls.

Then Linda saw Arch.

He was deep in conversation. Linda had seen pictures of the woman a thousand times; in newspapers, magazines, on posters and in newsreels – Madame Chiang, beautiful and influential third wife of the General.

It seemed that Arch hadn't seen Linda, and she felt excluded – and jealous. What a stupid, feminine reaction. She looked away and listened to McGovern. So large was the chamber that conversation all around sounded like echoing whispers. McGovern was saying, 'Do you recall that Chinese girl at the conference in Shanghai? She worked for Pacific Press – a Miss . . .' He clicked his fingers trying to remember. 'Miss Kuang, was it?'

'Yes?' Something stopped Linda from saying that Miss Kuang was in Nanking. 'What about her?'

'Just before I left Shanghai, police of the French district

raided the Pacific Press offices on the Avenue Joffre – the
word is that Dou put them up to it. They found three
officers of the Japanese Special Services Bureau and
escorted them out of the Concession, and they closed the
offices down.'

'You mean Pacific Press was a cover for spies?'

'It looks that way. And their Canton branch was raided
the next day.'

So what – what was Miss Kuang?

The hushed conversation in the mausoleum ended as a
short, slim man in plain uniform entered. His personality
immediately touched everybody waiting there. Energy
flooded from him. Shaven head, thin moustache, eyes steely.
He spoke briefly to somebody and Linda noticed that he had
false teeth. He walked with a spring in his step. And this was
the tough man of campaign after campaign – the man who
now held China together.

They followed him into the domed hall. It was a moment
of high drama – Linda knew now why the General had
decided on this place. She could grasp only fragments of
what he said as he stood by the marble effigy of Sun Yat
Sen, but it was evident that he was declaring his intention
never to give in until the Japanese were driven from China's
soil.

Then it was all over.

Linda left the hall with McGovern. Arch Rittenhouse was
waiting for her in the outer chamber.

'So you found your way here, Miss Bishop?' Arch smiled
down at her. 'I was anxious that you shouldn't miss this day.'
He nodded briefly to McGovern.

'Captain Rittenhouse isn't it? I saw your picture on the
cover of *Time* – you're getting more publicity than Clark
Gable.' McGovern glanced from Arch to Linda. 'Well.
Perhaps I'll buy you that drink next time round, Miss
Bishop.' And he turned away.

'I'm sorry I had to leave you with that guy . . .' Arch stared
unsmiling after McGovern.

'McGovern's okay. I nearly got myself picked up.'

'I noticed. Some of these people are like limpets.'

'I thought you were completely preoccupied.'

He looked out at the darkening hills. 'I knew you were here even before I saw you.' And he went on without a change in his tone, 'The first Ming Emperor is entombed – over there. Did you know that? This is the only time that you and I will be alone together.'

'All these people – we're not alone.'

'Yes, we are.'

She leaned on the rail, looking out with him. 'You look awful.'

'I'm tired, that's all.'

'Can't you rest?'

'After tomorrow. I'm joining the Generalissimo's staff. I won't be flying any more after tomorrow.'

'That will be a relief to Peggy – to all of us,' she added.

Arch smiled.

They started down the stairs together.

'If you are going to Hankow with the government, will you offer Peggy the chance of staying?'

'No.' Arch frowned and shook his head. 'No more. I make a poor husband. I have work to do. It's better that she goes home.'

Why do I have to talk about it? Why can't we just pretend there is nobody who could be hurt – except ourselves, Linda wondered. Guilt drove her to make a case for Peggy. 'She wants to go home to England, to see her mother. She wants you to go too – she thinks it might be better for you both. And she wants children.'

'Peggy will never be happy with me.'

'Did she say that, or is it something you decided?'

'I think you know it's true.'

Linda didn't answer for a while. They continued down the vast steps.

'You and Peggy must have been happy once?'

'In Cuba. We got married on Frank's last five dollars – he and I were just starting out in the bootlegging business. We had a little Curtiss seaplane. And we had a bungalow on the beach – Peggy cooked and washed, and went shopping in the village. She spent a lot of time in the sea – it was clear blue.' He smiled to himself, remembering. 'Frank taught her how to swim – he's a great swimmer.'

He meant Reed – Linda had to keep reminding herself.

It was bitterly cold, walking down the sloping path lit by lanterns. Linda could see small figures ahead, crossing the car park, and others far behind on the steps. We're really alone now, and I'm not in control of how the day will end, she thought.

Arch took her arm. 'That was what Peggy wanted, d'ya see? The beach and the bungalow, and me. But for me Cuba was just a place between other places. I always had work to do. Now I can give her the material things she needs, but . . .' and he stopped there on the path and turned Linda to face him. 'I can't make the dream come true for her.'

Quite so. Linda nodded.

It had begun to rain again. They passed through the three-arched gate and into the darkened car park. Dreams must match, and even then you counted yourself lucky if little bits of them worked out. Fine rain froze Linda's face and hands, and began to soak her coat. They reached the car and Arch pressed her back against it, his bulk protective. Could he feel her scar – as she could feel him? She had to tilt her head back for him to kiss her. 'What do you want – from me?'

'Everything.'

'Well, that's okay then – as long as that's all you want.'

I'm not going to worry any more, she thought as they got into his car. In a couple of days we'll part. And Peggy won't even know about this. 'We only have an hour – maybe two.'

'That's right.' He took his scarf and looped it over her head. 'There's a small hotel in the south-western district – the people who own it are discreet, and we won't be recognized.'

Arch started the engine and flicked on the lights. He'd sensed she was nervous and talked about the hills around them and the temples. The darkened road curved down the slope of Purple Mountain. Linda huddled next to him. Her legs were wet. She slid off her shoes and curled her feet up under her on the seat. She was suddenly shocked at what they were proposing to do. How could this ride seem so ordinary? They were making small talk about temples and religious customs, and within the hour they'd be in bed exploring each other's bodies.

In the reflected light from the headlamps she could make out the shape of Arch's greatcoat collar pulled up and his peaked cap set at an angle. Already her flesh was burning, quite independently of the small question that kept crossing her thoughts. How did he know about that hotel? It made no difference, of course, she was going to go anyway.

CHAPTER TWENTY-TWO

The faint sound was definitely gunfire. Reed slowed his pace to listen. Yesterday you could have believed it was thunder. Radio Nanking was still saying that the Japanese were twenty miles to the east but those guns were closer than that. And there was the unconfirmed sighting of an enemy destroyer only eight miles down river. 'What do you think, Russell – how far off are those guns?'

Russell shrugged and scowled, hands sunk deep in his coat pockets. 'The Japs will be here tomorrow so what difference does it make?'

They were at the northern end of the dock complex. The Pukow ferry, grossly overcrowded, was moving out from the SNR terminal on its final crossing. Reed kept walking, past China Maritime, to Jock Ming's shack on the floating wharf.

'Why are we going here?' Russell followed him in.

'Jock Ming is the only man left in Nanking with rye whisky for sale.'

'For God's sake, Reed!'

It was dark inside and crowded. Two Chinese were doing brisk business, selling bottles of spirit and cartons of cigarettes from crates behind them.

'They can't move the stock up or down river,' Reed said. 'So they have to sell it off cheap before the Japs begin the siege.'

Jock Ming was watching the transactions from his high desk, and he greeted Reed. 'Knockdown prices – best chance you ever have, Reed. What you want?'

'Two bottles of rye. Are you staying, Jock?'

'No. I make a friend.' He grinned and rubbed thumb and fingers together. 'I have first class passage on *Valdemar*. Start

272

new business in Wuhan.' He handed Reed two bottles in a brown paper bag. 'You want cigarettes?'

But Reed had seen the opened crate of black lacquered tins. Iron Buddha Tea. 'Let me have one of those, Jock.'

'Take care, Reed.' He licked his forefinger and counted the crumpled dollar bills. 'See you in Wuhan.'

'Maybe.'

When they got outside again Russell stared at him. 'At a time like this! Why are you buying *tea*?'

'You want Dalsager to do you a favour, don't you?'

A twenty-foot gangway connected the dock to Cruttwell & Prior's floating wharf. Dalsager's rust-streaked *I-cheng* lay alongside. The rest of the convoy was assembled a mile upstream.

Cruttwell & Prior's massive floating wharf housed check-out shacks and transit sheds, some of them occupied by Westerners, businessmen and a few anxious wives waiting passage up river. They milled around exchanging the same stale news. The Japanese were at the city gates. The Japanese were still eighteen miles away. Two British gunboats were arriving this afternoon – tonight – tomorrow. An attractive, middle-aged woman in a fur coat moved self-consciously along an isolated stretch of the wharfside, looking for somewhere to empty a bucket.

Reed crossed the wharf, with Russell limping after him. A mix of Asiatics and Westerners stood in a queue at the Cruttwell & Prior shed. 'As usual, the privileged and well-heeled will leave in some comfort before the unpleasantness begins.'

'People like us, you mean?' Russell scowled around. 'I don't feel privileged.'

The woman with the fur coat was carrying the bucket back to one of the tin sheds.

'You're particularly privileged, Russell. I reckon you're the most sought after man in Nanking. Let's go and see Captain Dalsager.'

The *I-cheng* had already taken on passengers at Chenchiang, they'd been on board for days, and they stared

273

down, eyes hostile, at the crowds forming on the floating wharf.

A wisp of smoke trailed from the single funnel of the ancient steamer. Three decks. Three hundred and ninety feet of her. Built by Swan & Hunter for the McMurray Steam Navigation Company; for seventeen years she'd hauled fruit and general cargo at a comfortable twelve knots between the West Indies and Liverpool. The Chang Seng Company of Shanghai had bought her in 1927 and changed her name, putting her to work on the Yangtze. The decade had left its scars. Parts wore out and were replaced by those locally made. Each year *I-cheng* became more Chinese.

'Let me do the talking – at first anyway.' Reed went up the gangway with Russell behind him. They climbed higher. 'And don't try any of that "Mister Dou will be displeased" crap. Dalsager is a Dane, and he's big, and he's likely to throw us over the side.'

Dalsager was in his cabin, one shoe and sock off, soaking his left foot in a bowl of water.

'Reed!' He looked astonished, then angry as he stood and limped water over the carpet. 'I waited for you at Chen-chiang, as I said I would. An extra *half hour*! How could I have been so foolishly indulgent!'

'I'm sorry, captain. I had to go to Hsai-kang to bring out some women. I didn't know I was going to miss . . .'

'The Japanese bombers raided Chen-chiang before we could get under way!' Dalsager pointed down with a large, squat finger. 'A piece of bomb debris – this big – fell on my *foot*!'

This wasn't the moment to give him the present. 'I'm really sorry about your foot. But I had trouble at Hsai-kang and . . .'

'A free passage I offered you – look at the trouble you have brought on me!' Dalsager hobbled back to his chair. 'What do you want?'

'Damn it, I really am sorry, captain, and if I could have got to the *I-cheng* I would have – you have my solemn word on that. This is Russell, the guy the Japanese have said they'll hang. He has two large crates containing aero engines for Chiang Kai-shek. All the air force people and the government are going or gone, so he wants to take the crates to Hankow. We've got them on an old junk.' He finished lamely, 'If we bring the junk alongside, would you winch up the crates and take them up river?'

Dalsager stared at him. 'Madness! What do you think I am? You think I would jeopardize my ship and passengers? Supposing I am stopped and searched by a Japanese naval vessel – how would I explain this breach of the embargo?'

How indeed? Reed didn't really care about the engines, but he made another small attempt to satisfy Russell, but not so forcefully that Dalsager would feel antagonized. 'A couple of Pratt & Whitneys would be useful to the Chinese.'

'Then let the Chinese move them.'

'That's a good argument,' Reed said. 'I'll grant you that.'

'But Captain Dalsager . . .' Russell was about to start reasoning with him, and Reed interrupted.

'We won't take up any more of your time. There's a little present for you,' and he put a bottle of whisky and the tin of Iron Buddha Tea on Dalsager's table. 'Take care of that foot.'

Dalsager weakened. 'Wait.' He lifted his foot out of the bowl and examined the bruise. 'I will not take engines, but I will carry you both as far as Wuchang.'

'There's seven of us, Captain, and we already have passage on the *Valdemar*. But thanks anyway.'

'Then you are fortunate. I cannot leave here until the eleventh. The *I-cheng* is old.' Dalsager looked weary. 'My engineers are replacing a mainshaft – we could have used you, Reed.'

'So you're sailing without the protection of the gunboats?'

The Dane raised one eyebrow. 'Who knows – that may be safer in the end.'

When they descended to the floating wharf, Russell turned his anger on Reed. 'You barely tried! You just went along with what he said!'

'It's his ship! Why *should* he take the damned engines?'

Russell stopped and stared at him. 'There's nowhere that you want to go and nothing that you'll struggle for. If I weren't so angry I'd feel sorry for you!' And he turned abruptly and limped away.

Reed stared after him, then called, 'Well you feel just what you like, this isn't my damned war! Lunatic!' he added savagely under his breath. First Arch, then Russell – that was twice in thirty-six hours he'd been called a man without purpose. But that wasn't going to stop them expecting an awful lot from him. And Linda Bishop asking him to fix this and fix that for her. His mouth hardened. What about her and Arch?

The remaining bottle slapped his hip as he walked. He ought to throw it in the river but he knew he wouldn't. Maybe he'd give it to Foster for medicinal purposes? He stayed with that self-deception and made his way across the floating wharf. A queue had formed at the shed where boarding passes were being issued. And he slowed, memory jogged as he saw Fletcher of YMCA standing there with a girl in a white trench coat. Long blonde hair – nice eyes. She was talking rapidly, and he recognized who she was as she turned her gaze on him. Daphne, who had so determinedly pursued Arch.

He was still smarting with anger over Russell's outburst, and his first impulse was to walk on, pretend he hadn't seen her. But she greeted him. 'Mr Reed, isn't it?'

'I'm none too sure today,' he said. 'Yes, I guess that's who I am. Nice to see you.' He smiled. 'Fletcher – how are you?'

'I'm remaining in Nanking so I'm apprehensive. And Miss Drummond has finally been persuaded to leave.'

Daphne Drummond. The name suited her.

'My uncle's imperative instructions.'

Reed wondered how much practice it required to shape each word so perfectly.

'Uncle threatened to send HMS *Capetown* to fetch me.' Her white even teeth showed. 'In chains, I imagine.'

'And not before time, Daphne,' Fletcher reproved. 'You've led us all a fine dance. I'd rather you raised a few pulses in Mayfair. Frankly, I can't think why you've stayed so long.'

Reed could guess one reason. And Daphne's eyes caught his briefly, reading his thoughts. 'Have you any word of Captain Rittenhouse, Mr Reed? I have been trying to contact him for a week.'

Poor Daphne, still dazzled by Arch. 'He's at the Chuyin

base, but he leaves shortly to join General Kai-shek's staff at Hankow.'

'If you should see him, would you tell him . . .' She paused then shook her head. 'No. Don't tell him anything.'

Fletcher said, 'By the way, Reed. I looked in on poor Brice. He said he'd like you to visit – just to pass an hour.'

'What's wrong with him?'

'Air raid. He has four broken ribs and a broken arm. They've got him in the Methodist Hospital. That German pilot of his was killed.'

So what had happened to the Stinson?

'Maybe I'll look in on him. Good luck, Miss Drummond. And you, Fletcher, take care.'

Reed reflected with sour satisfaction that Brice had got his come-uppance. There was some justice in the world. He walked back through the tunnelled River Gate. At the city end of the tunnelled gate there were abandoned carts, bicycles, even a couple of automobiles among the boxes and baggage. It was a graveyard at the point of exodus, marking the fragmenting lives of families heading up river. And of course there were scavengers picking through the leavings. Reed looked around for a rickshaw and for the first time there were none. He trudged through fine, cold rain to the centre of the city, and there he found an open bar.

It was his first drink of the day and he would have preferred whisky. The bar had only rice wine but he drank it. The bottle in his pocket would do for later. I've got to stop doing this, he thought. Every day I make up reasons for drinking. Today's excuse was a vague disappointment with Linda Bishop. He didn't know what was going on between her and Arch. All he knew was she shouldn't be doing it.

There had been no mid-day raid. As he left the bar in the early afternoon, Reed looked up at the sky. Paper filled his vision – thousands of fluttering white squares; lifting on an updraught, fanning out, falling again. And then the air raid siren sounded.

It was only a single enemy plane, bomb bays filled with

277

leaflets. Most of them fell into the river but many scuffed across the roofs and finally reached the streets. By then the plane was long gone.

Han Yu-lin leaned from the window of the cheap room he had rented and rescued one of the leaflets trapped in the guttering. It was soiled, wet in one corner, and he held it with distaste as he read aloud.

'"The Emperor Hirohito, divine upon the steps of heaven, wishes only peace and harmony, all Asians joined in partnership . . ."' Han lifted an eyebrow and scanned the print while Lao waited. '"Japan offers clemency to those Chinese soldiers and civilians who have misguidedly followed the war lord, Chiang Kai-shek. Surrender Nanking to the Imperial armies and you will be well treated."'

Han turned back to the window and resumed his watch of the bank opposite. Soldiers were removing long, heavy boxes and stacking them in the rear of a truck. Government bullion was being transferred. There were more soldiers, with rifles at the ready, guarding both ends of the street.

'The Japanese are within sight of the city. What would you do, Lao, if you were their general?'

Lao shrugged and took a small puzzle from his pocket. 'I would find a weakness in the wall.' He had bought the puzzle that afternoon and was already bored with it.

'No. Think. That is the *second* thing you would do.' Han was still watching the street. 'First you would surround the city – to make sure nobody escapes – just as you would do if Dou sent you with a dozen men to raid a club or a whorehouse.' He turned. 'The Japanese will use their dozen to cut off the river exit. That is our problem. We must remove the gold of our Brotherhood and be on the ship by mid-day tomorrow.'

Lao stroked the interlocking metal rings of the puzzle and they fell apart. He knew that the small trickery aroused Han's curiosity so he was careful not to let him see how he did it. 'If Dou wants the gold, why do we not go into the bank and take it? It is ours.'

'A complicated and delicate matter,' Han lied. He didn't know where Dou was. He knew only that the High Dragon had

278

left Shanghai with his mistress and a dozen henchmen, and he half expected him to materialize suddenly in Nanking. 'Dou needs the gold to pay off debts to the Hong-kong Triads. But Dou is also a friend of the Generalissimo and he does not wish to offend him by openly sending gold out of China now that we fight Japan.'

In fact, Han was very short of money, and unable to return to his master even if he'd wanted to. There was no longer any choice – he had to have the gold.

'Think I saw Dou today.' Lao looked up quickly to catch Han's unguarded fear, and he smiled. 'But it was another old man.'

'Dou instructs that the gold be taken on Saturday morning. We will go to the bank early and we will ask for Mr Wu, the fat man. He has access to the vaults. I will carry a gun – just as a precaution. When we have the gold we will go straight to the dock and board the *I-cheng*.'

Lao didn't like Han. He flicked the shining rings, joining them again. He was a reluctant accomplice, but Han held the rank of White Paper Fan – adviser and fourth from top in the Brotherhood hierarchy. Lao had taken the Thirty-six Oaths, his allegiance to the Green Society was binding for all his life.

Han examined him critically. 'People who handle gold wear suits. Go and buy one.' And he peeled dollar bills from his diminishing roll.

Lao walked eastwards. There was a shop he'd seen where they sold cheap Western clothes. He wished he was back in Shanghai. Nanking was strange to him; and the *I-cheng* would carry him even further away. Should he desert Han and try to find his way back to his own city? For breaking the First Oath the flesh would be torn from his bones.

Lao walked through the covered market – a small, frowning young man in worn tennis shoes.

Later in the afternoon, Radio Nanking interrupted its broadcast of martial music with news that Japanese troops were within a trench line of the city's south-western walls. Linda waited for more information but the music resumed, and she went back to her typing.

' . . . a young Chinese girl refugee, raped and mutilated by soldiers of General Matsui's 9th Division, died in one of the relief centres of Nanking's Safety Zone this morning. Such incidents have become commonplace in this grim, un-declared war . . .'

She paused and typed the word 'brutal' above 'incidents', then looked up as she heard Peggy's door open then close. Peggy was staying away. Did she know? Linda felt guilty, and worse – absurd.

' . . . and history may show that the claim made by many Chinese, that they are fighting our war for us, is justified. Japan has sufficiently indicated an intention to expand the Empire of the Rising Sun until the whole of the Pacific . . .'

She stopped again. How easy it was to move smoothly from the suffering of a young girl to these much larger, safer, stategic matters. The article was as bogus as she was.

Leaving aside the morality, why had even common sense forsaken her? Why couldn't she have believed Peggy? Arch was impotent after all. All her efforts at arousal. His bitter anger directed at himself. The embarrassment of rationalization in the drab hotel bedroom. Linda forced her attention back to the article – she'd think about it later.

She heard Reed talking to Mayling in the passage outside. He'd been drinking again; joking a little too loudly, enuncia-tion a little too precise. But he always makes jokes for Mayling because he knows how anxious she is, she thought. She even heard the Chinese girl laugh. Then Mayling's voice receded along the passage. Linda hoped Reed had moved on also, but there was a light tap on the door. She groaned softly. She couldn't even be alone with her guilt.

He looked in, and he was frowning. 'You busy?'

'A bit.'

'Yeah, well . . . We all have to have boarding passes.' He

took out cards, crumpled now. 'We all ought to have our own, in case we get separated. I've given one each to Peggy, and Mayling – have you seen Miss Kuang?'

'She went out before mid-day, to see her uncle at the Hotel Imperial, or so she said.' Linda could never quite bring herself to believe Miss Kuang.

'I'll hang on to hers.' He pondered. 'It's going to be crowded on the ship and we'll have to share cabins – me and Russell, and that kid Lao if he shows up. I assume you won't mind being in with Peggy and . . .'

'Oh! I'll double up with Mayling and the child, if it's all the same?'

Reed's eyes narrowed. He shrugged. 'It makes no difference.' But he paused, hand on the doorknob. 'You and Arch. You can say it's none of my business, but you shouldn't be doing this.'

She felt her face flush again. What exactly did he know? Certainly, when anybody says 'this is none of my business' they have every intention of interfering. 'You're probably right. Okay? Let's leave it at that.'

'I mean, a good time is one thing, but . . .'

Linda interrupted. 'Why don't you take up the matter with Captain Rittenhouse?'

' . . . but staying at a press party with Peggy's husband until gone midnight is something else again.'

God in heaven! He surely doesn't think we were innocently enjoying a party all that time? Amazed, flattered, and ashamed, Linda stared at Reed. He just doesn't think I would do a little thing like climbing into bed with Arch. 'I really am sorry about what happened.'

'You're getting to be a bit of a disappointment. All that earnest crap about wanting to be a writer.' He was scowling.

'Now just you listen, Reed!'

'I really admired you. But you're turning out to be one of those amateurs who hang about at parties, using the war to boost your ego.'

She stood quickly, knocking the chair backwards. 'We weren't at a party – we were in a drab little hotel bedroom. And when you're through being disappointed with *me*, take a look at yourself in the mirror.'

She instantly wished she hadn't said it.

'You're not just dishonest. You're also stupid.' Reed stared at her.

It stung like a slap. She felt her face burning.

Somebody banged on the door. 'Miss Bishop!'

Reed opened it. 'She's here,' and he walked off down the passage.

'What is it?' Linda went to the door. She could barely think straight.

The Chinese clerk looked worried. 'There is an urgent telephone call for Mrs Rittenhouse but I cannot find her. You are her friend – will you please take it?'

A friend? She hurried to the office. Damn Reed. He was right, he was right. And she did care what he thought.

The telephone earpiece was off its hook and she hesitated imperceptibly before picking it up. 'I'm Linda Bishop, a friend of Mrs Rittenhouse.'

The line was bad but she gathered it was somebody from the Chuyin base. 'I regret that Captain Rittenhouse is three hours overdue on a routine flight. There has been no message from him. Mrs Rittenhouse should know.'

'You mean he's missing?' How ordinary we sound, she thought, but her mouth had gone dry.

'Captain Rittenhouse is three hours overdue,' the voice repeated. 'Mrs Rittenhouse should be informed. I will telephone again when we have more definite information.'

'Yes – yes, of course. Thank you.' Linda hung the earpiece back on its hook. The clerk was watching her face. 'Bad news?'

Dear God, I've got to find Peggy and tell her. 'Yes, bad news.'

CHAPTER TWENTY-THREE

During the previous day they had climbed low hills skirting the sharpened peak of Purple Mountain, and then Sergeant Kimura had seen Nanking ahead and the river curving round behind it. They'd stood and stared. There lay the purpose of their journey. But it was Nanking's wall that held Kimura's attention; white and hard, and the closer they got the more awesome it seemed.

Night came and it started to rain.

They had come so far to face that wall – starved, fought, bled, all the way from Shanghai. Kimura stretched out in the wet straw of the barn. The wound in his buttock was suppurating. They had used up the field dressings and he had a woman's nightdress down his trousers to soak up the pus. Kimura's temper had become savage and unpredictable. He knew the men made jokes about his wound when they were out of his hearing. He let out a long sigh and unbuckled his belt. At least they had a roof.

The younger of the two Chinese women began crying piteously. Captured that morning, roped and burdened like a pack animal with all the spare equipment, she was exhausted. Some of the men planned to amuse themselves with her, but Captain Hashimoto's orders were that she was to be brought to him first – he'd been like a rapacious dog since the killing began.

Kimura called to the older woman and told her to clean his wound and dress it again. Expressionless, she nodded and fetched boiled water. Well into middle age. Kimura wondered briefly where her man was. Perhaps he was one of those they'd hanged back there? And he closed his eyes, too tired to remember the name of the village. The new order, passed to them by Captain Hashimoto was distasteful. "Kill all captives." It had come from Prince Asaka, and indirectly from the Emperor himself. But if that was what they were ordered to do, then that was what they must do.

The woman squeezed pus from his buttock. It took her a long time. Then she washed the wound and made a pad of clean cotton to cover it. Kimura felt better. He gestured to her to go back. Hashimoto had finished with the younger one and she wept uncontrollably as the men dragged her to the other end of the barn. We'll have to shoot them both in the morning, Kimura thought.

It rained until first light. Stars lingered in the western sky and colours were indistinct. Reed had been up and on the road since four o'clock and he was cold, huddled in the cab of the army truck. There was no heater.

The staff car ahead accelerated, spattering mud across their windscreen, and Reed stretched up and flicked on the wiper. But of course it didn't work. The skinny Chinese driver, shivering with the cold, grinned at him. 'Broken.' So also was the engine temperature gauge. A Benz Diesel truck, modified to take the maximum load. Tarpaulin covered a metal frame tent-like at the rear where Arch lay shrouded with blankets.

They'd collected the body from a military camp to the south of Shang-hain ho. Reed hadn't liked looking at the still, bundled shape. And God knows how Arch had come to crash so far south of the city.

Wet fields, brown and deserted, stretched off on either side of the road. Their sameness disturbed. And death nudged at Reed. There is a day somewhere in the calendar – it slips past unnoticed each year but it was there, waiting for you.

The staff car slowed, passing a column of soaked refugees heading for the safety of the city. Off to the left Reed could see the Sancha Ho where *Fushan* was moored at the CPC wharf, and even further off were the five ships making up the convoy. They would sail late afternoon just as they were burying Arch.

Gulls wheeled in the heavy sky and Reed watched them. I crawl across the earth, and they change their perspective whenever they are tired of looking at us, he thought. Like Arch said, I lost my nerve for flight.

Peggy had insisted on staying for the funeral even though it meant missing the convoy. He'd thought it was a mistake but how could he go against her? And in the end they'd all agreed to remain and sail with Dalsager tomorrow. Reed scowled to himself. An extra day in Nanking at a time like this made no real sense. If Arch had a soul it had gone to where dead heroes go, and saying prayers wouldn't make a scrap of difference. He stared gloomily ahead. When I'm dead they can put me in a sack and dump me in the river, he thought. I'll float with the tide like the pauper Chinese with a garland of drowned paper flowers.

Reed had heard no gunfire since last night. He wondered about that as the truck turned towards the West Water Gate. Out there to the east of the city the sky had cleared.

The Chinese driver was numb with cold – he was wearing only a thin cotton uniform and no greatcoat. His teeth chattered as he grinned at Reed. 'Dragon in sky.'

Reed looked. A Japanese blimp rose steadily over Purple Mountain and strained on its cable, like a tethered whale. They can watch every damned thing we do from up there, he thought. Last night the gunfire had been unnerving. Today we have silence and that all-seeing blimp, and not a Chinese fighter plane left to shoot it down – the last of them had flown to Hankow yesterday. No defence but the wall, and ten thousand Chinese troops.

The West Water Gate was still open but the driver had to steer slowly round oil drums filled with cement, and there were heavily sandbagged gun positions facing the south-western approaches. On the other side of the city Japanese advance units were reportedly a stone's throw from the wall. In a day, or two at the most, they'll encircle the town and the only way out will be the river, Reed thought.

The driver stopped and an officer climbed up into the rear of the truck and lifted the blanket from Arch's face. Heat had blistered the lower part where the goggles had given him no protection, and his hair was burned. Reed looked the other way and lit a cigarette.

They drove on, a staff car following through the crowded south-western district. Although the rain had stopped, water swirled rubbish along the gutter. There were people about, and some shops opening. Past the General Telegraph Office the truck speeded up along the wider thoroughfare to the American Methodist Hospital.

The driver's teeth were still chattering. Reed pulled the half-full bottle of whisky from his coat pocket. He took one swallow then handed it to the driver. 'You keep it.' And reading the puzzled expression on the man's face he repeated in Chinese, 'You keep it. I don't drink any more.'

They'd taken Arch's body into the hospital, and Reed followed. They'd fix him up here – make him look decent. The hospital was a convenient place, only a few hundred yards from the American cemetery.

He reached a cold, white-tiled chamber. Mortuaries didn't appeal to him and he tried not to look at what was going on. A Chinese military pilot from the staff car was talking to a doctor, and he lit a cigarette, dropping the spent match. It seemed unimaginative in this place and Reed picked it up and put it in his pocket. Assistants, grouped around a metal table, were removing the blankets from Arch. He forced himself to look briefly then turned away again.

It can't be Arch – that burned carcase and smashed limbs. He was going to run for Congress when he got home. And for God's sake – we flew in France together.

The officer smoking the cigarette came over with a small bundle.

'These were taken from the body of Captain Rittenhouse.' He smiled apologetically. 'I am afraid I have to ask you to sign for them.'

'That's okay. Let's take a look.'

286

And they spread Arch's things on a table. Leather flying jacket – the back and left arm were badly burned.

'You are a flyer? You know how it is?'

'Yes.' He nodded.

'Captain Rittenhouse's injuries were too extensive for him to crawl away from the burning aeroplane.'

Even the wristwatch strap was charred. 'And that's where the body was found?'

'Yes. Near the crashed aeroplane.'

Reed picked up Arch's wallet and started through it. Some money – he stuffed it into his pocket for Peggy. Identification. Inconsequential scraps of Arch's life; a list of books with ticks next to some of the titles, a torn-out and folded newspaper advertisement for a Nanking hotel – 'Good beds and friendly atmosphere' – membership card of the American Club in Shanghai, a bill for a pair of hand-made English shoes. Reed paused over a snapshot of himself, Peggy, and Arch, taken in Cuba. And there were two letters addressed to Arch in a neat feminine hand. They were from Daphne Drummond. He didn't read them.

'And the pistol, Mr Reed? It is not Chinese Army issue.'

It was Arch's own gun. 'United States Army – 1917, we were in France together.' Reed hefted the weapon, and on an impulse he stuck it in his belt. 'I'll get rid of the letters. You can burn the rest of this stuff.' He would concede now that Arch was twice the man he was. All that driving energy – it made him feel tired to think about it. He tore up Daphne's letters. And Arch might have become somebody to reckon with in this world – it had begun to look as if he was on the edge of it. Not that it made any real difference in the end.

> To Tao all under heaven will come
> As streams and torrents flow into a great river or sea.

The circumstances of Arch's death were inexplicable. He needn't have flown any more. He could have just packed his bag and left for the desk job in Hankow. Apparently it was the Japanese leaflet plane that lured him into the sky for the last time – though even this was in doubt. He'd gone off in the wrong direction and a mechanical failure had led to his crash. Or so it seemed.

Reed made himself go and look at Arch once more. As long as Peggy didn't have to see it. And he left the hospital and walked back to the Safety Zone.

It began to rain again.

There was muffled, sporadic gunfire in the hills to the east but Nanking remained quiet. Near mid-day two Japanese officers approached to within three hundred yards of the Mountain Gate and there waited under a flag of truce for the surrender of the city. A few of the remaining news reporters gathered on the eastern wall and watched through field glasses, but most of the population were unaware of this small drama. After a while one of the officers put up an umbrella.

At the Agricultural College within the Safety Zone, some of the volunteer staff were making their own arrangements to attend the funeral of Arch Rittenhouse. But where was Miss Kuang?

She'd left near mid-morning the previous day – somebody remembered that she was going to the Imperial Hotel to meet her elderly uncle. But she hadn't returned. It was a mystery. Could she be staying with her uncle? Perhaps she had hurriedly joined one of the ships in the convoy?

Miss Kuang had in fact been arrested at the Imperial Hotel. She was now in the jail adjoining the Court of Justice in Yenchiachiao district, close to the eastern wall of the city.

The jail was used largely for prisoners awaiting trial or transfer, and it was filthy and overcrowded. In the wet months water seeped through the walls of cells below ground level. They were more like animal cages, Miss Kuang thought. She could stand, or sit on the iron slats of her bunk, but if she wished to lie flat she had to pull up her knees. An oil lantern cast a dull yellow circle of light in the narrow passage between the cells.

The woman who shared the cell was urinating into the bucket. 'Who are you and why are you here?'

'My name is Kuang Tseng,' and she barely paused, thinking up a quick story. 'I'm a whore and I cheated a wealthy client.' That should make her popular.

'All men are animals.' Her cell mate rose from the bucket. 'I am Zhu Shu and I'm in for looting. Just a ring, that's all!' Her voice turned to a whine. 'I even offered to share the money with them but the soldiers dragged me here.'

Whereas I was requested, very politely, to enter this place. Miss Kuang bit her lip. I could have been on a ship – I even had a ticket.

A woman began howling further down the corridor.

Sometimes they all howled, the harsh noise swelling, and Miss Kuang supposed it was their way of relieving tension. She had read somewhere that zoo animals did that at certain times of the day. She stood to stretch her legs – there wasn't enough room to pace up and down. All the options are bad, she thought. And the convoy had sailed. Would that woman howl for ever?

After one day in the prison Miss Kuang felt physically low, and very depressed. Her limbs were cold – the guards had taken her shoes and clothes, and a woman had felt in her hair and in her mouth; everywhere, to make sure she had nothing concealed. Was this what the blind fortune teller had foreseen for her? They had given her a thin, foul mattress, a cotton smock and straw sandals. That was all. It was the loss of the bracelet with the cyanide capsule that had most depressed her. The final exit was no longer in her control. And I don't think I can evade death this time, she thought.

The howling sound grew higher and harsher, and a woman guard came and beat on the cell bars with her stick. The howler stopped abruptly. Miss Kuang sat again. 'Where are we taken if they want to question us?'

Zhu Shu scratched her thighs. 'I was taken into the court and the magistrates listened to everything. But when the men come it means they want evidence, and they take you to a room upstairs.'

289

A room upstairs. Miss Kuang wondered when she would be taken there. She drew up her knees and tried lying on her back.

'Men are pigs.' Zhu Shu spat into the bucket. 'No man has had me – I would never permit it.' She smiled slyly and wheedled, 'What do we need men for?'

Miss Kuang smiled back mechanically. 'You are right, Zhu Shu. What do we need men for?'

The door at the end of the corridor opened and two male guards entered. She felt her mouth go dry. They moved along the line, reading off numbers and names on the cell doors, and they took out the prisoner from across the passageway, dragging her as she attempted to hang onto the bars. Miss Kuang took deep breaths and slowly let her body go limp. She had noticed something – perhaps it was important.

'The pigs of magistrates gave me five years,' Zhu Shu was saying. 'Next week I go to the prison at Ma-an shan.'

Five years in a place like this! The executioner's knotted cord might be preferable. Miss Kuang pondered. Was there no other option? She thought again about what she had noticed – the men read the names off the cell doors.

'Another week in here.' Zhu Shu scratched her hair. 'My rheumatism will be the death of me.'

'No, Zhu Shu. The Japanese will take the city in less than a week, and *they* will kill us.'

'The guards would not leave us for the Japanese!' Zhu Shu looked alarmed. 'They would not do that to us?'

'Perhaps we will be saved.' But it might be wiser to keep Zhu Shu afraid. 'A good friend told me that the Japanese took all the women from Chen-chiang prison and roped them to beds – any passing soldier could have them. Then they stuck bayonets in them.' Miss Kuang rolled on her side and left Zhu Shu to ponder this.

Three hundred yards beyond the Mountain Gate the two Japanese officers awaiting the surrender of the city remained standing in sodden dignity until three fifteen. Then they turned and walked back the way they had come. Watchers in the blimp cranked their field telephone and informed General Matsui's headquarters, and within minutes a battery of guns began shelling the wall.

Peggy Rittenhouse paused to listen, then went on with her packing. 'Arch kept having a dream – did I say that? He used to have this dream about seeing his plane burning.'

Russell sat on the edge of the chair, leaning forward with his hands clasped and his thin forearms showing. 'Tomorrow you'll be on the *I-cheng*, gone from here. I think – I think you're managing very well.'

She wished people wouldn't keep saying things like that. Foster had told her she was brave when she insisted on staying for the funeral, and he'd offered her a sedative. Let them all assume my grief, she thought, if that's what they want to assume. Seeing Arch buried was a final duty, then she would be free.

'Do you want a scarf? You look as if you could do with a scarf – go on, take it. It was Arch's.'

Russell accepted it a little reluctantly. 'Thanks. Thanks a lot.'

'It's only a *scarf* for God's sake.'

Arch won't need it any more. And he won't need anything from me – no love, no worry, no guilt. Peggy picked up the red, high-heeled shoes and stared at them. If Arch hadn't taken Linda to that hotel I might have gone on feeling guilty for the rest of my life. Now I can go home, and I can start to forget Arch, and I can start my life again.

'How long will it take to get to England?'

'Five weeks from Canton or Hong-kong.' Russell frowned to himself and touched the ugly scar on his cheek. 'You'll be home in time for spring. All the ducks in the parks, and the sun getting warm.'

Sometimes he looks no more than a schoolboy, she thought. 'What about you – you'll be home too, won't you?' He must be six – seven years younger than her. 'What do you plan to do next?'

He stared at her. 'I don't know. There's one thing I *ought* to do.'

She had the feeling he was working up to saying something important, and an instinct prompted her to switch the subject. 'I have to change my dress. No, you don't have to go. Just look the other way.'

Russell talked, but she only half listened. She remembered that she'd been alone when she'd bought the dress. Arch was never there. Where was he *that* time, while I spent nights reading magazines in cheap hotels? 'You'll be coming to Hong-kong with us, won't you?' The dress made a rustling sound. 'I mean, *you* can't stay here.'

'It depends,' he said.

She fastened the zip. 'On what?'

'On whether you need me.' Russell went over to the window. 'If you need me I'll go all the way home with you, and glad to do it.' He stared out at the darkening day.

She hadn't expected him to come right out and say a thing like that, and she stood there looking at his gaunt shape. Could she have found anybody as completely different from Arch? He loved her, but how would she feel about him limping beside her?

'I don't know, love. I mean, we can go back to England together but don't expect too much of me. There's my bloody great family waiting there in Battersea – mum, four sisters, two brothers – they've all got kids, so I'll have a lot of catching up to do.' She thought he would turn and start making a case for him and her together, but he went on looking out of the window. 'It's not that I wouldn't want to see you – honestly. I really like you,' she added lamely.

'It's beginning to rain again,' Russell said.

'You *are* going home, aren't you?'

But at that moment Dr Foster tapped on the door, and the ritual of death and the disposal of Arch's body imposed itself. The others arrived, making deliberately ordinary conversation unrelated to the event. Mayling was explaining that the duty nurse had agreed to give Suyin her supper and put her to bed. 'But she will stay awake until I return, I know it.' Mayling looked worried again. 'She is afraid of the dark.'

Reed was wearing a tie, and Peggy thought it suited him but there seemed no opportunity to say so, and he was asking if anybody had seen Miss Kuang. Nobody knew where she was. There was discussion about how they would travel the short distance to the cemetery.

In the end Peggy rode with Russell, Foster, and two Chinese air force officers.

'There hasn't been time to do much.' Dr Foster blinked through his wire-rimmed glasses. 'The air force have sent a burial party and they'll fire a volley over the grave.'

'Thanks. I'm sure you've done everything you could.'

The dimmed headlights revealed vague, transient images in the rainswept streets. There were sounds of mortar fire from the south-west. The senior of the two Chinese officers lit a cigarette. Peggy coughed, and Russell leaned forward. 'Would you mind putting that out, please?' He opened a window slightly and the mortar fire sounded louder, echoing off the high buildings. Surprised, the officer apologized to Peggy and stubbed the cigarette.

She smiled at Russell to thank him, but it was too dark for him to see. How funny he was, and shabby, and clumsy. I must talk to him again later, she thought. He needs taking in hand, at least until we get back to England. The car stopped at the gates of the cemetery. There were other cars there, parked up close to the shoulder-high brick wall – two of them carried army pennants. A few newspapermen, McGovern among them, kept a suitable distance but moved through the gates with the mourners.

The gravediggers had barely finished their work. It had grown dark before somebody told them that the coffin measured six foot six inches and they'd had to enlarge the hole – it was covered now with a sagging tarpaulin but water was seeping in. The soldiers making up the firing party were in the chapel doorway, sheltering from the rain. They wore clean uniforms and puttees, and they'd been issued with greatcoats that afternoon.

Linda followed Reed into the chapel. It was small and the light was poor. The coffin, draped with a blue and white flag of the Chinese Republic, rested on three battered trestles – the middle one had been repaired with string. Linda had expected something more impressive – something grand for the air ace whose picture had appeared on the cover of *Time* magazine. Only the wreath from the Generalissimo and Madame Chiang suggested that Arch might have been important.

Dr Foster frowned and fussed. 'Somebody should have found an American flag.' And the Chinese major indicated his regret – they had tried but without success, and most of the prominent Americans had left.

'It doesn't matter,' Peggy said. 'I'm quite sure that Captain Rittenhouse would be proud to have his body draped with the flag of China.'

That was a pretty good thing to say, Linda thought, though it may have no real meaning. Peggy comes out of this with a whole lot more dignity than I'm able to feel. What *do* I feel? Numb, and foolish when I allow myself to think about it. Russell was at Peggy's elbow as if ready to steer her, as he'd steered the *Fushan*, through every difficulty and danger of the darkening day.

Dr Foster took a leather-bound service book from his pocket. He looked towards Peggy. 'I think we should begin, don't you?'

The low murmurs ceased.

Linda shifted her gaze to the flowers, rather than look at that angular, flag-draped casket. Poor Arch, and that shabby hotel bedroom just two nights back. And me there, talking too fast and too much. What a messy end to his life – there'd been no dignity in it.

'The eternal God is your dwelling place, and underneath are the everlasting arms . . .'

Does Dr Foster believe that? Do *I* believe it?

' . . . If there is a physical body, there is also a spiritual body. Just as we have borne the image of the man of the dust, we shall also bear the image of the man of heaven. I tell you this, brethren . . .'

294

The words are comforting whether you believe them or not. Are we never separated from the love of God? – even if we don't believe in Him? Is despair a sin? Is taking your own life worse? Linda hastily suppressed the thought. She'd had nagging doubts about Arch's accident.

Six soldiers carried the coffin out to the graveyard. They followed, Linda walking with Mayling and avoiding the puddles. Two storm lanterns cast circles of light, half illuminating Arch's grave – it already had three inches of water in it and the rain was splashing down.

One of the reporters put up an umbrella and handed it to Russell to hold over Peggy. Linda shared Mayling's prayer book. She looked straight ahead as the soldiers strained, lowering the coffin into the ground.

'Forasmuch as the spirit of the departed hath returned to God who gave it, we therefore commit his body to the ground . . .'

Peggy stooped to take a handful of wet earth, and she let it fall onto the wood below.

The ragged volley of shots startled a few birds and they flapped and cried out in the darkness. Then it was all over. The newsmen fired off their flashbulbs, and mourners were hurrying off. Linda went and joined Peggy. Peggy took a single flower from the wreath she'd made that afternoon. 'That was quite a good send off for him, wasn't it, love?'

'I guess so.' Linda suddenly wanted to cry.

'Bloody rain goes on, though. He wouldn't like that – it used to make his knee ache.'

'Oh God, Peggy. I'm so sorry!'

'Let's go home, love.'

Reed said, 'Those Chinese officers have to return right away. Fletcher can only manage four in his car, so two of us will have to walk.'

'You and me, Reed.' Linda hugged Peggy quickly then turned away.

Fletcher's car passed them within a minute of their

starting off. Reed offered his arm and adjusted his pace to hers. Nerves jagged, she felt emotionally strung out.

'How did Peggy find out – about me and Arch in that hotel?'

'*I* don't know. Maybe one of those women in the relief centre saw you and told her. Maybe she just guessed – Peggy's a lot smarter than you think.'

'She hasn't said anything. And you're being altogether too nice.'

'The impulse will pass,' he said. High up and to their right a sudden flare suffused the city with light. 'Which hotel did you go to?'

'The New Asia in Tibet Road.'

'The beds are good there.'

'Don't *say* that. I feel absolutely sick of myself. Have you ever felt absolutely sick of *your*self?'

He nodded.

'But I can't help feeling I've unwittingly done Peggy a huge favour.'

'That's true – all that guilt she carried around. You've freed her by having it off with Arch in a grubby hotel room.'

'Will you stop it! At least I know myself for what I am.'

'How can you know yourself? Nobody knows himself.' He shrugged. 'Arch knew *me* a whole lot better than *I* ever did.'

'You mean about not flying any more?'

'It was like having a wound and not daring to look at it. Arch ripped the bandage off for me.'

'Tell me about it.'

'Another time.'

'Arch said you were the only real friend he ever had.'

'I wasn't such a good friend. I envied Arch too much – it made me sour. Add all the good and subtract the bad – Arch was a better man than me.' Reed paused and looked up at the heavy sky. 'I wonder where he is now?'

'He might still be alive if it weren't for me.' They'd reached the college and Linda stopped outside the main entrance. 'That's an awesome thought to carry around.'

'And a stupid thing to say.' He stared at her angrily. 'Go

296

and pack or do something useful. Nobody wants to listen to you belly-aching about your guilt.'

'Good old Reed – always there with just the right words. I wasn't asking for your absolution.' Tears welled inside her. 'Any more stern words of censure before I go and face my responsibilities?'

'None.' He gripped her arms tightly. 'I'm no better. Right now I'm envying Arch that night with you at the New Asia hotel.'

She felt her face flush. 'Well, envying's about as far as *you'll* ever get!' She tried to turn away. 'You're *holding* me!' Her tense control suddenly broke and the tears ran down her face.

'Will you shut up? Will you just shut up a minute and listen?' And he went on holding her tightly until she nodded.

'You weren't really planning to take Arch away from Peggy. You went after him because he seemed certain. Right?'

She nodded again and sniffed.

'Arch wasn't certain. That was expecting too much – wasn't it?' He stroked her hair. 'Too much from Arch – too much from life?'

Linda thought for a moment then rested her head on Reed's shoulder. 'It's a tough old world, isn't it? Nobody seems to get what they want.'

'It's a little early to tell,' he said.

CHAPTER TWENTY-FOUR

Shells from the high velocity guns over on the right made a roaring sound through the darkness then dropped on the wall or just inside the city. In front and to Kimura's left two battalions from the 30th Division crouched in readiness for their assault. They were vague shapes, backs tensed. They'd fixed their bayonets. Kimura knew that two battalions wouldn't be enough. Perhaps General Matsui was merely probing – infantrymen were expendable.

Captain Hashimoto joined him briefly, staring ahead. 'They are late,' he said, and moved on. And bugles blared harshly in the night. Men rose and started forward. The barrage shifted abruptly into the city.

Kimura watched. The wall loomed massive, medieval – a crenellated silhouette against the starlit sky. He envisaged the Chinese defenders crouched ready, waiting for the attack. Flares popped high above, illumining the Japanese infantrymen – small figures with ropes and scaling ladders – and almost immediately the machine guns high on the wall began crackling.

Fifty feet and almost vertical. How will I climb when it is our turn, Kimura wondered – he knew that their turn would come. He could limp along, and even manage a hobbling run, but his leg wouldn't take the weight if he had to climb. The wound was dry and inflamed, swollen tight against his trousers.

Japanese troops reached the canal skirting the wall and were wading across. The defenders poured down oil and fired it – Kimura could hear harsh cries in the night. After nearly half an hour the red flare arced up to signal that the Rising Sun flag had been carried onto the battlements, but still Kimura waited. It was one thing to seize a section of wall, quite another to hold it.

After a while they started bringing in casualties: crushed, burned, shouting men. And the others came back in groups of ten or fifteen, their smoke-blackened faces streaked with sweat.

So *we* will try when light comes. Kimura tried to get some sleep.

The heavy shellfire had kept them all awake, and now it eased. Miss Kuang tried to rest, knees drawn up, taking deep breaths and exhaling slowly, but it was impossible to control the rapid beating of her heart. I could be taken upstairs for interrogation, she thought. A shell could fall on the prison. The prison building and adjacent law courts are near the south-east wall – perhaps the Japanese troops will storm this section. It seemed unlikely that she would survive the day and the important question now was *how* would she die? Miss Kuang suspected that the executioner's knotted cord might be quickest.

One of the women further along the corridor began to shriek, and Zhu Shu rose from her bunk and shouted at her. 'Shut up, you stupid whore!' She waited, satisfied with the sudden silence, then sat again. 'They are all ignorant, these cheap prostitutes – oh, I mean no offence to you, Kuang Tseng! You are not like them.'

Zhu Shu grated on her nerves.

Miss Kuang smiled at her. 'We are friends, you and I. Tell me about yourself.' And as Zhu Shu chattered, she again switched part of her mind to the possibility of escape. Prisoners came, were taken for questioning, moved to the command cells, transferred, sometimes released – a constantly changing population, she thought. And our names are not known to most of the guards.

Zhu Shu was whining. 'All I did was loot a ring from a dead woman's finger. Where was the harm? There were only her milksop children left alive and they couldn't use it. And for this I shall spend five years in prison.'

'Or be raped and mutilated if the Japanese get to us first,'

Miss Kuang reminded her. She lay back and watched Zhu Shu's small, foolish eyes turn fearful.

'No! That will not happen! The guards would let us go before the Japanese arrived!'

'By all means believe that, Zhu Shu, my dear friend, if it gives you some comfort.'

The door at the end of the passageway opened and murmuring in the cells ceased abruptly, each prisoner tensed. A male guard checked cell numbers and names against his list. Then he stopped and opened the door. 'Which of you is Kuang?'

Her heart thumped painfully as she walked ahead of him, up the stairs and past the communal cells. They had only sent one guard for her – was that a good sign? Would they have sent two or three if they intended to hurt her? Light-headed, and no longer completely in control of her limbs, Miss Kuang stood facing a wall while the guard frowningly checked his board. A brief moment to feel amazement at his total indifference to her plight, then she was bundled roughly through a door and it closed behind her.

There was a small window high up in the wall, and the sky was lightening. Early morning, she thought. She had lost track of time. There was a table and a single chair. A gutter set into the stone slabs of the floor emptied into a drain. That was all. The room smelt of fear. She stood and waited. If she had to scream, would anyone out there hear her? What had it all been for; the years of deception, the men she'd taken to her bed then blackmailed? Money – painstakingly accumulated in Shanghai and Canton banks, and useless to her now? Her fragmentary thoughts were interrupted by the rattle of the door bolt. She was afraid to turn her head.

Colonel Tang entered.

She had suspected that he was in the city, but face to face with him again she could still hardly believe it.

Tang sat and opened a folder. 'So we meet in Nanking,' and he looked at her, eyes expressionless, 'just as you suggested.'

'I hoped you would never find out what I am.' Her voice

sounded strange to her, husky. She tried to swallow but her mouth was too dry. 'This is not what I wanted for us.'

'No, it is not what you wanted. You are to die, madam. That is why you are here.'

Had the blind fortune teller seen all of this? She smiled wryly. 'I had a dream. I was afraid, but we were together, walking by the shore.'

'Time has run out, for me as well as you.'

The executioner would do his work on her, and Tang would probably meet his end out there, somewhere on Nanking wall. 'Does it have to be?' She knelt at the table and stretched out her hands, palms up. 'You desire me, filthy and ragged as I am now. I know it – I feel it. And I desire you. We could go to Canton. I have money there – enough for us both!' And she faltered, realizing how false she sounded.

He continued to stare at her. 'There is no greater calamity than underestimating the treachery of the enemy.'

'But I am *not* the enemy! I never was! I never did it for *them*! I did it all for money! Money for the girl sold into a brothel at twelve years! I vowed that men would pay. But not you – not now!' And she began to sob, chest tight and the tears running down her face. Part of her mind wondererd – am I acting?

'There is little time left.' He waited for her to stop, then said, gently, 'Whatever your reasons, you have helped bring the enemy to the walls of Nanking, and now we both must pay.'

'*You* don't have to – you could escape!' A last heavy sob and a sniff. She composed herself. 'Go to Canton – you can have the money I saved. I don't want it wasted. I don't want it all to have been for nothing.'

'I have lived my life by a warrior code, and I am content now to leave this world. The Tao teaches "he who knows where to stop can never be perishable". But your life must be ended before I die.'

She sniffed again and nodded. 'When is it – when is it to happen?'

'You will be taken from your cell and executed within the hour.'

'What of the others?'

'They are not my concern,' he said. 'I believe they are to be released when it is light. You will not see the sun rise, or greet the enemy you have brought to us.'

'Then this is our parting.' She paused, knowing that she must try to say it honestly. 'Because I came close to loving – just once – I find it difficult to die.'

'Then that is your misfortune.' Colonel Tang closed the file.

A different guard took her back to her cell. But Miss Kuang's fear had evaporated some time during the brief walk, and she felt an icy calm. Zhu Shu began questioning her as she sat on her bunk. 'What is happening – what did you learn?'

'I am to be released within the hour.' Miss Kuang shrugged. 'The pig I cheated has fled from the city and can't give evidence.' She drew up her legs and lay back.

'What about the rest of us?'

'I am sorry, Zhu Shu. Most of the others are to be freed before the Japanese arrive, but the convicted looters will be left here.'

Zhu Shu stared at her, aghast. 'They wouldn't!'

'They did the same thing in Su-chow,' Miss Kuang lied. 'Looters were left in their cells for the Japanese to rape and murder.'

Zhu Shu began crying, rocking from side to side. 'They said I would go to prison at Ma-an shan!'

'They said – they said. They always say things.' Suppressing her distaste, Miss Kuang stretched out her hand to stroke Zhu Shu's greasy, matted hair. 'I am very sorry. I did my best – I pleaded for you.'

'The Japanese will torture me! I cannot bear it! What shall I do?'

Miss Kuang sat up. 'You are my friend. I think I have an idea.'

'Yes – you are clever! Oh, tell me quickly!'

'If there was a mix-up over names . . .' And Miss Kuang frowned, pretending to ponder. 'I could always say later that I didn't understand and they would have to let me go, wouldn't they?'

'Yes – yes!' The dull, red-rimmed eyes registered hope. 'Oh, tell me what I must *do*!'

'When the male guard comes to the cell, you must pretend to be me.'

'You are such a good friend, Kuang Tseng!'

Grey early morning filtered over blotched walls and into the prison yard.

The streets of Nanking were almost empty when Colonel Tang left the prison and returned to the offices of the Military Governor near the old Ming palace. The seat of Kuomintang government was now deserted. Odd pieces of furniture littered the drive, abandoned in the hasty evacuation.

The Military Governor had also left. A second assault on the wall was expected before mid-day. But he would not leave. Tang walked quickly to his own office at the end of the corridor. He took the photograph of his son from its frame on the desk and tucked it inside his shirt. The two-handed Manchurian sword hung on the wall below the portrait of the Generalissimo. He lifted it down, testing its weight, then strapped it to his waist.

Tang knew where the assault would come this time. Japanese guns were pounding the weakest point near the Radiant Flower Gate only a short distance away. He climbed the ancient steps to the ramparts. It was now light enough to see, but dust and smoke partly obscured the crumbling stonework. Chinese provincial troops skulked in what cover they could find, and the wall shook at the impact of heavy shells thumping into its base.

Colonel Tang ignored the shellfire and stood looking down on the canal and the fields stretching away to the east. Thousands of small figures were moving towards the city. I am fifty-three years old, he thought. My son would have been twenty-two if he had lived. And he unsheathed the great sword.

Chinese soldiers watched, then one by one they came and joined him, forming a ragged line along the top of the wall. Some had used up all their ammunition and they held their rifles like clubs.

'This is a good place to die.' Tang smiled at them.

*

Although most of the shells were still falling well to the south of the Safety Zone, the incessant, earth-shaking thuds raked Linda's nerves. She stirred each of the buckets of thin soup in turn. A few air raids and they had assumed they were hardened veterans. Nanking was turning out to be an altogether different ball game.

Dr Foster looked over her shoulder at the soup. 'It has *some* nutritional value.'

'I guess so.' Linda forced a quick smile. 'It's the best we can do.' She still couldn't like him, but she admired him since they'd arrived in the capital. Foster never stopped working for the sick and the injured.

'Are you well, Miss Bishop – taking your tablets?'

'I feel okay . . . thanks.'

'It's better that you go home.' Frowning, he tried the soup then began to walk away. Some thought made him briefly pause. 'My wife was always ill here but it was more a condition of the mind. I should have taken her back to America.'

But you didn't. And she killed herself. Linda thought she'd begun to grasp what motivated Foster.

Mayling joined her – and she had little Suyin in tow and she looked tired. 'Those people out there are very hungry. Some haven't eaten for twenty-four hours.'

'The soup's done. No darling!' and she stretched out her hand to Suyin. 'It's hot! Burns!' And to Mayling she added, 'That's about all I can say for it.'

They wrapped rag round the handle of a bucket and carried it out to the college refectory. Mayling was tight-lipped. 'I will be greatly relieved when we leave here. But it is mainly for Suyin that I worry. Will you promise me something, Linda? If anything happens to me, you will look after her?'

'Oh, c'mon Mayling! We'll be on the *I-cheng* by mid-day.' But Linda was worried. Getting out of the city wasn't going to be nearly as easy as it would have been yesterday. 'Of course I'll look after her.'

'I will ask Peggy also, but you are the most determined of us, Linda.'

'Am I? I wouldn't have thought so.' She ladled soup into the bowls thrust towards her.

The refectory smelled of tired humanity. We should have got out – we could be safely on that convoy, with the British navy looking after us, she thought. And where is Reed? Linda turned her anxiety into anger. Why isn't he here when we need him? Damn it, *I* need him.

She emptied the bucket and went to fetch more soup. I'd expected one of those old-fashioned kind of sieges that take a week to get started then go on for months and months. Would we all have stayed for Arch's funeral if we'd known the Japanese were going to attack so soon? And why am I ladling out soup? *I'm* tired too. My hands are dry like paper, and I haven't slept, and I haven't washed. She hauled another bucket out to the refectory.

'Suyin fetch bread?' And Linda pointed.

The child stared up at her face, then turned and trotted to fetch a loaf seemingly as big as herself. Mayling glanced round at her, concerned.

'Stop worrying, Mayling. It's good for her – she can manage.'

A boy with boot-button eyes reached up on his toes, bowl held out to Linda, but he was lost among the adults leaning over him. 'Careful! Give the boy room!' She groped for a word in Chinese: '*Zhuyi*!' Tiredness and anxiety made her touchy. The refugees clamoured and jostled. Linda became unreasonably angry – and it was only seven o'clock in the morning. 'Why can't they make a queue?'

'The world treats them harshly.' Mayling cut up the loaves as fast as she could, and she smiled quickly at each face as she handed out the bread. 'They are large-spirited, kindly people when they can be, but they have to struggle so hard to live.'

Large-spirited and kindly. I'm high on justice and low on compassion, Linda thought. A missionary's daughter – why can't I be as loving as Mayling? But she recognized that sickness and poverty don't make people more lovable. The depressing truth was there, before her and in herself – suffering diminishes most of us.

305

She started back for more soup when the shells started falling much closer, rocking the building. Suyin clutched at Mayling's skirt.

'It's all right, darling – it's all right!'

The queue evaporated. Refugees crawled under furniture and covered their heads and necks with their arms. Linda copied them, scrambling under a table. The noise was constant and deafening, and fear gripped her. She crouched, her arm around Mayling as they sheltered Suyin between them.

The floor seemed to ripple in the shock wave of a shell close by, and somewhere along the corridor a sandbagged window collapsed. Linda gasped at the changes of pressure on her eardrums. She entreated silently, Save us, God! *Please* – if you can! Then Peggy ran in, and Foster followed – he tried to say something, but the roar of the bombardment defeated him. Linda felt stunned, as if she had been beaten about the head. Dr Foster's lips were moving – she realized he was praying. And then Reed was back as well, crowding in with her under the long table.

Linda suppressed her panic as the walls swayed and chunks of plaster crashed down from the ceiling. She leaned forward with Mayling and they covered the child with their bodies. Dear God, make it stop! Reed clasped her hand and shouted. 'It's all right!' He was only half protected by the table, head pressed close to hers. 'It's all right – it's shifting!'

Linda realized that the shells were falling further off. For a while they remained where they were, sheltered by the heavy table. The rapid thumping of her heart eased. She noticed that Reed smelled vaguely of cigarettes, and she was acutely aware of the stickiness of her own body.

Slowly they crawled out. Linda's hands were trembling. She couldn't think straight and it was a minute before she could grasp what Reed was saying.

'*Listen*! Listen to me! I came from the docks. There are thousands of people trying to get through the River Gate – it will be worse after this. If we're to get to *I-cheng* at the floating wharf we've got to leave right now!'

Linda was more than willing; but she turned to Dr Foster, waiting for him to release them.

'It's going to be bad here, Foster!' Reed grasped his arm. 'You should come with us!'

Foster shook his head. 'Not this time. I'm here, come what may.'

'Goodbye, Dr Foster.'

'Good luck to you, Miss Bishop.' He was already turning away.

Linda ran with the others to the hall of residence.

'Just one bag each.' Reed scooped up Suyin and sat her over his shoulders. 'No sign of Russell or Miss Kuang?'

'None.'

They had to pick their way over smashed glass and rubble strewn in the streets. A gold, glazed tile – Linda recognized it from the Confucian temple a mile away – had half embedded itself in the roof of a car. The air was filled with dust; and there were fires, and great craters and uprooted trees where the shells had fallen in the gardens and lawns of luxury houses along Sun Yat Sen Avenue. She could see people further on, and an ambulance bell was clanging. Somewhere a dog barked. Suyin clutched Reed's hair tightly.

As they neared the River Gate, a huge pall of black smoke rose from the docks beyond the city wall. Don't let it be the *I-cheng*, Linda prayed. She could see the same frightened question in Mayling's eyes.

'It's my fault!' Peggy tugged at Reed's arm. 'I kept us here because of the funeral – we should have gone with the convoy!'

'No.' Reed's mouth was hard. 'The convoy was attacked by the Japanese – they damaged two British gunboats and set the Socony ship on fire.'

Linda felt an icy chill. Maybe they were not going to make it.

CHAPTER TWENTY-FIVE

High above Purple Mountain the blimp strained in the wind, and the observers, half-frozen in the basket suspended beneath, watched through field glasses. They recorded the progress of the Imperial army, tracking the small figures of Nakajima's 16th Division as they reached the river to the north of the city. Yanagawa's 6th worked its way round to the west, and the "Black" 9th and the 114th were assaulting the south-east wall. The tunnelled River Gate was the only exit still open. General Matsui's guns rocked Nanking, cracking the great buildings and shaking tiles down. Whole blocks in the poorer district collapsed.

At the Mercantile Bank of China, five hundred yards from the now impassable West Water Gate, Han Yu-lin waited impatiently while Lao eased the heavy canvas bag from his shoulder and sprawled himself on the marble floor. Apart from Mr Wu, whose dead body lay slumped by the door, they were alone – their voices echoing in the large bank chamber.

'Did anybody see you enter?'

Lao shook his head. He was exhausted. Despite the cold, sweat ran from him. The sleeve of his cheap suit was torn.

Shells shrieked overhead, falling in the south-western district.

Han took the bag and tipped out the sticks of dynamite. 'Where did you steal it from?'

'Where bomb has fallen on Kincheng Corporation building.' What did it matter where he had stolen the dynamite from? It was enough that he'd been shot at by Chinese soldiers and nearly killed by a Japanese shell. 'Army engineers use to demolish.'

Han laid the sticks in a row, and frowned critically. 'I am not sure that we have enough.'

Lao had never blown a vault door. Han's plan for removing the gold had gone disastrously wrong. 'How do you know?' Anger made him cantankerous. 'You killed the bank clerk, but he knew how to unlock the vault – that was stupid! So I have to risk my life to steal explosive!'

'It was necessary.' Han concealed his anger at Lao's outburst – the boy would pay for that later. 'The clerk already had his hand on a gun.'

'All that talk of Dr Kung – you made him suspicious!'

The bank windows were heavily sandbagged, but the oak doors rattled with each shell burst.

'It makes no difference,' Han said. 'We still have time to blow open the vault, take the gold, and reach the *I-cheng*.' He was binding the sticks of dynamite into four bundles. 'Sticking plaster – search quickly!'

They found a First Aid kit and Han used the roll of plaster in it to fasten the bundles to the hinges and lock of the vault door. 'We did this twice in the old days, before you were born. We robbed Japanese banks in the Hongkew to finance the building of casinos in the French district. It is unfortunate that you didn't steal a detonator.' He carefully measured out fuse, cut it, and fastened it. Then he stood back, frowning at what he'd done. 'We must contain the blast for maximum effect. Help me pile furniture against the vault door.'

Lao assisted with growing reluctance. They ripped down the curtains, jamming them in the narrow gaps in the mound of furniture. Han was clever; he drew diagrams and did little sums and double-checked them. But all this, Lao knew, wasn't for Dou.

Han knew that his revised plan left no room for further improvisation. But what choice did he have? He was penniless, and by now Dou must have assumed that he had defected – or was dead. Either way, without the gold he could never buy his way out of China.

'Listen to the shells, Lao. They fall four in succession.

Then there is a gap of twelve seconds. You will light the fuse when the first shell drops and the dynamite will explode precisely at the end of the next salvo. If by some chance there are soldiers or police in the street outside they will not be suspicious. And we have just an hour to take the gold and reach the *I-cheng*.'

Lao lit a cigarette and waited. Was the Fifth Oath still binding if a senior member of the Brotherhood had turned renegade? He didn't know.

Han was counting ' . . . nine, ten, eleven, *now*!'

Lao put the tip of the cigarette to the fuse, and they took refuge behind the row of filing cabinets.

The explosion coincided exactly with the detonation of the last shell, blasting back the mound of furniture around the vault door. There was an awful ringing in Lao's head and the acrid smoke choked him. He groped, coughing, towards the vault but had to wait with Han for the dust to settle. The door was off its hinges but they could only see the top of it. A ton or more of rubble barred their way.

Lao stared. They could never get to that gold and still reach the *I-cheng* within the hour. So it was all for nothing! 'We leave without it!'

'Cretin!' Han had begun clawing away at loose bricks. 'We *must* have the gold!'

'But how we make getaway?'

'The *Fushan*. We'll escape Nanking on the *Fushan*!'

Reed could think of only one reason why the guns had stopped. He paused uncertainly in the open doorway of Jock Ming's storage shed and watched Dalsager's ship. Although there were perhaps two hundred would-be passengers taking refuge on the floating wharf, they still weren't allowing any of them to board the *I-cheng*. And neither was there any sign that the ship was preparing to sail. What the hell do I do now, Reed wondered. Three women and a child to look after.

It wasn't a role he had ever practised. Arch had picked a fine time to get himself killed, he should have been doing it.

And there was still no sign of Russell – he'd limped off immediately after the funeral. Reed felt vaguely guilty about that. He'd never made much attempt to get on with the guy.

There were Europeans and Americans settled in the abandoned wharf buildings, out of the wind. By tacit arrangement they had separated themselves from the well-to-do Chinese who were together in a rusting, corrugated iron transit shed. Smoke and the smell of cooking fanned out from a crooked chimney pipe jutting from the wall.

'Bloody Chinks.' A middle-aged Englishman with a black eye-patch joined Reed at the open doorway. 'If it weren't for them we'd be on board the ship now – they're just a liability.' And he gestured down river to the long, grey Japanese destroyer anchored forty yards off the torpedo depot half a mile away. 'And that lot – they're watching everything we do.' When Reed didn't comment, he turned and went back into the shed.

Reed walked across the wind-swept floating wharf to see if he could size up what was happening on the *I-cheng*. From here he could see the Japanese destroyer quite clearly. It had been there when they'd arrived, sleek, menacing, and somehow aloof from what was happening to Nanking. Two gunboats, small by comparison, busied themselves making sweeps to the upper limit of anchorage and back – Reed had heard the crackle of their machine guns.

He turned, hands sunk deep in his pockets, and walked back to Jock Ming's shed. Their perimeter had shrunk to just this wharf – it didn't feel very safe. There had been shots further along in the direction of the River Gate; and Chinese troops had tried earlier to get onto the floating wharf, throwing their rifles and belts aside. That, and the cessation of gunfire, suggested the Japanese were into the city.

The shed was crowded, people seated on their baggage – some had brought blankets with them – and they were anxious, wondering why the guns had stopped.

Jock Ming was making a few sales – his prices had reached rock bottom. 'Whisky, Reed? One dollar fifty.'

311

He'd got through thirty hours without it. Maybe he could keep on postponing that awful bender stored up inside himself. Reed shook his head. 'I'll wait. Another hour and you'll be giving the stuff away.'

He edged between seated groups and reached Peggy, Linda and Mayling. The Chinese girl was wrapping a small blanket round Suyin's shoulders, and she glanced at Reed and smiled. Linda Bishop said, 'Where have you been?' with just enough emphasis on 'you' to suggest he ought to be staying with them.

Peggy peered into a handmirror and renewed her make up – lipstick a little too red. 'No sign of Mr Russell?' She was frowning to herself.

'He's not on the wharf. But you know what a crazy man he is – he'll show up.' And, still uneasy, Reed turned it into a joke. 'Russell's probably trying to pump out the *Fushan*.' And as he said it he thought – by God, that's more than likely what he *is* doing!

Peggy stared as though he'd just revealed the truth.

'It's a joke! Get it? Russell shows up with the pump handle.'

'The Japanese will hang him if they catch him.'

Reed turned away, uncomfortable under Peggy's stare. 'I'm not Russell's keeper.'

'Hey, where are you going now?' Linda called.

'I've decided it's time I went to have a talk to Captain Dalsager.'

'Can I walk with you – just some of the way?'

'It's a free country – or this little bit of it is.' He suspected she had something she wanted to say. 'I'll show you the dimensions of our refuge.'

They walked across the huge, floating wharf. It moved very slightly under their feet, like a ship; and the river thudded the underside of the planking as one of the Japanese gunboats passed. The wind was raw. They stood in the shelter of the Cruttwell & Prior shed and Linda huddled deeper into her coat. 'You've looked after us pretty well this far,' she said. 'Would you stick close? We get nervous when you go wandering off.'

Anxiety was making him edgy. 'If I "go wandering off",
Miss Bishop, it's because we have a situation here that is
changing all the time, and I need to know what is happening.'

'I'm sorry. I didn't put that very well.' Linda avoided
looking at him. 'What I really mean is, *I* feel nervous when
you're not around.' She shrugged. 'Confession time.'

He wasn't used to her seeming to need him. He wasn't
even sure how he felt about it. 'We're neutrals, caught up in
this war. Right? And the Japs will be a bit damned careful to
respect American citizens – by God, *we've* got a gunboat too
– the US *Pannay* just a few miles up river. So you don't have
to worry too much. Right? But Mayling has no handsome,
embossed American passport, so she's at risk. I've got to
think about her first, d'ya see? I want to talk to Captain
Dalsager about maybe getting her and the kid on board
I-cheng.'

Linda stared at him. 'You do that, Reed.' Then she
smiled, looking suddenly young, though her hair was lifeless
and she was in the clothes she'd been wearing for three days.
She pulled up the collar of his coat for him. 'But tell me one
thing before you go. Arch said you wouldn't fly any more
because your nerve cracked. That isn't true, is it?'

'Yes, it is. I was flying a Breguet and I had this Bolivian
army officer along as observer – he hated *gringos*, particularly
Americans. And I had an oil leak – it must have been
seeping along the underside of the fuselage, and when I
landed sparks from the exhaust started the fire. The plane
burned like a torch.' He stuck a cigarette between his lips
and forgot to light it. 'I managed to jump clear but the
Bolivian guy was stuck in the rear cockpit. His clothes were
on fire. I couldn't get him out – I was scared even to try. I
had a pistol so I used it – emptied the damned magazine into
him.' He frowned to himself and flicked the cigarette away.
'I wouldn't fly again. And I wouldn't carry a gun, until now –
I've got Arch's forty-five, but I don't know if I could ever use
it.'

She rested her hands on his shoulders. 'You're a good

man, Reed. You go and see Captain Dalsager. I'll go back to Jock Ming's shed.'

He walked part of the way with her. 'You're a bit strange, did you know that?'

'And you're normal, dependable, well-balanced?'

'A normal, dependable drifter.' He stopped in his tracks. A squat man with a stick, arm in a sling, was passing the barrier onto the floating wharf. Brice!

Linda followed his stare. 'What's wrong?'

'It's nothing,' he said. 'Just an acquaintance. I'll see you in ten minutes.'

'I'll time you.'

He watched until she reached Jock Ming's shed, then he turned back. There was a near riot. More Chinese soldiers were trying to force their way onto the floating wharf, some attempted to swim out, but the police were holding them off. Reed didn't wait to see the outcome. He walked quickly to the moored, rusting *I-cheng*. A deck officer he knew slightly, and two seamen armed with pick handles were at the foot of the gangplank. 'It's no good, Reed. You can't go on board.'

'Ah c'mon! Turn your back for thirty seconds.'

The officer stared uneasily at the violence on the dock. 'All those damned Chinks! If it was just you, Reed, there'd be no problem. But if I let on . . .'

'Didn't I fix the captain's piano?'

'Yeah, but . . .'

'And his clock?'

'Oh, for God's sake! Tell the captain I let you by.'

'Thanks.' He ran up the gangplank. Passengers taken on days before at Chen-chiang were settled in every conceivable space and there was washing strung out on makeshift lines. He climbed to the boat deck and there had an altogether different perspective. The Japanese destroyer had its guns trained on the wharf, and one of the gunboats was bearing down on a flotilla of sampans putting out from the southern docks.

Dalsager was on the bridge. 'You were late again, Reed. Say what you have to say.'

All those stairs – he was out of breath. 'I've got three women and a child down there in Jock Ming's shed.'

'You're bad news, Reed. See my foot? I can still barely walk.'

'Two of the women have passports, but the other one and the child are Chinese. I fear for them, captain.'

'Look out there at my passengers. I have a hundred and fifty-six Chinese among those on board.'

Reed had already seen but he looked anyway.

'I was visited by two Japanese officers off the destroyer. They offered profuse apologies, medical assistance, fresh water, food. But they say if I take on any more Chinese the *I-cheng* will be detained here.'

Reed was getting angry as well as anxious. 'You're letting them tell you what to do!'

'The ship is registered to Chinese owners in Shanghai. I have to tread very carefully, Reed.'

'They can't do just as they bloody well like! The British aren't just going to accept having their gunboats attacked. And the US *Pannay* must be on its way. By God, there are still Americans in Nanking!'

Dalsager stared at him blankly. 'Haven't you heard? Japanese naval planes attacked and sank the *Pannay*. A British gunboat is searching for survivors. Face it, Reed, Japan means business this time.'

An alarm bell was sounding inside his head.

He went to the other side of the bridge and peered down at the floating wharf. Three light tanks were moving along the docks from the River Gate, and behind them were two lorries and an open-topped car bearing a fluttering Rising Sun flag.

'I must go.' He started for the stairs.

'Reed!' Dalsager called to him. 'I can't protect you and I doubt if anybody else can!'

He slid down to the next deck, his heels barely touching the stairs. The arrival of Japanese troops had triggered movement on the wharf. Westerners and Chinese surged towards *I-cheng*'s gangway – some had already abandoned their baggage. The deck officer and two seamen retreated slowly, trying to hold the crowd back, but there were more people running from the sheds. Linda and Peggy were either side of Mayling and the child.

As Reed attempted to force his way against the packed humanity, Japanese soldiers dragged aside the barricade and moved onto the wharf. And there was near-panic. A woman shrieked. Reed saw Brice lashing out with his stick, and Dalsager was shouting through a loud-hailer.

Then a single shot echoed off the bleak sheds.

All the heads turned. A Japanese army officer stood in the back of the open car. He held a pistol pointed up at the sky, and he waited until there was silence. Then he put the pistol back in its holster and said something to his sergeant. Soldiers jostled the crowd into a long, straggling line across the wharf. It seemed the sensible thing to do, and Reed breathed easier. Linda's head was stretched back, searching for him along the rail of the ship. He waved and she saw him.

The Japanese sergeant moved back and forth, bawling in parade ground fashion. He was wounded, Reed noticed, he had a bad limp. And he paused in front of Suyin and patted her on the head. Some of the soldiers were giggling, as if at a secret joke. Reed felt his gut tighten. The orderliness had a further purpose.

The two commandeered trucks trundled onto the wharf – one of them advertised Chefoo beer. The soldiers were moving along the line and taking out the Chinese – men and women into separate groups. Mayling struggled, then thrust Suyin into Linda's arms as she was dragged away.

Reed shouted and tried again to force his way past the seamen on the gangway. He was aware of the sick fear that intrudes on a dream just as it turns into a nightmare. The Englishman with the black eye-patch had stepped out of the line, and seemed to object until the limping sergeant slapped him hard across the face. Then the straggling line started to move, filing up onto the ship. Linda was stopped and Reed saw her holding Suyin tightly, then she moved on with Peggy following, and they reached him at the top of the gangway.

'We couldn't do *anything*!' Linda's face was white with shock. 'We just had to stand there while they did that!' And she went to the rail and peered down for Mayling.

'Bloody swine!' Peggy rubbed tears from her face. 'They were even going to take Suyin, Reed. A little girl! But Linda wouldn't let them.'

The male Chinese, prodded with rifles, were being herded off the wharf. Their women were crying. Mayling looked up at the ship, seeming to search for Suyin, and she raised her hand in a small gesture of farewell.

'What the hell do I do?' Reed said it aloud but he knew that there was nobody who could tell him.

Tight-lipped, Linda stared down at the wharf and hugged the sobbing child. 'Don't cry, Suyin – don't cry. I'll look after you.' To Reed she said, 'You can't help Mayling – nobody can.'

That was the trouble, he knew he could at least try.

The soldiers pushed women and girls into the Chefoo beer truck. If he was to save Mayling he would have to do something now. 'I'm going.' He hugged her briefly. 'I'm going.'

A Japanese soldier stopped him at the foot of the gangway. 'Go back!'

He forced his face into a grin and held his hands palms upwards. 'My bag – I left it over there.' He pointed to Jock Ming's shed. 'Case – valise – luggage.' And he took off his wristwatch and held it out. The soldier frowned and pressed it to his ear. Then he jerked his head towards the shed. 'Hurry!'

Reed walked quickly round to the back of the bleak sheds and shacks. The Chefoo beer truck was trundling off, leaving only a few soldiers – they showed no interest in him as they tipped out the contents of abandoned baggage and picked through them. The nape of Reed's scalp tingled as he walked casually off the wharf, and then he began to run again.

The truck reached the tunnelled Water Gate and there it stopped. Breath rasping, he caught up just as it began moving again.

It was clear why traffic here was slow. Two Japanese light tanks were forcing a path between jumbled carts, and burned-out automobiles with their dead – hair and clothes scorched black. Panicking when the south-east wall was breached, refugees had converged here and jammed up the last exit from the city.

Reed held a handkerchief over his nose and mouth and walked through in the wake of the beer truck now gathering speed as it moved towards Sun Yat Sen Avenue. There was nothing he could do – no point in running any more. He couldn't keep up with a truck. It was almost a relief. Then he saw the abandoned bicycle among the carts.

The handlebars were still hot from the fire. He mounted. He hadn't ridden a bicycle in twenty years. One tyre was nearly flat, but there was no denying the thing was ridable. Afraid now, another part of his mind was aware of how absurd he must look.

He had Arch's pistol stuck in his belt, it rubbed him raw as he cycled – a mile? Maybe a mile and a half. The truck had turned off to the left at the Bureau of Foreign Affairs. He could hear occasional rifle shots echoing around the deserted streets. It rained briefly, soaking through his trousers, and then he lost sight of the beer truck.

Japanese soldiers were looting. One shouted at him as he pedalled by, and he called back – 'American!' Another was carrying a sewing machine. They'd started fires in the shops; and drunk, laughing foolishly, they kicked in windows. Then he saw the Chefoo beer truck again.

It was parked in the broad driveway of the Chinese Military Governor's residence. Reed dismounted. Perhaps it was the incongruity of a down-at-heel American wheeling a rusty bicycle in a captured city, but the Japanese soldiers merely stared at him. The front wheel squeaked as he pushed.

Women and girls were being dragged from the truck and sorted into two groups. He leaned the bicycle carefully against a tree and walked over. Battle-weary, red-eyed infantrymen – they were all staring at him now. 'Where is your officer?'

They giggled. He wasn't even sure they understood him. 'I'm an American citizen. That young lady there is with me.'

Mayling looked terrified.

'She is with me. Mine. Savvy?'

They watched incredulously as he took Mayling's hand and began to lead her away, then a soldier with several day's growth of beard hauled on his shoulder and sent him sprawling.

'American!' he bawled. But he could read the huge joke in their faces – an arrogant Westerner made to appear ridiculous. Afraid, he tried to get to his feet but they held him down.

The bearded soldier grinned at him then dragged Mayling over to the grass. He ripped at her clothes until he'd exposed her breasts – Reed could almost feel her hopelessness. He struggled, lashing out. They forced out his left arm. No! Not my hand, he thought. Not my hand! A boot pressed on his wrist. The others were shouting and laughing as the bearded man threw Mayling onto her back and unbuttoned his trousers. Reed felt the pressure on his wrist increase, then a rifle butt smashed down on his clenched fist. Dizzy with pain and ready to vomit, he saw the soldier mount Mayling and rape her there on the grass while two of them held her.

He supposed it would go on. He wished he could lose consciousness. Pain thudded up his arm and into his brain. He turned his head on one side and was sick.

Then they were pulling him to his feet. A Japanese captain peered closely at his face. 'You are English?'

'American,' he muttered and felt himself swaying. 'I am an American. I protest at the bestial behaviour of your men.'

'Your name, please.'

'Reed. Frank Reed.'

'Which of my men did this to your hand?'

'Never mind my hand. Your men . . .'

'Answer, please. Who did this to your hand?'

Mayling was still lying on her back and sobbing. He couldn't bring himself to look at her. 'I don't know which of

319

them broke my hand, but that bearded bastard raped the girl.'

The captain didn't glance at Mayling. He rapped questions at the infantrymen then turned and led Reed into the Military Governor's residence. 'I am Captain Hashimoto. Sit please.'

An orderly entered, saluted, and opened his medical kit on the table.

'I am afraid we have no doctor. But this man will do what he can with your hand.' Hashimoto nodded for the orderly to begin. 'He is quite skilled.'

Reed slumped in the chair. Three of his fingers were curled inwards and he couldn't straighten them. And he couldn't adjust to what had happened out there in broad daylight.

Hashimoto offered him a cigarette. 'They are American.' He smiled. 'I studied engineering at the University of California and I acquired a taste for them.'

Reed shook his head. 'What about the girl?'

'You have stumbled into a war zone. You should not be here.' Hashimoto solemnly shook his head. 'I deeply regret what has happened to you, but you must understand that my men are tense. They have marched and fought their way from Shanghai – they deserve a little recreation.' He smiled again. 'And the Chinese must be taught a lesson.'

The limping sergeant led in a soldier and bawled at him to stand up straight.

'This is the man who damaged your hand?' Hashimoto bunched his fist and hit him repeatedly in the face. 'He wishes to apologize.'

'*Sumi-masen.*' The apology was muttered through split, bleeding lips.

'I'll accept that if you allow the Chinese girl to return with me to the ship.'

'I'm afraid the girl is an altogether different matter, Mr Reed.' Hashimoto jerked his head and the soldier saluted and marched out. 'The Chinese are now under our protection.'

'*Protection*? You call what has just happened protection!'

'Yes, Mr Reed. Soon the Chinese will be grateful to us. We will permit them to share our destiny. Our Emperor has said so. I will see that the soldier who molested the girl is disciplined. No more harm will come to her – you have my word as a Japanese officer.' Hashimoto peered out at the fading light. 'We have no quarrel with America. We seek only friendship. Soon it will be dark – it is better that you go now. My sergeant will see you safely back to the *I-cheng*.

And as Reed rose to leave, Hashimoto added with a final smile, 'Good luck. Do not leave the ship again. I would not want anything further to happen to you.'

Reed rested his hand in the front of his leather jacket as the limping sergeant led the way out to an open pick-up truck – it had the name of a Nanking garage on its doors.

He was trying to believe that Hashimoto would keep his word and protect Mayling, but as he squeezed into the cab with the sergeant he saw that the driver was one of those who had held her down. The man grinned at him, then put the truck into gear and pulled away.

He nursed his hand and the truck roared off towards Sun Yat Sen Avenue. A corpse lay in the road, severed head several yards away. The line of shops Reed had passed earlier was burning unhindered and drunken soldiers were pillaging those on the opposite side – they'd even impressed Chinese to carry the loot for them. And what good did I do? Reed thought as he stared out. Was it all a gesture to salve my conscience? I knew I couldn't save Mayling.

Near the Naval Academy all the lampposts were decorated with hanged Chinese – they at least would be spared Hashimoto's further protection. He could see soldiers herding civilians towards the blank brick wall of the Naval Academy, a machine gun was trained on them. The sergeant muttered irritably and the driver made a detour. He didn't want me to see, Reed thought.

The machine gun crackled.

Light was fading rapidly as the truck turned onto the docks. The sergeant gingerly stretched out his leg, thigh

321

swollen tight in his trousers. His driver glanced at the destroyer anchored out in the fairway and said something. Both men stank of dried sweat.

Animals didn't smell that bad. And animals wouldn't do what they'd done. Reed was aware of Arch's gun still tucked in his belt. It would be easy to wait until the driver stopped then blast them both. He could push the truck into the Yangtze. Nobody would ever guess what had happened to them. But he knew Arch had been right about him and he wouldn't be able to do it. Maybe it isn't Hashimoto, he thought, maybe it's myself I hate most.

Sergeant Kimura wasn't aware that his death had been considered and rejected. He had to ease his leg again – it had been dressed that morning and the medical orderly had seemed concerned. A few days in the field hospital, clean sheets, good food – Kimura was looking forward to it. The Nanking campaign was over – he had been part of history. The city was to be punished, those were the orders, but he wanted nothing to do with it. Let Captain Hashimoto enjoy the rape of Nanking, it was no proper work for a soldier.

Kimura leaned his head back and took out a packet of cigarettes he'd looted that morning. No more walled cities – for a while. And General Matsui would surely erase their disgrace. He thought about the American squashed up next to him. It had taken courage to try and save that girl, and Kimura wondered idly if perhaps she had been his mistress. He had only a vague idea where America was. Somewhere beyond the eastern sea.

There was a rank smell he wasn't used to. Decay. Kimura frowned to himself. He offered the cigarette packet and wondered why the American just shook his head and stared at him.

CHAPTER TWENTY-SIX

Russell's watch had stopped but he thought it must be around two in the morning. From *Fushan*'s stern he could see moving pinpoints of light, evenly spaced, as Japanese army trucks rumbled into Nanking. 'Hang me? You'll have to catch me first,' he muttered softly and thrust his hands under his armpits to warm them.

The deep red glow of fires streaked the night sky above the dark silhouette of the city wall.

Getting to the junk hadn't been easy. The city was sealed – he'd tried the West Water Gate but it was locked and barred, and Yanagawa's weary 6th Division troops were just fifty yards beyond the canal. So Russell had limped three miles north to Lion Hill and there lowered himself down the outside wall. Bitterly cold, he'd hid until evening then swum the Chinhuet Creek, unnoticed among the floating bodies; and he'd crawled ashore at the east end of China Petroleum's depot. It was deserted. *Fushan* was safe, chained fore and aft to CPC's pier.

Russell's clothes were wet from the swim across the creek, and his teeth chattered as he searched for the small burner. Stolen! Everything portable had gone: blankets, cooking pot, food, oil drum. Thieves had even broken open the top of one of the engine crates. He supposed they would have taken the bloody junk if they could have cut through the heavy chain.

He tried the diesel engine, wondering why he should expect it to work. But it began its familiar slow thump on the fourth swing of the crank and he quickly switched off, afraid that the sound would carry to the Japanese gunboat. 'How much fuel?' Russell speculated, rocking the junk and watching the rippling level of the remaining oil. Enough for thirty miles, maybe a little further. 'If that's all there is, I'll have to eke it out – move with the tide.' And I've got to stop talking to myself or somebody on this junk will begin to think I'm crazy.

Still shivering, he huddled in the bare stern shelter out of the wind. I'll wait for the incoming tide around ten tonight, he thought. That will give me my best chance. He would elude the gunboats and keep going up river as far as he could, and he'd hand the engines over if he could find somebody responsible. But whatever else, he'd scuttle the junk with the crates on board rather than let the Japanese have them. So that was all settled – except for why he was doing it. If Peggy had wanted him he would have abandoned the engines, and *Fushan*. Russell groaned to himself. What a sickeningly pathetic article he must have seemed, limping into her life and offering himself like that. And naturally she'd turned him down; so here he was, doing what he'd set out to do and no more bloody nonsense. Teeth chattering, he pulled up the collar of his wet coat. Knowing he was not giving in didn't help all that much – he still felt low.

Beyond CPC's silver tanks and maintenance buildings, bleak marshy flats extended along Sancha Ho to the Yangtze. There was nothing out there but Dong Ching Kee's wharf and a few scattered shacks. The two Japanese gunboats were making regular sweeps as far as the upper limit of anchorage. Occasionally their machine guns crackled, tearing apart a junk or sampan attempting escape. They were probing with their searchlights, and the cold, and the growing realization of how tight his situation had become, sapped at Russell's determination. If I get the engines across the river to Anhwei province, that will be enough, he thought. But if the gunboat intercepts *Fushan* I'll go down with it. I won't let them hang me. He listened. There was some other, extra sound out on the Sancha Ho. He moved cautiously and watched.

A small boat. Two occupants – he heard their paddles splashing. And when they drew close he saw that one of them was Lao.

'What the hell! Why are you here?'

The boat scraped along the quay and Lao climbed up,

grinning with pleasure. 'Damn good to see you.' He gestured, the torn sleeve of his cheap suit flapping. 'This is business associate, Mr Han.'

Their clothes and hair were thick with dust. And Han had something heavy strapped to his body, Russell thought, as he watched him climbing clumsily onto the pier.

Lao was still grinning. 'We have food. You hungry, Russell?'

Despite his anxiety, Russell was angry. 'Why did you go off?'

'Canned beans?'

'I thought we were friends?'

'Can-o' peaches? We need primus stove.'

'It's been stolen. Are you listening to me?' There was just sufficient light for Russell to recognize contempt and suspicion in Han's face, but he didn't care much beyond thinking that that was the swine who'd hit him from behind so he'd better not turn his back on him.

'We eat canned beans cold – in natural state so to speak.' Lao went on board *Fushan*, Han with him peering critically at the boat.

'It is in poor condition.'

'What the hell do you expect?' Russell followed them. 'I wasn't running a pleasure cruise.'

'Are you able to unchain the junk?'

'Yes, I am able to unchain the junk. Do you mind telling me why you are here?'

Han unbuttoned his coat then his trousers and urinated into the creek. 'How much fuel is there left in the tank?'

'That's nothing to do with you!' He was carrying money or bullion. Russell could see the pouched waistcoat as Han laboriously buttoned himself up again. 'There's enough fuel for *my* purposes – are you getting the picture?'

Lao interceded. 'First we eat.' He cut open the top of a can with his knife and handed it to Russell.

'You missed the convoy – am I right?' Russell was hungry enough to start on the beans before getting an answer. 'You think you can just take the *Fushan* out onto the Yangtze and sail away to safety?'

They sat on the floor in the stern shelter, and Han wolfed the contents of his can. 'You have guessed correctly. That is what I intend.'

'Well, I've got news for you. There are two Japanese gunboats and they are sinking every junk or sampan that puts out from the shore – see there?' And Russell pointed to the searchlight probing along the marshy flats.

'Nevertheless, I shall do it.'

Russell's irritation welled up in him. 'Now listen. I'm not necessarily opposed to you two coming along with me – God knows, I owe Lao that, but I make the decisions.'

'*Fushan* is the property of Mr Dou and I am his agent.' Han threw the empty can overboard. 'You have no claim on the vessel. And *I* will make the decisions.' He pulled himself awkwardly to his feet.

'I can't deny that the junk is Mr Dou's.' What do I do now? Russell wondered.

'You come with us, Russell?' Lao said it as though he really wanted him to join them.

'I'm not sure we'll get very far.'

'You – me. We got out of Shanghai.'

'That we did.'

Han was smiling thinly. 'Your voyage was not wasted – you have provided me with a boat.'

'It would be wisest to wait for the tide to turn, then seize our opportunity as the gunboat completes its sweep and turns back.' Russell decided to give the appearance of going along with them. 'Get well clear of Nanking; and three of us to work the boat – we could use the sail.'

'No, Russell. Your interests conflict with mine. I could never turn my back on you. You will not be coming with us.' Han groped in his coat and took out a pistol.

'Edge backwards towards the stern, Russell.'

Russell didn't have time to feel fear. Lao leapt at Han in the moment the gun went off, and the bullet struck Russell's foot, knocking him down like a skittle. He rolled in the filth, aware of the gouting wound and a numbness. There were frenzied sounds of Han and Lao struggling.

Still twitching with shock, Russell dragged himself across the deck. Lao's hand was under Han's jaw, pushing him backwards over the side. And there was a second shot, muffled by the two bodies locked together. Han clutched at air then shrieked as he splashed into the creek, and his heavy burden took him straight to the bottom.

Russell's shoe was soaked in blood. Pain would come later – he reached Lao who was doubled over, head pressed to his knees.

'Done for.' The little gangster groaned softly. 'Russell?'

He sat clumsily and put his arm around Lao's shoulders. 'I'm here.'

'I fix the sonofabitch?'

'More or less.'

'We go back to Shanghai now?'

'Sure we will – sure we will.'

The first faint grey light softened the angry red of fires. The turning tide washed bodies up along the Hsiakwan shore, and bits of rammed junks. In the dock area corpses bobbed under the wooden piers and collected by some trick of the current round the stern of *I-cheng* still moored at the floating wharf.

I-cheng was isolated between Japanese warships and the stricken city. All the cabins had been occupied for days, and the new arrivals from off the floating wharf filled every available space. Linda was camping with Peggy and Suyin in the saloon on the boat deck. They had established a claim to one of the worn leather sofas and took turns to rest there. Peggy was stretched out on it with Suyin. She muttered something and twitched.

Most of the passengers slept restlessly, but Linda had abandoned all attempts. Uncarpeted floor was hard on her limbs. The saloon was warm with tightly packed humanity. Only one light burned and the fans were off – Captain Dalsager was conserving power. And there had been no water except for drinking. Linda couldn't remember when she'd last washed.

Reed was sprawled next to her. The pain killers were working and now his eyes were closed, and he snored softly,

327

splinted hand held out awkwardly. Linda watched him. He needs a haircut, she thought. The hard lines of his mouth suggested that his dreams had touched something bitter. He hadn't told her what had happened out there in the city. Now he turned, banging his hand, and mumbled.

'It's all right.' She touched his shoulder. 'Go back to sleep – it's all right.'

Was she the only one awake? Linda leaned up on her elbow and tucked the blanket round Suyin, then she stretched out again and stared at the darkened ceiling. I remember, only a few days ago, being unable to understand why Mayling worried so over Suyin – I was even smugly condescending about it, she thought. But now I'm worse than she was. Dear God, how soon an obligation can turn into commitment. All those times my mother said to me, 'Take care'. And I never knew the anxious thought behind the words.

There were sounds of a generator starting up somewhere in the ship, then water gurgling in pipes. She lay there listening. The night seemed endless. If Reed was awake I'd talk to him. I only worry when he's asleep or going off to do this or that.

Gratefully, Linda was aware of the first grey light outside. Soon there would be queues to use the toilets. Maybe there was water for washing? She woke Suyin and picked their way across the crowded saloon.

There were a few people already lining up, and while she waited in the queue Linda listened to the new rumours. A fat American woman in a badly crumpled dress had heard that a British cruiser was on its way to Nanking. 'It's true! I got it from one of the ship's officers. The *Capetown* has steamed all the way from Hankow – it will be here by mid-day!'

I doubt it, Linda thought. The sinking of the *Pannay* had left her sceptical of rescue. No, we're stuck here – dependent on the Japanese, God help us.

The attentions of Japanese naval officers off the newly arrived warships was a puzzle. One of them, a doctor, had lectured passengers about the health hazards of overcrowding, and he'd left them soap but was unable to promise water. Another had addressed them on the longstanding friendship between Japan and the West and smilingly assured them of their safety. But he had removed bits of the ship's wireless equipment so that they were unable to receive news. And they'd put up "Wanted" posters for Russell with a hand drawn picture that was quite unlike him.

There was a trickle of water. Linda stood at the sink and washed Suyin's hands and face, then her own. 'That will have to do.' And Suyin smiled, uncomprehending, and hugged her leg.

'That child is Chinese!' The woman behind stared accusingly. Linda noted her expensive tweed suit and high-necked white blouse.

'That's right. She's Chinese.'

'If we had no Chinese on this ship the Japanese would have allowed us to sail.' 'Tweed-suit' tightened her lips. 'The Chinese are trying to hide behind us – it's intolerable! I had to *sleep* between two of them!'

'Well, I hope you had a good time.' Linda took Suyin's hand and pushed past the woman. All that crap about crisis bringing out the best in people! Arrogant bitch – she'd throw the Chinese off just to get more room for herself!

Instead of going straight back, she took Suyin for a walk. It was raw outside, and the air was clean though Linda could smell smoke. Fragments of black ash floated down from high over the city. She saw Brice, the man Reed knew, leaning at the rail. Other passengers were about but there wasn't much room to walk and they'd bunched in the stern, looking down. Bodies were jammed up close to each other in the water. She steered Suyin away.

When I left America I never thought to see anything like that. Thousands – maybe a million have died along the delta. And poor Mayling. She supposed, from Reed's silence, that Mayling was dead as well. Innocent, beautiful, truly good. And Linda forced herself to think about what the Japanese officer and his men had probably done to her.

Reed had tried to stop them – she was sure of that. The damage to his hand was no accident. And it was no longer possible to think of him as a drifter, even though that was how

329

he seemed to see himself – she suspected he'd been pleased enough with the image until quite recently. I guess he was always a lot more than that, she now decided.

The child kept pulling away and pointing a tiny finger at windows and doors. 'Mayling?'

'No, Suyin. Mayling isn't there.' How long before she forgets her? 'I'll look after you.' I'll take care of her until we reach Hong-kong, but what then? An orphanage? – Peggy said there was one run by English nuns. I could give them money to look after her and send more when I reach home. 'No, darling, Mayling isn't there either.' And will she search the orphanage looking for *me*? I could send her birthday presents, but nobody knows her birthday.

She noticed the blonde girl, further on but walking in the same direction. Daphne somebody – she'd seen Reed talking to her last night. Attractive. Very expensive clothes. Not his sort of thing, surely? What *was* Reed's sort of thing? She was no longer sure about that. He wants *me*, she told herself. She'd known that all along, and it pleased her now. Despite her anxiety, the thought of bed with Reed made her flesh tingle.

Suyin trotted ahead, and then fell flat. The blonde girl helped her up.

'Poor little button. Did you hurt yourself?'

English, Linda thought, and she stooped to examine Suyin's hands. 'No, she's okay. They do it all the time.' How matter of fact and like a mother I've suddenly managed to sound. 'You're all right, Suyin. Don't cry.'

'She's a lovely child. Aren't you, Button?' Daphne Drummond touched the girl's upturned face with a well manicured finger.

Linda was curious. 'I believe you know Mr Reed?'

'We're merely acquaintances, but we had a friend in common.'

'A friend?'

'He was killed a few days ago.'

'I'm sorry.'

Daphne Drummond smiled faintly. 'It's good to be going home, isn't it?'

'Yes.'

'Goodbye, Button.'

Linda stared after her. So I wasn't the only one. And Reed had known that but he hadn't said anything. Suyin was tugging at her sleeve. 'Yes, darling, we'll go back now.'

She felt a small anxiety when they returned and found Peggy alone. 'Where's Reed?'

Peggy folded blankets. 'He's gone to clean up.'

'He's always going off somewhere.'

'He's shaving, for God's sake! You were always complaining because he didn't shave.' Peggy paused, frowning. 'I told him to ask around about Russell. One of the men might have heard something or seen him.'

'And Dr Foster. And Miss Kuang. I wonder what has become of them?'

'I'm not concerned with *them*.' Peggy looked almost angry. 'I feel responsible for Russell.' She handed Linda two corners of the blanket and they folded it between them.

'Russell offered me something – love, I suppose. But I didn't give him an answer. He knew I was worried about taking home a man with a limp – I mean, after Arch. I was so proud of Arch when he met my family. And Russell is sort of thin and funny looking.' Peggy shrugged. 'Anyway, I was no use to him.'

'There's still time for him to find us.' If he's still alive, Linda added to herself.

'I needed a little while to get used to the idea of him and me. D'you see that? I didn't think he might just *disappear*. I wish he hadn't done that.'

'Supposing he turns up and makes the same offer again. What will you do?'

'*I* don't know.' Peggy folded the last blanket. There were sweat stains under her arms and she paused, unhappy. 'How do *I* know what I'd do?'

Poor Peggy. Life is moving too fast for her. Neglected for years by Arch, and betrayed by him the night before his death . . . Linda hastily suppressed that thought. Peggy is aware that Russell would be good for her but she doesn't know which of her instincts to trust. And me? What of me? I've never committed *myself* to anything.

She watched Reed edging his way across the saloon, and noted almost clinically her own small feeling of relief. I guess I'm working up to the belief that, imperfect as we are in an uncertain world, we eventually have to commit ourselves and hope.

Still several paces off, Reed saw her and smiled.

I'm going to have to give him a haircut, she thought, and she smiled back.

'We sail tomorrow,' he said. 'The Japanese are giving us an escort to Shanghai.'

'Shanghai!' Peggy laughed incredulously. 'Thank God for that!' And she scooped up Suyin and hugged her.

Across the saloon they were cheering.

'Is it absolutely certain?' Linda asked.

A Japanese warship came alongside the rusting *I-cheng* to fill her water tanks. In mid-afternoon supplies of fresh food arrived. The tensions and bickerings ended. Captain Dalsager reluctantly agreed to a party in the saloon on the upper deck.

The range of tide at Nanking is four feet in the winter months. Ships in the fairway swing to the flood for a while. The great river feeds creeks, and the canal curving round the south wall of the city. Dead from the 114th Division's assault moved with the turning tide and mingled with dead from the "Black" 9th, and Chinese who had fallen from the wall during the battle. They bobbed and bumped gently together, no longer enemies. Colonel Tang's corpse lodged half submerged against *Fushan*'s hull until the retreating tide sucked it out into the Yangtze.

The seams of the ancient junk had let in a lot of water. Each haul on the pump sapped Russell's strength. Pain wearies the body – he sweated. It would be all right, though. All the decisions were made. Now he could write the letter inside his head. *My dear Peggy, It is nearly dark and there is little time left to Lao and me. I shall say quickly what I have to say . . .*

He slumped for a minute after he'd finished pumping. 'It's going to be a fine night, Lao. See out there – stars.'

Lao didn't reply. He slid down from his seated position and was doubled up on his side. For a moment Russell thought he was dead. 'Lao!' and the little gangster gestured slightly with his hand.

'We'll make a start as soon as we see the gunboat's lights change direction.' Russell dragged himself to the stern. 'I reckon we might get right out into the river before that boat begins its next sweep.' Where had he got to with the letter? *You were the woman to whom I always addressed my thoughts. Without you I'm just a crazy man who talks to himself.*

The wound in his foot was leaking blood. 'I think we have enough fuel to get as far as Yu-chi-kou thirty miles down river on the other side. That's free China, Lao, as far as I know. We'll get help there.'

Lao made no sound.

Russell lowered himself to the diesel engine. This is going to be difficult, he thought. And more – it's going to hurt. *When you were on the* Fushan, *that was the best time of my life . . .*

To reach the crank he had to drag his damaged foot into the confined space. 'I'm going to start her up. Say a prayer, Lao.' And as he changed position to take hold of the crank, pain savaged the torn nerves, his head span, and he was ready to vomit. The slumped form of Lao was next to him, head resting on the side of the hatch. 'Who did you pray to, Lao?'

'Guan Yin,' the boy's voice was so soft he could hardly hear him.

'Guan Yin? You make a good choice. How do you feel?'

'Dying more or less.'

Russell nodded. 'Maybe – maybe not.' He took the crank again. The pain stabbed through him but the engine began to thump slowly. He dragged himself back to release the stern chain. In that moment before you turned the crank you had to believe with all your heart that it would work.

Fushan drifted, turning in the creek. Russell banged in the gear lever and opened the throttle a fraction. He had to get to the rudder before the junk drove itself into the far bank. Lao's

333

eyes were open, watching him as he crawled up to the stern, and he managed just in time, pulling the heavy rudder and heading the junk along Sancha Ho to the Yangtze.

The pain eased now he was seated. He rubbed sweat from his face. 'Your prayer worked, Lao.' *Our lives are pared down to the very simple,* he thought. *If the Japanese finish us off they'll also sink the cargo in deep water. We'll have done our best.*

As they neared the mouth of the creek, Russell saw to his astonishment that Dalsager's lighted ship was still moored at the floating wharf. Peggy was there, only a few hundred yards away! *I've got to get Lao to a hospital, and maybe then I could go home. And I'd find you . . .*

'If only it would rain or mist, we might get out unnoticed, we're going to need a lot of luck.' He turned quickly at Lao's harsh breathing. 'Lao! Are you all right?'

'Luck all gone,' the boy murmured.

'Don't say that! You mustn't give up – that's the worst sin of all!' Russell kept steering but he stretched out and clasped Lao's hand. 'We're friends! We've got to get to Shanghai!'

'Guan Yin comes for me.' Lao's eyes opened wide, then the life went out of them.

Russell steered out into the river. It was no good him crying like this. One short prayer. 'Guan Yin, Goddess of Mercy and Captain of the Boat of Salvation, carry Lao safely to the next world.' That was all he had time for.

Then he groaned out loud. The gunboat was turning back towards *Fushan*, searchlight scanning. No chance now of getting away unnoticed. He opened the throttle wide.

'Faster, you bitch!'

Only a hundred yards separated *Fushan* from *I-cheng*; and the Japanese gunboat was bearing down. His luck had run out – the probing searchlight fastened on the stern. And Russell cringed, waiting for bullets to tear into him.

CHAPTER TWENTY-SEVEN

Hashimoto's soldiers were guarding the wharf below. They sheltered from the cold wind. And in the bowels of *I-cheng* half-naked stokers were raking and shovelling to build up a head of steam.

From the boat deck it was evident that there were more fires in the city. And the shooting was organized now – or so Reed thought. He peered across the dark river and only half listened to Brice. That damned gunboat was back again.

' . . . and I came to under a pile of bomb rubble – it took them near an hour to dig me out,' Brice was saying. 'Three cracked ribs, and my arm's fractured in two places . . .'

The gunboat's searchlight was flicking across the water, probing at boat debris drifting on the current.

' . . . and that frigging bomb wrecked the entire hotel. They didn't find the Hun until the next day – he'd been crushed right there in his bed. How d'ya like *that*! So there I was; stuck in hospital, the city about to fall, and no pilot to fly me out. That's why I wanted to see you – you could have flown me.'

'Too bad.' Reed didn't care. He was sorry about the Hun, though. 'Where d'ya hide the Stinson?'

'There.' Brice pointed down river to where lights indicated the lower limits of anchorage. 'There's an abandoned torpedo depot.'

'I know it.'

'That's where we stashed the frigging thing – nobody else knows. There's all my baggage aboard.' Brice grunted in disgust. '*And* it cost me two hundred bucks to fill the fuel tanks! All wasted!'

What did it matter now? Reed thought Brice was a pain in the ass. Tomorrow they sailed down river. He'd leave this place behind him for ever.

A machine gun in the city crackled continuously for fifty seconds.

'Mopping up operations?' Brice leaned against the rail and listened.

'No.' Reed shook his head. 'A massacre.' Russell had been right all along. The fate of Nanking was decided before the first shots were fired in Shanghai.

'Troops get out of hand. I gotta cousin with the Republicans in Spain. Rape, murder – it's the same over there.' Brice shrugged. 'And they've got no respect for property.'

Reed timed the next burst of machine gun fire. 'How about carefully *planned* rape and large-scale premeditated murder?'

'That's crazy!'

'Is it? Then how about victory by terror? The Japs compel Chiang Kai-shek's submission by destroying the popular will to resist.'

'You really are a crazy bastard!' Brice stared at him. He thought a moment. 'But just supposing you're right. It would make sense, wouldn't it? To force the frigging Chinese into a decision and end the war with the destruction of just one city?'

'Absolutely right. Such a plan is perfectly logical, and the sons of bitches who thought it up should be hanged. Maybe they will be one day.'

'What the hell are you going on about, Reed? War is war. There are no frigging rules.'

'I *know* that! I fought in two damned wars – d'ya think I don't know that!' Brice depressed him, so Reed left him leaning on the rail and walked the deck along the outside of the brightly lit saloon. The party was just starting, and the contrast between laughter and music within and what was happening out there in the city was too sharp. It was hard sometimes to go on believing that people are good even though some are downright evil.

336

Heaven's net is wide:
Coarse are the meshes, yet nothing slips through.

Linda would be anxious if he was gone for too long. He went
back to the saloon.

All the remaining liquor on *I-cheng* had been opened, and
four crates of champagne sent from the Japanese cruiser.
The party had begun. A worn, portable gramophone
scratched out a Rodgers and Hart song, and the words,
GOOD OLD SHANGHAI, cut huge out of coloured paper
decorated much of the end wall. There was space now that
more of the Chinese passengers had been taken off, but the
saloon still felt crowded. And the chatter was light-headed –
Reed caught snatches between loud laughter. 'Tweed-suit'
was telling the man with the eye-patch that she'd lost her
clothes. 'Not *all* of them, silly! My servants will steal what I
had to leave – they're all thieves.'

Reed moved round the edge of the saloon. He couldn't
entirely account for his mood and felt boorish when a young
woman spilt champagne over his coat. 'Okay – forget it. It's a
party, isn't it? They've even got bonfires and rockets out there.'

She said she was sorry and backed away. Why am I taking
such a high moral stance? he wondered. Mayling is probably
dead and I haven't protested very loudly.

He was aware that Linda had seen him from where she
sat with Peggy and Suyin. She had that tight-lipped anxious
look he'd come to recognize, as though she thought he
might go off or do something to disturb her precarious
composure.

A Chinese steward offered him champagne. It would be
easy to drink and he might have if he hadn't seen the two
officers from the Japanese cruiser. Immaculate uniforms.
And white gloves – to keep their hands clean? They were
seated with Captain Dalsager and Walter Schutz of Eurasia
Aviation. What were Japs doing here? Dalsager looked
weary, resting his foot.

The man with the black eye-patch was creating a scene.

337

He'd forced the purser to stop the gramophone. 'I insist! I insist that we all drink a toast to Captain Dalsager.'

Everybody drank. Dalsager rose, irritated, and bowed stiffly.

Encouraged, the man refilled his glass. 'Now I propose a further toast, to the officers of the Japanese cruiser, *Atago*; and to those of the gunboats *Sumida* and *Saga* for their assurance of our safe conduct to Shanghai.'

There was a short, embarrassed lull, then a few glasses were raised and the purser quickly put another record on the gramophone. Couples began to dance to the music of "Good Old Shanghai". The girl who had spilled champagne on Reed's arm sang the words with an untrained and unexpectedly attractive voice – she knew she was good, and sounds of machine gun fire in the city were lost in the applause.

Reed scowled and clumsily lit a cigarette with his bandaged hand. A small pocket of privileged people in the middle of a storm.

A paper streamer arced over the dancers, and then another. A young man lifted the girl who had sung and deposited her, light as a feather, on a chair. She posed with her new paper hat.

The purser was asking Peggy to dance with him, so it was time to go and talk to Linda. Reed was half way across the saloon when a dull boom rattled the windows. Everybody stopped for a moment and peered out at the red-tinted column of smoke rising against the dark sky over the city. There was just the music scratching from the gramophone, then the dancing went on.

'What was it?' Linda jogged Suyin on her lap. She didn't look up at Reed standing there.

Somebody was handing out party masks.

'I dunno. A pile of ammunition maybe.' He touched Suyin's hair and she smiled to herself but buried her face between Linda's breasts. 'Are you all right?'

'Yes, we're fine.'

'Dalsager says we sail for Shanghai at dawn.'

'That's good.'

She's fixed her hair, he thought, and used a little lipstick. 'You'll be getting a boat straight home from there?'

'Not right away.' Linda lifted Suyin off her knee. 'Don't stray darling – *bu keyi*. I'm going to take Suyin back to America with me.' And now she looked up with that questioning expression as though she expected him to argue with her. 'It'll be difficult – I mean, I guess I'll have to get permission from just about everybody, and exit papers. *Then* Suyin and I will go.'

He was surprised. He hadn't thought she would take it so far. 'Well, that's . . . that's a good thing to do.' But for a moment he wasn't sure how he really felt about it. All day he'd kept remembering huddling with her from the shell-fire, and the warmth of her, and the smell of her. 'So you'll get something out of all this?'

She looked at him steadily. 'What I'm getting, Reed, is a whole lot of trouble.'

'Yes, but it's by your own choice.' Hadn't he heard that she couldn't have children of her own?

Her mouth tightened fractionally. 'If you're saying I shouldn't bitch about it, I promise I don't intend to.'

'No, that's not what I meant.' She could be so damned touchy. 'It's your decision and I admire your determination.'

He sat with her and rested one worn boot on his leather bag. 'I'll stay in Shanghai with you for a while – if you want me to?'

'I'd appreciate that.' She didn't look at him.

'What will you do after that – go home to Connecticut?'

She frowned slightly. 'I have a little money left by my grandmother but it won't be enough to keep me and Suyin. I'll have to find work, freelancing, I guess. I'll go to New York.'

'Well I'm going east as well.' Reed made the decision in that moment. He picked up a balloon and gave it to Suyin. 'The Seversky Company on Long Island – they build airplanes and they needed skilled workers when I left.' He added casually, 'I'd be close by you. Maybe I could – I could help?'

'That would be nice.' Linda smiled to herself. 'You're not suggesting that we play house?'

'Hell, no!' he said hastily. 'Nothing immoral like that.'

She watched Suyin and she talked. Reed felt the magic flowing off her.

The dance ended and Peggy came back breathless. 'I don't have the energy for this any more – or perhaps my heart isn't in it.'

'That doesn't sound like you,' Reed said, watching a Chinese steward edging his way towards them. He had a sudden presentiment.

'Sir, captain wantchee see in cabin chop chop.'

It was cold outside. Light from the saloon illumined most of the upper deck. And beyond the wall of the city, huge fires burned uncontrolled, flecking red the dark water of the river below.

At his knock the cabin door opened a crack, and a deck officer peered out then spoke to somebody inside. 'It's Reed.'

The cabin was dimly lit. Dalsager's bulk partly obscured the man lying on the bunk. 'Ah, Reed! *Another* problem you have made for me.' He stood aside. 'Your friend, I believe?'

He felt his jaw drop open. God in heaven! His first thought surprised him – he would have preferred not to see Russell again. And for a moment he wanted to deny that Russell was any friend of his. But Russell slowly pulled himself up on his elbow and smiled faintly. 'Spectre at the bloody feast, Reed.' He looked deathly pale.

'The Japanese are searching for this man. I would have dropped him back in the river if he had been Chinese.' Dalsager paced up and down. 'What am I to do with him? They will search the ship before we leave. If they find him on board they will create endless difficulties. They need only flimsy excuses to delay us – take people off for questioning.'

'And they'll hang him.'

The Dane waved a large dismissive hand. 'I have a ship

with passengers to worry about. I am making Russell your problem, Reed. If he is caught I will disown you both.'

Reed nodded. It could all start falling to pieces – that dream of his life beginning to make sense; Linda, the passage home, New York. 'Have you some dry clothes for Russell?' He thought quickly. 'I'll take him into the saloon.'

'There are two Japanese naval officers in there!'

'Then that's the last place anybody will think of looking. I'll find a paper hat and a mask for him. I'll hide him in the crowd.'

He half supported Russell, and that was okay because several of the passengers were already a little drunk.

'Easier to push me over the side.' Russel dragged his foot, and Reed realized with shock that they were trailing blood along the open upper deck.

'I would prefer to, Russell. Believe me, I would.' Music from the party spilled out into the night. 'Now, we're going in there. Try not to bleed over every damned thing. You know the words to "Good Old Shanghai"? Well, you sing what you can remember as we cross to the far corner where Linda and Peggy are. Got it?'

He was sure every head would turn in their direction, but nobody seemed to notice. A woman even banged clumsily into Russell, and apologized before turning away. Some, already the worse for drink, started singing 'Land of Hope and Glory'.

Reed caught Linda's shocked surprise. But Peggy was already on her feet; and as Russell sat clumsily on the leather sofa she deftly dropped a blanket over his damaged foot. 'You've had me worried *sick*, Mr Russell!'

Someone here might betray him – Reed glanced quickly round. There were dark stains on the wooden floor.

Peggy had in the instant taken over the care of Russell. 'He's exhausted! How could you let him *bleed* like that?'

'I didn't have much goddam choice!' Reed felt aggrieved as well as scared. 'When the ship's underway I'll take him somewhere and bind up his foot.'

'*I'll* bind it!'

341

'No! You'll stay out of this. If the Japanese come searching it's just Russell and me.'

Linda stared up at him and he could read in her face that she too had realized what they might lose. But she grasped his hand tightly. 'You're doing fine, Reed, for an ox dung man.'

He held her hand for a fraction longer. 'Russell should have a drink – it will seem more natural.' He'd gone only half way across the saloon when Miss Kuang stepped through the doorway.

She looked as if she'd just left Shanghai's Cathay Hotel; white coat over a green silk dress, elegant high-heeled shoes, her hair gleamed blue-black. With her was Captain Hashimoto.

The man with the black eye-patch handed the pair glasses but most of the people near the improvised bar started to move away – small, ineffectual protests.

Hashimoto took the glasses and smiling handed one to Miss Kuang. She stared at him coldly. Reed saw that she had a dark bruise on her left cheek, and he guessed that Hashimoto had hit her.

The mood of the party changed, passengers talking loudly as though reassuring themselves. Hashimoto smiled around him. He enjoys our fear, Reed thought. Miss Kuang sipped champagne, and when one of the younger men spoke to her she raised a white-gloved hand to conceal the bruise on her face. The two Japanese naval officers eyed Hashimoto expressionlessly.

Reed forced himself to think. There was no reason to panic. It was the Japanese navy that sought Russell, not the army. But he avoided Hashimoto as he made his way back with a drink for Russell.

'It's cognac – take it down slowly. Now we'll all carry on a normal conversation. It'll help if we smile.'

' . . . and I know this guy, Jordan, at the US consulate in Shanghai – he might help with the papers for Suyin.' Linda chattered, glancing anxiously at Reed's face.

Reed watched as Captain Hashimoto moved with complete assurance towards Daphne Drummond. People stood aside

342

...om him, and Daphne looked embarrassed, glancing
round.

'You're not listening to me, Reed.'

'Yes I am. You think Jordan may be able to help.' He picked
p Suyin's balloon and balanced it on her head. She giggled
nd it fell off. He glanced at the windows along the port side
f the saloon to see if there was any sign of daybreak.

There were Japanese sailors out there – half a dozen of
tem!

'Jordan's a bit of a pain. But he knows just about everybody
nd he's not a bad guy.'

They've seen the blood, he thought. And now there was an
fficer with them – he was peering through the window at the
arty.

'I'll need you with me when we reach Shanghai.' Linda
atched the saloon door. She bit her lip. 'They're going to
ome in here and search, aren't they?'

'I guess they will,' he said softly. 'I'm sorry.'

'Oh God! What are we going to do, Reed?'

'Keep them occupied.' He stood, and he couldn't look at
er any more.

Russell tried to get to his feet then fell back. 'You don't
ave to do this, Reed!'

'Yes I do, Russell. And it has nothing to do with you.'

What option was there? He started across the saloon. He
as sick of being on the losing side. They weren't going to
ave Mayling *and* Russell.

He intercepted Hashimoto just as he was attempting to
teer Daphne onto the dance floor. Hashimoto's eyes nar-
owed, and then he remembered. 'Mr Reed, is it? How is your
and?'

'Your guy broke two of my fingers.' There was an odd
ensation of release. He'd stopped feeling afraid.

'I am extremely sorry.' Hashimoto smiled at Daphne. 'Mr
eed had a small accident.'

'That's right. I was trying to prevent the captain's men from
aping a Chinese girl.' Reed said it loud enough for those
earby to hear.

343

Daphne's expression turned icy. 'I hope you succeeded.'

'I'm afraid not. The captain's men are scum, you see.'

Hashimoto froze. He glanced quickly round at the circl of shocked faces and he murmured, 'I shall assume that yo are intoxicated, Mr Reed.'

'Believe whatever you want.' The gramophone recorc finished and now everybody was listening. Reed spoke loudly, 'And I shall assume that you are a pig posing as man.'

The Japanese sailors had entered the saloon, and the watched as Hashimoto struck Reed hard across the face.

Reed swayed back, then smiled and spat blood. He'd have to knock Hashimoto senseless – one blow with his good hand, that's all he'd have. 'You're a pig. Your men are scum. Your General is . . .'

Hashimoto's eyes opened wide and he drew back his hand again.

' . . . a pig.' Reed hit him first, sending him crashing backwards in a welter of food and glasses.

The two Japanese naval officers reached him through the crowd. 'You are under arrest!'

Hashimoto was out cold.

I guess the party's over, he thought, and nursed his aching knuckles. The passengers were watching in fascinated horror as armed Japanese sailors ringed him round.

'I'm Russell,' he said. 'I'll go quietly, just take your hands off me.'

He deliberately didn't look back at Linda, Peggy and Russell as they led him out of the saloon.

A cold wind caught at his coat. The river was vast and dark, but that was the only way out. The thought and the action were one – he broke through the guard of sailors and vaulted over the rail. And he dropped. It was a long way down – time to wonder if he'd hit floating debris or a body. Lighted windows, lighted lower deck, people, portholes. He splashed, shocked, into the river.

He must have gone down a long way. As he kicked up to the surface his arm scraped the hull of the *I-cheng* and he stayed close, seeking the protection of the hull's curve. Dear God, the water was cold! He kicked off his boots and clung with his finger tips to the mottled, rusting side of the ship. Bullets splashed into the river – the sailors were firing at anything and everything. It could only be a matter of minutes before they lowered boats, and they'd find him. He swam along the length of the hull then went below the surface as he cleared the stern.

Half-submerged bodies – they seemed to grope at him, and his lungs were near bursting. He surfaced briefly then dived again, swimming under water for as long as he could. The current was with him, carrying him down river towards the lights at the lower limits of anchorage. He peered back each time he came up. When *I-cheng* was far behind, he stayed on the surface.

The cold ate into him, numbing his limbs. Millions of lives, millions of final thoughts had been absorbed into the awful hugeness of this river. Harsh beams flicked over the water, but they also were far off now. Half a mile ahead were the abandoned sheds of the torpedo depot. And the Stinson was there; gassed up, waiting for Brice who'd never come. Reed didn't know if he could survive the cold to swim that far. He found the floating debris of a smashed junk and clung to it. And the river carried him on.

CHAPTER TWENTY-EIGHT

Sergeant Kimura had no clear memory of his actual arrival in the hospital. He'd had a fever – yes. His leg had swollen badly and he'd had a fever.

He could smell ether – and something else. He frowned, trying to identify what it was but his attention kept shifting to sounds. A trolley clattered somewhere outside. He was too weak to raise his head but he was aware of the vast room lined with beds. It had an ornate ceiling, now palely lit by two shaded oil lamps. Most of the room was in shadow. Someone murmured in their sleep and turned, bed creaking. Kimura dragged his attention back to the sickening odour. It couldn't be his leg, the surgeon had taken it off almost to the hip.

The windows were draped but a small chink in the curtaining revealed stars in the early morning sky. A machine gun crackled at intervals and Kimura assumed they were still shooting the Chinese prisoners. It was not his concern. He was going home.

He focused his mind on what it would be like with only one leg. Captain Hashimoto had been encouraging when he had visited two days before – he'd need a stick, but with a light, aluminium limb he'd be able to get about. 'You must look after the girls, Kimura, until I return.' It was the captain's joke. And as a veteran NCO with a good record, the government would train him for something back in their home city. There was plenty of work in Nagasaki.

Sergeant Kimura frowned to himself. His thoughts had drifted once more – he seemed to have little control over them. That stench! As if the whole of Nanking had died and was putrefying. He'd begun to suspect it was in his mind.

Black smoke gouted from *I-cheng*'s single funnel and fanned back towards the larger, newer ship eighty yards astern. Watching, Miss Kuang could see washing strung out between the lifeboats, and three overcoated girls walking on the main deck. They had been part of that other convoy attacked up river.

She felt a grinding vibration along *I-cheng*'s rusting hull, then she saw the debris of a rammed junk float off to the rear. Smashed timbers, roped fragments of bamboo impossible to identify.

It was nearly mid-day. Nanking was slipping away behind her. Miss Kuang left the stern and walked along the starboard side to find somewhere sheltered from the wind. Escape from Nanking had been a very close thing – even thinking about it disturbed her.

The shore was a faint line as *I-cheng* steamed further out into the deep channel. Only one vessel, a Japanese destroyer, steered an opposite course and it was two miles away. She preferred this isolation. *I-cheng*, crowded with card-players, women gossiping, and their noisy Western children, felt safe from the war. She had already decided that she wouldn't step ashore until the ancient, creaking steamer reached Shanghai. A new identity awaited her there. I'm tired of the old one, she thought, and perhaps it will be like starting life again. All Miss Kuang's clothes, shoes, jewellery, and baggage were new.

There were white caps on the water and wind span the gulls. Miss Kuang looked up. Prison has made me envious of them; free, able to change their perspective with just one beat of their wings, she thought. In those hours after escape, and almost immediate capture by a 9th Division patrol, it had begun to seem that Zhu Shu had had the best of the bargain. What if the Special Services Bureau had failed to find her in time? She shivered slightly and huddled deeper into her coat. Better to think of something else.

The weak winter sun gave a light colour wash to the river scene, like a Ching Dynasty painting she had seen in the University of Nanking. And it was strange, her subconscious attempts to suppress even that inconsequential thought of the city.

The Special Services Bureau officer had seen the marks on her body from Hashimoto's beatings, but he'd said nothing – such hazard was part of their work. And there had been only two hours to transform her from a half-naked, filthy prisoner, and put her aboard the *I-cheng*. They'd ransacked the Sincere Department Store for suitable clothes, shoes, and a watch snatched hastily from a display case. He had promised her the assignment outside China, and for that she was profoundly grateful.

The jewellery was very good imitation, like her hastily replaced passport. She didn't care about the rings and clasp taken from her in prison, but the loss of the jade bracelet had left her feeling particularly vulnerable – so much so that she had put a gold chain in its place.

I-cheng slowed where the deep channel narrowed at Morrison Point. There was a cut-off ahead round the north side of Deer Island but it was navigable only by small junks – like *Fushan*. The thought triggered her memory of the dream. She'd had it again last night – a lonely shore and a boat far out.

I-cheng turned along the south of Deer Island, wash rippling over the marshy flats. Miss Kuang paused for a moment out of the wind. In the last few weeks she had become aware of a growing dread that she might have to live her whole life over and over again.

Linda was approaching, moving slowly, with Suyin clutching her hand. Some women seek out burdens for themselves. Guilt over this, guilt for that – Westerners seemed particularly prone. But more, there was a change in the set of Linda's face – Miss Kuang noticed such things. Gone was that tense enquiry; and the mouth was firmer, more determined.

Suyin pointed, arm outstretched as a gull planed on the air beside *I-cheng*.

'Bird, darling. It's a bird.' And Linda spoke to Miss Kuang

348

as she drew near to her. 'I'm learning shortcuts. I figure it's easier for Suyin to master English than it is for me to speak Chinese.'

Miss Kuang smiled. She'd seen the ship's purser. He'd said he might find better accommodation for her.

'We're going walkies. You want to come with us?' Linda asked. 'Suyin's pace isn't likely to wear you out.'

They walked, Suyin between them, passing other passengers. Overworked stewards were clearing the mess of last night's party in the saloon, sad paper streamers, limp balloons, a few broken glasses. Miss Kuang noticed the man with the eye-patch seated in a recess, good eye closed, face turned towards the pale, winter sun.

Linda paused briefly to wipe Suyin's nose. 'What are your plans?'

'I believe my employers will have work for me overseas.'

'That sounds exciting?'

She noticed Linda's curious sideways glance, but natural caution prevented Miss Kuang from explaining further. A rest. Then Honolulu – it was promised her. Special Services Bureau was interested in the military and naval dispositions at Ford Island and Pearl Harbor.

They reached the bows. The Japanese gunboat *Saga* was ahead, gleaming white, its machine guns covered.

On the deck below, Russell was leaning on the rail and watching the river. He seemed uninterested in their escort.

'And you, Linda – you will take Suyin back to America?'

'Yes – we'll go. But not immediately.'

She is anxious for Reed, Miss Kuang thought, lifting Suyin so that she could see the gunboat. 'And you, small one, will go to an American school, and get to like jazz music. China will sink to a very small part of your memory.' She put the child down again. Why should she want Suyin to remember her? 'I will think about you, Suyin, as the years go by. What is this?' Miss Kuang fingered the bracelet of blue glass stones on the child's wrist.

'That awful woman in the tweed suit gave it to her. She's suddenly become attentive now that we're safe.'

349

'Blue means ill-fortune.' Miss Kuang took off her gold chain looted from the Sincere Department Store, and she wrapped it twice round Suyin's other wrist. 'Gold brings good luck.'

'It must be expensive! Thank you so much.' Linda was frowning slightly. 'I'll be very careful that we don't lose it.'

Peggy approached. She'd slept well and even managed a thirty-second shower. 'I've been looking everwhere for you. Shall we fly, Suyin?' And she picked her up and swung her round while Linda watched.

'Honestly, Linda, you worry more than any mother I've ever known. What will you do when Suyin goes to school?'

'I'll take that hurdle when it comes.' A child was a constant nagging anxiety, she had discovered.

Peggy looked down at Russell on the deck below. 'David says you have to stand back every now and then and let them take risks.'

'*Who* says?'

'David. David Russell.' Peggy looked self-conscious. 'Well I can't keep calling him Mr Russell all the way back to London.'

'Bird!' Suyin said, and pointed.

'How *clever* you are!' Peggy hugged her. 'They fly all the way to heaven.' She looked suddenly wistful. 'Do you remember how they used to scavenge from the *Fushan*?'

'One of them stole the fish from my bowl – d'you remember that? It just swooped right down and carried it off.' Linda smiled. 'And you all laughed.'

'We laughed at your outrage.'

'Two gulls followed us for days.' Miss Kuang was smiling as well. 'I think they brought us luck.'

'*Luck* you call it! We nearly drowned at least twice! Don't you remember when Reed had to . . .' Peggy stopped in mid-sentence. 'We're alive. Maybe they did bring us luck. D'you know what? I've begun to think that was a good time in my life.'

Miss Kuang glanced back along the deck. The purser had just left the saloon. 'I must write letters. We can send them ashore for posting at Chen-chiang.'

Peggy watched her disapprovingly: slim, elegant, she had a way of walking that caused men to turn their heads. 'Those clothes! They're all brand new, and from the same store – I had a good look at the labels while she was up here with you. Now she's talking to the purser – I'll bet she has a cabin by tomorrow.'

'She's a survivor.'

'Reed's pretty good at surviving too, love.'

'I hope so.' She took a deep breath. 'We'll see. What about you, Peggy – what do you plan to do?'

'Go home. Settle. Arch had quite a lot saved. I'm going to buy a house with some of it – a small house in Battersea, with a backyard, and noisy neighbours who know everybody's business. And my mum can come round to tea, and my sisters and their kids.'

Linda was glad for her. 'How about a handsome gentleman caller?'

'He doesn't have to be handsome, as long as he loves me and works hard. I want children. And I want to be needed next time.' Peggy paused. 'He sounds like David Russell, doesn't he?'

'That thought crossed my mind.'

'Well, maybe it will be him.'

I-cheng's engines slowed as they followed the Japanese gunboat past smaller islands covered with reeds. Here the deep channel curved where silt had formed a new sandbar.

'I'll visit you – or you visit me?' Linda knew as she said it that they never would. 'We'll at least write. I'll give you a forwarding address before we reach Shanghai.'

'How will you manage with Suyin?'

'I'm going to have to find work to support us both. We'll go to New York – I've got a few contacts there and I can freelance. And I'm going to have to find a place for us to live. Reed was going to help me.'

'Promise you'll let me know how you are?'

'I promise.'

Peggy nodded, satisfied. 'What's the date?'

'Thirteenth of December.'

'It's exactly four months since we arrived in Shanghai.'

Russell left the bow, limping towards the companionway. He looked up and smiled before climbing the steps. Peggy waved to him. 'I have to change the dressing on his foot. You okay?'

'Go ahead. Suyin and I are fine.'

Linda remained, watching the gunboat's wake. Four months. Who would have thought I'd become so possessive about Reed in four months? He'll turn up in Shanghai – I'll *will* him to, she told herself.

On the shore to the right she could see a white pagoda and a few shacks, then she recognized the single stone building jutting up behind rickety piers and frail houses. 'Look Suyin! It's the village where we put in to repair the *Fushan*!' And she lifted her.

Suyin smiled, uncomprehending.

The whole episode seemed remote now. Linda watched as the piers and ramshackle buildings receded. Then only the top of the stone building was visible above the curve of the shore. She frowned to herself. She'd have to write about it all, and soon before the detail blurred. She could make a start tonight when Suyin was asleep.

In the bleak fields off to the right, children were scrubbing the back of a water buffalo. A small aeroplane crossed between clouds, heading east.

The horn on the Japanese gunboat blared an unnecessary warning of shoals and thousands of wild fowl squawked and lifted, flapping in a wide circle. Suyin was pointing.

'Yes, darling. Birds.'

THE END